Our Land of Palestine

OUR LAND OF PALESTINE

Malcolm Archibald

Prelude

Gully Ravine, Gallipoli
28 June 1915

It was hot. Major Andrew Selkirk of the Royal Borderers smoothed a hand over his forehead and ducked as the movement brought an instant response from a Turkish sniper. The bullet smacked into the sandbag behind his head, so a small trickle of sand eased out.

'I thought our artillery would keep Jacko's heads down,' Lieutenant Turnbull sounded nervous.

Selkirk looked at him. 'It seems that Jacko Turk has other ideas.'

The British guns fired non-stop, pounding the Turkish positions on either side of the ridge. Dust, smoke and the stink of lyddite filled the air. Selkirk narrowed his eyes at the evil orange petals of explosions and the occasional chunk of rock thrown high above the ground.

'There shouldn't be anything left after that,' Turnbull sounded impressed. 'And look!' He gestured out to the calm waters of the Mediterranean where the ships of the Royal Navy were giving support. Every few moments the lean grey vessels were obscured by smoke as they unleashed a broadside. The rip of heavy artillery overhead should have been reassuring, but Selkirk doubted that it was effective. He had been in too many battles to expect everything to go well.

'They are firing hard enough,' Turnbull grabbed his pith helmet as another bullet zipped overhead.

'Aye, but not on our front,' Selkirk pointed out. He crouched low behind the sandbags and indicated the ground ahead. 'The guns are plastering the Turks everywhere else. Our divisional artillery is still sitting in some quayside back home.'

'The Navy boys will change targets soon,' Turnbull shouted above the constant roar of the guns, 'then Jacko will know all about it.'

Selkirk grunted and said nothing. He looked along Fir Tree Spur, the broken ground along which 156 Brigade, including his Royal Borderers, was to advance. There was a succession of ravines which might give cover to his men if the Turkish machine guns opened up, but conversely, the Turks could be lurking inside them, waiting. Knowing the high calibre of Turkish infantry, and very aware that his men were untried weekend territorials, that thought was unsettling.

The sun was high, bursting the sweat from his forehead and dampened his armpits and the back of his shirt. Selkirk checked his watch. It was coming up to 10.30 on 28th June 1915. The attack was scheduled for 10.45, fifteen minutes ahead, but so far the guns had not dented the Turks positions on the spur. He cautiously raised a trench periscope above the line of sandbags and peered forward. There was hardly a single shell-burst on the Turkish positions, yet his men had to advance fifteen hundred yards and capture them.

Over there is the *Asakr –I Shahaneh*, he thought, the Ottoman Army, once the most feared military force in the world. Over there sits Jacko Turk, representatives of the same army which had held Christian Europe in fear for centuries, which had conquered the Middle East, North Africa and much of Eastern Europe. Over there, in well-dug trenches and behind rows of sandbags, crouched over machine guns and grasping modern German Mauser rifles, the Asakr –I Shahaneh waited for his few hundred Territorials, his part time soldiers who had never fired a shot in anger or seen the face of the enemy.

'We're giving them Hell, sir,' a high-pitched voice said, and Selkirk saw a very young boy crouched low in the bottom of the trench. His uniform was at least two sizes too large while his rifle looked taller than he was.

'I hope so … Semple isn't it?'

'Yes, sir.' The boy looked very pleased to be recognised. When he smiled, the adolescent spots on his face merged.

'So what did you do before the war started, Semple?'

'I was an office boy, sir, in a mill in Galashiels.' He looked about fifteen and probably was.

'Well, you take care, Semple, and keep your head down.' Selkirk nearly patted him on the shoulder but knew that was not what majors in the Royal Borderers did. He crawled along behind the sandbagged trench wall, talking to the men, checking their equipment, encouraging the nervous and smiling at the crude jokes of those who pretended they were not scared.

'Pringle!' Selkirk saw Captain Pringle standing upright to face the enemy positions, 'get down!'

Pringle did not move. 'It is an officer's duty to set an example to the men.' He looked down his long nose at the crouching Selkirk. 'It is undignified and un-British to cower before the enemy.'

Selkirk dragged him behind the sandbags. 'It's an officer's first duty to look after his men. You are no good to your men when you are dead!' He saw the expression of near contempt on Pringle's face. 'What were you before the war started, Pringle?'

Pringle frowned, 'I am the Honourable Walter Pringle of Westriggs …'

Selkirk interrupted him, 'and how long have you been in the Army?'

'I was in the Officers' Training Corps at Fettes College and joined the Territorial Army immediately I left school.' Pringle flicked slender hands at Selkirk, 'I have been training twelve weekends a year for just this opportunity, plus annual camps.'

Selkirk nodded. 'You call me sir.' He held Pringle's eyes and waited for him to acknowledge the fact.

'Sir,' Pringle seemed to force out the word. Selkirk knew that Pringle was from an old Berwickshire landed family, a man who considered himself born to lead and a man desperate to prove his mettle in battle, no doubt incredibly brave, but inexperienced. 'Have you been in action before, Pringle?'

'No, sir, but I am ready...'

Selkirk pointed over the lip of the trench toward the Turkish positions. 'Well, you will be in action soon, Pringle. These are the Asakr-I Shahaneh, veterans of Balkan wars, Greek wars and Russian wars; top quality soldiers with far more experience than we have. I know you will set an example of bravery and duty when we go into action, but it would be a waste to have some Turkish peasant sniper kill a man like you before you show how to do it.' He leaned closer to the young officer. 'So keep your bloody head down!'

Selkirk glanced along the shallow trench where his Royal Borderers were sheltering, waiting for the artillery to stop so they could go forward. 'Bayonets, lads,' he shouted, 'it won't be long now!'

One man was shaking; some looked at him with red-rimmed eyes. All were tired and most very young. Selkirk mentally compared these Territorials to the long service men he had fought alongside in the South African War and wondered how these children, mill workers and office clerks would cope with the horrors of combat. A sergeant, one of the few veterans who had been transferred to stiffen the ranks, snicked his bayonet in place. His long face was tanned nut brown with the sun.

'Sergeant Crosier isn't it?'

'Sir,' Crosier nodded.

'You were a regular once,' Selkirk accused.

'Aye, sir.' Crosier did not flinch as a shell scattered a red-hot patter of shrapnel a few yards in front of their trench. He gave a faint smile. 'I did ten years in the Gordons, sir; the Frontier and South Africa.'

'You look after these men, Sergeant,' Selkirk felt some reassurance that there was a man such as Crosier to help his weekend soldiers.

Selkirk ducked as a British shell fell short to explode no more than twenty yards in front of them in a great orange ball of flame that clouds of brown dust and fragments or rock instantly obscured. One of his men yelled and clutched a hand to his forehead. Blood eased between his fingers. 'I'm hit!' he shouted. 'Mother help me; I'm hit!'

Moving in a crouch, Selkirk approached the man. He was about eighteen years old, with wide, terrified eyes and a face as smooth as a baby. 'Let me see... Hunnam isn't it?'

'Yes, sir,' the boy kept his hand over his wound. Flies already sought the fresh blood.

Selkirk pulled the hand away. 'It's only a wee scratch' he tried to sound cheerful. Taking a field dressing from Hunnam's pouch, he applied it to the wound. 'It's nothing at all to worry about, but you'd best get back to base and have an orderly see to it.' In this heat, any injury could fester. He watched as the boy limped to a communication trench that led back toward the beach and relative safety.

The ships fired another salvo, with the shells screaming overhead to explode in tall columns of smoke and dust on either side of Fir Tree Spur. Selkirk swore; he remembered the carnage of Magersfontein when Boer riflemen had decimated the Highland Brigade in that earlier South African war. Here, with machine guns, the Turks could do even greater damage unless the artillery softened them up first.

He checked his watch: 10.37. Seven minutes to go. He looked behind him where the few guns of 52 Division fired a desultory barrage that barely scratched the surface of the ridge. He had no desire to attack the Turks in their prepared positions. What in God's name was Hunter-Bunter thinking? Where was the artillery support for this brigade?

Pringle pointed to the great hill of Achi Baba that dominated this southern tip of the Gallipoli peninsula. 'I want to plant the British flag on top of that before nightfall.'

Selkirk nodded. 'Very commendable.' Achi Baba had been their objective since the landings on 29 April when the 1st KOSB had lost nearly 300 men in eighteen hours of non- stop fighting. The hill rose only a few miles ahead, but in this campaign where an advance of a hundred yards was a good day's work, Pringle's plan was very ambitious.

Selkirk heard a change in the pattern of bombardment. The Navy had altered their range. It was 10.42; there were three minutes until the attack.

'The guns are preparing to stop,' he told Turnbull and pushed one of his men back down. 'Keep your bloody head down, Fraser' he ordered. 'I'll tell you when you can move!'

The shell fire intensified, landing in a concentration of bursting steel that smothered the Turkish positions facing the left flank of the British at Gully Ravine. Dust and smoke drifted across the lines, all but blocking the once clear sky. It must have been steel and hot hell in the Turkish positions, swamped by heavy and medium artillery, blasting trenches and men with no mercy or compassion.

All at once the bombardment ended. The silence was so sudden that it hurt the ears and for a moment nobody moved. Somewhere in the distance a hopeful bird called.

10.44: a minute until the attack.

Selkirk took a deep breath and pulled out his whistle. The metal was hot against his lips.

The silence continued; somebody gave a hysterical giggle. Somebody was praying, the words soft in the hard hush. 'Our Father, who art in heaven...' Somebody else was singing a music hall song with lyrics that the composer had not intended for innocent ears. There was the sound of a single shot, then the chilling rattle of a machine gun. A shell exploded above, the smoke acting as a harbinger of the hell to come.

'Come on Royal Borderers!' Pringle shouted and began to rise to the lip of the trench.

10.45: time.

God help us all.

'That's us, lads!' Selkirk's long whistle blast reached along the length of the Royal Borderers lines. 'Up we go!' He would have liked to hear the Border Pipes now, the thin wail from his native green hills combating the dust and heat of this parched land, but instead, there was a grim growling cheer as his young part-time soldiers rose from their trench and began the desperately long advance toward the entrenched Ottoman army.

It was time to be an officer. Selkirk stood tall, fully aware that he would immediately be a target for dozens of Turkish rifles and machine guns on the ridge, but determined to set an example. Regulars would not need such direct leadership, but these youngsters were only part-time soldiers, catapulted into this nightmare by circumstances that nobody completely understood.

He looked around, temporarily enjoying the freedom from the constriction of the trench. He saw the crest of Fir Tree Spur stretching before him until it merged with its parent hill of Achi Baba that rose in threatening dominance to the north. A series of ravines and rugged ridges blocked the Borderers' path, plus the stone walls of the town of Krithia, all defended by some thousands of Ottoman soldiers. Smoke and dust from the bombardment hazed his view so that Selkirk could see little but yellow-brown rocks and scrubby olive green vegetation. He could see nothing of the enemy, but he knew they were there, hiding, waiting behind their rifles and machine guns for the British to present themselves as a target, willing to defend their land with all the courage and skill for which the Turks were famous.

'Move lads!' Selkirk glanced along the trench line as the Royal Borderers emerged, some with their shoulders hunched, others upright with rifle and bayonet at the high port as screaming sergeants had trained them to do, as they had done on weekend exercises at Barry Buddon and among the long green hills of Ettrick. The trembling man was biting his lip but still moving; another had a pipe firmly clenched between his teeth. The praying man was a Corporal Scott, broad and ugly, a Kirk Elder from Selkirk who had joined the Territorials on the urging of his wife. 'The quicker we move, the less chance there is of being killed!'

'You heard the major,' Sergeant Crosier bellowed, 'follow my lead, lads and take the bayonet to Jackie Turk!'

For the first hundred yards, there was no defensive fire, and Selkirk ushered his men onward, hoping to cover as much ground as possible before the Turks realised what was happening. With luck, Jackie might be dazed from the bombardment, or believe that the British would not attack along the spur. He felt the ground hard and stony beneath his boots as he forced himself to walk at a steady pace. If he ran, some of the men might charge, and then their advance would be ragged, uncoordinated and much less effective. He wanted his Borderers to arrive at the Turkish trenches like a solid wall of steel rather than a disorganised rag-bag of individuals. Selkirk knew that the younger men needed encouragement from their more experienced fellows in this first step into war. The dust was clearing now, settling down and there was a spatter of musketry but whether from the British or the Turks he could not tell.

'On to Achi Baba!' Pringle shouted. He drew his revolver and fired wildly in the general direction of the Turkish lines.

'Keep together!' Selkirk shouted. 'Pringle! Look after your men!' He saw Pringle break into a run and surge in front of his company.

There was a new sound now: singing. He did not recognise the tune, but suddenly realised it was coming from the Turkish lines. The men that the bombardment was intended to blast out of existence were singing.

'Follow me, Royals!'

Selkirk stopped and looked around. The entire British line was moving in a general advance to break through the Turkish lines and capture Achi Baba. If they could capture that dominant hill the whole Turkish line might collapse, and the Allies could push up the peninsula to Constantinople and knock Turkey out of the war. That would enable a secure supply line to Russia and free up hundreds of thousands of troops, British, Imperial, French and Russian for the campaigns against Austria and Germany.

'Come on lads: Royal Borderers! On to Constantinople!'

His Royal Borderers were only a small part of the attack, but they were moving well. They were grim of expression, white faced, shaking, but none had dropped out. They maybe only weekend soldiers, but they were Borderers, with two thousand years of warrior tradition behind them and they would do their best. One small group began to follow after Pringle, breaking into a shambling run that disrupted their formation as they struggled across the uneven ground.

'Stay with me, lads!' Selkirk coughed to clear the dust from his throat. He took a quick swig of his water bottle, tipped back his pith helmet and swore at the distinctive, all-too-familiar buck-up crackle of Mauser rifles and the rapid rattle of the Maxim MG09. The Turks had recovered from the bombardment and were firing on the advancing troops.

'Here we go lads; keep together as you were trained but don't bunch up; leave the wounded for the stretcher bearers; if a machine gun opens up spread out!' Selkirk raised his voice to a roar: 'Royal Borderers!'

The call echoed his words as he had expected, with Crosier first to take up the call: 'Royal Borderers!'

Lieutenant Tweedie was next, yelling as loudly as he ever had on the rugby field at Peebles. 'Royal Borderers!'

The name was repeated from man to man, so it became a rolling cry that stretched the length of the battalion's front, a reminder of their shared heritage back in the peaceful valleys and bustling mill towns of the Borders. They may be bank clerks or mill workers, shepherds from the lonely cleughs or carters from the highways and byways, but they were all Borderers.

Their calls caused the Turks to increase the volume of their singing as if they were taunting the oncoming British soldiers.

'Cocky bastards,' Sergeant Crosier said. He turned around to check his men.

'Royal Borderers!'

And then the Turkish song stopped. As the volume of rifle fire increased, the Royal Borderers began to take casualties.

'The bastards have found our range,' Crosier warned.

Selkirk saw a stout middle aged man drop without a word while a young soldier whimpered and looked at his stomach, from where blood seeped into his khaki tunic. Some of the men were kneeling and firing blindly into the dust. One blonde haired giant stood still, mouth open in horror as his comrades, with whom he had trained and marched and served for years, crumpled all around him.

The machine gun found them, raising spurts of dust and splintered rock from the ground as the gunner sprayed the advancing British infantry. The blonde giant lurched as a bullet smashed into his left hip, and then fell backwards as two more thumped his stomach. Another bullet took his right foot clean off as he sprawled on the ground. He began to scream, high pitched and hopeless as his blood pumped onto the baked rock.

'Spread out! Forward!' Selkirk shouted as memories of Modder River, and Magersfontein came again into his mind. 'Remember your training!' He lifted the rifle from the crumpled body of a youngster, worked the bolt, fired a quick round and began to run forward. They were still some hundreds of yards from the Turkish trenches. 'Come on Royal Borderers! Give them the bayonet!'

He saw Crosier leading from the front, gesturing to his men to follow, and then a Turkish shell exploded, throwing up a cloud of ochre dust. The sergeant vanished from sight.

This battle epitomised the sort of fighting Selkirk despised, wasteful, pointless, putting men's lives in the path of bullets to gain a few yards of dust. He heard screams and cries for help from behind him but pressed on. A battle was not the time for compassion or sticking to the letter of the training manual. The quicker they reached the Turkish trenches, the fewer men he would lose.

'Charge!' he roared. 'Give them the bayonet, Royal Borderers!'

Selkirk flinched as bullets kicked up dust and chips of stone around his feet. He fired back blindly and swore as he realised the advance had come to a halt. The Territorial soldiers had dived for whatever cover they could find and were firing madly forward, hoping to unsettle the Turks.

The ground changed here, with patches of scrubby olive green vegetation clinging to the thin soil. Sharp thorns scraped against Selkirk's ankles as he moved, shouting to his men, still urging them forward.

'Close with them! Up and advance, boys! Royal Borderers!'

Selkirk realised that his efforts were useless. The advance on the spur had ground to a halt before the massed Turkish Mauser and machine gun fire. The men tried to make themselves as small as possible, burrowing behind minuscule folds in the ground or isolated rocks, clinging to the plants for comfort as the machine gun raked them with its insistent mechanical chatter.

'Up!' Selkirk ducked as that Turkish gunner swung the machine gun in its killing cone. He heard the whine of a ricochet and swore again as a bullet tugged at the sleeve of his jacket. 'Up Borderers! Forward!'

There was no reaction as the men hugged themselves closer to the ground or tried to find what cover they could. Selkirk realised he was nearly the only man standing, and it seemed that every Turk in Gallipoli was aiming at him.

Crosier was still on his feet, bleeding from a wound on his face but striding around the prone soldiers, kicking at legs and feet as he urged them forward.

'Sir! Get down!' That was Turnbull, his smooth face smeared with dust and blood and one ear hanging loose where a bullet had ripped it half off. He did not look scared.

'No! Press on! Show them your cap badge, Royals! Get forward!' Selkirk hauled one man to his feet and shoved him in the direction of the Turkish lines, kicked another on the boots and swore at a third. 'Charge, Borderers! Forward!'

Other machine guns were firing now, so bullets kicked and pinged and whined around them as the Royal Borderers rose and rushed forward, now desperate to reach the Turkish lines. Some had fallen before they had the chance of a single step forward. One man looked behind at the dubious security of the British lines until Selkirk grabbed his shoulder and pushed him in the right direction. If one man headed back, the others might follow.

'Forward! Cut the distance!'

Then the Turks found the range again, and men fell in ones and twos and then in dozens. Selkirk ran forward, swearing and firing. He saw Pringle in front, his long legs covering the ground at a fast pace, but a burst of machine-gun bullets ripped into him, and he was thrown backwards, dead before he hit the ground. Turnbull yelled something incomprehensible and looked at his left arm, shot clean away from his body.

'Sir,' he looked at Selkirk in surprise, and then crumpled to the rocky ground.

Thomas Wright, a confectioner from Alnwick, screamed and fell on his face, but a Turkish bullet caught his ammunition belt, and he burst into instant flames. His screaming redoubled as he burned alive in the midst of his companions.

'Oh dear God!' David Johnson of Dumfries screamed in horror and rose to run, but the machine gun found him and blew the top of his head off. Selkirk looked around for something to douse Wright's flames, but there was nothing; the scrub vegetation around Wright began to smoulder and spark, and then the ammunition in his pouches began to explode. The men around Wright rose; some fled back to the British lines but most charged forward to fall in the vicious fire of the Turkish machine gun.

'That's the way lads: remember Wright and take the bayonet to the Turks!' Crosier's roar sounded even above the hellish din of battle.

More men were advancing, some cheering, others swearing, but when Selkirk glanced around, he saw Khaki-clad bodies smeared across the ground. He counted ten Royals; fifteen, maybe twenty still moving forward and then there was another sound as the Turks countered.

That deep Turkish music began again, backed by the staccato hammer of drums; the machine guns ceased fire. Only the spatter of Mausers poisoned the air. And then the Turkish singing intensified and abruptly stopped. Hundreds of Turks exploded through the dust haze, pouring out of cover toward the scattered Royal Borderers. Bayonets glittered through the dust, and then the two forces met the battered Borderers, shocked by the impact of massed machine guns, and the roaring veteran Turks defending their territory and their nation.

A Turk rushed toward Selkirk, the cross belt startlingly white against his brown uniform and his mouth open beneath a black moustache. Selkirk parried the wild bayonet lunge, but the Turk was muscular, and he crashed into Selkirk, sending him staggering back. The Turk powered forward, raised his rifle and levelled the bayonet at Selkirk's chest. His mouth opened in a roar of triumph, which gave Selkirk the opportunity to level his rifle and fire, and then lunge upward with his bayonet.

Selkirk felt the sickening slide of steel as it entered the Turk's body, gave a slight twist and withdrew. The Turk stiffened; bright blood spurted over his cross belt, and he coughed, spewing blood. Selkirk shoved him aside and looked around.

The Turkish counter attack was successful. The Royal Borderers had reeled back from the ground they had captured, and the survivors were in their original trenches, desperately firing all they had. Rather than sit and wait for the British, the Turks were surging forward, brave, stalwart men who moved from cover to cover as they advanced. A tall officer in an immaculate khaki uniform and bush hat led the most advanced group.

For a second his gaze met that of Selkirk. It was not the bright blue eyes or the prominent Roman nose that caught Selkirk's attention so much as the brilliant boyish smile. This man was no older than Selkirk's recruits, an enthusiastic young officer leading his men into battle. Selkirk frowned: the uniform was wrong. It was not Turkish: this man must be one of the German advisors he had heard about, and the burly man at his side must be his NCO, a German Crosier; Selkirk saw the officer lift a hand in hesitant salute, and then a drift of smoke concealed him. Selkirk realised he was the only Briton standing on the field of battle, with a score of enemy rifles firing at him.

When a bullet zipped past his ear, and another kicked up a fountain of dirt an inch away from his left foot Selkirk swore and ran back, leaping over the bodies of Border and Turkish dead.

'Right lads,' he yelled as he slid over the parapet of the trench. 'Hold fast now! The Turks will come at us!'

The young faces of the Royal Borderers were shocked at this introduction to warfare. Some were openly weeping; others ashamed that they had turned and run. Many cradled open wounds.

'Buck up, lads! Face your front and blast the buggers back!'

That singing started again, the words harsh but strangely moving. These Turks were good soldiers, well trained and brave as anybody Selkirk had ever encountered. They came forward in a rush, still singing as the long blades of their bayonets glinted in the sun.

'Here they come!' Selkirk hefted his rifle. 'Shoot them flat, lads!' From being the bold attackers now the Royal Borderers were the desperate defenders, firing from shallow trenches at an unknown number of Turkish infantry. The Turks charged through the dust, an amorphous mass of brown-khaki uniformed men, yelling, singing, stabbing with their long bayonets. Selkirk fired until his magazine was empty, reloaded and fired again, working the bolt of his Lee-Enfield as he shouted encouragement to his men.

'Come on Borderers! Push them back!' He reloaded, fired, swore and glanced right and left to see his men. He had an instant snapshot of them, some firing, and two lying in crumpled heaps on the bottom of the trench, one with blood pouring from a head wound.

Sudden silence. Selkirk stopped; he had experienced this phenomenon in previous battles when for some inexplicable reason men stopped firing and shouting. He heard the ragged gasping of frightened men, the moaning of the wounded, and the high screams of the mortally hit. He took a deep breath and then the singing began again. It was strangely beautiful, this deep throated singing. It started quietly and then quickened until it rose to a crescendo.

'Here they come again!'

Reinforcements had joined the Turks, so a solid mass of khaki-brown ran toward the British trenches. The whole of Selkirk's vision seemed full of advancing infantry and long bayonets. He stood behind the sandbags, firing until he was sure the barrel of his rifle was red-hot.

One group advanced in front of the rest, led by the smiling German officer. Selkirk fired, cursed as he realised his rifle was empty and fumbled for an ammunition clip.

'Out of ammo,' he yelled, 'ammo!'

In the confusion of battle, nobody heard his call, so he dropped the rifle, pulled his Webley revolver and aimed at the Turks.

In the few moments when he had searched for ammunition, the situation had altered. The Turks were right at the lip of the trenches, with the German officer firing a Luger. A man to Selkirk's right fell, and then the Turks were among them, and it was bayonet to bayonet and butt to butt. A grenade exploded with a vicious crump, a machine gun chattered and then fell silent, and Selkirk was face to face with the young German officer.

Both men fired and missed. Before Selkirk could squeeze the trigger again, the German officer was at his throat, growling. The man was taller that Selkirk's five foot ten, broader in the chest and about fifteen years younger. As soon as Selkirk felt the strength of the German's grip he allowed his body to go limp. The sudden dead weight surprised the German, who staggered forward, momentarily unbalanced and Selkirk rammed a knee hard into his groin, following up with a punch to his kidneys.

As the German screamed, Selkirk reached for a discarded rifle. He ignored the lunge of the German sergeant over the lip of the trench; one enemy at a time was sufficient for anybody. The German officer lay in a foetal ball, groaning and holding his groin with both hands. Selkirk lifted the rifle and plunged the bayonet between his ribs, twisted to increase the wound and withdrew. The German gave a long gasp and arched his back so for a second Selkirk stared directly into his pale blue eyes.

'Sir! Major Selkirk!'

Selkirk spun around, prepared to thrust his bayonet into the speaker.

'It's me, sir!' Crosier barely managed to deflect the blade. 'They're running, sir!'

Selkirk took a deep breath to try and control his racing heart. He looked back over the parapet, but the Turks were no longer surging forward but withdrawing in very good order. The German sergeant looked directly at him.

Selkirk checked his watch. 13.45; three hours since the attack had started, but it seemed like only seconds. What had happened to the time?

Semple slid over the lip of the trench and crumpled to the ground. As Selkirk reached to help him, he stood up. 'I'm all right, sir.' He was still the spotty adolescent of that morning, but his eyes were ancient. One morning of war had turned the boy into a man. He would never be the same again.

'What's all this?'

Selkirk looked up as Colonel Palgrove marched along the trench, 'Selkirk! I ordered you to take the Turkish positions, not run from them!' His carefully trimmed moustache seemed to bristle.

'We need more artillery support, sir!' Selkirk pointed ahead. 'The Navy ignored Fir Tree Spur and concentrated on the other fronts, and we have only weak divisional artillery.' He felt his anger rise, and faced up to the colonel, 'there's the result, sir,' he pointed to the dead and broken bodies that lay in obscene profusion across over the parched ground. 'These lads died because there was no proper artillery!'

Palgrove took a deep breath. 'I know all about that, Selkirk, but General Hunter-Weston wants us to advance and take the position. Where's Major Humble?'

Selkirk looked around. 'I have not seen him since the action began, sir.'

I did not see him during the battle either.

'Right; he must be dead or wounded. I want you to take the left flank of the battalion, and I will take the right. I have brought forward the support lines, so we have fresh men. You have ten minutes to get them organised, and then we will advance on my whistle.'

'Yes, sir.' Used to impossible orders, Selkirk moved to obey.

The supports were also Territorials; they looked in horror at the scattered bodies on the battlefield, the crumpled dead and the writhing wounded. They winced as a Turkish machine gun rattled somewhere to the north, and when one of the injured let out a series of long drawn out howls. Wright still burned, with the stench of his body an added horror.

'Don't fret boys,' Crosier tried to restore morale that was evidently flagging. 'You'll get used to it.' He watched as one man turned aside and vomited onto the ground. 'That's the way lad, better out than in.'

Colonel Palgrove ignored both. 'This time you will press on Selkirk and no hesitation. The general wants Fir Tree Spur captured by two this afternoon, no matter what the cost. No stopping this time; no matter how many casualties. Do you understand?' Palgrove pushed his face close to Selkirk's.

'Yes, sir,' Selkirk nodded. He knew that was a virtual death sentence for him and what remained of this battalion of the Royal Borderers, but General Hunter-Weston, Hunter –Bunter to nearly everybody, was known to be a commander who cared nothing for the men under his command.

'Wait!' That was a different voice. 'Are you Major Andrew Selkirk of the Royal Borderers?'

Selkirk hesitated for a second, and then admitted the fact.

'Then I must talk to you.' The man was small and slight, with a clean shaven face, the red tabs of a staff officer and the insignia of a brigadier.

Palgrove looked round. 'Who the devil are you, sir?'

'Brigadier John Smith,' the man said calmly. He did not flinch at the renewed rattle of a machine gun. 'And I am afraid I am going to deprive you of the use of this officer.'

'What?' Palgrove stared at him. 'We are about to go into an attack, sir. I need all my officers!'

Smith glanced over the parapet of the trench just as a Turkish machine gunner sprayed it with fire; spurts of sand and dust bounced into the air, hung in a faint haze and slowly descended. 'If you need all your officers,' he said, 'then I suggest you do not send them forward into machine gun fire. You won't keep them long that way.'

'Orders must be obeyed,' Palgrove said.

'Indeed they must.' Smith took a folded document from inside his tunic and handed it over to Palgrove. In the distance, there was the sound of cheering, the rapid rattle of a machine gun and then silence.

'You continue with your duty to this regiment, Selkirk,' Palgrove ordered, but as Selkirk moved to obey, Smith put a delicate hand on his sleeve.

'No, Major. You had best stay here until Colonel Palgrove has read my orders.'

The nearest men were listening, inching closer to see what was happening. 'Be about your business lads,' Selkirk said. 'Check your ammunition and tell the supports what it's like out there. We will be back over the top in a few moments.'

The men looked at him with haunted eyes. They knew that there was no hope of breaking through along the spur, but they were soldiers and they obeyed.

'I'll look after them, sir,' Crosier promised.

Palgrove scanned the document. 'What the devil?' He seemed to like that expression. He looked down at the diminutive Smith. 'Is this from Hamilton himself?'

'It is,' Smith said. He turned aside for a second and helped a private soldier check his rifle. 'Have these men not been trained how to be soldiers?'

'Not properly, sir,' Selkirk told him. 'They are Territorials just off the boat yesterday and thrown into action.'

'Damned shame,' Smith said. 'Damnable bad luck that.'

'Damnable,' Selkirk echoed.

Palgrove folded the document neatly and handed it back to Smith. 'Well Selkirk, it seems that you are needed elsewhere. The battalion will have to manage without you. You go along with the Brigadier.'

'Sir ... my men?' Selkirk faced Smith directly.

'They are no longer your men, Selkirk,' Smith told him. 'As from this minute you are under my direct command. Come on.'

As Selkirk walked down toward the beaches, the cry 'Royal Borderers' reached him, high and faint, and then the rattle of Turkish machine guns. He was ushered into a steam launch and taken out to sea.

Chapter One

Selkirk admired the opulence of the room. Just a few days previously he had been hugging the bottom of a filthy trench as Turkish machine gunners tried their best to perforate him, but now he was surrounded by incredible luxury.

The golden frame of the mirror that hung on one wall would be worth a king's ransom alone, while the leather armchairs were thick and comfortable and the desk surface was polished perfection. A map of the Middle East spread across the entire opposite wall, with coloured pins showing the position of the various armies, red for Britain, blue for France and green for the Ottoman forces. There seemed many more green pins than red or blue. Behind the desk, an open window allowed in all the heat of a Maltese summer, while the musical tinkle of a fountain reminded Selkirk that the room overlooked a secluded courtyard in the very centre of Valletta.

Outside the door, a Royal Marine stood on guard. Unlike many sentries, the marine carried a fully loaded rifle, and his fixed bayonet glittered under the lights. The chevrons on his sleeve and medal ribbons on his breast confirmed he was a veteran, there to keep out intruders and not just for ceremonial effect.

There were four men in the room apart from Selkirk. Brigadier Smith sat on the left side of the desk, his face expressionless as he scrutinised Selkirk. There was a bald civilian in an immaculate old fashioned suit with a winged collar on the far right while two red-tabbed generals occupied the other seats. One had a central parting and a plump face, while the other was tall, moustached and frail look-ing with a withered left arm. It was the tall general who looked up at Selkirk and gave a surprisingly friendly smile.

'Major Andrew Selkirk, I presume.'

Selkirk smiled at the attempted humour. 'That's right, sir.' He stood at attention until the tall general motioned for him to sit down.

'General Iain Hamilton,' he introduced himself briefly, 'and this is General Sir John Maxwell,' he indicated the plump faced second officer, 'and Mr Jones of the Government. You already know Brigadier Smith of course.'

Selkirk shook hands with each man. Smith's grip was like iron while Jones merely touched the tips of his fingers and withdrew. Maxwell nodded; his eyes were bright but disinterested.

'You will be wondering what this is all about, Selkirk?' Hamilton smiled across to him.

'Yes, sir.' Selkirk studied the general. Everybody in the Army knew Hamilton by reputation. As a young officer, he had lost the use of his left arm fighting the Boers at Majuba; he had fought through the Great Boer War, and on the North- West Frontier, he had fought the Mahdis in the Sudan and had been an observer at the Russo-Japanese War. Now he led the Allied army at Gallipoli; not a bad collection of cam-paigns for a man with a bad limp and a very delicate appearance.

'Sit down, man,' Hamilton indicated a seat. 'Cigar?' He proffered a box.

'No thank you, sir. I don't.' Selkirk shook his head.

'Quite right; filthy habit,' Hamilton grinned. He did not offer the box to Smith or Jones, but Maxwell took a cigar and slowly lit up. 'Now, let me get this straight before we begin. You are Major Andrew Selkirk of the Royal Borderers?'

'Yes, sir.' Selkirk glanced down at his battered khaki. It compared unfavourably with the splendid dress uniforms of Maxwell, Smith and Hamilton but he had come straight from the front without time to pack anything smarter.

'You served throughout the South African War, fighting at Modder, Magersfontein, Klip Drift and the siege of Kimberley?'

Hamilton did not refer to any notes. He held Selkirk's eyes throughout his recitation.

'Yes, sir, I was in the ranks in those battles...'

'I am well aware of that, Selkirk,' Hamilton said cheerfully. Smith nodded but Jones the civilian, if he was a civilian, gave Selkirk a glassy-eyed stare.

'I remember you in the later stages,' Maxwell spoke with a slight Liverpool accent, 'when I commanded in the Western Transvaal.'

Selkirk nodded. 'Yes, sir.' He had never met Maxwell before but knew him by reputation as an honest commander who was skilled in dealing with the Boer population.

'You were given a field commission and raised a body of irregular horse, known as Selkirk's Reivers, to act as scouts for the mobile columns: correct?' Hamilton continued.

'Yes, sir,' Selkirk agreed. He compared those free ranging days on the veldt with the terrible yard-by-yard trench warfare in Gallipoli and France.

'Your Reivers were also used as a special force for more...' Hamilton hesitated for a significant second, 'clandestine operations in areas out with the principal campaigns.'

Selkirk nodded. 'Yes, sir.'

'And since then you have been farming in South Africa, but the war called you back to the Colours.' Hamilton finished off Selkirk's career with a neat flourish.

'That is correct sir.' Selkirk agreed.

'Good,' Hamilton leaned back in his chair. 'I had to make sure we had the right man. There are quite a few Andrew Selkirks in the Army, but only one who led Selkirk's Reivers.' He perused Selkirk for a few moments while Smith and Jones sat like sphinxes, silent and inscrutable. Maxwell was busily writing notes, with the sound of his pen loud in the room. 'I may have a little job for you, Selkirk, if Brigadier Smith and Mr Jones think you are up to it, and General Maxwell agrees you are suitable.' A wave of his hand indicated his companions.

'Yes, sir.' Selkirk glanced at Smith, who nodded and at Jones, who stared at him through basilisk eyes. Maxwell looked up and gave a small inclination of his chin.

'I remember these irregular units,' Maxwell said quietly. 'They played a part in suppressing the Boer commandos, but I am less convinced that they will be of use in more conventional warfare.' He put down his pen. 'Tell us what you think of the present military situation in the Middle East, Selkirk.'

Selkirk blinked. 'That's a big subject, sir,' he said, but all four men on the opposite side of the desk gazed at him unblinkingly. He walked to the map and pointed to the various areas about which he spoke.

'Well, we are facing the *Asakr -I Shahaneh* – the Ottoman Army - across the Suez Canal, in Gallipoli and further east in Mesopotamia, from Basra northward.' He stopped; hoping that was enough but the four men said nothing. Hamilton raised his eyebrows as an encouragement to continue.

'When the Gallipoli campaign succeeds,' Selkirk pointed to the area from which he had just come, 'it should force the Ottoman Empire - Turkey out of the war, but until then we are fighting on three different fronts, and we are already heavily committed in France and various places in Africa.' Selkirk had paid little attention to the wider issues of the war. He thought as a regimental officer, caring for his men and intent only on achieving the next objective. 'The Turks attacked Suez earlier this year, and we pushed them back, but apart from that it has been quiet there.'

Hamilton shook his head. 'Not quite, Selkirk. The Ottomans attacked at the end of January, and a couple of their companies managed to cross the Suez Canal near Ismailia. General Maxwell here kicked them out, but it was no rout; they fought well and withdrew in good order.' He smiled; 'Jacko Turk is a bonny fighter.'

'But we forced them back,' Selkirk insisted.

'Not all the way to Palestine,' Maxwell leaned forward in his chair, 'we had to abandon Sinai to them. The Ottomans once owned Egypt, as you know, and they want it back while we are busy elsewhere. We are stretched pretty thin until Kitchener's volunteers come through in strength, and even then the French theatre will still take priority.'

Selkirk thought of the casualties in Gallipoli. The army surely could not afford to lose men on such a scale.

Maxwell continued. 'A German named Frederich Von Kressenstein commands the Turks in Sinai, and he is an active officer with raids and attacks. Only two months ago his forces mined the canal, and he continues to probe and test our defences along the Suez border.'

'I see, sir.' Selkirk said.

'Do you, Selkirk?' Jones spoke for the first time. 'Do you understand exactly how important the Suez Canal is? The lifeblood of the Empire passes this way; it is the main artery of trade between India and all points East, and Egypt and all points west, including Great Britain. Under British rule it is open for free trade and every nation in the world can use the canal. Now; could you imagine world – not just British but world – trade under Ottoman or German control?'

There was silence in the room, broken only by the faint sound of people in the square outside. Selkirk nodded. Until now he had thought of the war only regarding Britain; the greater meaning and the possible outcomes, apart from the loss of prestige and hideous loss of life, had not occurred to him.

Maxwell glanced at Smith and then Jones, who gave a brief nod, as though granting permission to continue.

'I see you understand, Selkirk.' Maxwell said. 'Now this German fellow, Von Kressenstein, is sitting pretty somewhere in Sinai but we have information that the Turks are planning a major push to overrun us at Suez and seize the Canal.' He paused there and glanced at his companions.

'Carry on, Maxwell,' Hamilton said at once, while Smith gave an imperceptible nod.

'Sources have told us that the Turkish commander in Sinai, Dermal Pasha, is shortly meeting Von Kressenstein to organise a much larger attack on the canal. As I already said, this is to be no mere raid, but a full blown advance to capture Suez and disrupt Britain's lines of communication and supply. The Gallipoli campaign,' he glanced toward Hamilton, 'has diverted troops from Von Kressenstein's force, but has also weakened the potential of our defence.'

'Yes, sir.' Selkirk looked from face to face across the table.

'The thing is, we are not sure where Von Kressenstein is, or in what force.' Maxwell spoke slowly, 'and that is what we want you to find out.' He glanced at Hamilton and Smith. 'We have aircraft from the RFC out there, but they have seen nothing so far. We remember your exploits from the South African war and Hamilton thinks you have the imagination and expertise for the job, but I wanted to see you first.'

Selkirk felt that familiar surge of excitement. 'Yes, sir,' he glanced at Hamilton, who beamed at him. 'Thank you, sir.'

'Oh don't thank me, Selkirk, this is a dangerous job we are giving you, but it is critical and may advance your career.'

Maxwell grunted, apparently unhappy at this unwarranted attention paid to a junior officer. 'As from now, Selkirk, you are transferred from General Hamilton's command to mine.'

'Yes, sir.' Selkirk said. 'Do you wish me to raid against Van Kressenstein's force?'

'No, I want you to locate him and wait for my orders.' Maxwell snapped. 'This is not South Africa. There is no place in the modern British Army for tip-and-run raids and breaking windows with golden guineas.'

Jones glanced at Smith. 'Is this man trustworthy?' He asked bluntly.

'He is a British officer...' Hamilton interrupted, but Jones grunted at that.

'Selkirk is only an officer by default; he rose through the ranks so is hardly a gentleman.' Jones fixed Selkirk with eyes like acid. 'He joined the army rather than be jailed for horse theft. I ask again: can he be trusted?'

Selkirk felt his temper rise at the slight but kept his tongue firmly behind his teeth and said nothing. The class consciousness of the British Army was nothing new to him, and he had learned to ignore it whenever possible.

'General Hector MacDonald rose through the ranks...' Hamilton began, but Jones interrupted him.

'That is exactly my point, Hamilton. MacDonald committed suicide rather than live with the disgrace of his homosexuality. Can we trust this man Selkirk to maintain the necessary high standards of a British officer?' Jones spoke as if Selkirk was not in the room.

'I fought in the South African War...' Selkirk struggled to control his rising temper.

'My dear fellow, nobody doubts your courage,' Smith said, but again, Jones interrupted.

'Not your courage, Selkirk, but do you have the qualities of a British officer and gentleman? Do you have the moral strength necessary to deal with the temptations of the East? Do you have the perspicacity to discern the better of two hard choices?' Jones' voice was like ice as his gaze bored into Selkirk. 'If I agree that you should become involved in this operation, I must have assurances that you will not let us down.'

Selkirk noted the use of the word 'I.' Jones had revealed that he was the real power in this meeting: he was political then, something from a government office. 'What assurances do you require, Mr Jones?' He refused to call this man 'sir'.

'Assurance that you are of the right quality, Selkirk,' Jones said bluntly.

'Selkirk is a proven fighting officer,' Hamilton spoke up for his protégé.

'But can he operate out with the chain of command in this theatre?' Jones pressed home his point in a soft, unemotional voice. 'Can he maintain discipline among a disparate group of individuals when far from the support of superiors? Can he show the attributes of a British gentleman in a foreign land and impress upon those he meets the essential superiority of Great Britain over other nations?'

Selkirk blinked; that had come out of the blue. What, he wondered, was the 'essential superiority of Great Britain over other nations'? And why did he have to impress that over those he met? There was obviously more to this operation than a mere straightforward raid on an enemy force.

'May I ask what exactly I am supposed to do, sir?' Selkirk thought it best to direct the question to Maxwell.

There was no answer at first. Maxwell glanced at Jones, who frowned, obviously not used to such a junior officer asking such direct questions.

Selkirk pressed home his advantage. 'Am I leading a military raid, sir, or is there a political angle to this?'

Maxwell's face closed. It was Smith who looked toward Jones, ignored his slight shake of the head and grinned. 'As we are going to ask you to risk your life once more, Selkirk, I think you are entitled to know the truth.'

Jones drew his breath in sharply, but Smith continued. 'You must treat everything we say in here in the strictest confidence, you understand, Selkirk?' He lifted a finger to silence Jones' protests. 'This is a military matter, Mr Jones, and should be decided by army officers.'

'Of course, sir,' Selkirk said.

Smith looked at Jones and the generals: 'do we all agree that Major Selkirk is the man for the job?'

'Without a doubt,' Hamilton said at once.

Maxwell gave Selkirk a hard stare. 'I would prefer a regular soldier rather than a reservist, but Selkirk has experience in irregular warfare.' He tapped stocky fingers on the desk and looked directly at Jones. 'Sometimes it is better not to have a gentleman in this sort of operation, Mr Jones, in which case Selkirk may even be preferable to a real officer.'

Selkirk said nothing but was sure that Hamilton gave him a wink to take the sting from the insult.

Jones gave what may have passed as a smile. 'I agree. Nothing in Major Selkirk's background suggests that he is a gentleman, despite my questioning. He was, and remains, a ranking soldier promoted beyond his social standing.' Jones spoke as if he was discussing a tabby cat among pedigree Siamese. 'A gentleman may hesitate to undertake such a mission as we propose, but Selkirk appears to have the necessary background and experience.' He began to shuffle the papers that lay in front of him and relapsed into a silence that stretched for some time. The fountain in the courtyard outside seemed very loud. Movement caught Selkirk's attention as the harsh sun shot a shadow across the window; a woman's face momentarily appeared in the mirror, there was a brief bouquet of floral perfume as she walked past the open window, but before Selkirk had time to register details Jones was speaking again.

'We want you to raise a small, very mobile force of horsemen and observe what is happening in Sinai,' Jones said at last. 'We want you to find Von Kressenstein, watch his movements and send regular reports back to Cairo. In other words, Selkirk, we want you to be a spy.' He spat out the last word as if it fouled his mouth and immediately began to put his papers in order as if that statement ended his day's work.

Selkirk digested the implications. A hundred questions crowded his mind. He had a momentary vision of once again being mobile and leading a company of horsemen rather than cowering behind sandbags. He thought of the sounds of hooves drumming across hard ground, the excited whinny of the horses and the laughter of confident warriors.

'Yes sir,' he said. 'How many riders will I have?'

'We will send you some men.' Smith sounded surprised as if he had not expected a question from a jumped-up ranker. 'No more than twenty troopers as you have to be fast and invisible. God only knows what Jacko Turk would do if he captures you. We will provide an interpreter and any other specialists you may need.'

Selkirk studied the map on the wall; the Sinai Peninsula east of Suez seemed wild desert land.

'Do we know roughly where the Turks are sir?'

'No, but Brigadier Smith will furnish you with details,' Jones had obviously spent enough of his time with a man such as Selkirk. He rose from the table like a jack in the box. 'If you will excuse me, gentlemen...' he did not look at Selkirk as he left the room.

'Well now,' Hamilton passed around the cigars again, and this time Maxwell accepted one. He lit it carefully, drew slowly and leaned back in his chair. 'That's better. I don't envy you working with that man, Smith.'

Smith shrugged. 'He is what he is,' he said enigmatically as he also selected a cigar.

'It's always best to avoid politicians' Hamilton said, 'you'd be advised to remember that, Selkirk. You do know who that was, don't you?'

'No, sir,' Selkirk admitted. 'I have been involved in regimental duties since the war started and before that, I was farming in South Africa. I don't know Mr Jones at all.'

'That is not his real name,' Hamilton looked very pleased to give the information. 'That is C, the head of the Secret Service Bureau...' he stopped suddenly, glanced behind him at the open window and tapped a finger along the side of his nose, 'but we'd be better not to say any more, eh?'

'Perhaps not, sir,' Selkirk agreed. 'Now, sir, could I have Sergeant Crosier of the second battalion, Royal Borderers. He is in Gallipoli if he is still alive. And if I have twenty riders I need at least forty horses, preferably more, and time to train them for this sort of warfare.'

He crouched at the table as he explained his requirements and demands. He looked up and inhaled deeply of that hint of perfume in the room.

God, how I miss Helena. It is two years now. I want to hold her again and smell her hair and listen to her sensible, quiet talk.

Chapter Two

Egypt
August 1915

It was hot. Selkirk wiped the sweat from his face, sat back on Kimberley, his black stallion, watched his unit form up and shook his head.

'Oh dear God, is that the best you can do? Try again! I have seen one-legged blind spiders ride better than that!'

General Maxwell had kept his word and sent him twenty men, but except for Crosier, they were unknown to him. It seemed as if the regiments at Gallipoli had conferred together to get rid of their most unwanted.

'I've seen better, Crosier' he said. He sighed as one man in the rear slipped sideways out of his stirrups, balanced at an acute angle and tumbled to the ground.

'You!' Crosier rode up to the man, 'what's your name?'

'I'm John Wells,' the man said and for second Selkirk thought he was going to proffer his hand.

'So we are on first name terms are we?' Crosier's voice was laden with sarcasm. 'My name is Sergeant Crosier; you will call me Sergeant!'

Wells smiled, 'yes all right Sergeant.' He spoke with a rich accent that Selkirk could not place until he added, 'we don't have sergeants in Herefordshire.'

Selkirk turned away as Crosier introduced Wells to the volume of sound that a British Army sergeant was able to produce. When the recruits' horses began to back away, Selkirk guided Kimberley forward and soothed the most agitated. The rider dropped the reins and grabbed hold of the horse's mane.

'All right, son,' Selkirk calmed the horse and handed the reins back to the rider. 'It's only a sergeant shouting; that's what they do best.'

The soldier was red faced and perspiring in the heat. He gabbled a quick thank you and added 'sir' as an afterthought.

'What's your name?'

'Batsford, sir,' he was about twenty, with a thin face that he had not properly shaved. Nor had he correctly fastened his buttons, and he sounded terrified.

'Where were you before here, Batsford?'

'I was in the depot sir; the sergeant there said he had never seen anything like me before. He said he didn't know what to do with me and had me doing the training again and again until he sent me here and…'

Selkirk held up a hand to silence the torrent of words. 'Well, Batsford, you are in an elite unit now. You will be one of the best soldiers in the British army. Just do your best and do what Sergeant Crosier says.'

'But I'm useless…'

'Nobody's useless, Batsford; you have a new start here.'

Oh God, what has Maxwell sent me?

Selkirk waited until Crosier had shouted himself silent and rode up to him. The sergeant was staring at the assembled men as if he could not believe his eyes.

'Not quite the Gordon Highlanders, then?'

'They'll get there sir,' Crosier said. He was from Liddesdale and rode his horse as perfectly as he did everything else. 'Give them time; a lot of time.'

'That's just it, Sergeant; I don't know how much time we have.' Selkirk raised his voice as Batsford slid sideways on his saddle and let out a scream. 'Control your horse, Batsford! Don't let it control you!' He looked away and lowered his voice. 'Oh dear God what do we have here?'

'Just swaddies, sir,' Crosier said quietly. He looked sideways at Selkirk as if measuring his man. 'You know how the army works. The General would send a request for men for a particular mission, and the regiments would take the chance to dispose of the soldiers they don't want, the misfits, trouble makers and useless. We have the dregs of the Army here sir.'

He nodded to the men. 'Only two are volunteers; that fellow there…' He indicated a slight, smooth skinned man, 'William Walker, and that one, James Matthew…' a burly man with dark hair and a prominent hooked nose. Crosier shook his head, 'neither is up to scratch sir,' he paused, 'yet.'

'I am sure we can do something about that, Sergeant,' Selkirk said.

'Yes, sir.' Despite his show of pessimism, Crosier seemed pleased at the challenge. He turned back to the men. 'Form a straight line you useless bastards! Line up stirrup to stirrup! Did God not give you eyes when he plucked you from your mother's womb?' He swore when Batsford fell off his horse for the fifth time that morning and swore again as Batsford rolled in the sand as his mount delighted in this new freedom and shied away. Selkirk walked Kimberley forward and calmed the animal down.

'Up you get Batsford and try again. Don't be scared of your horse; you are his master.'

'Yes, sir,' tears rolled down Batsford's cheeks. 'Yes, but nobody told him that.' Batsford reached for the saddle, slipped and fell once more on to the sand.

Walker and Matthew backed away; Wells dismounted to help.

'Get back on that horse, Wells you idle bastard!' Crosier sounded nearly demented. He rode around the men, pushing and gesticulating before returning to Selkirk's side.

'They're hardly the best material for a force that has to survive in the desert and ride rings around Jacko Turk.' Selkirk said.

'Maybe not sir,' Crosier was too diplomatic a soldier to disagree with his officer. 'They will come round though.' He lowered his voice, 'or I'll break them. They may not look like soldiers, but I will make them act like them!'

Selkirk nodded. He had argued that his men wear a more comfortable uniform than was usual in the British Army, with the pith helmets replaced by Australian slouch hats and their leggings by loose fitting trousers that kept the wearer cooler in the burning heat. Crosier had disagreed violently but with respect; Selkirk, drawing on his African experience, overruled his protests.

'Get back in line, Kelly!' Crosier's roar could have awakened the Pharoes in the pyramids, but Kelly merely glowered at him and aimed a deliberate kick at Private Rourke.

In a minute the two men were at each other's throats, exchanging punches and kicks as their horses bucked and reared. Crosier bounded over and rode between them.

'Break it up you two, or it will be field punishment number one for the both of you!' He pushed them apart by sheer muscle power.

'Dirty Orange bastard!' Kelly tried a final kick that Rourke blocked and responded with a punch.

'Papish Scouse bugger!' He retorted.

'I'll rip your bloody Orange head off!' Kelly swore, but then Crosier had hauled them both off their horses.

'At least they have spirit, sir,' he said to Selkirk.

'Some have sampled too much spirit,' Selkirk nodded to one bleary-eyed incorrigible who swayed in the saddle.

'That's Sinclair, sir. I think his unit got rid of him because he prefers a bottle to a battle.'

What a perfect selection of men to take into Sinai: drunkards, brawlers and incompetents.

Selkirk and Crosier spent the rest of that day teaching the recruits the basics of horsemanship, having them mount, dismount and walk their horses. Of the nineteen men, three had been cavalry, and two had some mounted infantry training, but the others were complete novices. They sweated and cursed and fought their horses while Selkirk and Crosier roared orders and demonstrated every single step of horse management.

By the second week, the men were a little better. Every day Selkirk wondered when the call would come to lead them into action, and every day he prayed for more time.

'Ready to fight, sir? They are hardly able to stand,' Crosier shook his head. 'They might be capable of carrying a heavy object in a straight line under constant supervision, but I doubt it.'

'You know the difference between a hoof and a saddle now,' Selkirk addressed his men, 'and that's more than you did last week. Let's try something different. Let's try riding in the desert.' He glanced at Crosier. 'I will lead, Sergeant, and you take the rear.'

'Yes, sir,' Crosier rolled his eyes in mock dismay.

'We won't go far; the Senussi are quiet just now, but you never know if they could rise again.' Selkirk allowed his words to reach the troopers. The Germans and Turks had stirred the tribe of the western desert, the Senussi into rebellion, but the British had temporarily subdued them; however, there might well be a few malcontents ready to take a swipe at a weak British force. It would do his men good to be watchful; for once they were in Sinai, they would be in danger every minute of every day. 'Keep alert, boys.'

Within ten minutes of leaving their tented camp, the unit was in chaos as the stronger riders kept together but, the weaker lagged behind.

Selkirk slowed the march to allow Crosier time to round up the stragglers, but the sergeant was soon hoarse with shouting at them through clouds of desert dust. Batsford managed to lose his rifle and in doubling back to find it, quickly lost himself. Selkirk halted the troop and searched for both. He found the rifle muzzle-down in the sand, but Batsford was harder to locate. Selkirk rode in ever increasing circles for two hours before he saw him riding determinedly in the wrong direction.

'Sorry, sir,' Batsford said, 'I am useless sir; just no good at anything.'

'Keep with me,' Selkirk ordered and wondered if he could tether their horses together.

'I can look after Batsy, sir,' Wells volunteered, then yelled as his horse stumbled and he had to haul hard on the reins to control him.

'You learn to look after yourself first!' Crosier advised.

Selkirk had intended to keep them all day in the desert, but after four hours he knew they were not ready. Two more men wandered into the desert; others lost control of their horses, three finished the contents of their water bottles despite orders to ration water and one drew his rifle in near panic when a passing Arab lifted an arm in greeting.

'Back to camp,' Selkirk said, and Crosier nodded grateful agreement. He took a position in the rear and blasted them into formation as they returned in a state of drooping exhaustion. They halted outside the gateway to their tented encampment and stood in a dejected clump while a lone horseman watched from under his broad slouch hat.

'Water, feed and groom the horses first,' Selkirk ordered, 'take care of your equipment and then get water and food for yourselves!'

He knew that Crosier would ensure the orders were carried out.

The lone horseman walked his horse closer and spoke around the long pipe that hung from his mouth.

'Are these supposed to be horse soldiers?' His tone was laconic, the accent undoubtedly Australian.

'They are,' Selkirk said. He knew Australians well enough not to be surprised at the lack of any sign of respect to an officer.

'Not very good, are they, mate?'

'They're getting there,' Selkirk defended his men. 'They just need time.'

'Some ability would help, too,' the Australian said. He held out his hand. 'Thomas Black.'

'Andrew Selkirk,' Selkirk waited for a second. 'Major Andrew Selkirk.'

The Australian's grip was like iron. 'Christ, you're a major! Should I bow and scrape and call you "my lord?"'

'I expect nothing less; call me Your Majesty if you wish,' Selkirk said. 'You're a bushman aren't you?'

Black nodded, 'not many British officers would shake my hand, yet alone know that.'

'I rode with Australians in South Africa.' Selkirk noticed the gold wound stripes on Black's sleeve. 'Where did you pick that up?'

Black shrugged. 'I was at the landings at Gaba Tepe. I never even cleared the beach before Jacko got me.' He lifted his left arm and tapped his right leg.

They were silent together for a few moments as Selkirk considered what he wished to say. 'I rode with men from New South Wales. They were the best bushmen going.'

'You thought that the Walers were good bushmen?' Black shook his head. 'They couldn't find their arse with both hands tied behind their back.'

Selkirk hid his smile. 'I found them more than adequate. How good are you?'

'I'm South Australian,' Black boasted, 'I can track the footprints of Jesus Christ through a bloody thundercloud blindfolded and with a bottle of rum in each hand.'

Selkirk grinned. *You'll do me.*

'So what are you doing with this mob?' Black indicated Selkirk's sweating riders as their attempt to form a column to ride into camp ended in total confusion. Batsford lost control of his horse and ended face down in the desert once more. Selkirk allowed Crosier the dubious pleasure of reprimanding the unfortunate man.

'Just training them,' Selkirk said and ignored Black's sneer. 'Which unit are you with?'

'Australian Light Horse,' Black said at once, 'so they used us as infantrymen in Gallipoli.'

'That's the military way,' Selkirk agreed. He shook his head. 'I expect you'll be returning to Gallipoli when you are fully fit.'

'I expect so,' Black puffed at his pipe and watched as Crosier berated the riders. 'What are you training them for?'

'Operations,' Selkirk said.

Black nodded. 'This will be the secret force that is going to ride into Gaza to find Johnny Turk.'

'That's it.' Selkirk was not surprised that Black knew all about them. Rumours spread around the army so quickly so that any secret was virtually bound to be heard and passed on in the interval between being uttered and reaching the ears of its intended recipient.

'Djemal Pasha must be quaking in his fez,' Black said as Wells stopped to fondle his horse and disrupted the column of march into the encampment.

Selkirk smiled. 'He will be by the time we have finished.' He gave Black a sidelong look. 'I am going to put in a request to have you volunteer to join us.'

'I thought you'd never ask, mate,' Black took the pipe from his mouth. 'It looks like you need all the help you can get.'

Sergeant Crosier had finished his most pressing task with the trainee horsemen and caught the last few words of the conversation. 'He noticed Black's total lack of badges of rank. 'You call the Major, sir, Aussie!'

Black slowly removed the pipe from his mouth. He looked at Selkirk, winked and said nothing.

Crosier straightened to attention in the saddle. 'I said you address the major as sir, private!' His voice was like the stab of a bayonet.

'Stand easy, Sergeant,' Selkirk spoke quietly; 'This is Thomas Black of the Australian Light Horse.'

'Yes, sir,' Crosier glared at Black but said no more.

'He'll be joining us shortly,' Selkirk added.

Crosier gave Black a look that had terrorised hundreds of private soldiers but which bounced off the Light Horseman like rain off a slab of granite. 'As you wish, sir.'

'As a sergeant,' Selkirk added and grinned at Black's expected denial.

'I'm not a bloody sergeant!'

'I'm not a bloody sergeant, sir!' Selkirk saw the sudden amusement in Crosier's eyes. 'You can either be a sergeant with our very irregular horse or a private hiding in a trench in Gallipoli.'

'You're a devious man, sir,' Crosier said quietly.

With Black giving horsemanship instruction, the training speeded up. 'Your shooting is standard British Army,' Selkirk told them. 'You are fast, and by European standards, you are relatively accurate.' He left the sentence unfinished.

'I will alter that. By the time I finish with you, every man will be a proficient marksman.' He looked over his twenty-one faces, with colours ranging from peeling scarlet- recruit to the nut brown veterans of India and Africa. 'No fancy weapons, lads; just the Lee-Enfield, which is as fine a rifle as exists.' He grinned, 'we'll start with the basics.'

'This is the short magazine Lee Enfield .303.' He had them lined up in the desert a mile outside the encampment with the pyramids of Giza prominent on the horizon and a small group of Arabs watching with some curiosity. Selkirk held up the standard British Army rifle as if none of them had ever seen it before. 'But nobody ever calls it that. You know it as the SMLE or the Smellie.' He waited for the inevitable ripple of laughter to die away. 'It is a bolt action rifle, forty-four and a half inches long and holds ten rounds loaded in two clips' he held up the clips and demonstrated how to press them home with his thumb. 'Smellie is a killer. At two hundred yards, a round fired from this little darling will smash through two bricks and kill Jacko or Fritz hiding at the back.' He waited for his words to sink in. 'We each routinely carry 120 rounds. When we go on field operations, we will be unsupported so that we have to carry more. At Le Cateau, last year, the Royal Scots faced the Hun at five hundred yards and slaughtered them. The Royal Scots Fusiliers did the same to the Turk at Suez. We will do better.'

'Now this is not merely a rifle.' Selkirk held the weapon high. 'It is your lover; treat her properly, and she will save your life. Abuse her, and she will jam, and you will not be able to fire so that Jackie Turk will emasculate you with his bloody sharp bayonet. Second to your horse, she is the best friend you will ever have.'

Selkirk could see that the veterans were resentful of his previous words about their standards of musketry, so he explained further. 'As you know, the British Army takes great pride in its marksmanship. Company commanders are expected to have at least half their men wearing the marksmanship badge.'

There were a few of nods from the assembled troopers. 'The Army expects you to hit a twelve-inch square target from a range of 600 yards, and every soldier has to be able to fire fifteen rounds a minute at a target 300 yards distant.'

He waited for the recruits to assimilate that information and then continued. 'Last year Sergeant Alfred Snoxall set the standard with thirty-eight rounds on target at 300 yards.' He waited for the murmurs of admiration from the veterans to fade, and repeated the words, 'thirty-eight rounds: pull back the bolt...' He demonstrated as he spoke, 'allow the round to click into the chamber, push forward the bolt, lock, aim and fire. He did that thirty-eight times, plus he changed the magazine three times all within a minute.' Selkirk tossed the rifle to Black. 'I want forty a minute from everybody, and we will start now.'

Selkirk started their practice marksmanship until every man could hit a two-foot square target ten times out of ten at fifty yards, and then increased the range to seventy- five yards and then a hundred. When Batsford complained that he could not do it, Selkirk held his gaze. 'The German snipers carry Mausers sighted to 2200 yards, and they seldom miss. Now get to work.'

They got to work.

The next day he increased the range to two hundred yards. Within a week the majority of his unit could hit the target eight times out of ten at five hundred yards, and the best of them were scoring at six hundred. Selkirk was moderately satisfied.

'Good,' he said. 'Now we will try at moving targets.'

He had men pull a wooden framework behind them while others fired, but he had to increase the length of the lead when some shots came perilously close to the pullers. He taught them the simple mathematics required to calculate where the target would be by the time the bullet reached it, and the widest part of the human body at which to aim.

'Hip to hip' Selkirk demonstrated. 'If you are not sure, aim for a body shot; we are at war, and it is our job to kill or disable the enemy before they do it to us.' He looked over his men, sensing the reluctance in some of them. 'How many of you are married?'

Four hands rose.

'Would you like Jacky Turk to rape your wives?' He allowed the question to hang unanswered in the air. 'Well, they will. If we lose this war, the Kaiser has promised that a Turkish army will garrison Britain.' That was a blatant lie, but he saw the sudden consternation on the faces of the married men.

'Anybody have a sister or mother?'

Most of the men answered to that one, and Selkirk repeated his warning. 'So when you shoot, lads, shoot to kill, and when you train, train as hard as you can. The better a soldier you are, the better the chance of us winning this war and the better the chance you have of returning home alive. Train hard: fight easy.'

It was a simple enough speech, but when the men resumed their training, there was a new purpose to their movements and a new drive as they rode or fired. Selkirk showed them a captured Mauser rifle and ensured they familiarised themselves with it. 'You might lose your weapon in battle,' he said, 'so it's best that you can use anything handy.'

He trained them to load and unload blindfold and showed them how to whitewash stones to use as range markers when they were in a fixed position. Drawing on his experience in the South African War, he advised them not to attract the attention of a sniper by acting or dressing in a manner that made them distinctive and watched them slowly learn the arts of soldiering away from the barrack square. He saw some of them eye the women among the Arabs who attended their training and knew his men were far from ready for irregular war.

By the end of the third week, the strongest personalities were coming forward. Selkirk kept his promise and promoted Black to sergeant, split the men into two sections of ten, with Crosier in command of one group and Black of the other. He made sure that Kelly and Rourke were in different sections. Rather than try and bring the two men together, Selkirk exploited their antagonism by making Crosier and Black's men compete against each other, with the hope that rivalry brought out the best in each man. Then he stood back and watched results.

He requisitioned two Lewis guns and ensured that everybody, including himself, was at least adequate in loading and firing. 'You never know when extra fire power will come in handy,' he explained, 'and once we can handle the Lewis, we will get back in the saddle.' He grinned at his men. 'When we are ready, we will be able to outride anything any anybody the enemy has, outshoot their best and outfight ten times our number.' He gave one Lewis gun to each section and offered a twelve-hour pass to the section with the best score.

'But keep clear of the Wazza district of Cairo,' Selkirk warned and saw the immediate spark of interest in every eye.

Crosier won the contest of the Lewis Guns, and Selkirk watched his section celebrate before they clumped together to discuss how best to spend their precious free time. He knew they were not yet ready for war, but the clock was ticking, and every day he wondered when the order would come to lead his men into the Sinai and face thousands of veteran Turks.

I cannot relent; I must push them as hard as I can.

They spent days on horseback as Selkirk trained them in dismounting and mounting the instant an order was given, in using the horses as shields and in shooting from the saddle.

'I don't recommend this,' he said, 'but it looks spectacular and can unsettle the enemy, particularly if we have half a dozen unseen marksmen in cover picking off their men.' Once they had mastered the basics, Selkirk expanded on their training with fire and movement, with five men firing from cover as the others charged forward in flame and glory. 'And make sure you don't shoot your colleagues: are you listening, Rourke and Kelly?' He watched them pick up the techniques but noticed Walker trying to make some conversation with the Arab women and Rourke eyeing Kelly with contempt and knew they were not ready for war.

Selkirk trained them in every aspect of horsemanship, but in rough riding and bush skills Black was Crosier's undisputed master, and his section picked up the twelve-hour pass Selkirk offered for horse mastery. Selkirk watched as they celebrated, knew they were not yet ready for war.

He trained them in the sudden night time swoop on an enemy position, and the fighting withdrawal with the men split, one section covering the other, so the pursuing enemy was constantly under accurate fire. He trained them in night picketing; he checked the heavy cavalry saddles with which they had been issued and had them lightened for long rides, so the horses travelled faster without fatigue. He taught them every irregular horse trick he could remember and watched them grow in skill and confidence. He trained them how to recognise the size of an approaching body of cavalry by the volume of dust they created, and how to gauge the number of men approaching by the vibrations they made on the ground. Black won the round on irregular warfare, and when his section celebrated, Selkirk watched and knew they were not yet ready for war.

He trained them in the gentle art of grenade throwing, and in camouflaging themselves, in using dead ground for cover and in knife fighting. He showed them how to use the buckles of their belts as weapons and where to kick to maim and kill, with Kelly and Rourke proving themselves expert in the more ugly aspects of close combat. In this contest, Crosier's section won, and Selkirk watched them celebrate their twelve hours of freedom, but he knew they were not yet ready for war.

Crosier's men were a little the worse for wear when they returned. 'When do we go against the Turks, sir?' Crosier asked.

'Whenever higher command orders us to,' Selkirk said, 'and when I think we are ready. In the meantime, we train and ensure that we are fit to face whatever the enemy throws at us.'

Not yet, please God, not yet; my boys are not ready yet.

But somewhere within him, Selkirk knew he wanted the urgency and terror and excitement of war. He wanted to forget the heartache with which he lived every night of his life.

He trained them in bayonet and close quarter fighting, with Black and Crosier adding their quota of skills to Selkirk's offerings. He trained them in camping overnight with their horses in the desert and celestial navigation, so if any of his men got himself separated from the unit, they could find their way back to Egypt by the stars. He brought in a specialist from Cairo and trained them in pigeon handling and tying the delicate message to their legs without causing any injury. Wells proved the most gentle with the birds, with a morose thirty-year-old man named Wilson nearly as good.

He trained them in signalling with flags and the heliograph so a scout could send messages from twenty miles away. The first time was a disaster, with an indecipherable message being misunderstood by everybody, but after half a dozen attempts Selkirk found satisfaction in watching his men read the blinking light on a dark desert night, but he knew they were not yet ready for war.

He stationed one man on top of the great Giza pyramid and had his men ride deeper and deeper into the desert, each mile sending message, by flags by day and heliograph by night to test the range of that flashing light in desert conditions.

'This is nothing like Hereford,' Wells said, 'there's not an apple tree in this entire country.'

'Not a single one, and no workhouse overseers either,' Batsford said in a quiet voice. He watched as Wells struggled to untangle his reins. 'Here, I can help there.'

Selkirk heard that comment and watched Batsford. He was still clumsy, still naïve and still slow, but he was a different man who now merged with the other troopers far more and was no longer the butt of all their raucous humour.

'There,' Batsford untangled the harness. He looked around him. 'This is a man's life' he said.

Selkirk looked at the tiny light flickering across the desert and agreed. Irregular warfare in the wilderness was indeed a man's life, but he missed Helena with her slow smile and practical outlook on life that could dissolve into laughter at the most unexpected times. This wild training was also a bachelor's life, and it was many years since he had been a bachelor.

But Helena is not here, and my men are not yet ready for war.

The sudden surge of homesickness forced him away from his men, so he climbed part of the way up the great pyramid and stared south. Down there, some thousands of miles away, Helena lay quiet at home. He should be with her, not up here fighting a war for a country in which he no longer had much interest.

Selkirk obtained the best available maps of the Sinai and Palestine and spent hours poring over them with Crosier and Black.

'I feel as familiar with Sinai and the Negev as I am with the Outback,' Black said.

They discussed where Von Kressenstein might base himself and the best routes to attack him and his supply columns. Each of his sergeants had a point of view founded on their own military experience, and when they refused to compromise or listen to the other, Selkirk knew they were not yet ready to go to war.

August passed in blistering heat as the men gradually became hardened to the climate and accustomed to long hours in the saddle. September arrived with a slight drop in temperature, but Selkirk did not relent, driving his men to their limit. They rode with more confidence, relaxed in the saddle and shot like veterans, but still, Selkirk was not satisfied.

On the 15th of September, he split his command into their two halves and had them compete, Black's red section against Crosier's blue. He equipped each unit with rifles, packs and water, ordered each to find their way to the oasis of Al Fayoum in the Western Desert, capture a palm frond and bring it back to the summit of the Great Pyramid of Giza, just to the west of Cairo. To make things more interesting, he persuaded the colonel of a resting battalion of Fusiliers to set ambushes and pursue his men with an object of capturing them.

'My lads are keen as mustard,' the Fusilier colonel warned, 'they might be a bit rough with your boys.'

Selkirk nodded. 'I'll take that chance,' he said. He thought of Kelly and Rourke loose among the Fusiliers and wondered if there would be any fatalities. The British Army had a long history of inter-regimental rivalry that could erupt into bloody battles with fist, boot and belt-buckle, so his unit would merely be following an ancient tradition.

He gave his men a few hours and then rode to the platform of hard sand on which the pyramids were built and unfastened his pack and portable heliograph from Kimberley. This area was always popular with off-duty British and Anzac soldiers, so he had no difficulty in finding a group of Australian cavalrymen to look after the horse while he slowly ascended the steep steps of the pyramid.

A body of Egyptian police watched him without interference, while a crowd of guides clustered hopefully, no doubt cursing the war that deprived them of tourist money. He waved them away and looked up-ward. The Pyramid of Kheops had once been smooth, but centuries of use as a quarry for Cairo had deprived it of its limestone covering so now it was a succession of huge stone steps that climbed to the apex. Aware he was mounting history; Selkirk hefted his burden and hauled himself slowly upward. He stopped about half way and looked over Egypt and the immense expanse of desert that stretched to the straight gouge of the Suez Canal and beyond to Sinai and all the way east. 'Ship me somewhere east of Suez' he murmured and wished he had brought his Kipling with him.

Getting as comfortable as he could, Selkirk took his binoculars from his pack and looked westward where his men were riding. He searched for any tell-tale clouds of dust but could only see a group of camels. He scanned north and south and as far west as he could, but a heat haze distorted his vision; he knew that the palm trees floating above the horizon were only mirages, while the many clouds of dust could conceal anything tangible out there.

Selkirk put his binoculars down, adjusted his hat to compensate for the glare of the sun, took a drink from his water bottle and waited. His men had to trust their section leaders, and he had to trust his men. He wanted them as self-sufficient as possible, unlike the ordinary British soldiers who were trained to follow orders blindly, implicitly and without question. The sheer scale of the view drew his attention, but the sense of history eased him away from the troubles of the war to his own life. He thought of his years with Helena on their farm in South Africa with their children Andrew and Helen, and he did not know that he was smiling. He thought of the decade of happiness he had enjoyed and then the horror of disease that had robbed him of his wife and his children.

There is enough evil in this world, enough sadness; how many thousands of families would this war destroy?

He felt the punishing heat of the sun, contemplated the vast void of space above him and wondered at the majesty of God in this place where contrasting desert wastes and fertility spawned gods and religions.

And he waited. He heard the distinctive sound of camels passing beneath and experienced the timelessness of the East. Out here, life continued as it had for centuries, even while the most modern armies in the industrial world planned the most efficient methods of massed slaughter. He heard voices floating from below and guessed that the tourist guides were haggling with a body of British or Anzac soldiers; he hoped everybody would leave him in peace.

Tipping back his bush hat, Selkirk once more focussed his binoculars to the west. He no longer expected to see his men but the movement provided a feeling of connection. The desert sprang into focus, mile after mile of bugger all, as Black called it.

Night fell, swift as the horsemen of the apocalypse. The temperature plunged from unbearable heat to chilling cold, but Selkirk remained where he was. His men were out there, and he would wait for them. There was a massive part of him that yearned to ride out and guide them in, but he knew that would defeat the purpose of the exercise.

Most of his men were the undersized, the undernourished and the unwanted from the back streets of British cities; they had rarely ventured into their local countryside yet alone seen the vastness of the North African desert. An exercise such as this would increase their confidence in themselves and their ability in a manner in which they would never have dreamed Or it would destroy them.

Their lives would have been full of constrictions and rigid constraint from the moment of their birth, through schooling that emphasised their need to conform as it taught them only what was considered fitting for their station in life, to menial jobs and then the lowest rank in the army. Now they were experiencing a form of freedom that would either make them or terrify them. If it succeeded, they would never view life in the same narrow manner again.

His musings so preoccupied Selkirk that he nearly missed the first stark blink of the heliograph. He read the message as the Morse flashed over the desert. 'Red section successful' it said, and was followed a few moments by another: 'blue section successful.' He acknowledged at once; both his sections had located the oasis and cut a palm frond. Now all they had to do was find their way back to the pyramid, avoid the Fusilier ambushes and present him with their trophies. That should be an educational trip for them.

Selkirk waited as the soft glow from nearby Cairo increased until it chased away the security of the desert night. The moon rose, the same moon that had risen above Moses and dozens of dynasties of Pharaohs, and Selkirk wondered if they had ever wanted peace and solitude and a return to their wives and families rather than anticipate the onslaught of another round of war. Silver light ghosted across the pyramid, highlighting the hard edges of the steps. Selkirk could nearly taste the age of the structure and hear the moaning of the centuries it had endured.

He heard them in the stillness, the soft pad of hooves through the dark, then a sharp command in pure South Australian. Selkirk nodded; Black's section had won the race despite distance and unfamiliar territory, and all the Fusiliers could do to stop them. He waited as Black's men clambered up the high steps of the pyramid, listened to the scrape of iron-studded boots and an occasional curse as a shin or ankle barked on ancient unforgiving stone. Selkirk looked downward and saw the moon gleam on slouch hats and khaki.

'Sir! Major Selkirk?' That was Crosier's voice from the ground far beneath. 'Right, men, keep in step!' Only a regular sergeant would insist on his men maintaining step while ascending a pyramid in the light of an Egyptian moon.

Selkirk heard the disciplined stamp as Crosier's section marched up the opposite side of the pyramid from Black's more stealthy approach. He lit a lamp although the moon made that unnecessary, and stood up, waiting.

Black's section arrived first, grinning with triumph despite the dark patches of sweat that disfigured their uniforms and the weary lines of their faces. 'Here we are, sir,' Black produced a single large palm frond, 'taken from the oasis and carried to you.' He made a gesture with his hand that Selkirk chose to interpret as a salute.

He acknowledged. 'Thank you, sergeant.' He held up his lantern, 'how was the operation?'

As Black began his explanation, Crosier arrived, stamped to attention and threw a smart salute. 'Blue section reporting back, sir, with palm fronds.' He raised his voice, 'Batsford!'

Batsford stumbled up, failing to hide his grin as he handed over two palm fronds. 'The bloody Fusiliers tried to stop us, sir,' his smile widened, 'and there was a bit of a bobbery.'

'You got through though,' Selkirk said.

'Yes, sir, and we got souvenirs,' Batsford gave a sly smile as the other members of the section crowded round. Rourke wore a grin on his face that Selkirk thought was pure evil.

'Souvenirs?' Selkirk held up the lantern.

'Right, lads,' Crosier said, and each man of his section dipped into a pocket and produced a small metal object. They piled them on the second top step of the pyramid. Selkirk lifted one up; it was a Fusilier cap badge; the second was the same, and the third.

'Are they all the same?' Selkirk wondered what the Fusilier colonel would think.

'Yes, sir,' Batsford said, 'and we got these two.' He reached into his pack and hauled out what looked like a bundle of off-white cloth.

'Batsford...' Crosier's voice was like steel, but Batsford continued.

'There was this Fusilier sergeant that tried to stop us, a right four-letter-man he was, sir. He tried to ambush us, but we heard him moving about miles away, sir and the Sarge, Sergeant Crosier I mean, led us around the back of them, sir, and we put the kybosh on the bastards.' He shook out the cloth to reveal a pair of long woollen underwear. 'The Fusilier sergeant lost this, sir.'

Most of the men of blue section laughed, obviously enjoying the memory of the sergeant's discomfort.

Selkirk wondered if it would be bad for discipline to approve the disrobing of a non-commissioned officer, but decided his men were not part of any conventional unit and allowed himself to smile. 'Well done, lads!'

The resulting grins and nudged from the assembled soldiers told him that he had made the correct decision.

Only Wilson did not smile. He sat on the step and touched the ancient stone. 'This is an uncanny place,' he said quietly.

'It's nothing like Hereford,' Wells moved closer. 'You all right, Wilson?'

'There is death here,' Wilson said. He looked upward to the moon. 'This is a bad place.'

'It's a place like any other,' Crosier said. 'And that's the end of it. Now stop talking nonsense and celebrate like the other lads!'

Black stepped up, 'while you Blues were wasting time playing with the Fusiliers, my section just passed them by and got here first.'

'You're useless!' Kelly taunted, and others of the Red section joined in, so the opposing halves of the unit squared up to each other on the steps of the pyramid. When Black and Crosier also exchanged unfriendly glares, Selkirk knew that they were not yet ready to go to war.

'Twenty-four-hour pass,' he decided, 'for both sections. But avoid Wazza!' His attempt to intimidate them with a glare was completely ineffectual.

* * *

Brigadier Smith lifted the report from his desk, read it and raised his eyebrows. 'That is not good,' he said. 'That is not good at all.' He read further. 'So the Central Powers are meeting to co-ordinate a rising in Bengal with attacks from Germany and previously neutral powers,' he scribbled notes on a small pad of paper. 'This is worrying.'

Jones tapped his fingers on top of the desk and glanced outside. Rain battered against the Whitehall window and ran down the panes in constant streams. 'If the Germans are successful in this endeavour it could put an intolerable strain on the Empire and may also lead to another Mutiny.'

'Our forces are already dangerously overstretched,' Smith said. 'If there is an internal and external threat to India, it might be impossible to hold on to it, and if India falls, the rest of our Empire in the East would also go. We dealt with the February Mutiny quite efficiently, but this Jugantar group appears even more dangerous.'

'The Indian Independence Committee is a threat,' Jones said. 'If you read the report to the end you will see that they plan uprisings in Bengal and Burma, together with a German navy raid on Madras and the Andaman Islands.' He walked to the window and looked at the traffic bustling past. Wartime London, the hub of the greatest Empire the world had ever known, still bright and unbowed. 'Our position is very tenuous in the East,' he said. 'We must nip this in the bud. We know that a man named Jitendra Gupta is vital in this plot. He is the Indian Independence Committee liaison between the overall leader, Mukherjee and the Germans. At present Jitendra Gupta is the most dangerous man in the East.'

'Do you have people in location to find out where he is?' Smith asked.

'We have a few double agents in the organisation but none of our own in Palestine, where they're holding this meeting.' He repeated the name. 'Jitendra Gupta,' In Jones' mouth, it sounded flat and sinister. 'If we had him in captivity we could get names and dates and unravel the whole organisation.' He grunted. 'We must have him; it is top priority. We will suspend all other clandestine operations until this traitor is in our hands.'

Smith sighed. 'You said we have no operatives of our own in Palestine. Do the Russians or French have anybody there? Anybody that we can use?'

'Not that we can trust.' Jones opened the window and allowed a blast of autumn air into the room. 'There is a Zionist group there.'

'Jewish? Would they work for us?' Smith scribbled more notes on his pad.

'With the right incentives they might,' Jones said.

'How much would we have to pay them?' Smith looked up. 'If India is at stake...'

'Not money. If we promised the Jews an independent state in the Middle East after we defeat the Turks, they would help. Naturally, I would have to square it with the Secretary of State for the Colonies and the Secretary for Foreign Affairs.'

'Bonar Law and Edward Grey? Will they agree?'

'The Canadian may, and Grey will do as I tell him,' Jones' smile was laden with malice. 'I had him as my fag in Winchester you see; he was a most indolent youth, and I had to beat him quite often.'

'I see.' Smith knew how the old school tie system worked. 'That sounds promising then.'

'The Jews will find out what is happening, but we must send in somebody to capture Gupta.' Jones said. 'As we have no reliable agents there, what units do we have that might do the job?'

'Scottish Horse, Australian Light Horse and the Lovat Scouts are all in Gallipoli,' Smith said, 'we could pull one of them out and stage a quick raid.'

'Lovat is a gentleman; he would never agree to use his men for this sort of operation. The Scottish Horse is dismounted, and I want the Australians for something else.'

'That leaves Selkirk's lot then,' Smith said slowly. 'We were going to use them in Sinai.' He hesitated, 'you met Selkirk in Valetta, Jones.'

'The horse thief raised from the ranks. He'll do.' Jones closed the window. 'Get this Gupta in our hands, Smith, by any artifice you wish. I don't care what it costs; Selkirk's rag tag and bobtail are expendable; we can replace them easily; just get me the traitor.'

Smith made a final entry in his notebook and stood up.

'Oh, and Jones, if you think these Jewish fellows could be useful later on, feed them whatever story you like and take any measures to get them on our side.'

* * *

The military police sergeant stood at rigid attention outside Selkirk's tent. His uniform was immaculate, with a sharp crease in his trousers and his tunic fully buttoned to the throat. He seemed impervious to the high sun and refused to blink as sweat beads formed on his eyelashes.

'There is trouble in Wazza sir.' He reported. 'Some of your men are involved.'

Selkirk reached for his hat. 'What sort of trouble?'

'Your men are brawling with a Fusilier unit. The military police have been called and are dealing with the situation. There are some casualties.' The sergeant's expression did not alter.

Selkirk stilled the words that came to his mouth. 'Are any of my men seriously injured?' He headed for Kimberley, shouting for his batman to bring his saddle.

'I don't know, sir,' the sergeant said, but Selkirk had not waited to hear the words. He sped out of the tent, knowing that he needed every one of his men.

There were two Cairos, the modern city with wide streets, banks and hotels where the Europeans and wealthy Egyptians lived, and the old Cairo of tangled narrow streets, shacks, and low-roofed houses. Wazza was in the old quarter, where doorways opened onto mysterious courtyards, women sheltered behind faceless veils and Coptic churches survived in a city long since Moslem. Kites hovered on outspread wings; there were exotic aromas of musk, coffee, incense and humanity around the booths and the slender minarets of mosques. Wazza was also the red light district that attracted British and Anzac soldiers like iron filings to a magnet, despite strong official warnings to the contrary.

Selkirk heard the noise while he was only a few streets into the area; the loud roaring of disputing British soldiers, the snarl of orders from the redcaps and the occasional shout of triumph or yell of pain. He grinned; the off duty British Army was notorious for the occasional riot. It was good that this mixed army of territorials, reservists and Colonials maintained the fine old tradition.

Pushing Kimberley around a steep corner and past a crowd of interested local men in long robes, he saw the first casualty. A Fusilier leaned against the wall of a mosque, bleeding profusely from a head wound. In the next alley, there was a group of Fusiliers happily battling it out with half a dozen redcaps, with a couple of New Zealanders joining in for good measure. In one corner a corporal of Fusiliers was arguing with a redcap over the custody of a tousle-haired private who seemed to have had the worst of an encounter with the Prussian Guards, yet alone a rival British soldier. A few yards away a score of bush-hatted Australians threw bottles through a window and shouted in triumph at the sound of breaking glass.

Selkirk ignored them; it was not his place to interfere with the pleasures of men from other regiments. He pushed Kimberley on to a slightly broader street, which was a confused mass of brawling bodies. Every redcap in the British Army seemed to be in Wazza, with a sprinkling of headquarter troops as well, and all intent on putting down the trouble his men had allegedly caused.

'Sergeant Crosier? Sergeant Black?' Selkirk shouted above the background roar. In the confusion of Wazza, the weight of the revolver at his hip was reassuring. He had no fear that any of his men would attack him while sober, but a drink-maddened Fusilier or an Anzac just back from Gallipoli may well wish to even some score with a British officer. There was no response to his hail, but he heard Crosier's roar: 'Blue section; this way!' and Selkirk pushed Kimberley into the crowd.

Some of the khaki clad men parted before him, but others ignored him, intent on doing as much damage as possible to somebody, anybody, as long as they could vent their frustration.

'Red section!' That was Black's voice, and then Selkirk reined up and stood Kimberley still in the centre of the heaving street. He listened to what Black had to say: 'Go to help the Reds!'

Well done, Black; that's what I wanted to hear.

Selkirk hid his smile and waited to see what happened next. He saw a couple of Fusiliers fall on an unfortunate redcap; he saw Rourke backed against the wall, swinging punches and swearing nonstop when he kicked a redcap savagely in the groin. Three more military police took the place of their injured colleague and while two grabbed Rourke's arms the third set about him with a wooden truncheon. Crosier roared and thrust forward, until a mob of Fusiliers crowded around him, boots and fists thudding.

'Enough of that!' Selkirk moved to defend his men, but Black led a surge of his Reds through the street.

'Come on boys,' Black's distinctive South Australia accent rose high. 'We're all together in this; we're Selkirk's Riders!'

'We're Selkirk's Reivers!' Crosier re-instituted a name from the old Anglo-Scottish Border, the same name as Selkirk's irregular horseman had been known in the South African War.

Selkirk felt a surge of pride. He patted Kimberley and watched as Black led his section to merge with Crosier's men, and only then did he un-holster his revolver and fire a single shot in the air.

The effect was instantaneous as the battling British soldiers stopped. A hundred faces peered round at this tanned officer on the black horse.

'Sergeant Crosier has given us a name,' Selkirk spoke through the sudden hush. 'Reivers! Form up in column of four and follow me!' He did not wait to see the response; these were his men, and he knew they would obey. The redcaps and Fusiliers could do what they liked or think what they desired; Selkirk's Reivers had come together; Selkirk's Reivers were ready to go to war.

Chapter Three

October 1915

A rising wind whipped sand across the tented encampment as Brigadier Smith handed over the packet in person. 'Here are your orders, Selkirk,' he waited until Selkirk broke the seal and scanned the contents. 'Not what you were expecting, eh? I know you are training for raiding in the Sinai, but something has occurred that we need to rectify.'

'Yes, sir,' Selkirk waited for more information.

'The situation here is fluid, and you command the best unit for the job.' Smith's smile appeared sincere.

Selkirk sat back in his chair and reread the orders. 'It says here that we take a boat to Palestine, meet a man named Abraham and follow his advice, sir,' he looked up. 'I thought we were a military unit formed to locate Von Kressenstein and harass the Turks in Sinai.'

'You are a military unit,' Smith's smile did not disguise the steel, 'and as such it is your duty to obey any order of higher command.'

'Yes, sir,' Selkirk said. 'Who is this Abraham we have to meet?'

'You have his name,' Smith said. 'You will be told more when you are on board the boat.'

'One man? Is Abraham a senior officer, sir?' Selkirk already guessed the answer to that.

'He is a man who may influence the entire region,' Smith said, 'and perhaps more than that.'

'Is he a spy?' Selkirk asked.

That's why they gave this mission to us; it is too dirty for the established units.

'He is a man whose information could alter the whole course of history,' Smith dropped his smile. 'I really cannot tell you any more about him than that.'

Selkirk nodded. 'Yes, sir. Will there be space on the boat for our horses?'

'I can tell you that,' this time Smith's smile was genuine. 'You will be going as a complete unit, Selkirk, men horses and equipment. You are landing in a far more densely populated area than Sinai, with Turkish troops everywhere, so you will need all your guile to avoid capture.' He leaned forward in his seat. 'Palestine is a vastly different proposition. I can also tell you that the Turks and Germans are planning something nasty there, so we may need a highly mobile force of men; that is you.'

Selkirk nodded. He thought of his men, trained, united and eager. 'Yes, sir. Are we being picked up by ship as well, once the operation is complete?'

'I am not *au fait* with all the arrangements yet, Selkirk,' Smith said.

Either he does not think we will survive or they intend to abandon us once the mission is complete.

'Could you tell me where we are landing, sir? And where this Mr Abraham chap is?'

Smith shook his head, 'sorry Selkirk, I am afraid that everything is hush- hush as from this minute. Your boys are being put in isolation until you sail.'

'When is that, sir?'

'Two days' time,' Smith said.

'When will I have more details, sir?'

'Not until you board the ship,' Smith said. 'Security is paramount on this operation. He held out his hand, 'you'll be in and out within three days, a week at most; one simple job and then you'll be back doing what you have trained for.' His eyes were so sincere that Selkirk knew it was a lie. His hand was hard. 'Now you won't see me again until you return. Good luck.'

Selkirk gripped hard. 'Thank you, sir.'

And that is the last you expect to see of Selkirk's Reivers. Brigadier Smith or whatever your real name is.

* * *

The redcaps had surrounded them for two days, restricting their movement in every way possible. The Reivers had been confined to their small circle of tents and the horse lines outside, with Kelly and Rourke grousing, while Walker and Batsford, in particular, fretted at the restrictions. Batsford merely resented the redcaps' presence, but Walker had other reasons for looking for free access.

'He's got a bit skirt in Cairo,' Matthew told the world, 'and he wants to kiss her farewell, and with knobs on.'

'She's not just a bit skirt.' Walker protested, 'we're serious.'

'She's a bint from the Wazza; she gave him a dose, and he wants another, so he doesn't have to go back to war,' Sinclair stirred things up until Walker was nearly frantic and Crosier had to intervene and hustle them about their business.

Selkirk did not interfere. Sometimes it was an officer's job to be like the three wise monkeys, hearing, seeing and saying nothing. That was why he had two good quality sergeants between him and the men. He looked through the entrance of the encampment where four redcaps stood guard and wondered what sort of mission the powers-that-be were sending him on this time.

Patience Drew; time will tell; one day at a time.

They rode out in the dark hours of the early morning before the sun dragged the heat of the day across the never ending wastes of the desert. They rode in silence except for the pad of hooves on the hard packed sand and the usual jingle of accoutrements now muffled with old rags. Selkirk acknowledged the salute of the NCO at the gate and did not look back as he led his men northward toward the coast. They rode two by two with each man leading a spare horse, as they had so often before, but now they knew that their lives had altered forever. Their training was over: now they rode to war.

'Don't take anything you don't need,' Selkirk had advised, 'the lighter we are, the faster we ride, and even a few yards might make the difference between life and death.'

Two horses carried the Lewis guns and panniers of ammunition. Others walked under the burden of extra water and ammunition, two heliographs and rations. One brought two baskets of pigeons, with Wells detailed to look after the birds. All was as ready as it could ever be in wartime.

They rode through Alexandria with the sound of their hooves echoing from the surrounding houses and the bustle of the awakening city strangely muted as their thoughts wrapped around them. Selkirk looked back over his men and wondered how many he would lead back.

I prefer being a leader than a follower, but the responsibility of lives in my hands is difficult to bear.

He watched them as they boarded their ship, *General Gordon*, in the Eastern Docks, noting the serious faces of the veterans and the nervous excitement of those who were preparing to face the enemy for the first time. Some of the men were unhappy at being parted from the horses they had once hated but now viewed as close companions.

'You'll see them on the voyage,' Crosier grated; he understood the bond between man and horse, 'now get fell in.'

General Gordon was a nondescript tramp steam vessel with a funnel that sat at a perilous angle to the hull. She was old and slow and leaked rust from every metal surface, but there were stalls for the horses and space for the men and all their equipment, while a squad of Royal Naval gunners manned the single Lewis gun that was all the defence they had against marauding German submarines or any other maritime menace.

'I think I saw Noah just now,' Matthew said. Nobody laughed. They looked back at the spreading city of Alexandria and then out to the Mediterranean.

'Here we go again,' a voice Selkirk recognised as belonging to Private Mackay said. Mackay was a soldier old in sin who had campaigned and drunk his way across half the Empire, but he was steady on his horse and popular with his fellows.

As they left the harbour, a Mediterranean dawn greeted them, swift and silver and bright as a politician's promise. Selkirk stood near the stern of the ship, looking forward to where the prow pushed through to the north, and a brace of listless seamen scraped rust from the bulwark. There was a woman in the bow, tall and dark haired as she stood like a living figurehead. She did not move when a sharp wind ruffled her hair and flicked her skirt around her legs but stared forward as the bows of the ship slid into the waves and kicked up a bucket load of spindrift that spattered as far aft as the funnel. She remained static as the ship rose to an oncoming sea and altered course, first to the west and then directly north.

Selkirk watched her, wondering who she was and why she was on board this vessel as it steamed toward the coast of Palestine. She was a peach, he decided and smiled at the thought.

What would Helena have said if she knew I was looking at another woman?

General Gordon began to zig-zag to confuse possible enemy submarines, taking him to war, further from the memories of his wife, further from the graves of his children, further from everything that mattered to him.

The dark haired woman was alternatively silhouetting against the horizon and standing in profile as *General Gordon* altered course, but she did not move. The wind rose again, pushing her long cotton dress against her, highlighting the contours and curves of her body.

Who are you? I am intrigued. Why are you on this ship of fighting men?

It was many years since Selkirk had looked at any woman other than Helena. He felt the contrasting pangs of interest in her and guilt at his feelings; then he turned away, and his attention returned to his command. When he looked forward again, his flicker of desire had altered to resentment and anger. This ship was no place for a woman, and she had no right to tease him. He stomped below in a foul mood.

'Sergeant Crosier! Get these men moving! They are meant to be soldiers, not school boys on holiday! Get these horses cared for, and I want all the equipment checked!'

Selkirk gave his men an hour's hard work before he mustered them on deck for an inspection.

I hope that bloody woman has gone.

The seamen stopped work to mock the Reivers as they staggered on the bouncing deck.

'You'll be wondering why we are here,' Selkirk began and smiled at the cat calls and whistles that he had expected. 'Well, the powers-that-be have decided that they like us so much we can travel in comfort.' He also expected the jeers and exclamations of disbelief. 'We are off to Palestine, for a mission so important that nobody can do it except us: they need the Reivers.'

The cheers were a bonus. Selkirk waited until they died away. 'We will be operating in Jacko's territory, so we have to use all the skills we have.' That sobered them a little, as it was intended to. The comments faded as they staggered across the blue Mediterranean with the sun beating down on them and the crew already losing interest and drifting away. The woman was back, leaning against the rail and listening with her head cocked to one side and her mane of hair cascading from her head like a gleaming black waterfall.

From where had that thought come? If I had Helena, I would never notice anybody else.

'At present, we don't know exactly what we have to do,' Selkirk admitted, 'but we're the Reivers; we can take whatever they throw at us and come back for more.'

Only the younger men smiled at that. The veterans, bitter with memories gave no reaction at all.

'I don't know if I can answer them, but are there any questions?' Selkirk was surprised when a trooper raised his hand.

'Yes, Walker?' He noted that the sun had tanned Walker, so he was as dark as any Arab. That could be useful later.

'Do you know where in Palestine we are going, sir?'

'Not yet Walker.'

I hope they tell me soon. There must be a message waiting for me from the captain or somebody.

Walker was quiet for a moment or two. 'Do you think it could be near Bethlehem, sir? Or Jerusalem?'

'I know as little as you do, Walker,' Selkirk admitted. 'But it would be good to see the old Biblical places, like in Sunday school eh?'

'Yes sir,' Walker said.

'Have you got a bint in Bethlehem too, Alex?' That was Sinclair, 'it's nothing to do with the Bible, sir; Alex has a woman in every town from Valetta to Rangoon.' Walker joined in the resulting laugh.

Selkirk waited for the noise to subside. 'I have some good news for us all...' he waited for their interest and said the two words that were always welcome, 'mail up!'

News from home was a small oasis in the misery of a soldier's existence. It was a reminder that there was a life beyond the radius of a sergeant's barking orders, a past before the donning of stiff khaki and a nudge that there would still be hope after the last rifle had fired the final bullet. As Selkirk produced the packet of letters, he saw the joy on faces young and old.

They crowded around him, eager for news from wives and sweethearts, mothers and sisters and friends that connected them to that strange civilian life that seemed so quaint and alien and reassuring.

There was none for him, of course. *How could there be? I have buried everybody in this world that mattered to me.*

'Major Selkirk?' The voice was light and feminine, with a throaty burr that he had never heard before.

Selkirk tore himself away from Helena's memory to look at the woman who had appeared beside him. She was about thirty, a few years younger than him, with a blue linen band now holding back her mass of dark hair and a long dress that looked out of place on board this ship. An hour before she had been acting as the figurehead, but now she was standing in front of him with serious dark eyes fixed on his.

'I am Rachel,' she said, unsmiling. 'Brigadier Smith sent me as your interpreter and guide.'

For a second Selkirk did not know what to say. He had not imagined that the interpreter would be female. 'You're a woman,' he said foolishly.

Rachel nodded. 'Obviously.'

'We will be in dangerous territory,' Selkirk knew he was talking nonsense so stilled his tongue. He held out his hand, 'welcome aboard, Rachel.'

She hesitated before accepting, but her hand was slim and firm. 'I speak Arabic, Greek, Hebrew and Turkish,' she told him abruptly.

'And English,' Selkirk tried to make amends for his earlier words.

'Obviously,' Rachel said.

'Can you ride a horse?' Selkirk wondered if this woman would slow them down. 'We may have some hard riding ahead of us.' He wondered which of the spare horses would be quiet enough for the interpreter. 'Do you have your own horse?'

'Obviously.' That seemed to be her stock reply to what she considered a foolish question.

'I have this for you from Brigadier Smith,' Rachel handed over a small envelope with the ubiquitous red seal. He checked to ensure it was unbroken. His name was printed neatly across the front of the envelope with the instructions 'not to be opened until noon on the 17th October.'

'Thank you,' Selkirk said. He wondered why there was so much secrecy but did not ask. It was just after nine in the morning; there were three hours to wait.

'We will get to know each other better,' Selkirk finished the conversation and walked away to check on his men. The woman accompanied him, unsmiling. Despite Rachel's apparent efficiency, he was uneasy about taking a woman to war.

The Reivers were less concerned about such niceties than Selkirk. Most smiled when Selkirk introduced Rachel to them, or avoided her eyes, with only one or two being slightly too forward, but Selkirk expected that Rachel could deal with them quite adequately. Sinclair held out his hand and gave a slight bob, nearly a bow, which made Selkirk wonder what he had been before he joined the army. For all his womanising reputation, the handsome Walker barely nodded and quickly backed away.

Selkirk left them to get acquainted and retired into the relative privacy of the cabin he shared with the mate of the ship. He tried to forget Rachel and concentrate on his map of Palestine.

The names were so familiar from his childhood Sundays that Selkirk found it hard to think of them as places of war: Jerusalem; Nazareth, Judaea and the evocatively beautiful Galilee. He studied the coast and looked for possible landing spots, familiarised himself with the topography and followed the lines of the roads and the few railways. In Selkirk's opinion, irregular cavalry was less effective in such a densely populated area, and he wondered if the tactics they had practised would work there. He shrugged; it was too late now. He had a shipload of highly trained horsemen and a female interpreter of unknown nationality, with a partly known mission. He hefted Smith's envelope and wondered what horrors it would take him.

At ten to twelve Selkirk's patience snapped and he broke the seal and took out the stiff folded paper inside. The message was short and to the point. 'Rachel will take you to the house of Abraham. Follow his instructions. Destroy this letter.'

This is like a child's game, Selkirk told himself as he ripped the stiff paper to fragments and tossed them into the sea. Rachel stood at the rail, a solitary figure watching the surge of the sea.

'Did you know what that letter said?' He asked Rachel, who shrugged and turned away.

'No,' she said, 'I have to guide you somewhere and be your interpreter. That is all I know.'

'You have to guide us to a man named Abraham,' Selkirk said. 'Can you tell me where he lives?' He resisted the desire to raise his voice to a shout. He was used to not being in charge of his destiny, as were all soldiers, but this secrecy brought frustration to a new level. 'I need to plan the safest route for my men.'

Rachel looked at him without any expression in her dark eyes. 'Jerusalem,' she said. 'I will show you our route.' As she spoke, the wind carried a whiff of her perfume to Selkirk. He inhaled unconsciously with the scent transporting him back home where Helena smiled to him across the width of their living room.

Selkirk shook away the image and tried to immerse himself in the matter at hand. Taking a body of horsemen through Ottoman territory would be difficult enough without the added complication of thinking about his late wife.

* * *

They landed in Palestine two hours after dark on 28th October 1915. General Gordon steamed as close to shore as possible and heaved to, swinging on two anchors as the Reivers loaded the horses onto small boats.

'Get a move on there,' the shipmaster, a red nosed Welshman with gravel in his throat, ordered, 'I don't like lying so close to a hostile shore. Get these blasted soldiers off my ship.'

Selkirk was in the leading boat, keeping his hand over the muzzle of Kimberley to keep him quiet and watching as every stroke of the seamen's oars brought them closer to the shore of Palestine. He saw the phosphorescence around the oar blades and fancied he smelled the scents of the fabled land of Israel.

Jerusalem; I am taking my men to Jerusalem.
Bring me my Bow of burning gold;
Bring me my Arrows of desire:
Bring me my Spear: O clouds unfold!
Bring me my Chariot of fire!

The words of Blake's poem echoed through his mind as he stroked his horse and wondered how many thousands of soldiers from scores of different nationalities had led their men to this troubled land. He was just one more insignificant pawn in the complicated chess-game of Palestinian history.

Using the shaded beam of an old fashioned bull's eye lantern, Selkirk checked the map. They were a mile north of the vanished city of Ascalon, on a beach of hard yellow sand. Shattered pottery and slivers of glass glittered in the reflection of the silver surf. Behind the beach, a ridge of dunes hid the interior, mysterious yet comforting in the dark. Selkirk jumped into the shallow water. 'Come on!' He whispered, and urgently motioned his men ashore. They splashed through the tepid surf, talking too loudly as they comforted their horses. 'Keep the noise down; Jackie could be nearby!'

Rachel was at his side, her eyes bright. 'Congratulations Major Selkirk' she said, 'You are the first British soldier to begin the recon-quest of Israel.'

'The reconquest?' The significance of Rachel's words was lost on him.

'For the Jewish people,' Rachel explained. 'That is why the British are here, is it not? To help us build a homeland in our own country?'

Selkirk nodded. 'I am here because I have a job to do,' he said. 'Once the Turks are defeated it's up to the politicians to decide what happens next.' He felt Rachel withdraw from him as her enthusiasm evaporated.

'We have to be five miles inland before dawn.' Her voice was de-tached as she looked around, 'there is not a Turkish garrison in this part of Palestine, but we must ensure that nobody sees us.'

'Get these men moving, Crosier!' Selkirk hissed. He grabbed the reins of Mackay's spare horse and hauled it toward the range of dunes that backed the beach. 'Come on! *Ak Dum!*'

He heard the peculiar snorting of camels somewhere behind the dunes and nodded: that would do. The camels would be useful in a few moments.

When Selkirk had the last man and last horse on the beach, he motioned the boats away. 'Best of luck mate,' the leading seaman said, then pushed into deeper water and rowed back to General Gordon. Selkirk saw the last flash of phosphorescence from the oars and suddenly felt very lonely. That was the Reivers last link with Egypt gone; now they were on their own and half the *Asakr-I Shahaneh* lay between them and safety. God alone knew what waited them out here. He heard the soft rumble of engines and knew *General Gordon* was heading back south.

Inevitably Batsford had managed to detach himself from his colleagues and was wandering alone in the direction of Damascus, one boot undone and the lace trailing on the wet sand.

'That way, Batsford,' Selkirk rounded the errant soldier and pointed him toward the sand dunes, 'give Sergeant Crosier my compliments and tell him I have sent you to help him.'

That should keep Batsford out of trouble for a few moments at least.

Once in the dunes Selkirk checked his men, formed them into their two sections and ordered them to follow Rachel. 'Black, you and Walker are with me. I want some camels rounded up.'

'Sir?' Walker looked confused, but Black nodded.

'Right, Major.'

As the Reivers slipped away from the dunes, Selkirk took Black and Walker in the direction of the camels. 'This way Major, I can smell them,' Black said, 'we have them in the Outback too.' His teeth gleamed in a grin. 'Who owns these bastards?' he wondered. He nodded to the score of camels penned behind a barricade of thorn bushes.

'I don't know, but if you ever find out we can thank them later,' Selkirk said, 'now set them loose and drive them to the dunes.' He followed Black's lead in flapping his bush hat at the confused camels. 'Come on Walker.'

'Yes, sir, Walker took off his hat and waved it in the general direction of the camels. 'Why, sir?'

'We have left a trail even a blind Turk could follow,' Selkirk explained. 'The camels will wander over the beach and the dunes and obscure it for us.'

'The Arabs won't like you for losing their camels,' Black pointed out.

'No doubt,' Selkirk agreed. 'You go ahead as scout, let me know if you see anything unusual.'

Leaving the camels to trample over the dunes, Selkirk called Walker to him and pushed Kimberley after the Reivers. The dunes ended in a belt of flat, fertile countryside, with the winter wind crisp and the occasional bark of a dog in the distance. There were houses nearby, flocks of sheep and small fields in which the stubble of oats and barley crunched under the horse's hooves, while the scent of onions sweetened the air.

The night sounds were different here to the Egyptian desert; closer, more intimate and Selkirk found himself jumping at the harsh bark of a camel or the distant bleat of sheep. He loosened his rifle in its sheath at his side. He had not expected to be leading his men through settled countryside.

'Something ahead, Major,' Black loomed out of the dark. 'I'm not sure what but it's undoubtedly military.'

'We'll have a decko,' Selkirk said. 'Crosier, keep the men here and together. Make sure Batsford does not wander off by himself.' He kicked his heels and ushered Kimberley forward, 'Rachel, you're with me.' He was surprised that the woman had kept up so well, riding astride and in silence.

Perfumed tobacco drifted to Selkirk and the rough cadences of male voices. There was the sound of metal scraping on metal and a deep laugh. 'What are they saying, Rachel?'

Even in the dark of night, he could see that she was unnerved. 'They are speaking Turkish,' she whispered, 'but I can't make out the words.'

'You said there was no military in this area,' Selkirk reminded.

'There were none last time I was here,' Rachel sounded worried.

'All right; let's see what's happening. You stay here Rachel. Black, you and I.' Selkirk dismounted and walked softly toward the voices. He could not hear Black but knew the Australian was there. When it came to the silent murder of night assaults, there was nobody he wanted more at his side than an Australian bushman.

Cigarette smoke drifted to him, and the guttural tones of a Turkish soldier, a hard laugh and the clink of metal on stone. Selkirk crouched slowly and followed the twin steel tracks of the coastal railway that stretched north and south into the distance. He tried to work out how many Turks there were.

Black held up four fingers and then slid one finger across his throat in an obvious query. Selkirk shook his head and motioned for them both to return. They backed off slowly to where Rachel waited; her breathing was nervously harsh in the night.

'Sentries,' Black said quietly. 'They could make things awkward' He looked over to Rachel. 'Did you know about the railway?'

'Obviously,' Rachel said, 'but I did not know about the guards. There were none last time I was here.'

'Maybe they heard we were coming,' Black tapped his bayonet, 'what do you think, Major?'

'They must have second sight if they knew about us,' Selkirk said. 'It was only yesterday that I found out where we were landing.'

'We have to cross the railway,' Rachel said. She looked directly at Selkirk. 'You have to kill the Turks.'

'We'll avoid them,' Selkirk decided. 'Murdering a handful of sentries won't help win the war and may alert the Turks that we are here.'

Rachel looked at him in disgust. 'They are Turks,' she said. 'They are the enemy: kill them.'

'There is always plenty killing,' Selkirk turned away. 'Can you find us a safe way over the railway, Sergeant?'

'Give me half an hour, Major,' Black disappeared into the night.

'We don't kill unless we have to,' Selkirk whispered to Rachel.

'They are Turks,' she responded fiercely, 'they are the enemy!'

'We don't kill unless we have to,' he repeated. 'We are soldiers, not murderers!' He met her glare. 'Is that clear?'

Rachel looked away, wordless, and Selkirk cursed silently. This woman was going to be trouble.

Black was back within twenty minutes. 'Jacko has standing patrols every quarter mile or so,' he reported, 'but I can't see any sign of anything moving.'

'We slip between them then,' Selkirk decided. He checked his watch, 'four o'clock; about two hours until dawn. Let's get moving.'

With Black on the opposite side of the track, he sent one of his veterans a hundred yards on either flank to watch for the Turks.

'If the Turks come, whistle,' Selkirk ordered, 'but don't shoot unless your life is at stake.'

'Yes, sir,' Sinclair was laconic, as he always was when not raging drunk. He loped into the dark with scarcely a sound.

Selkirk gave him two minutes and then sent his men across in pairs, with strict orders to keep silent. He started at every slight link of hoof on steel rail and every scuff or rattle of equipment, but the men were well trained and crossed within five minutes.

'They're doing well,' Black said as they mustered on the inland side of the railway. 'Where to now?'

'A small farm outside Jerusalem,' Selkirk said flatly, 'where there is a man who sympathises with us.' He nodded to Rachel. 'Lead on.'

'They'll see our trail,' Crosier glanced behind him where their hoof prints were becoming visible in the growing light.

'I am hopeful that the Turks will only see the trail of a body of horsemen,' Selkirk said, 'but they can't trace it back to the coast anymore so that we could be anybody.'

'The local people might tell the Turks,' Crosier continued.

'Let's hope not,' Selkirk glanced over to Rachel. 'You're the local expert here, what do you think?'

'The local people are Arabs or Jews with a few Christians of different types,' Rachel shook her head; 'I do not believe they will tell the Turks.'

Selkirk nodded, 'thank you.'

Rachel led them on into the heart of Judaea, and the British soldiers followed, fingering their Lee-Enfields much as the Roman soldiers must have fingered their swords as they marched to face the Jews at Masada. In the East, the sky was still dark, and Selkirk could sense the presence of the vast wilderness that stretched half way to India.

It was nearly five when they reached their destination; a small farm tucked into a fold of low bare hills that rose on either side.

'Bad place to get ambushed,' Crosier said at once, glancing around. 'With your permission sir, I'll post men on the heights.'

'Do that, Sergeant,' Selkirk agreed, 'and spell them regularly.'

'Yes, sir.' Crosier's tone was sufficient to tell Selkirk he knew his job.

Selkirk's first impression was of incredible age, and then of a ramshackle collection of buildings that seemed to have been cobbled together over centuries by a succession of builders who did not care about aesthetics or practicality.

Selkirk would have halted the men at the door, but Rachel showed no hesitation in riding right inside. He followed her through a high arched doorway into a courtyard, off which there was a collection of low, flat roofed buildings, while an elderly, bearded man appeared with a lantern that might have come straight from the Bible.

He looked at the foreign soldiers who crowded into his property and spoke urgently to Rachel, waving his hands around in what might have been agitation or just natural excitability. Selkirk dismounted and moved closer.

'I am Major Selkirk of the British Army,' he introduced himself. 'Thank you for putting us up here.' He waited for Rachel to translate as the man continued to talk loudly and long.

Rachel was also talking, with her hands equally busy. Her voice rose a semi-tone.

'What's happening?' Selkirk asked as his patience stretched.

'There is trouble,' Rachel said. 'The Turks have captured Abraham.'

Chapter Four

'And if Selkirk has both Gupta and Abraham?' Smith tapped his fingers on the desk. The smell of beeswax polish merged with the sharp aroma of brandy to create a scent of luxury and comfort in the room. There were coloured pins thrust into the map of the Middle East on the wall behind the desk.

Jones stepped onto the veranda outside, cradling his balloon glass in his hand. 'I used to come here before the war you know,' he reminisced, 'Shepheard's was Shepheard's in those days before all these young officers moved in and lowered the tone of the place.'

Smith smiled, 'we all have to make sacrifices in wartime' he said.

'The food is gawd-awful of course,' Jones continued, 'but it always was.'

'To return to the matter in hand,' Smith followed Jones to the veranda and looked over the city of Cairo. Despite Shepheard's being British Army headquarters for the area there was more civilian than military traffic on the road below. 'What do we do if Selkirk gets his hands on both Gupta and Abraham?'

'He would have to be very lucky,' Jones sipped at his brandy. 'But it might happen.'

'In that eventuality,' Smith said quietly, 'we will have to think how to get both out of there?' He swirled his brandy around the balloon glass but did not drink. 'One option would be to send a ship and pick them up on the coast. It is either that or Selkirk can ride right through Palestine and Sinai to Suez.'

'We will not be bringing him out by ship,' Jones said. 'The Turks will notify the Germans of events, and they would undoubtedly send a submarine to the Palestinian coast.' He placed his empty brandy glass on the stone balustrade of the veranda and pulled a Havana cigar from his inside pocket. 'As for Selkirk bringing Gupta and Abraham through Ottoman territory all the way to Egypt,' he snipped off the cigar band, then cut the end and lit it. 'No: that just won't do. The Turks will swarm after him as soon as they know. We must try and ensure that Abraham is in our hands so we can use his organisation when we come to invade Palestine, as we will.' He drew in the rich smoke and allowed it to seep slowly out of his mouth. 'As for Gupta; we desperately need him. The information he has is the key to the whole incipient insurrection in the Indian Empire.'

'If not by sea or land, then how do you suggest we retrieve this Indian fellow? By balloon?' Smith allowed sarcasm to creep into his voice.

'Near enough; we use the Royal Flying Corps.' Jones drew on his cigar. 'All we need is three aircraft to carry Gupta, Abraham and Von Stahl to Egypt, some deserted areas of flat ground in Palestine for the machines to refuel and somewhere safe to pick them up.'

Smith withdrew into the room and lifted the brandy decanter. 'You have worked this all worked out. Where have you in mind for the pickup?'

'Just here,' Jones followed him. He pointed to a spot on the map. 'Right there; it is prominent enough to be seen and flat on top for the aircraft to land.'

Smith peered intently at the map. 'And how do Selkirk and his ruffians back?'

'They won't,' Jones poured himself another brandy. 'If they get Gupta, Von Stahl and Abraham on to the aircraft they will have done their bit for the Empire. Selkirk is disposable.'

Smith studied the map again. 'Interesting place to choose; very historical too, I believe.' He swirled the brandy in his glass. 'We are assuming that Selkirk is successful of course. Do we have a second plan if he fails?'

Jones blew slow smoke across the map so for a moment it obscured all of Palestine. 'No, Smith. If Selkirk does not get his man, all India may go up in flames.'

'That would be a damned shame,' Smith said.

'Damned shame,' Jones echoed. 'Shall we dare the dinner menu? I am getting peckish.'

* * *

'The Turks have captured Abraham?' Selkirk repeated. He could hear his men moving their horses into the stables around the courtyard, with what seemed like a hundred children chattering at the top of their voices and a score of women in long robes watching silently from the doorways. The men were either watching suspiciously or grinning from ear to ear as they allowed the children and British soldiers to do the work.

'Water,' that was Crosier's voice, bellowing in broad Liddesdale, 'we need water for the horses, see? Tell your Barrow Wallah that we want water, jildi, right? Esma, you useless buggers, mafeesh the baksheesh; just water the bloody horses, see?'

Selkirk left it to him. If anybody could make these people understand, a sergeant of a British infantry regiment could, using whatever medley of languages he had picked up in a score of years of service across the Empire. 'What do you mean, the Turks have captured him? What happened?'

Rachel lifted a hand for quiet. 'This is Benjamin. He is one of us...' she did not explain who 'us' was as she indicated the agitated man who had greeted them, 'and he told me that the Turks came and grabbed Abraham three nights ago when you were safe in your bed in Egypt.'

Selkirk bit off the words that came to his mouth.

'We'd better turn back,' Rachel's voice rose in near panic. 'Once the Turks question him, he will give all our names, and they will take all of us.'

Selkirk looked around at his men as they cared for their horses and exchanged the ribald pleasantries common to every unit of British soldiers. 'Where is Abraham now?' He asked.

'The Turks have him!' Rachel began to remount her horse. 'If we hurry we can be back on the coast.'

'And then what?' Selkirk asked, 'swim? The ship is half way to Alexandria by now.' He pointed to Benjamin, 'ask him where the Turks hold Abraham now.'

'Why?' Rachel asked, 'they have him, and that is that.' She leaned down from the saddle, 'you don't know the Turks, Major Selkirk, you don't know what they are capable of, and I tell you that they will make Abraham talk and then we will all be rounded up and tortured until we tell everything. Then we will be hanged.'

Selkirk shook his head. 'You have twenty British soldiers around you, Rachel. You are in no immediate danger. Now, if you ask this gentleman, Benjamin was it? If you ask Benjamin to tell us where the Turks have Abraham, we can see what we can do about it.'

Benjamin seemed nearly as excited as Rachel, but when she translated the direct question, he calmed down sufficiently to merely explode. The torrent of words left Selkirk thoroughly bemused.

'The Turks hold Abraham in the army headquarters in the heart of Jerusalem,' Rachel pronounced the city as Yerushalayim, 'he is chained to a wall in a dungeon, with soldiers beside him and on guard all around.'

Selkirk nodded. He had momentarily contemplated the idea of breaking Abraham free, but although he had every confidence in his Reivers in open country, he could not see them groping around in the narrow streets of the ancient city. The riot at Wazza had proved how difficult that had been. He realised that Benjamin was still talking.

'It is worse than I thought,' Rachel was close to tears. 'They are holding him in Jerusalem but are taking him further away, to Damascus.'

'Taking him?' The idea came to Selkirk fully grown, 'by rail?'

'There is no railway between Jerusalem and Damascus!' Rachel sounded scathing, 'they will take him by road, with a full military escort.'

Black wandered across the crowded courtyard, hands in pocket and pipe clenched between his teeth, to see what was happening. He removed the pipe from his mouth. 'Do we need this Abraham fellow, Major?'

'We do,' Selkirk said, 'he is the whole reason for us being here.'

'There's no option then, is there?' Black did not hide his grin.

'None at all,' Selkirk felt the old familiar surge of mingled excitement and dread. He understood what Black meant. 'We have to find out where and how first,' he said, 'and how large the escort is.'

'We'll be through them before they know we're even there,' Black said.

'What? What do you mean?' Rachel looked from one to the other, lost in the quick fire exchange of ideas and thoughts.

'Ask Benjamin when the Turks will be taking Abraham away and what road they will leave by.'

'Why?' Rachel looked confused

'Just ask him!' Selkirk was used to instant obedience in the Army, so Rachel's questions irritated.

Rachel spoke again to Benjamin and listened to the man's long tirade in return. 'He does not know for sure, obviously, but he says there is a daily... 'She looked bemused, 'I am not sure of the word ... A caravan? That goes from Jerusalem to Damascus every week with messages and mail, and it is likely that Abraham will be on it.'

'A convoy,' Selkirk said. 'Ask him how big the convoy normally is.'

'Convoy,' Rachel repeated. 'Thank you.' When she smiled, her entire face altered, so Selkirk found himself smiling back. She spoke to Benjamin again, and Selkirk heard her say the word 'convoy' three times.

'He does not know this time, but it can be as few as ten men and one wagon, and as many as a hundred men and ten wagons.'

Selkirk glanced at Black, 'a hundred Turkish soldiers against twenty Reivers?'

Black frowned and shook his head. 'Those are long odds, Major.' He looked at the courtyard, now empty of men. 'Where do we attack the poor buggers?'

'Are you planning to attack the convoy?' Rachel looked astonished. 'You have only a handful of riders, and these are strong Turkish soldiers.' She shook her head. 'You have not met the Turks!'

Black laughed outright, the sound honest in this courtyard of fear. ', Rachel, we have, in Gallipoli. But the Turks have never met the Reivers.' He looked at Selkirk and winked, 'there are a hundred against us, Major; it will be a massacre.'

'If they will massacre you, why do it?' Rachel appeared on the verge of tears.

'Oh no, Rachel,' although Black spoke softly, his Australian accent was very pronounced, 'they won't massacre us. We will do the massacring.'

Selkirk squeezed every last piece of information out of Benjamin, studied his maps of Jerusalem and the area northward and decided on a strategy.

'An ambush,' he said to his sergeants, 'right here.' He pointed to a spot on the map where the road between Jerusalem and Damascus passed through a range of hills. 'As you know, a convoy travels at the speed of the slowest vehicle, and if they have wagons, they move between two and three miles an hour, sufficiently slow for their infantry escort to keep pace.'

Crosier nodded agreement, 'yes, sir' but Black had not experienced years of military discipline and was more vocal.

'There is a town nearby,' he jabbed at the map, 'there might be a garrison there. Why not try there,' he indicated a spot ten miles further north, 'there is no village, and the hills are deeper, easier for us to escape into.'

Crosier stiffened, still unsettled by Black's freedom of expression with an officer.

'No,' Selkirk had made his decision. There was no reason for him to explain anything to a ranker but he wanted everything to be clear in his unit. He pointed to his original choice. 'They will reach that spot at the end of their first day's journey. They will have travelled about seven hours, they will be weary, and they will be looking forward to a halt. They will be off guard and at their most vulnerable. However, if we hit them there,' he indicated Black's preferred location, 'they will be two hours into the next day's journey, refreshed and vigorous.'

'We could attack at night, sir,' Crosier broke years of military tradition by venturing his own opinion. 'That's what the columns did in South Africa.'

'Thank you, Sergeant,' Selkirk had no desire to curb this new initiative from his sergeant, 'but the Turks will know the territory far better than we do. A night attack gives the possibility of some of our men straying and maybe losing themselves, or worse, the Turks capturing them. I do not want that.' He lightened the tone, 'could you imagine Batsford in the dark?'

'No, sir,' Crosier nearly smiled. 'He is bad enough in full daylight, and some of the others are not much better.'

'But can you imagine Batsford as a prisoner?' Black countered. 'He would give them so much misinformation they would be utterly confused!'

This time Crosier did allow himself a small smile. 'Maybe so, Black, maybe so.'

'Benjamin told us that the convoy always leaves by the Damascus Gate and keeps to the Nablus Road,' Selkirk said, 'so we have no difficulty about the route. Now we spy out the land and organise.' He saw Black's frown, 'it won't do any harm to have a look at your spot, Sergeant.'

'That's Nablus,' Rachel pointed to a small village in the shelter of a tall, smoothly rounded hill, 'and that's Gerizim.'

Some of the Reivers bunched forward to look. 'So that's Nablus, and Gerizim is it,' Walker said. 'I've heard of that; it's the sacred mountain of the Samaritans.' He sounded quite animated, so Selkirk wondered which Sunday School had educated him to such a high standard, yet had omitted to advise him not to sleep with a succession of girls. 'That's where Yahweh wanted the Holy Temple built!' Walker nudged Rourke, who looked less than impressed. 'The Samaritans are the purest of the pure, you know.'

'That's you out then,' Rourke mocked, 'you and your hundreds of women!'

Other Reivers joined in the laughter. Selkirk hid his smile. When his men were miles inside enemy territory and could still joke, he was satisfied.

They rode out at sunset the next day, twenty troopers, two sergeants, a major and one interpreter bound for the hills north of Jerusalem to rescue a man named Abraham.

Immediately to the north of Jerusalem, the road was on a level dusty plain, with no cover from the sun for man or beast. It rose slowly, with most travel at the pace of a donkey or one of the strings of camels that walked, aloof and as timeless as the East itself. Bands of blue beads encircled their necks to ward off predatory spirits as their owners, Mohammedans to a man, reverted to earlier beliefs to ward off the evil eye. Behind them, Jerusalem spread out behind its high golden walls, looking much as it must have in Biblical times except for the addition of mosques and minarets. Selkirk would have liked more time to explore this most famous of cities, but duty forced him away.

Selkirk and Crosier watched the road through binoculars, noting everything that moved. 'Not much military traffic,' Crosier said, 'just camels and civilians.'

'Good,' Selkirk approved. 'I was concerned there would be more Turks.' He lowered his binoculars. 'Jerusalem seems to be a bit of a backwater here. Their main base is Damascus; luckily for us.'

They rode parallel to the road, avoiding centres of population and hoping that they looked like Turkish soldiers on patrol.

'Look slovenly,' Crosier advised. 'Not you, Batsford: you are a natural scruff.'

'Thank you, sergeant,' Batsford took the words as praise.

The ground rose to dusty bald hills that shimmered in the heat, with only a thin scrub covering the limestone beneath.

'What do you think of these hills, Wellsie?' Sinclair asked.

'The Malverns are far better; this is nothing like Herefordshire!'

There were occasional Bedouin passing by, but they ignored the Reivers as if they lived in different worlds.

'Strange buggers, these,' Black kept a hand close to his rifle.

'We are the strangers here,' Crosier said, 'the Arabs have been riding these roads since time began. They belong here while we are just passing through.' He looked back at his men, 'the Arabs will be here a thousand years after we are gone and forgotten.'

'That was very philosophical,' Black sounded surly, 'who told you all that?'

'We saw caravans in the Khyber,' Crosier said, 'and all along the Frontier, men following the same routes their ancestors had for centuries,' he glanced around. 'This sort of landscape brings it all back.'

The sun was at its zenith, evaporating the sweat from their bodies even before it had formed as they reached the spot Selkirk had chosen for the ambush.

'Here we are; a perfect place for murder,' Selkirk said softly. He guided Kimberley to a secluded dip just below the skyline and looked down. The road coiled through the hills beneath, broad and dusty, with a trio of sad donkeys trudging past, each with a robed man sitting astride. There was no cover, not a single tree or building, just the heat shimmer from the limestone and the rising dust from the passage of the donkeys. Selkirk surveyed his chosen site, where the road swung around the flank of one hill, curved toward the Reivers and then slid away to border the next. There was a bare slope rising steeply on the opposite side and a steep, ten-foot gulley nearest to them, speckled by rocks and with an occasional spiky plant giving a brief hint of greenery.

'No cover, nothing,' Crosier sounded cheerful. He swatted at a fly that hovered at his face.

Selkirk nodded. 'We will set up a block there,' he pointed to the far curve, 'and there,' the curve on the left. 'Let them pass the first block, then the bulk of the men sweep down and rescue Abraham. The second block will stop any attempt they make to escape with him.'

'How will we know where he is?' Crosier asked. 'If it is a long convoy he could be anywhere in it.'

'Benjamin said that prisoners are either shackled in a wagon or chained to the back and made to walk.' Selkirk explained.

'Let's hope there is only one wagon,' Black said.

'Let's hope so,' Selkirk agreed.

We won't have much time if there are a hundred Turkish soldiers.

'This will be the lads' first action together.'Crosier glanced toward the Reivers as they stood beside their horses, surveying the desolation of the Judean Hills. 'I'd prefer something easier to blood them gently.'

'They are soldiers,' Selkirk tried to sound professional, 'they will do their duty.'

God that sounds callous.

Selkirk posted sentries on the slopes of the hills to give warning when the convoy came, or if any other body of Turkish troops appeared. He posted a stop on either side of the ambush and gave each man instructions what to do. Three Reivers manned each stop; two to operate a Lewis gun and the third to act as lookout and signaller. He divided the remaining fourteen Reivers into two unequal parties. He posted Black and his two best shots, Walker and Wells on the near side of the road, while he and Crosier would lead the remaining twelve to pick out the wagon and free Abraham. Once the prisoner was released, his men would ride hard to the hills beyond and meet up with the other Reivers.

It was a simple plan that he repeated to all the Reivers until he was sure that even Batsford understood what to do. He made every man repeat his part, and then he posted them at their allotted places and settled down in a convenient hollow to await the arrival of the convoy.

Waiting was the worst time, the calm before the storm, the period when the nerves stretched and began to jangle, when the imagination took hold and reminded of all the horrors that could occur. This prelude to battle was the time when men could panic over nothings, or when a passing Bedouin could stumble across them and give the alarm to the Turks.

A horse whinnied, with its owner shushing it into silence. Selkirk saw a small lizard scuttle from rock to rock while overhead a trio of birds of prey was circling, sensing food.

'Short toed eagles,' Rachel noticed Selkirk's upward glance.

He nodded, 'thank you' and she gave a small, haunted smile then began to explain more about the birds, speaking in short nervous phrases until she realised what she was doing, stopped and looked along the road in the direction from which the convoy was expected to come.

There was silence. Somewhere a rock exploded in the heat, causing Batsford to start and reach for his rifle. Crosier put a hand on his arm, 'easy lad.'

'Will you succeed, Major Crosier?' Rachel bit her lower lip, her eyes wide. They darted from side to side.

'We've done all we can do,' Selkirk replied. 'Now it is all up to the men, and the Lord.' He looked over his Reivers as they sheltered behind a fold of ground, each man caring for his horse, each man hopefully ready.

A succession of camels walked the road, some decorated with bells, all roped together. An occasional overloaded donkey plodded past, and a few pedestrians suffered the appalling heat. The sun slowly slid across the sky, scorching the ground beneath, creating optical illusions, so the road appeared to waver in the heat. The Reivers waited, cursed, drank from their water bottles and stared into space. Sinclair played patience with dog- eared cards.

'This will be your first action, Moffat,' Selkirk sat beside a youth of about nineteen. The sun had burned him, so his forehead was scarlet and peeling.

'Yes, sir.' Moffat could not keep the nervousness from his voice.

'Keep calm and remember your training,' Selkirk patted his shoulder. 'Do what Sergeant Crosier or I say, and you will be all right.'

Moffat nodded. 'I'm not scared, sir.'

'I did not think you were, lad.'

'Sir,' Crosier caught Selkirk's attention, 'something's happening.'

The flags were raised and lowered as the observer of the first stop sent his message. 'Convoy in sight, sir,' Crosier read.

'Stand ready, men,' Selkirk ordered. 'Signaller, pass the message on to the end stop.'

'Civilians, sir,' Crosier said quietly.

There were ten of them; graceful camels that swaggered toward Jerusalem in the care of four Bedouin adults and three children who dressed and acted like miniature copies of their elders. They reached the centre of the ambush area at the same time as the head of the military convoy came into sight from the opposite direction.

'Attack them,' Rachel gripped Selkirk's arm. 'Kill the Turks.'

Moffat half rose and took hold of the reins of his horse, but Crosier pushed him back down. 'Easy lad; wait for the order.'

'Wait,' Selkirk said. He watched the Arabs amble along the road, moving at the same apparently leisurely pace that their ancestors had adopted for countless centuries to combat the heat of the deserts. The advance guard of the convoy was filing past the first stop, twenty Turkish infantrymen looking deceptively un-military in untidy uniforms. Their appearance did not fool Selkirk; he remembered how efficient they had been at Gallipoli when they stopped the British, French and Anzacs with their stout defence. The Turks were superb soldiers and dangerous enemies.

The camels ignored the oncoming Turks as they ambled along with their noses in the air and their attendants strolling long legged beside them. The children stared at the approaching military convoy; a small boy pointed, but one of the adults must have said something, for the child dropped his hand and moved closer to the camels.

'Give the order,' Rachel whispered urgently, 'give the order to attack! We must free Abraham.'

'Not yet,' Selkirk said. He watched the sedate progress of the Bedouin family and remembered the terrible concentration camps of the South African war; he would not endanger civilians for the sake of a man who had chosen to put himself in danger.

'Give the order!' Rachel was nearly pleading, 'we must save Abraham; all our lives are at stake. The future of Zionism is at stake.'

'Stay still and keep quiet!' Selkirk whispered urgently. He tried to judge the respective speeds of both parties, the family of Arabs with their camels and the steadily increasing column of Turkish troops. Benjamin had told him there would be a maximum of a hundred soldiers and ten wagons, but already there was twice that number of Turkish infantry, and still, they marched around the bend of the road. Unless he gave the order soon, the advance guard would be level with his end stop, compromising the whole ambush.

'Signal sir,' Crosier sounded as calm as if he was on exercise on Salisbury Plain, 'ten wagons and two hundred and fifty infantry plus five mounted officers.'

Selkirk nodded. 'Thank you sergeant' he scanned the wagons with his binoculars. If the Turks had any sense, they would put Abraham in the middle of the convoy so soldiers surrounded him and he was secure. Selkirk focused on two wagons that were nose to tail in the centre. There was a file on infantry on either side of these wagons with a moustached NCO haranguing the men.

These men are not for decoration. One of these wagons must hold Abraham, but which one?

'Attack now!' Rachel pulled at his sleeve. 'Now! Before it is too late.'

The Arabs were abreast of the convoy, with the camels and adults walking as if the Turks did not exist and the children waving and pointing until a bearded and dignified Bedouin pulled them back. Some of the Turkish soldiers were making comments, shouting across to the Bedouin, making gestures; one burly man tried to make friends with the children, but all the time the convoy drew closer to the end stop. Selkirk thought of his tiny force of three Reivers and a Lewis gun there;

he had not thought there would be so many Turks, or that they would be so close to his men.

He calculated times, speeds and distances, watched the advance guard approach the end stop and wondered if his soldiers, the unwanted, could cope with Turks on both sides if he allowed the advance guard to pass them. The leading Turk, a young officer, pulled up his horse so he could light a cigarette. His men instinctively slowed down, and the advance guard coalesced into a more compact group.

'Good man,' Selkirk approved. 'Just you stay there and hold the column up until the civilians are out of the way.' He returned to his scrutiny of the two central wagons. Both were solidly built, with no side windows, much like the Black Marias of the British police. Selkirk swore softly, he had expected the Turks only to transport Abraham, but it appeared that they had taken the opportunity to empty their jail at Jerusalem and send the lot to Damascus.

'We'll have to break into both wagons,' he said to Crosier, 'there's no help for it.'

'Aye, sir.' Crosier did not appear perturbed at the prospect.

The Arabs were at the tail of the column now, moving agonisingly slowly, and the advance guard was nearly at the end stop when one of the Arab children broke away from his parents and ran to look at the nearest wagon. A Turkish soldier grabbed at him but missed, the child panicked and screamed, and the soldier landed a back handed cuff that sent the boy sprawling to the ground. The bearded Arab, presumably the boy's father, drew a knife and jumped at the Turk and a second soldier fired a hasty shot.

'Attack!' Rachel screamed. 'Major Selkirk says to attack!' She pulled a small revolver from inside her jacket and fired into the mass of Turkish soldiers.

'That's put the kybosh on it,' Crosier said; 'keep still, lads; wait for orders!'

Selkirk saw Rachel mount her horse and spur alone for the Turks. He swore, 'Right boys, charge! Black: open fire!'

He threw himself on Kimberley and spurred out of the dead ground and down the steep slope. The horse's hooves slipped on the thin soil over the limestone, but Selkirk could ride before he could walk and corrected her, recovered and kicked in his heels.

'Reivers!' he yelled, 'Reivers!' Releasing his rifle from its holster, he aimed and fired into the mass of Turkish infantry. 'Come on lads!'

The Turks had not expected an attack so deep in their territory. They certainly had not expected a deluge of British horsemen to explode from the hills of Judea just as they were looking forward to stopping for the night. Taken by surprise, some dived for whatever cover they could find, while others ran in any direction. Only a few had the wits to try and fire back, but by the time their first shots rang out, Selkirk had overtaken Rachel and was among them. He targeted the young officer with the cigarette, shooting him in the body, and then looked for other targets.

'Kill the leaders,' he shouted, aware how cold blooded that order was. 'Fire away, boys!'

Selkirk saw Rachel haul on her reins, so her horse pulled up with a loud neigh and its two front hooves flailing. She fired point blank at a cowering Turkish soldier, with the bullet sending him staggering back. She fired again, and then Selkirk was past her and at the wagons. He glanced over his shoulder; the Reivers had followed, whooping and yelling to create the maximum confusion as he had ordered.

'Reivers!' that was Crosier's voice, 'Selkirk's Reivers!'

They fired into the mass of Turks, wheeled their horses, worked the bolts of their rifles and shot, again and again, killing or wounding the disorganised infantry. Loyal to their training, they kept moving, making themselves difficult targets as they rode in a circle around the two central wagons to screen Selkirk and Rachel.

A driver and guard sat on the first wagon, with the close escort of twenty men already reduced by the Reivers fire; the driver lashed at the two horses to try and escape while the guard aimed his rifle at Selkirk.

Leaving his men to deal with the milling escort, Selkirk shot the guard through the head and pointed his rifle at the driver. 'Halt' he said, and killed the crazy impulse to add: 'stand and deliver.'

He heard the whinny of horses and crackle of musketry behind him, heard a long scream as a man was agonisingly wounded, saw a man in Turkish uniform thrown backwards by the force of a .303 bullet, thrust the muzzle of his rifle into the driver's chest and shouted again: 'Halt!'

'Kill him!' Rachel pleaded, 'please kill him!'

The Turk was a brave man. He spat at Selkirk and lashed the horses on. Selkirk shot him without compulsion, reached out to grab the reins and pulled the horses to a halt. The driver's body slumped in his seat; his eyes were open and hot with hate. Something whizzed past Selkirk and raised splinters of raw wood from the body of the wagon. He heard the staccato bark of a Mauser close by, then a loud grunt as a bullet smashed a Turk's shoulder.

Selkirk yanked at the door of the wagon and swore as it was locked. He threw himself off Kimberley, ducked as a bullet smacked against the iron surround of the door, had a quick glance around and saw his Reivers still held firm as the Turks were still in confusion. He shouted a warning, pressed the muzzle of his rifle against the lock and fired. The recoil was savage, and for an instant, he smelled burning timber, but this time the door answered to his tug. It swung open, dense wood with a reinforced iron frame, and Selkirk peered inside, gagging at the reek of confined humanity.

'Abraham!' he yelled. 'Abraham!'

There was no immediate response, and then voices in a medley of languages. Selkirk heard the rattle of iron chains, but the contrast between the brightness outside and the dark of the interior prevented him from seeing any details.

'Abraham!' Selkirk shouted again. 'Is there an Abraham in here?' There was no clear response, merely the gabble of men and the rattle of manacles and chains. Selkirk swore and looked around. Crosier had formed the Reivers in an uneven circle around the two central wagons, riding their horses to make a moving target. They were continually firing, ducking and weaving as the Turks recovered their composure like the excellent soldiers they were. 'Rachel! I need a translator!'

Selkirk could not see Rachel. He heard the insistent rattle of a Lewis gun and wondered briefly which of his stops were in action. Somewhere horses were screaming, and a man was shouting. Selkirk did not know the language, but he knew the man was calling for his mother; that seemed to be universal with young unmarried men of any nationality when mortally wounded. He raised his voice again, 'Rachel!'

'Major Selkirk!' she was panting, reloading her revolver. There was blood spattered on her face and the front of her jacket. Her eyes were wide and wild.

He took hold of her shoulder, 'is Abraham in here?' He gestured inside the wagon. Now he looked closely he could see that the prisoners inside were shackled to the internal walls; that would be the sound of chains he had heard.

Rachel peered in. 'No,' she shook her head. She looked around and pointed to the second wagon, which lay on its side with one horse dead and the second wounded, kicking and screaming in its harness. 'He will be in there.'

Leaving the frantic prisoners in the first wagon, Selkirk ran to the second, reloading his rifle and shouting across to Crosier as he did so.

'How are we doing, Sergeant?'

'All right, sir. Jacko is recovering now, though; we'd better be quick.'

Terrible screams of pain from the second wagon raised the hairs on the back of Selkirk's neck. This time he did not waste time trying the handle but just shot out the lock and wrenched the door open. The interior was in chaos; the prisoners chained to the uppermost side of the wall were suspended by their wrists and lying on top of those on the lower side. One man lay with both legs at a terrible angle and his femur protruding through the skin. He screamed, high-pitched and horrible.

'Oh Jesus,' Selkirk looked away. He only hoped the injured man was not Abraham. 'Abraham? Is there an Abraham in here?'

Rachel pushed past him, ignored the screaming man and spoke rapidly in what Selkirk assumed was Hebrew. It seemed as if every man in the wagon spoke in return, rattling their chains as they demanded release.

'That's Abraham,' Rachel pointed to a man at the very back of the wagon. She crawled in, with Selkirk following. The man with the broken femur continued to scream.

Abraham was about fifty and balding. When he looked up, Selkirk saw he had a badly bruised face, while a recent cut on his forehead was seeping watery blood.

'Are you Abraham?' Selkirk asked, and the man glanced to Rachel, who translated. The man nodded.

'I am Major Andrew Selkirk of the British Army. We have come to get you out of here.'

The chains were stapled to the inside of the wagon and padlocked between Abraham's wrists. 'Where are the keys?' Selkirk pointed to the lock and repeated: 'keys?'

Rachel spoke to Abraham. 'The guard has them,' she said, and Selkirk swore loudly. The shooting was constant now, with bullets thumping the body of the wagon and raising wicked splinters as they passed through the stout wood.

'I'll get them,' Selkirk hurried outside, glad to escape from the sounds and scenes of suffering. Crosier had the defence well organised, but the Turks were pressing hard, with a moustached officer dashing around his men.

'How much longer, sir?' Crosier yelled. 'We can't hold them much longer.'

'Can you give me three minutes?'

'Aye, sir.' Crosier was astride a different horse, so Selkirk guessed that the Turks had shot his own.

The guard was nowhere to be seen; either he was dead or had fled, but the guard of the first wagon lay in a crumpled heap. Selkirk searched his pockets, flinched at the bullet that thudded into the ground between his legs and hoped Black and his marksmen could keep the Turks busy. He heard the rattle of keys and hauled a bunch from a hook on the man's belt. 'Thank God.'

Both Lewis guns were in action now, their sound strangely reassuring as a background to the sharper crack of the Mausers and Lee-Enfields, but he ignored them and ran back to the second wagon. 'Here,' he threw the keys to Rachel, 'release Abraham and get him on a horse!' The man with the broken legs was silent now, hanging loosely with blood dribbling from his mouth but the other prisoners held out manacled hands in desperate pleas for release. Selkirk ignored them all, struggled past the clutching hands and added his firepower to Crosier's protective ring.

Rachel appeared a moment later, supporting a limping Abraham.

'Can he ride?' Selkirk asked. He saw the moustached Turkish officer gathering a squad of soldiers behind one of the other wagons. 'Is he fit enough to sit a horse?'

Rachel nodded, 'yes; I think so!'

'Get him mounted then!' Selkirk knelt and fired three rounds at the Turkish officer, but the man had ducked behind the wagon. He raised his voice: 'Crosier - pull out now!

A bullet smacked into the side of the wagon an inch from Abraham's head, and Selkirk swore yet again; they had risked too much to lose his man now. 'Get Abraham out of here,' he yelled and dragged a horse to Rachel. 'Move now – you know where to meet.' A second bullet hissed past. Selkirk frowned; that had not come from the Turks in the ambush, the angle was wrong.

'There are more Turks up the hills,' he yelled, 'break and run, lads; go to the rendezvous.'

He helped Rachel push the bewildered Abraham onto a horse, slapped its rump to get it moving and looked for Kimberley. The horse was waiting for him, frightened but loyal.

'Break off, lads! Take them away, Crosier!' Selkirk flinched as he saw one of his men thrown backwards by the strike of a bullet. He fired toward the Turks, grunted as a Lewis gun opened up and saw three horsemen explode from his end-stop trio and head for the hills opposite.

Selkirk had trained his men in staged withdrawals and nodded approval as Crosier took the first group away, halted twenty yards into the hills and opened rapid fire on the Turks as the next group leapfrogged him and did the same. Selkirk turned Kimberley's head toward the hills and had a last look around the ambush site in case any of his men were wounded and left behind.

One of the camels lay dead, but the others were nowhere to be seen, although the Arab family were still there, lying in a huddle with the bearded father protecting two of his children. Selkirk met the man's eyes and started at the anguish there. The Bedouin pointed, left handed, with his right arm still around his family. Selkirk followed the direction he indicated and saw the third child, the inquisitive boy, cowering in the shelter of an abandoned wagon, howling in terror as a Turkish soldier used him as a shield as he fired at the Reivers.

Selkirk levelled his rifle, but in the noise and confusion, he was not sure if he could shoot the Turk without endangering the boy. He glanced again at the father and understood his agony of indecision; he could not run to save one of his children without leaving his wife and remaining two children in danger.

Selkirk swore again; he was responsible for the lives of twenty-two men, his men; his duty was to them and his mission, he could not neglect that duty for the sake of a foreign child. But he thought of his children, and then he was dismounted and moving, cursing the Arabs, the Turks and this bloody war that saw British fighting Turks in a land that was supposed to be holy for both. Selkirk felt a quick surge of fear, but he could not run from that small boy and look himself in the mirror again; he knew that Helena would not wish him to abandon a child to save himself. He dismounted and ran toward the boy.

The Turkish soldier was too intent on firing at the rapidly withdrawing Reivers to notice Selkirk running at him. He aimed and fired, muttering to himself as he held the boy down; he did not even look up as Selkirk pressed the barrel of his rifle to his head and squeezed the trigger. Blood and brains and fragments of bone exploded in an obscene spray; Selkirk scooped up the screaming boy and ran to the Arab family, but two more Turkish soldiers lunged into view, one with his bayonet fixed and the other young and scared.

The bayonet wielding Turk was obviously the most dangerous, so Selkirk turned to him, fired his rifle one-handed and swore as his shot went nowhere. The Turk flinched at the report of the rifle, realised that Selkirk had missed and yelled again, thrusting forward with the bayonet. Selkirk turned away to shield the boy, felt the keen blade rip through his tunic and swivelled round, to see the Turkish soldier with the bayonet straightening up with a curious expression on his face. A trickle of blood from his mouth quickly grew to a spurt, and then he collapsed. The young Turk screamed and ran, leaving Selkirk alone with the boy, but with a score of Turkish infantry staring at him in seeming astonishment.

At a shout from the moustached officer, the Turkish soldiers began to move, some levelling their rifles, others running to block his escape. Selkirk held the boy close, ducked and weaved across to the Arab family and nearly threw the child into the outstretched arms of his mother.

Then he was astride Kimberley and spurring hard. He forced the horse to trample down the nearest Turkish soldier, fired his rifle at another and jumped over a third as he ducked away. He heard somebody shouting his name, looked up and saw Black leading three Reivers down the bare, bald slope to cover him.

Black's men fired and moved in the manner in which Selkirk had trained them. Selkirk flinched as a bullet ripped through his saddle and nicked the side of his thigh, and he twisted and weaved to break the aim of the Turkish soldiers. Kimberley made a final leap over a thorn bush; Selkirk's men were all around him, yelling, shooting over their shoulders and spurring as hard as they could to put distance between themselves and the Turks.

Chapter Five

November 1915

'We've done it, sir!' Black was so exultant that he forgot his carefully nurtured disrespect.

'Spur,' Selkirk yelled, 'Reivers! Get away from here!'

His men echoed the call. 'Selkirk's Reivers!'

They crested the hill and halted in a rocky hollow half a mile distant, with the men panting or grinning or exhausted; one youngster was openly crying, and others were wounded.

'Not bad, sir,' Crosier was grinning, 'seven minutes flat!'

Seven minutes? Was that all? I thought we had been in action for an hour at least. Fighting always distorts time

'Roll call,' Selkirk looked around at his command. 'Three men missing: Kilner, Anderson and Syms.'

'Anderson was killed in the first rush, sir,' Crosier reported, 'and Kilner as we withdrew. I did not see Syms.'

'I did,' Kelly said. 'He went down at the second wagon, and a dirty Turk bastard bayoneted him as he lay on the ground.'

The rest answered their names, although Mackay, Moffat, Charlton and Pembroke were slightly wounded.

'How are you lads; are you fit to continue?' Selkirk wondered if it was better to leave them at a friendly house if he could find one, or take them with him and hope they did not hamper the rest of the Reivers.

'We showed them, sir,' Pembroke was a veteran of Gallipoli. 'We got them back.' He nursed his side, where a bullet had grazed him.

'We did that,' Selkirk agreed. 'Are you fit to ride with us?'

'I am that, sir.'

Moffat and Mackay had minor injuries that did not hamper them; they answered Selkirk's query with forced smiles but high morale. Reaction was setting in now as some of the men began to shake and most reached for cigarettes.

'I hope he was worth it,' Black nodded his head at Abraham, 'I don't think one buckle is worth losing three Reivers for.'

Nor do I; my men are too precious to squander.

'He is an important man, Black. He could save hundreds of lives.'

Black gave Abraham a look that should have consigned his soul to eternal cleansing in Gehinnom. 'Anderson was a Melbourne man,' he said, 'One of the best.'

'He was,' Selkirk agreed. 'There are too many good men killed in this war.' He caught the buzz of conversation as his Reivers began to talk about the action.

'That Turkish officer had a charmed life,' Wilson said, 'I shot at him three times and missed each time.'

'I got four of them, maybe five,' Rourke sounded satisfied.

'Six for me,' Kelly had to be one better.

'Did you see the woman?' That was Sinclair's voice.

Mackay answered: 'She just killed and killed.'

'That woman has no fear at all.'

Selkirk called Rachel over. 'Ask Abraham why he is so important that he cost the lives of three British soldiers,' he said bluntly and added, 'bring him to me.' He gave his sergeants a few moments to settle the men down and then called them over.

'Black, Crosier, the Turks were aiming specifically at Abraham; they must be very keen to get him back. There was at least one Turkish sniper on the other side of the valley particularly trying to kill him.'

'I did not see any Turks on my side of the valley,' Black said at once.

'I saw the shots strike,' Selkirk said, 'they undoubtedly came from your side of the valley.' He did not press the point as Rachel and Abraham arrived.

Selkirk had not been very impressed with his first sight of Abraham, thinking him overweight, bald headed and ungrateful, but when Abraham looked him directly in the eye, Selkirk realised the force of the man. Abraham's eyes were deep and dark and intense, despite the blood around his mouth and the spreading bruise that disfigured the left side of his face.

Abraham touched a hand to his face 'the Turks' he said, and gave a small smile. He looked to Rachel and spoke in Hebrew.

'Abraham wants to say thank you,' Rachel said. 'You saved his life and possibly the lives of a great many more people.'

Selkirk took the hand that Abraham offered. It was small and soft. It did not feel like the hand of a hero, but there was something heroic about this little man. 'You are not safe yet, Abraham. The Turks seem to think you are valuable; they will certainly be hunting us as soon as they get organised.'

'Why does Jacko want you?' Black asked bluntly as Rachel translated Selkirk's words.

Abraham gave a small smile and shrugged. 'Maybe they don't; maybe the Turks held the wrong man. Either way, I thank you, Sergeant.'

Black grunted and turned away. 'Bloody buckles.'

'We lost three good men rescuing you,' Selkirk reminded, 'so you had better be worth it.'

He held Abraham's eyes but got no response. The spy was inscrutable.

Night had fallen as swiftly as always in this latitude, and crisp air caressed them as they collected in the bowl between two hills with stars gradually appearing in the black abyss of the sky.

'I know the Turks,' Abraham spoke through Rachel, 'and they will be confused. They do not know who you are or how many you are. They do not know where you came from or to where you vanished.

They will take a day or two to get organised, and then they will raise an army and sweep Judea from north to south and west to east. The Turks are methodical and will not rest until they have scoured these hills and killed any British soldier.'

Selkirk nodded. 'We are safe here for some hours, but we had better be out of here before dawn.' He waited for Rachel to translate. 'But to where? I was told to pick up Abraham and follow his instructions. What are these instructions?'

Abraham squatted on the ground and rubbed his ankles, where the manacles had scraped weeping abrasions. Selkirk sent the sergeants to settle the Reivers down, post sentries and apply first aid to the wounded men. He realised that the wound in his thigh was throbbing abominably, but he had no time to dress it.

'Go on, Abraham,' he nodded to the spy.

Abraham listened intently to every word that was said and replied in short, urgent sentences that managed to convey a sense of seriousness even although Selkirk did not understand a word of the language.

'There is to be a crucial meeting,' Rachel translated, 'in Jerusalem. The Germans have organised it. There will be representatives from Germany, the Ottoman Empire, Afghanistan, Persia and a man from India.' She had difficulty with the words and asked Abraham to repeat them. 'The Indian is disaffected; he wishes to break India free from British control.'

'Disaffected men?' Selkirk repeated. 'Does he mean traitors to the Raj; to the Crown?'

He curbed his impatience while Rachel engaged in a long conversation with Abraham. His men were settling in for the night, caring for those of the horses that had been injured, mourning the loss of comrades and the five horses that had died. He looked up, where the stars gleamed in the velvet night; the same stars that had shone on Christ and the Apostles when the Romans held sway here. He wondered if some Roman centurion had grouped his men here, waiting for Herod's order to slaughter children and wishing he was back home in the gentle climate of Tuscany.

'They are planning an attack on India,' Rachel said at last. 'The Germans are encouraging Persia and Afghanistan to join Turkey and raise a pan-Islamic movement along with the Muslim peoples in India to attack the British Empire. The Germans will also urge the Hindus of Bengal to rebel.'

'Christ!' The enormity of the plan ripped the blasphemy from Selkirk's lips. In common with every schoolboy, he had learned of the Mutiny in India in 1857 when the sepoys of the East India Company had rebelled. It had taken three years, and tens of thousands of lives before the Mutiny had been quelled and ever since that event the British had been wary of a similar outbreak.

Afghanistan was also a constant worry for the British, with the wild tribes along the North West Frontier needing little excuse to raid British India and spread devastation among the more settled peoples there. Sergeant Crosier had fought in one of the more major outbreaks in 1897, but the Frontier was always an eagerly anticipated posting because of the opportunities for action and distinction; it was rarely quiet for long. Britain had fought two wars against Afghanistan itself, with mixed fortunes in both cases, while Persia was a mysterious country of oil fields and sheikhs, with the potential to cause significant trouble. Britain had also fought a small but bloody war there back in 1856.

The possibility of a pan-Islam alliance of Persia, Afghanistan and Turkey, allied with the discontented among India's tens of millions was a frightening thought, particularly when the war already stretched Britain's military and the Indian Army was heavily committed in other theatres of war. There were Indian units in France and Mesopotamia, he knew, and East Africa as well.

All these thoughts crowded through Selkirk's head, so he had to jerk himself back to the present when Abraham stopped talking, and Rachel translated again.

'Abraham and Brigadier Jones wish you to disrupt the meeting and capture the Indian delegate.' She gave that information as if she was asking him the time of day.

'Do we know this traitor's name?' Selkirk already hated the man, whoever he was and whatever his reasons. Loyalty to the Crown was one of the fundamental reasons for Selkirk's existence.

Rachel asked Abraham and came back with the answer: 'his name is Jitendra Gupta.'

'Jitendra Gupta; that is a Hindu name.' Selkirk took a deep breath as the implications hit him; he had spoken to many Hindi orderlies and stretcher bearers during the Boer War and knew them to be brave and loyal, but if they joined the Moslems against the British in India the result could be catastrophic.

We are in the centre of something huge here.

This meeting was between diplomats, including those from powers who were friendly, or at least ostensibly neutral. These were highly influential people from the top echelon of society, and if he killed the wrong man, a diplomat from Persia or Afghanistan, he could precipitate war rather than preventing it. The responsibility for a junior officer of Irregular Horse was frightening.

'They are meeting in Jerusalem,' Rachel continued, 'but you will need a guide to take you there.'

Selkirk swore. This cloak and dagger work was not the sort of operation for which he had trained his Reivers. They were intended for lightning raids in the open spaces, not for creeping around behind walls to hunt diplomats and traitors.

'Where in Jerusalem?' Selkirk asked, 'inside or outside the city?' He hoped it was outside, where his Reivers could at least operate in an environment they understood.

'In the city, in the Citadel.' Rachel dashed Selkirk's hopes.

'Oh Jesus,' Selkirk blasphemed again.

The difficulties were immediately apparent. Selkirk had eighteen men trained to operate in the wide-open spaces of the desert, and he had been given a task within the close confines of an ancient city.

'That's just the Army way,' Crosier said later when they were discussing the problems. Train the men for desert warfare and send them to Burma, or equip them with sun helmets and send them to Canada.'

Black shrugged, 'they'll adjust,' he said, 'it will be like the Wazza again,' he grinned, enjoying the memory of that street brawl.

'Not quite,' Selkirk said. They sat under the fading stars with the horses tethered in the centre and the men sleeping or mumbling all around. He looked up and momentarily saw the silhouette of a sentry against the skyline. Walker looked timeless, with his slouch hat angled so it could be a helmet and his rifle taking the place of a lance. 'We can't charge in and shoot everybody.'

'Why not?' Black asked at once. He raised his eyebrows and pulled at his pipe until the tobacco in the bowl glowed red.

'Killing neutral diplomats is not the best way to keep friends,' Selkirk explained.

'But these people are not friends,' Black pointed out. 'Friends would not talk to Germany and Turkey. If they act as enemies, we should destroy them when we have the chance.'

Selkirk saw Crosier shift uneasily and wondered if he agreed with that.

'Depending on exactly where the Turks are holding the conference,' Selkirk said, 'I don't think I will take everybody. Nineteen mounted men riding through Jerusalem would undoubtedly raise the alarm.' He saw a nod of approval from Crosier, and decided to strengthen his case, 'could you imagine Batsford trying to be inconspicuous?'

'Dear God almighty,' Crosier shook his head. 'He'd fall off his horse or invite a Jacko for a drink or break a mosque window with his rifle, sure as death.'

'Exactly,' Selkirk saw Black nod agreement and puff happily at his pipe. 'So we will need a small, select number of men. The best we have for this type of work.'

'Sir!' Trooper Walker emerged from the dark. 'I thought I saw someone moving outside the perimeter.'

'Are you on sentry duty?' Crosier demanded, 'then go back to your post!'

'Yes, sir,' Walker spoke with a slight hesitation as if he was not quite sure which words to use.

'It could have been a shepherd,' Black said, 'or some wild animal.'

'Or a Turkish patrol,' Selkirk decided to take no chances. 'Take a decko, Black and see what you can find.' He had every confidence in Black's bush skills ahead of any possible Turk.

That was the end of any rest for the men. Selkirk wakened them, ordered Wells and Sinclair to act as bodyguards for Abraham and had the rest prepare for a quick departure.

'Jildi, lads. But quietly, Jacko might be nearby.' He took Rachel aside, 'do you know anywhere we can stay safe until this conference?'

'Obviously,' Rachel said, 'I know the exact place,' she gave one of her rare smiles; 'I hope your men are not scared of the dark.'

'And the horses?' Selkirk asked.

Rachel thought for a few moments before she replied. 'Obviously,' she said at length, 'but we will have to get you to look like Turkish soldiers first.'

'In God's name, how ...?' Crosier looked at his men, 'Walker may, or Matthew, but Batsford, say? Or Sinclair? His red hair would be a dead giveaway...'

'Not as hard as you think,' Rachel said, 'a tired sentry sees what he wants to see, and a dusty rider is just a dusty rider.' That smile hovered at the corners of her mouth. 'We have to visit the battlefield first.'

Black slid out of the dark. 'Nobody out there,' he reported, 'it was probably an animal of some kind.'

'All the same,' Selkirk decided, 'up-saddle and move on.' He glanced at Rachel, who stood with her eyebrows raised in query. 'We are going back to the ambush site first.' He accepted her nod. 'It seems we must all be Turkish for a while.'

* * *

They halted as the sun threatened the eastern horizon and streaked the dark sky with bands of fiery orange. As it slid upward, they peered at the golden mediaeval walls and the thrusting minarets and towers of Jerusalem. Selkirk had heard of this city all through his childhood in

Sunday school and church, and now he was leading a band of desperadoes and two Hebrew spies a few hundred yards from the Damascus Gate. He focused his binoculars on the square towers soaring a few yards on either side of the gate, and on the pointed arch above. The surrounding walls were castellated, with a lone Turkish sentry peering languidly toward the country, with his form dwarfed by the enormous Ottoman flag on its tall pole with the white crescent serene against its crimson red background.

It was beauty encapsulated with iron security, spiritual history encased within an enemy empire, a centre of pilgrimage closed to travellers by war and religious enmity.

'Here we are then,' Black said. 'Bloody Jerusalem.'

'I hope this haven is close,' Selkirk said, 'for the Turks must be up and about soon, and then we are bound to be seen.' He glanced at his men; even wearing looted Turkish helmets and a few Turkish tunics they looked exactly like British soldiers to him.

'Sir,' Crosier pointed. A column of Turkish troops appeared in the gateway, with a mounted officer at the head. The sentry on the wall stiffened to attention as two others joined him.

'That looks dangerous,' Selkirk said quietly.

Abraham turned to Rachel and spoke rapidly. She listened and faced Selkirk. 'Abraham thinks that they are looking for him now. He recommends that we do not go through the Damascus Gate.'

'Is there an alternative?' Selkirk grasped the butt of his rifle.

'We can go to Herod's gate, down that way,' she indicated the wall to the east.

'Lead on,' Selkirk ordered quietly. He pulled Kimberley to the right, so he could watch the Turkish column march out; the infantry looked frighteningly formidable as they passed through the gate, rank after rank of soldiers, marching with the indefinable swagger of veterans.

'There are plenty of them,' Selkirk said, as Rachel joined him.

'They will be marching to search the Judea hills for you,' Rachel allowed herself to smile. 'Even the Turks will never think you will be under their very noses, in Jerusalem.'

'I hope this place you know of is very secure,' Selkirk watched the last of the Turks swing past.

'No Turk will find you there,' Rachel promised.

Only when the last of his Reivers had passed did Selkirk trot to their head, where Wells supported Abraham and Black studied the high limestone walls of the city.

'That is Herod's Gate,' Rachel said quietly. It was smaller and less ornate than the Damascus Gate, a single arched doorway set within a square tower. There was no flag above, and the sentries looked bored as they cast desultory eyes over the slow trickle of donkeys and people who passed in and out.

'Through the gate,' Rachel said, 'and look neither right nor left.'

'Turkish kabalaks, lads,' Selkirk ordered softly, 'and slouch a bit. Remember you are Turkish soldiers returning to your city. This entry is just routine for you; don't stare like virgins in a knocking shop.' He winced as the wound in his thigh began to throb; slow blood seeped through his uniform.

The Reivers slipped off their Australian hats, replaced them with the slightly pointed Turkish kabalaks they had recovered from the ambush spot and followed Selkirk straight to the Herod Gate.

Rourke had difficulty getting his kabalak to fit until Crosier jammed it over his ears with impatient force. 'Bloody stupid Turkish hat,' Rourke gave his muttered opinion and then rode in with the rest.

Selkirk could only admire the courage of Abraham. Already a fugitive from the Turks, he knew he would be at best harshly treated if they caught him a second time, and probably faced torture and death, yet here he was wearing the uniform of a Turkish officer and returning to Jerusalem in plain view. Selkirk hoped that the brass crescent of the Order of Orta that was resplendent on the front of Abraham's kabalak would increase respect for him so any Turkish soldier would ignore any flaws in his vocabulary or accent.

If the Turks discovered Abraham was an imposter, then the entire unit would be destroyed, and they were riding into the heart of the *Asakr -I Shahaneh* without support.

The gate was open, with the flagpole above the tower thrusting bare to the sky and the languid Turkish sentries barely watching the Reivers approach. One gave a half-hearted salute as Selkirk and Abraham rode through, but the other did not even look up. One body of troops would be much like another to them, and none should dream that British soldiers would dare ride into Jerusalem through the front door.

The more alert of the Turkish soldiers within the gate grunted a short challenge, but Abraham replied confidently and, duty done, the soldier returned to his post and began talking to his companion. He did not look up again as the Reivers filed past.

Selkirk lingered in the flank until the last of his men were safely through before once more passing them to move to the head of the column, but already he saw the difficulty of riding in formation through the streets of Jerusalem. Immediately through the gate was a small open area with dusty narrow streets leading left and right and a confusion of flat topped buildings in front. Men in long robes led laden donkeys and barely looked up as the Reivers halted in the open space immediately behind the gate. The men sat on their horses, some trying to look nonchalant but others staring at this holiest of cities.

For a moment Selkirk wondered what to do next. He had trusted Abraham so far, but now he was inside Jerusalem's walls he began to feel trapped. This city was the very opposite environment to that in which he had trained his Reivers.

'This is nothing like Hereford,' Wells said, but Rourke replied:

'No, but it's like the Trongate on a Saturday morning,' and Selkirk remembered that many of his men came from the squalid streets of industrial Britain, not the open countryside. They would feel more at home in a city than he ever did. He had a quick look around as Rachel spoke with Abraham.

The city was hectic. What appeared to be the principal street was crammed with men busily setting up stalls, of fruiterers and pastry cooks, of fish merchants with an assortment of strange looking fish that must have been caught in the rivers of Palestine and maybe the Sea of Galilee. Beside them were cloth merchants and bread sellers and a host of running, shrieking children and traders all shouting to advertise their wares.

The air was soft, and the people looked much as they must have done for the past thousand years or more, with long robes, olive-skinned faces and dark eyes.

'Keep moving,' Rachel said softly, 'and don't let your men speak English. We are in the Moslem Quarter; there is more likelihood of some Turkish sympathy here.'

'Thank you for the warning,' Selkirk passed on the word. 'Keep your voices down, Rourke and Wells.'

Abraham led them on a street that led roughly right, following a long curve that passed a succession of ancient buildings in a display of mingled architecture that was like the layers of a badly made cake.

The long wailing, strangely beautiful call made him start until he realised that it was a muezzin calling the faithful to prayer from a minaret.

'Bloody hell,' Matthews said in pure Yorkshire until Crosier shushed him to silence.

'This way,' Rachel said as Abraham turned into an even narrower cobbled street, where the horses could barely squeeze without the knees of the riders brushing against dirty walls. Selkirk looked up: enclosed balconies projected from walls that stretched up to a sky that was now bright with the risen sun. Already the heat was apparent.

The narrow street ended in a wall of blank stone, but there was one of the ubiquitous pointed Jerusalem doorways to the left, wide enough for two horses and tall enough for a man to ride through without ducking. Abraham glanced over his shoulder and passed through without comment.

'Where are we?'

Selkirk felt for the butt of his rifle as he entered what seemed like a vast gloomy cavern, but the slightly musty smell was familiar, and he patted Kimberley's neck. 'Easy boy, we are among friends.' He breathed deeply of the scent of horses; horse men the world over shared a common heritage. One by one the Reivers filed into what proved to be a vast stable with scores of stalls on either side, some occupied but most were empty. The scent of straw and hay and horses was friendly and reassuring.

'The Turkish military stables for this part of Jerusalem,' Rachel said calmly. 'It is the best place to hide horses; in plain view.' She shouted out a name and a man appeared from the gloom.

Rachel held out her hand: '*Netzah Yisrael Lo Yeshaker*,' she said.

The man raised his hand, and they spoke together for a while, with Selkirk watching intently and his men fidgeting on their horses. Eventually, the stable man laughed, and Rachel said, 'this is Joseph; he is the head stableman for the Turks. He will be looking after your horses.' She lowered her voice, 'he is one of us.'

Selkirk saw Walker and Mackay pushing forward to listen to what was happening and motioned them back. He wanted to ask who 'us' were, but not with so many people present.

'Will the horses be safe here?' Selkirk had a vision of some rough Turkish cavalryman abusing Kimberley. 'I mean, will the Turks not use them for remounts?'

'Joseph will ensure they are safe,' Rachel said.

'My men can't stay here,' Selkirk pointed out, 'not in a stable.' Once again the Biblical association came to him.

'Trust us,' Rachel said. 'Leave the horses here and follow.'

Who is us?

'How about my pigeons, sir?' Wells asked, but Rachel assured him that Joseph would also care for them.

There was a period of confusion as the Reivers dismounted, placed their horses in individual stalls and said a last farewell before grabbing their packs and forming up.

'We have a short walk,' Rachel said, 'and then your men will be safe.' She gave Selkirk a sidelong look, 'I only hope none of them is scared of the dark or is claustrophobic.'

'You said that before,' Selkirk pointed out. 'Where are you taking us?'

'Me'arat Tzedkiyahu,' Rachel told him, 'Zedekiah's Cave.' She seemed to find Selkirk's confusion amusing. 'You'll see. Now follow.'

They left the stables for the awakening streets of Jerusalem, complete with the rising tide of noise and assorted aromas that Selkirk associated with every city in the Near East. Rachel led; walking quickly along the narrow lanes, where men in long robes hunched in doorways and women hid behind veiled all- encompassing clothes.

'This is nothing like Hereford,' Wells said, still helping the limping Abraham along until Crosier growled at him to keep his mouth shut.

'If this is the Holy Land you can keep it,' Wells refused to be subdued. 'It's Herefordshire for me from now on … all right, sergeant, no need to swear at me.' He relapsed into silence as they moved on.

Rachel stopped at a filled in archway in a wall of dressed limestone blocks. For a moment Selkirk could see nothing, and then he noticed a small arched doorway beneath a window shielded by a once ornate but now sadly battered grill. What looked like a bundle of old rags in front of the door moved when Abraham nudged it with his foot, but not until it stood up did Selkirk realise it was a man.

'Netzah Yisrael Lo Yeshaker' Rachel said. The man looked at her through narrow eyes and pointed wordlessly to the column of soldiers, still wearing their Turkish headgear.

Rachel spoke rapidly and poked the man in the ribs, so he produced a large key and inserted it; despite its appearance, the door opened without a sound, and Abraham stepped in.

'Take the rear, Crosier,' Selkirk said and followed Abraham into the dark.

They were inside a small courtyard, surrounded by low walled buildings with square windows. The heat was already oppressive as it bounced off the walls, but Abraham limped to the opposite corner and straight through a wide doorway. A woman grinding grain barely glanced at them.

Abraham spoke softly, but Selkirk heard the same words: '*Netzah Yisrael Lo Yeshaker*'. He tried to remember them, but languages had never been one of his talents.

The woman looked up briefly, stared at the crowded soldiers, spoke to Abraham with a tone of surprise and continued with her work.

'Follow,' Rachel said.

Selkirk checked his men. They were all there, looking around them at the reality of the exotic East, some holding their rifles firmly, others mumbling to their neighbour. The wounded men were white faced with fatigue and supported by their comrades.

'How much further?' Selkirk saw Moffat stagger until Sinclair held him tight. Blood stained the front of his tunic.

'Not far,' Rachel said quietly. 'Follow.'

'This is nothing like Hereford,' Wells said, and then there was silence as the Reivers formed a single line and marched on, looking around them and talking in subdued tones, except for Kelly and Rourke who put on a swagger and raised their voices in defiance.

The building was surprisingly long, with a small doorway set low into the far wall, beside which two men were weaving on an ancient loom. They looked up as Abraham approached, spoke briefly to him and opened the door.

'Through here,' Rachel said. She lifted an oil lantern from its hook beside the loom and lit the wick. 'Nearly there.' She disappeared through the door. Selkirk followed and stopped. By the light of Rachel's lantern, he saw they were at the head of a long rock hewn passage that sloped steeply downward into unseen depths.

'Where is this place?' Selkirk asked.

I am trusting the lives of my men with this woman that I had never met until a few days ago, and I do not even know her last name.

'Me'arat Tzedkiyahu,' Rachel repeated the name. 'You might know it as King Solomon's Quarry?' When Selkirk shook his head, she sighed. 'It does not matter. What is more important is that the Turks never come here.'

The passage swooped down, with the ground underfoot worn smooth by tens of thousands of feet over many centuries. Selkirk could not see into the depths but followed Rachel and Abraham as they walked on. The Reivers followed their voices echoing amidst the ancient rocks.

'It's the road to Hell,' that was Wilson. 'There is death here.'

'There's death everywhere with you, Wills' Sinclair said.

'Careful Batsford!' Crosier roared, 'you'll break your bloody fool neck doing that, God but you're clumsy!'

Selkirk did not waste time wondering what Batsford might have done; Crosier would have him well in hand. They descended deeper with every step, but Selkirk did not feel any sense of confinement. It was much more than a cave; it was a complicated system of chambers that long-dead hands had hewn out of the living limestone.

There was the sound of running water as they passed a small spring and then they entered an immense cavern with limestone pillars holding up the roof and a score of tunnels probing off into the unknown dark.

'This is a tomb,' Wilson said, 'our tomb.'

'I hope there's a pub,' Sinclair replied.

'Stay together, lads,' Selkirk heard his voice echo in the gloom. 'Don't go wandering around until we know where we are.'

They gathered around one of the rock pillars, with the lantern light highlighting the angle of a jaw here, a deep eye socket there, a strained white face in the corner.

Rachel lifted the lantern high. 'Welcome to Solomon's Quarry' she said grandly as if she was a guide and they a party of care-free tourists in the happy days of peace. 'This is where people hewed out the stones for half the temples and buildings of Jerusalem. It extends for hundreds of yards and has many offshoots and small caves attached. You will need to walk with care as there are many hidden pits where a man may fall and be injured.'

'Thank you,' Selkirk said. 'I'll warn the men.' He looked around, 'could you tell me exactly where we are?'

Rachel pointed upward. 'We are beneath the Moslem Quarter of Jerusalem, but they cannot hear a thing and they certainly never come down here, so you are as safe as...' she sought a suitable comparison 'as safe as the Bank of England.'

'We will need food and water,' Selkirk said, 'and I have to talk to Abraham about this conference.'

'There will be food provided,' Rachel said, 'and there is a spring here with fresh water.'

'Make yourselves at home, lads,' Selkirk said, 'this will be our home for the next few days, or until our work here is done.'

'Break out the iron rations, sir?' Crosier asked.

'Yes, scran and rest.' Selkirk agreed. 'Take care of the wounded. They look all in.' He did not mention the nagging ache in his thigh. 'We'll catch whatever sleep we can get and then find out about this meeting we have to disrupt.' He looked around at the alien landscape of the cavern and wondered how life had taken him here.

I should be with Helena now, working the farm, watching my children grow, tending the animals, exchanging news with the neighbours and living my life. God! When I left the Army back in 1903, I vowed never to go to war again. Three years of soldiering in the Veldt of South Africa cured me of any feelings of romance toward the profession.

I saw too many good men killed and maimed, too much suffering to believe there was anything in war except bloodshed and horror

'Helena' Selkirk murmured, and sat upright. The Reivers surrounded him, snoring or muttering in their sleep.

The thoughts of home and Helena cascaded through Selkirk's head as he tried to relax in that vast man-made cavern underneath Jerusalem. He felt as if he could reach out and touch her, but when he did so, she would vanish, as if made of smoke. Helena was dead, and Selkirk felt very alone and far from home.

Chapter Six

November 1915

Jerusalem was a small city within its guardian walls, teeming with life but always with the pressure of history a burden that bore down on it. It was noisy, bustling, and filled with a mixture of aromas that either made him gag or which enticed him to explore the streets even more.

With the long flowing robes of an Arab concealing his uniform, Selkirk followed Abraham through lanes made even more constricting by overhanging balconies and vendors selling their goods by volume of sound. He tried to follow his progress by comparing the route with a mental map of the city, but he was soon hopelessly lost and merely kept Abraham in sight.

'It is a bad time to be a Jew in Palestine,' Rachel said as they stopped outside the burned out ruins of a synagogue. 'The Turks are trying to remove us from our land.'

'Are you from Jerusalem?' Selkirk tried to find out more about this woman.

'No; I am from the Carmel Mountains, further north by the coast,' Rachel said quietly, 'but we are all the same.'

'We?' Selkirk asked. He looked inside the synagogue; the remains of painted decoration and colourful curtains hinted at a previous beauty, but the interior was now a blackened ruin, with charred beams fallen onto a litter of burned papers and books. He shook his head; he had no knowledge of the modern history of this part of the world, but any nation that burned religious places and books was wrong. Knowledge was too precious to be destroyed.

'Who are we?' Selkirk asked.

Rachel glanced down the street where a water carrier was selling his wares; festooned in an array of shiny brass cups, he rattled as he walked. 'We', she repeated, 'are the true people of this land.'

The water carrier passed them with a smile on his bearded face, followed by a brace of stately Greek Orthodox priests and then a young Arab boy leading a heavily laden donkey. A group of Jews stopped to look at the synagogue; they wore black clothes and kippahs and spoke in a language that might have been German but was not Hebrew.

'The Jews?'

'This is our land,' Rachel said softly, but with such feeling that Selkirk knew he had touched on something important to her.

'Would you share it?'

'Would you share yours?' Rachel parried, and Selkirk wondered how he would feel if a horde of foreigners demanded the right to live in Scotland.

'No,' he said at length. 'We fought too hard and too long for what we have.'

'So did we.' Rachel still spoke quietly. Her eyes held his; dark and profound, they seemed to yearn for understanding. 'And we are fighting still.'

'The Turks seem to be pretty thin on the ground in Jerusalem,' Selkirk said.

'They are all hunting for Abraham,' Rachel raised her eyes to meet his, 'and you.' Her expression was unfathomable. 'I did not thank you for rescuing Abraham. Three British soldiers died.'

'They were good men,' Selkirk said.

'They died for a good reason,' Rachel sounded genuinely sorry.

Selkirk wondered if their families would agree that saving a middle-aged Zionist Palestinian was worth the loss of their men. He did not voice his thoughts.

'Why is Abraham so important?' Selkirk faced him, 'who are you and how do you know so much about Turkish intentions?'

'Have you heard of Aaron Aaronsohn?' Rachel asked. She stepped back to allow a pair of Arab women to pass. They moved slowly, without seeming to notice her.

'I have not,' Selkirk admitted.

'You will,' Rachel told him, 'he is an agriculturalist and leader of NILI...' she looked away for a second to watch the Arabs pass, 'of which you have also not heard, I see.'

'I have not,' Selkirk saw an expression of disappointment cross her face.

'The initials stand for *Netzah Yisrael Lo Yishaker*: the Eternity of Israel will not lie.' Her eyes were hopeful as she looked at him. 'We are on the British side, and we are fighting for our land; we are Jewish.' She saw his nod, 'Abraham is one of our leaders.'

'I see; very hush hush,' Selkirk nodded, 'so if the Turks succeeded in making Abraham reveal details of this NILI, he could give some of the names and the Turks could cause severe damage to the organisation.'

'That is correct,' Rachel said. 'Abraham knows all the leaders of the NILI. The Turks would torture him until he told them.'

'He is a vital man indeed then.' Selkirk said, 'no wonder the Turks want him.'

Abraham was moving again, walking through the narrow streets with his back erect as a Guardsman on parade. Selkirk followed, wondering anew at his confidence and courage to walk openly in a city where the Turks would arrest him on sight.

'Here we are,' Rachel halted at a massive stone structure, overlooked by a series of towers and the slender minaret of a mosque. 'This is the Tower of David, otherwise known as the Citadel.'

'It is huge,' Selkirk said. 'Is that where the Turks are holding the conference?'

'In there,' Rachel agreed. 'There are five main towers, but we are only interested in that one,' she used her chin to point to a massive square tower on the opposite side of the fortress from the mosque. 'It is not as large as you may think, Major Selkirk. The walls are very thick, and the room in which the meeting is on the first floor.'

Selkirk studied the building, wondering how he could get in, disrupt the meeting and escape with a prisoner. 'How well is it guarded?' he pointed to the large Ottoman flag which hung lifeless above the citadel, 'I presume the Turks have soldiers in there.'

Rachel nodded. 'Obviously.' She gave a small smile, 'that is the Turk's main garrison in the city.'

That makes things a bit awkward.

Selkirk drew a deep breath. 'How many men are there inside?'

'I don't know; there might be hundreds.' Rachel shrugged. 'The numbers change from week to week, but we saw a convoy march out to search for your men, so there will be less than usual.'

'A column, not a convoy,' Selkirk corrected, 'but that is good news.'

He withdrew into the shadows of a doorway as a group of Turkish soldiers walked past, talking and laughing much like their British counterparts would do. He watched them from beneath his kaffiyeh, the ubiquitous Arab head dress, wondering about their quality and numbers, and then they were passed, and he was left to contemplate the huge problem that faced him.

He had eighteen highly trained horsemen and two Hebrew spies, but four men were wounded. He had to break into a mediaeval fortress garrisoned by an unknown number of Turkish soldiers, disrupt a high-level diplomatic meeting, capture a traitor while leaving neutrals unharmed, and escape. He also had to keep Abraham safe from the Turks, and then?

How in God's name do we get out of Palestine?

Selkirk drew a deep breath. *Brigadier Smith must have some idea of getting this Indian traitor and Abraham safely away. Hopefully, he would send a ship so there would be a quick dash to the coast and back to Egypt.*

'I have seen enough for just now,' he said.

* * *

There was the constant sound of dripping water within the vast quarry under Jerusalem, but the Reivers had adapted to their circumstances and made themselves as comfortable as possible. There were flaring torches set in niches, and the local Jewish nationalists had supplied food, so the men did not have to resort to their iron rations.

'You've done well,' Selkirk complimented the sergeants, who merely grunted in response.

'Some of the lads are getting a bit edgy,' Crosier reported. 'They miss the open air.'

'That's not surprising,' Selkirk sympathised. 'It's been a week now. I might be able to give some of them an opportunity to get out shortly, at least into Jerusalem.'

They sat on a small ledge of rock, with Black puffing at his long stemmed pipe and Crosier casting hard glances at his men. Torchlight threw dancing shadows over the Reivers as they sat in small groups, playing cards or Crown and Anchor or merely tried to catch some sleep, as British soldiers seemed able to do in any circumstance.

Selkirk explained what the situation was and waited for his sergeants to comment.

'As we said before, Major,' Black gave his opinion, 'we need a small strike force to break into the castle, kill or grab who needs to be killed or grabbed and get out quickly.'

'That's how I see it,' Selkirk agreed.

'How many men will we need, sir?' Crosier asked.

'No more than six. Enough to have fire power but not too many to attract attention when we march through the barracks.'

Black puffed at his pipe, 'we could use the same technique as we did coming into Jerusalem, pretending to be Turks.'

Selkirk nodded. 'If the Turks catch us in their barracks they will believe we are spies and shoot us – if we are lucky.'

Black took the pipe from his mouth and grunted. 'They will do that anyway.'

'We'll need more than just Turkish helmets then,' Crosier pointed out. 'We will be close to the Turks, so we'll need full uniforms. Where in God's name can we get them?'

'From the Turks,' Selkirk said.

'Just walk up to the stores and ask them for a uniform?' Crosier asked.

'Something like that,' Selkirk agreed. 'We need some of our more disreputable Reivers for the job.'

'They are all disreputable,' Crosier spoke with feeling. 'I've never served with such a bunch.'

'What have you in mind, Major?' Black thrust his pipe into his mouth and raised his eyebrows, 'nothing legal, I hope?'

'Nothing legal at all,' Selkirk told him and explained his plan.

'I know just the men for the job,' Black said, and Crosier nodded.

* * *

While the streets of Jerusalem had seemed noisy and crowded during the day, at night, they were dark and cool and slightly sinister. Selkirk had given strict instructions to the four men who accompanied him but still walked very warily as he moved toward David's Tower.

'Remember,' he said, 'we are not here to start a fight. We are using violence for a purpose, not for its own sake.'

'I'll keep an eye on them,' There was iron in Crosier's quiet voice.

Kelly glowered at Rourke; 'best watch that Orange bastard then,' he said, 'he'll rip anyone he sees.'

Crosier intercepted Rourke's lunge at Kelly. 'I'll have you, Rourke! And you shut your mouth, Kelly.'

Selkirk winked at Rachel who he had reluctantly agreed should accompany them because of her linguistic skills. 'They understand each other,' he said.

'Obviously.'

Selkirk had chosen a narrow street that lay between the Armenian Garden and the Citadel. He was the officer, but he knew that in this kind of operation his two most troublesome private soldiers had a better idea of what to do. Both were brought up in the urban jungles of their respective cities and knew the rules of this kind of operation as well as anybody in the army.

There were fewer Turkish soldiers abroad than he had expected. If the Citadel had been a British base, there would have been a constant movement of men to and from the city, but instead, there were only a few stragglers who were returning from the city and one weary patrol that marched in the opposite direction.

'What was your plan, Major Selkirk?' Rachel asked.

'Catch Turkish soldiers coming back from visiting the brothels, knock them down and strip them off their uniforms.' Selkirk held her eyes.

Rachel did not flinch. 'There is a better place,' she said, 'if you want me to take you? It is not far away.'

The streets were even narrower, the darkness more intense. But there were lights in some of the barred windows and sounds of exotic music drifted to their ears.

'This is more like the East,' Kelly said softly. He looked around, 'It feels like Scotland Road on a Saturday night. You can feel them watching you.'

'Feel who?' Rachel rarely spoke to the men.

'The boys that want to rip us,' Kelly said. 'We can't see them, but they'll be there, in the doorways and behind the windows.' He tapped his side, where his bayonet sat snug under the ubiquitous dirty white robes, 'well come on then, boys, and see what I've got for you.' He jerked his head toward the nearest window, 'let's see if you are as good as the Scousers!'

'You'll bloody run if anybody even blows on you, you Papist bastard,' Rourke spat on the ground.

'Enough!' Crosier silenced them.

They moved on, deeper into the labyrinth of streets and lanes, with Arab voices now floating in the night air and the occasional bleat of a goat or bray of a donkey. Rachel stopped them at a curving street, broader than the surrounding lanes, where men crouched at lit doorways, smoking hookahs and talking to each other in low tones. Somebody giggled, high pitched and hair-raising, and a woman screamed in the distance. A dog barked, once.

'These are the brothels the Turks use,' Rachel explained.

'That's why they call this the Holy City,' Kelly said, and for once Rourke joined in his vicious bark of laughter. They stopped immediately and glared their hatred at each other, two men who were far more similar than they knew; products of virtually identical backgrounds but divided by opinions of religious ideology.

'Now we wait,' Selkirk said. 'We want them coming out when they are sated and relaxed, not going in when they might be more alert.'

The street was busier than he liked, with groups of men passing through and an occasional heavily veiled woman. Men and women spoke together with a freedom he had not expected, and more than once he saw a couple strike a bargain and disappear into one of the doorways.

'Lucky buggers,' Kelly whispered.

'Not so lucky, Kelly;' Crosier said, 'God alone knows what sort of disease they will pick up here. Have you not noticed how many of the men have pock-marked faces? Why do you think they call it the pox?'

'Turks!' Rachel spoke the word as if it was a curse.

'Where?' Selkirk peered into the semi gloom of the street, where lights from the windows provided arcs of lesser dark through which robed figures flitted and in which the hookah-smokers sat.

'I can smell them.' Rachel put a hand inside her clothes and Selkirk guessed she was touching the handle of her revolver.

'Ready, lads; quiet now.' Crosier dropped the sandbag from his sleeve. About eighteen inches long and made of heavy linen, it was filled with sand and soaked in water to give it extra weight. 'It's more supple than a cosh,' he had explained to Selkirk, 'but deadly when you get up close.' He had smiled at a distant memory. 'We carried them on guard duty on the Frontier. The Pathans would always go for sentries with rifles, but we used to have a few lads with equalisers as well, just in case.' His laugh had lacked humour.

Rachel was right. Two Turkish soldiers emerged from a doorway and rolled into the street. Selkirk judged them to be in their late teens or early twenties, smooth faced, sturdy young men who probably wished they were back home in Istanbul or Ankara, but who made the best of their lives in the circumstances war had forced upon them.

'They're coming this way,' Kelly whispered.

Selkirk nodded. He had hoped for men walking alone, but a pair was better than half a dozen.

The Turks talked and joked like old friends as they walked straight past the alley where the British waited.

Crosier held Kelly back as the Liverpool man edged toward them,

'I will bring them in,' Rachel said, and before Selkirk could stop her, she stepped out of the dark directly in the path of the Turks.

Rourke grinned. 'We know that trick in the Trongate' he said and hefted his weapon of choice, a lead weighted leather cosh that showed signs of wear and tear.

The Turkish soldiers stopped as Rachel removed her head scarf and tossed back her long black hair. She stood exactly in their path and slowly lifted the edge of her robe to expose the calf of her left leg, jerked her head toward the alley and stepped back.

'If they fall for that they are total bloody fools,' Rourke said but grinned as the Turks hurried after Rachel.

'Country yokels,' Kelly agreed and smashed his iron bar across the head of the second soldier.

The man fell without a sound, but his companion gave a little shriek of surprise before Crosier felled him with his sandbag.

'Nice work,' Selkirk approved.

'Kill them,' Rachel pleaded. There were tears in her eyes. 'Kill them both.' She dropped the hem of her skirt, replaced her head dress and stared at the two prone Turkish soldiers.

'No,' Selkirk shook his head, 'we are soldiers, not murderers.'

'Why not?' Rachel demanded. 'They are the enemy; they are Turks.'

'No,' Selkirk said. 'Strip them.' He watched as Kelly and Rourke undressed the unconscious men. When one of the Turks groaned as if he was awakening, Rourke smashed him across the back of the head without any compassion. Kelly kicked the prone man in the ribs for good measure as Rachel fingered her revolver.

'I could kill him if you like, sir,' Rourke half drew his bayonet. 'It would save fighting him later.'

'No.' Selkirk said again, yet Rourke's logic was inescapable. Why save this man's life now, when he could be the Turk who fired the rifle that killed him the next day or the next week? There was no sense in that, but there was no sense in the war anyway. War was a pointless sordid slaughter.

'That's enough,' he stopped any further violence. The young Turkish soldiers lay on the ground, pathetic and vulnerable in their underwear. 'Drag these lads into a doorway in case somebody sees them. We'll move elsewhere; Rachel: you know this place best.'

Bundling the uniforms into a bag, they followed Rachel out of the alley and into the street, where the hookah smokers looked up, hopeful for custom, and then returned their attention to their pipes.

'Here,' Rachel led them to a very similar alleyway on the opposite side of the street. 'This is the way the Turks come in from the Citadel.'

'I want the next one,' Rourke said.

'Obey orders!' Crosier's whisper was savage.

'You honestly hate the Turks, don't you?' Selkirk asked Rachel.

'Obviously' she said and relapsed into silence.

They heard the singing before they saw the men. The sound was so familiar that Selkirk and Crosier exchanged glances. 'Fir Tree Spur,' Crosier said quietly, 'it's the same song the Turks sang there.'

Six Turkish soldiers were walking together. These were not recruits but men in their late twenties with the swagger and confidence of veterans. They marched purposely, two abreast and three deep and the leading pair pushed aside an unfortunate elderly man who left his house just as they passed.

'I want them, sir,' Crosier spoke quietly, but Selkirk saw the dark hunger in his face. 'We lost hundreds of men on that ridge.'

'There are too many,' Rachel said, 'six of them and only five of us.'

'Ready lads?' Selkirk remembered the carnage on Fir Tree Spur and knew he had to get these Turks. This ambush was nothing to do with professional soldiering; this was pure revenge for the loss of so many of his men.

'Ready sir,' Crosier hefted his sandbag and looked to Kelly and Rourke. 'Keep it quiet now lads, but we want these bastards.'

There were no smiles from the two privates. They could calculate odds as well as anybody else and were past masters in this situation of sudden savage street assaults.

'And keep quiet: don't speak English whatever you do. We can't let them know that there are British soldiers in Jerusalem.'

'Yes, sir,' Rourke said.

'Rachel – do your act!' Selkirk ordered.

'There are too many!' Rachel protested.

'Do it!' Selkirk's order was savage. He wanted these men; he had a score to settle for the Borderers he had left behind in Gallipoli.

Rachel hesitated, but took two steps outside the alleyway, glanced at Selkirk with huge dark eyes and then at the approaching Turks. Selkirk could see her trembling as she removed her head scarf, but she collected herself, straightened her back and tossed her hair loose once more. It flowed over her shoulders like a glossy black waterfall, shining in the light that escaped from a partly shuttered window.

The leading Turkish soldier shouted something, and his companions joined in with a series of calls, yells and gestures that made their immediate intentions obvious.

'Enough now,' Selkirk whispered, but Rachel now seemed determined to play her part to the full. She swivelled in front of the Turks, lifted the hem of her robes well above her knee, thrust out her hip and smiled over her shoulder.

The Turks were forty feet away, close enough for Selkirk to note they wore the dark green collars of the infantry and one had a bandaged arm. They had stopped to watch and roared their delight as Rachel flicked her robe even higher, turned around and spoke to them. Selkirk did not understand the words, but the meaning was clear when she walked, swaying her hips, into the alley where the Reivers waited. Only then did Selkirk notice that her eyes were liquid.

'Well done, Rachel,' he said. 'Well done. That took courage.'

'Kill them,' she pleaded, 'please kill them.'

They came with a rush, six soldiers intent on lust cramming into the narrow dark alley where four British soldiers waited with the opposite intent. Selkirk used the same tactics he had at the ambush; he had stationed Crosier at the entrance of the alley while he waited at the far end, with Kelly and Rourke in between. As soon as the last Turk passed Crosier, he gave the signal, and they pounced. Kelly and Rourke took a man apiece, with Selkirk advancing down the alley with his knobkerrie and Crosier waiting for any who turned to flee.

Taken completely unawares, the Turkish soldiers stood no chance. Kelly and Rourke dealt with their men with relish, felling them with quick blows to the head and adding another as the Turks slumped to the ground. Crosier smashed his sandbag over the skull of the rearmost Turk while Selkirk was less efficient. He ran up to his target and swung his knobkerrie, but his man saw him coming and ducked. He was a sturdy soldier with the hard eyes of a veteran, and threw a roundhouse punch that missed, but put Selkirk off his stroke, so his next swing only caught the Turk on the arm.

The remaining two Turks saw their comrade struggling with Selkirk and lunged forward, so Selkirk faced three at once. He brandished his knobkerrie and tried to look ferocious as they came forward. Ignoring the man with the bandaged arm who was farthest away, Selkirk thrust the end of the weapon into the throat of the first man, then withdrew and swung the weighted tip at the legs of the second. The first man stopped dead, clutched at his throat and gagged, while the second yelled as the solid knob at the end of the weapon smashed against his knee cap, but then the third had pounced, his one hand grabbing at

Selkirk's throat. As he closed, Selkirk had time to notice the man had the shoulder straps of an *onbasi,* the equivalent of a corporal.

The force of the *onbasi's* attack knocked Selkirk backwards. He dropped his knobkerrie and took hold of the man's grasping hand, but the Turk was immensely powerful and matched him muscle for muscle. For a moment Selkirk thought the onbasi would strangle him, but he managed to bring his knee up smartly into the onbasi's groin. The man grunted in agony and slackened his grip, so Selkirk smashed his forehead into the Turk's nose. He felt the spurt of warm blood, heard the crack of something breaking and saw the Turk lurch back, hands to his face.

The other two Turks had recovered, but before they could attack him, Rourke cracked one over the head and Kelly grabbed the other in a choke hold. Rachel stepped forward to the injured *onbasi* and pressed her revolver against his neck.

'No!' Crosier pulled her arm away and removed the pistol. He said no more but thumped his sandbag against the back of the Turk's neck. As the man collapsed, Selkirk hoped that single word had not betrayed them all, but it was too late now to worry about what might be.

'Strip their uniforms,' Selkirk ordered, 'and let's get away from here. We have lingered far too long already.'

'They might have heard us speaking English,' Rachel did not help in the stripping process, 'if we kill them they cannot say.'

'There will be no killing,' Selkirk ordered. He saw the disappointment on Rachel's face.

What drove you to this level of hatred?

Rachel looked backwards at the Turks on the ground, but only Selkirk saw the expression on her face. She was weeping, with large round tears rolling down her cheeks and dripping from her chin.

* * *

Oil lamps pooled uncertain light over the map of the Citadel that Selkirk spread on the ground. Selkirk crouched opposite Rachel, with

Crosier and Black on either side. Abraham sat on a square block of rock a few feet away, watching but saying nothing.

'There is an outer wall with towers and buildings around a court-yard,' Selkirk pointed out the buildings one by one as Rachel gave the names, 'but this is the only one we need to bother about.' He indicated the tower opposite the slender minaret and the furthest away from the entrance. 'This is where they're holding the meeting.'

'That's part of the city wall,' Black said. 'Is there an entrance from the outside?'

Rachel shook her head. 'No; just from inside the citadel.'

Crosier peered at the plan. 'So that means crossing the courtyard in full view of the Turks,' he said. 'The Turks are not stupid. They will know that somebody has stolen eight of their uniforms and they will wonder why. They'll be looking for strangers wearing their uniforms.'

'That is a chance we have to take,' Selkirk said. All war involved risk. He remembered the advance along that terrible ridge in Gallipoli when the Turkish machine guns opened up. That battle had cost hundreds of lives, yet he was more concerned about this small operation than he had been about that murderous day. Perhaps it was because there was so much as stake, with this meeting between diplomats from foreign powers, and one mistake on his part could increase the danger to the Empire and Britain itself. Perhaps it was because he was responsible for this one, and he knew each man involved.

'Do we know the exact date yet?' He asked Abraham.

'You will know as soon as we do,' Rachel translated Abraham's reply.

Selkirk spent the next few days alternating between planning the mission in the citadel and watching the movement of the Turkish garrison. He noted down the different insignia on the uniforms and hoped to identify the units to judge the approximate size of the garrison.

'There are a lot of wounded men,' Crosier said, 'probably from Gallipoli or Mesopotamia.'

Selkirk nodded. He watched a white coated Turkish officer adjust his belt buckle with its crescent and star insignia. 'That is an artillery-man,' he said, 'but I have seen no sign of guns.'

'I think this is a garrison of odds and sods, sir,' Crosier said. 'There seem to be men from every unit under the sun.' He looked at the notes he had been making, 'Artillery, infantry, firemen, snipers; the Turks must think Jerusalem is a quiet area, so they use it to rest their wounded and sick. With men from so many different units, I can't see any way we can calculate the numbers.'

'Nor can I,' Selkirk agreed. 'So our next move is to try and remove as many as possible, so there is merely a skeleton garrison in the citadel when we are in.'

'We already know that some are searching Judaea for us,' Black pointed out. 'Maybe we can stage another raid, so the rest leave Jerusalem as well?'

'That might work,' Selkirk agreed.

'It would do the boys good as well,' Crosier said, 'some are getting fidgety being confined underground for so long.' He glanced toward the main cavern, where the Reivers were gathered in a muttering mass, playing cards or checking their rifles. 'They were asking me if they had come to Palestine to be locked in jail.'

'A few of them know all about jails,' Black put in with a smile. He thrust his long pipe into his mouth. 'This place may be a bit too familiar for them.'

'There have been some quarrels, sir,' Crosier said. 'I have had to intervene.' He hesitated for a fraction of a minute, 'and I caught one or two of the boys trying to sneak out, but they did not get far.'

'Who was that?' Selkirk asked.

'Matthew and Kelly sir, and then Walker as well,' Crosier said.

'We will be out of here as soon as we can,' Selkirk made a promise he hoped he could keep.

'I am not so sure about having another raid,' Crosier said. 'With a lot of these Turkish lads injured, their officers may not think them sufficiently fit to send up country if we make another appearance, and then there is the problem of getting out and back into the city with the horses.'

Selkirk nodded. You are correct, Sergeant. We were lucky the first time; we may not be so fortunate again.'He pondered for a moment. 'All right: I will talk to Abraham and allow the men to visit the horses on a rota, so they are at least out of here for a while. We can't leave the city, but we have to create some diversion...'

'A Wazza, Major,' Black said. 'When the lads rioted in Wazza, all the redcaps in Cairo came in, and a whole lot of other headquarter troops as well. If we get a good riot going, the Turks have to put it down. The garrison will empty, and we can get in, knobble the Kaiser's boys, shake hands with the Persians and Afghans, grab the traitor and run.'

Selkirk considered. 'What do you think, Crosier?'

'It's an idea, sir, but how do we start a riot in Jerusalem?'

Selkirk glanced at Rachel, 'is Jerusalem volatile? Are there riots here?'

'I think we could arrange one,' she said seriously.

'That is what we do then,' Selkirk accepted that as assent. 'Let's work out details.'

Chapter Seven

December 1915

Helena was there, just on the periphery of his vision. He could sense her; he knew that subtle perfume that she wore on very special occasions. He reached out, but she was not there. He peered into the opaque landscape, where the desert dust of the Kalahari hazed everything and saw her form, plumper now after two children, but even more desirable for that.

'Helena'

She did not reply.

'Helena'

She turned to him, unsmiling, with her eyes invisible. He tried to step forward but could not move. His legs failed to respond. She was drifting away, sliding into the ethereal distance. She was leaving him.

'I had to go, Andrew,' she said. 'I did not wish to.'

Selkirk recalled that day on the stoep watching the huge orange sun set across half the continent, casting shadows on the graves of his wife and children.

There was a small figure on either side of her now; their children had joined her, looking at him across the width of the world. He reached for them, but Helena hustled them away, so his hands clawed at empty air.

'Helena' he said, 'Helena' but she was no longer there, and the desert sky was red with blood and dark with despair.

'Helena...'

'Major!' Black shook him awake. 'You're needed.'

Selkirk started. 'Helena?'

'Sorry Major; it's Sergeant Black.'

Selkirk staggered to his feet. 'What's the matter, Black?'

'That buckle bint says she has information for you.' Black said bluntly. He jerked his head backwards. 'She's waiting out there.'

Abraham was clinging to Rachel's arm. He looked frail and old, with the bruises on his face having merged to one large purple mess that completely closed his left eye. He slurred when he spoke.

'Abraham says that you had better start getting organised, Major Selkirk,' Rachel translated and then listened to Abraham again. 'He says that there is a fresh company of the First Division marching to Jerusalem; that can only mean the Turks will use them for some particular reason.'

'The diplomatic meeting?' Selkirk asked, and Rachel shrugged.

'Obviously.'

'The First Division?' Black had remained to listen. 'That's bad news, Major. They're the best they have. If they are in the Citadel we won't just be facing odds and sods, but prime soldiers.'

Selkirk felt Rachel's eyes on him. 'In that case, we'll just have to be that much better,' he said. *His rag bag collection of odds and sods were opposed to a company of the best soldiers in the Ottoman army. That was not good.*

* * *

Sunset over the city of Jerusalem was something that Selkirk would always remember. He sat on a small knoll on the Mount of Olives, with the ancient olive trees of the walled Garden of Gethsemane beneath him and the yellow limestone walls encompassing the most famous city in the world with the Golden Gate forever closed. The western horizon was brilliant red as the sun dipped low, with horizontal rays catching the golden dome of Al Haram al Sharif, the Dome of the Rock on Temple Mount.

As I sit upon the hillock of tears
Without skin on either toe or sole
O, king! – Peter and Paul
Far is Rome from Loch Long

Selkirk intoned the poem of Muredhach Albanach, the Gaelic pilgrim who went on crusade in the thirteenth century, and wondered why swords and rifles should visit a place of such incredible beauty and holiness.

'You are singing, Major Selkirk?' There was the suggestion of a smile at the corners of Rachel's mouth.

'It is a song of homesickness' Selkirk told her, 'from hundreds of years ago.' He gestured to the city that was spread out before him. 'This is the Holy City that we all learn about at school and in the church. I should feel blessed to see it, but here I am planning death and destruction and thinking of my wife.' He stopped abruptly. He had made it a rule not to discuss his personal life with anybody who did not already know him.

The sun seemed to hover on Jerusalem's skyline, creating shadows from the scattered olive trees of the Mount. Selkirk watched as a solitary lizard, bright with colour, emerged from the shelter of a rock and moved in small spurts of speed to hunt its prey.

'I was born in Jerusalem,' Rachel seemed willing to talk, 'although I moved north when I was married. Do you miss her a lot?' She sat on a rock a few feet from him and turned to face him directly. Her eyes were hooded, her face an expressionless mask within the blue and white scarf she wore around her head.

'Yes,' Selkirk said. He thought of his recent dreams where Helena had appeared.

'And?' Rachel probed further, 'you should smile when you talk about your wife, Major Selkirk, but you did not.'

Selkirk shook his head. 'I wish she were still here to see all this,' his wave encompassed Jerusalem and much of Judaea.

'You might bring her back after the war,' Rachel said, 'but would you introduce her to me?'

'She is dead,' Selkirk said abruptly.

'Oh,' Rachel was quiet for a long moment. 'I am sorry Major Selkirk; I did not know.' She reached across and placed her hand on his sleeve.

'There is no way you could have known,' Selkirk said.

'Can you talk about her?' Rachel allowed her hand to linger on his sleeve for longer than was necessary. 'It might help.' She waited as Selkirk gathered his thoughts. 'Would you have brought her here? Would she have liked me?'

Selkirk wondered how Helena would react to the Holy Land, 'you would get along very well,' he said. 'She was a warrior when I met her.'

'A warrior? A Scottish woman warrior?' Rachel inched slightly closer. She put her elbow on her knee and rested her chin in her cupped palm, waiting for an answer.

'No, Helena is- was - a Boer – Dutch South African.' Selkirk was going to stop there, but Rachel raised her eyebrows in encouragement and inched even closer to her legs were nearly touching his.

'Don't stop there, Major Selkirk.'

It was months since Selkirk had spoken to a woman and the sound of Rachel's voice was somehow a reminder of home. Yet he could not talk to her of Helena. That felt wrong.

'We were on opposing sides in the South African War,' he said slowly. 'We fought each other half a dozen times' he smiled, 'good practice for marriage I suppose.'

Rachel met Selkirk's smile. 'And then you met after the war?'

'After the war, I left the Army, sailed to South Africa and married her.' Selkirk said. 'We had two children.'

'You *had* two children? That is past tense is it not?' Rachel's eyes were dark with compassion.

'They died of fever,' Selkirk said. 'One after the other.'

'Oh,' Rachel's hand has warm on his arm. 'Talk to me.' She said. 'Tell me about your home in Africa.'

Rachel inched even closer, listening to every word as Selkirk told her about their farm on the edge of the Kalahari Desert, with the wildlife all around and the everlasting peace of the horizon that stretched to infinity and the great void of the sky as a never ending bowl above their heads.

'I would like that,' Rachel said at last. 'I would like the peace and the sense of newness over everything. Here. 'She looked all around at the ancient city beneath them and the settlements that crowded flat roofed and slightly ramshackle outside the walls, at the plethora of minarets, domes and churches from every denomination under the sun. 'Here, history presses upon us with sad memories in every corner.' She touched his arm with a surprisingly gentle hand. 'I envy you, Major Selkirk. I envy you the chance of a new start, but,' she looked around, 'this is my country, our country, our land. I may make a new start here, once we have cleansed the land of the Turks!' Once more she said the word as if it was a curse.

Selkirk tried to suppress his discomfort as he recalled Rachel's hatred of the Turks. 'Are you married, Rachel?'

She stiffened on her rock, and all expression drained from her face. 'I was married,' she said. As she spoke, she looked away in the direction of the Dome of the Rock.

'Were married?' Selkirk waited until she recovered her composure.

'The Turks killed my husband,' Rachel stopped and again stared at the dome as the sun glared a brilliant gold from the dome. 'They shot him like a dog at the door of our house, and they raped me.' When she looked at Selkirk, her eyes were unreadable. 'I will kill Turks until I cleanse our land.'

Selkirk tried to hold her eyes. 'I wondered why you hated them so much,' he said, 'now I understand.'

'You are a long way from your Helena,' Rachel spoke quietly, 'and you must miss her greatly, as I miss my husband. When your war is over, you can return to your country. I have neither a nation nor a husband. The Turks have taken both.'

'I understand, I think.' Selkirk watched the sun slide away. 'War is man's greatest obscenity.'

Rachel leaned forward and touched him, lightly, on his arm. Her smile was soft. 'Soldiers must be used to being away from home.' She raised her eyebrows again, 'you need to talk more about your wife,' she said.

'Do I?'

'You want to release yourself from this burden,' Rachel told him. 'And to whom else can you talk? Sergeant Crosier? Private Kelly?' She taunted him with unlikely names. 'And here I am offering to listen.'

Selkirk could not face her. He looked in the direction of the holy city, but in his mind, he was on his farm with Helena at his side and the children running at their feet. 'I have said all I ever will say,' he said. 'They are always with me.

Rachel nodded. 'As you wish. And now you are fighting for your country and me for mine.' She came closer, so she pressed against him, hip to hip on a slowly cooling rock above the Garden of Gethsemane with the skyline of Jerusalem highlighted against a flaring sunset. 'Is that such a bad thing, Major Selkirk?'

'War is always a bad thing,' Selkirk said. 'I am using it as an excuse not to think about Helena and the children. When it is over ...' He shrugged. 'I don't know.' He watched the sun dipping fast toward Jerusalem and felt that his own life had also sunk into the abyss.

Rachel said nothing but held out her arms. Without any conscious thought, Selkirk accepted her unspoken invitation and came to her. He was immediately aware that this was not Helena. She felt different and acted differently, and the scent of her hair under his nose was different. He held her close, with no intention to do anything but offer and accepting support and sympathy.

The sun dipped with that suddenness he had learned to expect in this part of the world, so different from the prolonged dusks of his native Berwickshire. Rachel did not move from her position in his arms, and Selkirk knew that he did not wish her to. For the moment she was

Helena, and he was her husband, not as a replacement, not in soul or body, but in memory and for the comfort of a lost love.

She was firm against him. Not for Rachel the yielding softness of city women with their subtle emotional games and layers of laundered clothing. Rachel was muscle and openness and hurt, bitter anger against circumstances that had robbed her of her man and her reason for existence and a given her a primaeval desire to strike back. She was a microcosm of this tortured Holy Land to which everyone laid claim. She was an elemental force, a Helena of her land, a flesh and blood scream against the sordid horror of war and the hopeless limbo of stateless humanity.

'Rachel?'

She began to tremble against him.

'Rachel?'

She was all of these things and none of them; she was a woman deprived of her man, and he was a man bereaved of his woman. They were similar but opposite, a human oxymoron in this land of tortured hopes and religious fundamentalism.

He looked closely and realised she was in tears as all her anger dissolved and the underlying grief came to the surface. It was only natural to wrap his arms around her and pull her closer, and only natural that she should respond by placing her head on his shoulder.

They remained like that as the night cooled and the lights of Jerusalem came on, one by one and then in a rush. Selkirk felt her sobbing. He said nothing, knowing that words would not help until she had drained herself of emotion. He held her as the moon slid into the sky and the stars appeared, pinpricks of hope against the eternal blackness of the night. He held her but thought of Helena, a survivor of a war in which her people suffered as they strived against the mightiest Empire the world had ever known, only to die of disease alongside her family.

Why?

In the name of God: why?

And then it was not Helena, but Rachel and the walls of Jerusalem were before them with the muezzin's haunting call to gather the faithful to prayer, the minaret pointing to the stars and her dark hair soft against his face and the air was from the desert.

Eventually, Rachel stilled, leaning against him as the wind rose and chilled her tears that had soaked through his shirt.

'Rachel?'

She shifted, blinked and pushed herself upright. 'We had better get back,' she said, 'they will be worried about us.' She looked at him gravely. 'I think we understand each other Major Selkirk.'

'I think we do,' he agreed, 'but you can call me Andrew or Drew when the men are not around.'

She smiled although her eyes were still bright with tears. 'I will call you Major Selkirk,' she said.

* * *

The men of the First Division marched in through the Jaffa Gate in a column of four; rifles sloped over their shoulders and a rope circlet holding their kabalaks in place on their heads. They marched in silence save for the drum and scuff of boots on the road and an occasional barked order from the bimbashi in command.

'They look like they know what they're doing,' Crosier said quietly. He pulled the scarf further over his face.

'They are regulars,' Selkirk agreed. 'But we are the Reivers.' He ignored Crosier's murmur of 'scruffs and scourings of the gutter.'

'They are a division protection company,' Rachel said. 'See that square cloth on their sleeve with the red and white triangles? We are not sure what that means, but we believe they are specially trained as bodyguards and to protect officials and staff officers.'

'Or diplomats,' Selkirk said.

'Or diplomats,' Rachel agreed.

'We need these red and white triangles,' Selkirk decided. 'They will be our pass port into the Citadel.'

'I will have some made.' Rachel told him.

'Thank you,' Selkirk knew not to ask for details. Rachel was naturally secretive about the organisation to which she belonged.

'The boys are getting restless,' Crosier reminded. 'Kelly and Rourke are at each other's throats more often than not, and Walker is going doolaly.'

'It won't be long now,' Selkirk said. He thought of his men fretting in that dripping underground chamber and hoped they would survive to breathe fresh air again.

'I'll be glad to get out of this town,' Crosier echoed his thoughts.

The Turkish infantry passed them, looking neither left nor right, and continued into the streets of the city.

'A hundred and twenty,' Selkirk counted. 'Soldiers presumably expert in this sort of occasion, and we have a handful of men trained for raiding in the open spaces.'

When Rachel touched his arm, the fleeting contact was like a shock. 'It is important, Major Selkirk. If these other countries join in the war on the Ottoman side, Great Britain may not prevail, and Israel, my country will still be under Turkish control.'

Crosier said nothing. He watched the last of the Turkish infantry disappear into the streets of Jerusalem.

'I know,' Selkirk said. He thought of his men cocooned in that underground chamber that had been a sanctuary but now felt like a prison. 'We will be ready.'

* * *

The pigeon came at dawn; landing on Selkirk's designated spot high on the Mount of Olives. He skimmed the brief note, reread it with more concentration and took a deep breath.

Jesus: Brigadier Smith does not just expect the impossible, he demands it.

Selkirk read the note a third time, memorising the strange names, committed the dates, times and details to memory, tore the flimsy paper to fragments and scattered it to the Palestinian winds.

I am a soldier, not an explorer; how am I meant to find this place, yet alone do what Smith demands?

* * *

The constant sound of dripping water was now a major irritant. He looked around his men, noting the strained white faces and the occasional nervous twitch. 'The pow-wow is confirmed for two day's time,' Selkirk said. 'We will go with a stealth raid and then leave the city.'

'Where to, major?' Black asked.

The Reivers crowded around, some sitting cross legged in near Arab fashion, others with their legs stretched in front of them as they leaned against the walls of the cavern. In the flickering light of the lanterns, they looked haggard and old. They needed a release from this enclosed place.

'We are going to a place called Masada,' he decided to trust them. 'We are to take Abraham, the German delegate if we can capture him, and the Indian traitor to a place called Masada.'

He could sense the change in atmosphere as they heard the name. Abraham's back straightened as he looked at Rachel, and then he nodded, slowly and just once. Rachel gave a small smile and patted Abraham's sleeve as some of the more Biblical aware of the Reivers caught the significance of the name. Walker was leaning against the wall of the cave; he frowned, shook his head and began to drum his heels on the ground, but it was Crosier who posed the question.

'Masada, sir? Is that not where the Romans massacred the Jews back in the old days?'

'I believe so, Crosier,' Selkirk agreed.

'It's bloody miles from the sea,' Crosier said. 'How can we get picked up at Masada?'

Selkirk remembered the last sentence of the message. 'We will wait and see what happens,' he said. *Some things were best left unsaid.*

Crosier opened his mouth and closed it again. 'Yes, sir.'

'Masada is a sacred sight for us,' Rachel corrected, 'a place of pilgrimage.' She spoke to Abraham and added, 'it is a good place to die.'

'Well that's comforting,' Black said, 'but I've no intention of dying there.'

'There will be death,' Wilson spoke quietly. 'But it won't be you, Sergeant.' He stood up, tall and dark headed, with the lantern casting deep pits of shadows where his eye sockets were. 'I can see a coffin in the sky above the rock of Masada.'

Kelly crossed himself, and a broken-nosed Irishman named O'Brien said a short prayer that Selkirk did not catch. 'Holy Mary,' Kelly said, 'a premonition.'

Crosier raised his eyebrows to Selkirk.

'Our mission will drive a nail in the coffin of Ottoman rule in Palestine,' Selkirk tried to lift the mood.

'Not much chance of that, sir' Wilson was morose. 'We're getting nowhere in Gallipoli, and they pushed us right out of Sinai.'

'Enough!' Crosier blasted him to silence. 'We are the Reivers. We pummelled them in the pass, and we'll destroy them in Jerusalem!'

Rachel stood up and waited for the murmur of dissent to dissipate. 'You are soldiers,' she spoke quietly but her words penetrated every corner of the vast cavern, 'and you come from foreign lands and you all learn about my country and its history.'

The men listened to this dark haired, intense woman who had shared their hardships and lived among them as one of their own.

'If you succeed in your endeavours,' Rachel said, 'you may change history, for the campaign you are fighting here is more important than that in France.'

She waited for the grumbles of disbelief to subside.

'The war in France is among European powers, where Empires rise and fall in succession. The war here is eternal.' She raised her voice slightly, but every eye was on her, from the cynical Rourke and Black to the morose Wilson. 'You are helping remove an alien power from my homeland, and the homeland of millions of people that history has scattered around the world for many centuries.' The idea seemed to inspire her, so she appeared taller, more forceful; she raised her hands in the air. 'You are doing God's work, not Man's.'

Selkirk forced his eyes away from her and watched his Reivers. They said nothing as Rachel stood there, arms raised and mouth open, with her hair a dark halo around her head. Wilson and Walker stirred a little, but Rourke and Kelly seemed completely under her spell.

'What is happening in France, even in Gallipoli,' Rachel continued, 'is transient. It will not last; within a generation, maybe two generations, the balance of power will shift and nations now dominant will slide and new empires will take their place, as has always happened.' She let her words enter their minds as she walked among them, moving gracefully as a deer through a field of corn. 'Thank you, gentlemen,' she said, 'for here you are rectifying an ancient wrong and restoring a people to their proper place.'

Selkirk saw the impact of her words as some of the men smiled and others squared their shoulders. Selkirk wondered if they had ever been called 'gentlemen' before in their lives, or spoken to in such a manner by an educated and intelligent woman.

'You are making history and helping to re-create one of the oldest nations in the world,' Rachel ended softly, and, unbelievably, she stepped through the throng, shaking the hand of each man and thanking them individually.

'Now we have to get everything ready,' Selkirk said. He had never seen British soldiers as thoughtful as they were at that moment.

* * *

The noise started in the late afternoon, echoing through the narrow streets of the city and rising upward to compete with the muezzin's call to prayer. Selkirk stood in the doorway of the burned out synagogue and watched as the police hurried to the spot.

'An hour until we go in,' Rachel said.

'Will your people manage to keep it up?' Selkirk asked

'Obviously,' Rachel pushed him further back into the doorway as a squad of police hurried past. 'They know how important Abraham is to us.'

The noise increased, and Selkirk thought he heard a gunshot. 'I hope the Turks don't take it out on the rioters too much.'

Rachel sighed. 'We are Jewish; everybody persecutes us.' She pulled further into the shadows, 'it is time for us to strike back.' Her voice hardened, 'it is time we lived in our land where we made the laws for ourselves, and we decided how we should live.'

'You are taking a huge chance then,' Selkirk told her.

'The prize is also huge,' Rachel said. She looked at him through narrowed eyes. 'That is why the British government sent you here, is it not?'

Selkirk saw the smile waiting at the corners of her mouth. 'I don't know,' he admitted. 'My orders were to meet Abraham and obey his instructions. That is all I know.'

'Were you not told that you were to help create a country for us?' Rachel's smile touched her eyes. 'You are making history. We want our land back.'

Selkirk shivered. War in the Middle East was an eternal conflict, one that had continued for countless generations. He thought of his own people's attachment to Scotland, a nation they had defended for a thousand years against foreign invasion; to the Jews, a thousand years was merely a fragment of the time they had battled for their home.

He could not imagine the Diaspora, with the people scattered to the four corners of the globe and denied the chance of their homeland, with alien people of opposed religions dominating sites that had been sacred as long as humanity. He shook his head, aware that other races and peoples also called the same land home, and in the case of the Arabs, their claims may well have equal validity.

Selkirk nodded. 'I hope you get it' he said, and when he remembered what he knew of the history of the Jewish people he added, 'I hope I can help'.

The noise in the city increased, augmented by a hint of smoke in the air. 'We'd better get back down; the boys will be ready for us now.' He glanced at Rachel, 'let's hope that your people manage to divert at least some of the garrison out of the Citadel.'

'They will,' Rachel said. 'The Turks will be afraid of a Jewish uprising. They know about Masada as well.'

* * *

There were to be seven in the strike force. Selkirk had selected the solidity of Crosier over the guile but sometimes indiscipline of Black, with the street fighting skill of Rourke, the quiet professionalism of a sober Sinclair, the dogged acceptance of Wells and the language proficiency of Rachel, with the wounded and weak Abraham to identify the men they needed to spare. Crosier might also be useful as he had a smattering of the languages of the Indian sub continent. It was a mixed bag to take into the heart of the Turkish garrison of Jerusalem, but they were all men of steady nerve and as professional soldiers as the Reivers had to offer. 'Just as important,' Selkirk explained to Crosier, 'these boys will obey orders, so the neutral diplomats will be fairly safe.'

'Even Rourke, sir?' Crosier glanced at the Glasgow man who was slowly sharpening his bayonet on the limestone walls of the cavern.

'Yes,' Selkirk said quietly. He raised his voice slightly. 'Stay together lads; keep calm and do exactly as Rachel and I say. She will translate what Abraham wants.'

Dressed in Turkish uniforms squeezed over their own, they looked much like soldiers of the Asakr –I Shahaneh. Selkirk was familiar with the German Mausers and had ensured his men could handle them nearly as well as they knew their own, except it was not possible to have live firing practice in the confines of the Quarry. Hopefully, they would not have to fire a shot.

After months in the East the men were fundamentally sun bronzed and fit, and after two weeks in Solomon's Quarry, they were eager for activity in the fresh air. Selkirk looked them over and took a deep breath. When he had been a young soldier, he had always felt a tingle of excitement before setting out on any mission, but now he just hoped not to lose any men.

There was more smoke hazing the evening air as they stepped into the street, and the noise from the distant riot was a constant background to everything they said.

March quickly,'Selkirk ordered. 'If we look as if we are on an important mission even Turkish officers will be less inclined to interfere.' He glanced at the square patch on his sleeve, 'let's hope that we look like we belong to the divisional protection company.' He tapped Abraham on the arm, 'are you sure you're fit for this?'

Abraham raised his eyebrows to Rachel, who translated for him. 'Abraham says he is as fit as he needs to be,' she said.

'Good man,' Selkirk said. 'Tell him that we all depend on him; Great Britain depends on him.' He saw the hint of a smile on her face as she replied:

'Abraham is not doing this for Great Britain,' she said. 'He is doing this for Israel.'

'I know,' Selkirk said, 'Please tell him that Israel depends on him.'

I have orders to deliver this man alive to British hands, and here I am leading him into the heart of the Turkish garrison.

Selkirk halted his men as a section of Turkish infantry force marched past. The NCO in charge gave Abraham a smart salute without stopping. Abraham acknowledged with a casual lift of his hand.

'That's the first test passed,' Selkirk said, 'but there are a lot tougher to come.'

The gate of the Citadel loomed ahead, tall and arched and sinister in the gloom. The sentries looked nervous, more interested in the commotion in the city than in checking for credentials as Selkirk's party hurried past. Their salute to Abraham was perfunctory.

'Where to now?' Selkirk looked around. He had studied the citadel from the outside every day of the last ten and had looked at plans that Abraham had drawn for him. Now that he was inside, it seemed a confusion of walls and towers, with fixed lamps pooling light on ancient stones where sentries stood guard and corners of utter darkness in which anything could hide.

'This way,' Rachel whispered as Abraham limped confidently across a bridge over a deep moat and into a small courtyard. Selkirk grasped his Mauser firmly and followed to an inner wall where a sentry looked at them with total disinterest.

'Bloody Turks' Rourke said under his breath until Crosier hissed a savage order to keep quiet.

'Careful here,' Rachel said. 'We are going inside.'

There was an arched doorway into what seemed a blank wall, and two Turks with the green collars of the infantry on guard. Selkirk could only admire Abraham's courage as he marched straight in without a glance at either man. Selkirk knew that Turks could quite legally shoot him or any of his Reivers for wearing the uniform of the enemy. He also knew that they would treat Abraham far more harshly. A political prisoner of the Turks could expect extreme torture and possibly execution.

The Citadel interior was gloomy, with a peculiar musky smell that reminded Selkirk of the interior of Edinburgh Castle. He kept close to Abraham as he limped on, acknowledging salutes from several soldiers and acting like any officer in any army in the world.

'How far?' Selkirk mouthed to Rachel.

'Not far,' Rachel replied.

Selkirk felt as if the walls of this place were closing in on him. He checked his men. Rourke looked as casual as if he was walking along the Trongate; indeed Selkirk wondered unkindly if Glasgow's Trongate was not more dangerous than the Citadel of Jerusalem. Sinclair was white under his tan but looked as determined as if he was assaulting an entrenched position at Gallipoli, while Wells looked thoughtful.

'This is nothing like Herefordshire,' Wells mouthed.

Crosier appeared unmoved. He marched at the rear, his eyes were everywhere, and his boots crunched reassuringly down on the stone floor.

There was another courtyard, larger this time, with fragments of a ruin set on the ground, and surrounding towers and the minaret of the mosque looming into the now dark sky beyond. Selkirk called a halt. He pointed to the tower opposite the minaret, where the red flag of the Ottoman Empire hung limp and barely seen in the night.

'That's our objective.' A window on the second floor spread yellow light to the courtyard beneath. 'Are you ready boys?'

After a final check, Selkirk nodded to Abraham, and they marched across the last courtyard to David's Tower. He felt his heart hammering within his chest but also that surge of excitement that had been lacking until now. There was no going back now; Selkirk knew that he and his small group held the future of the Middle East in the palm of their sweating hands. Selkirk straightened further; it was a huge responsibility for a ploughboy from the Berwickshire Merse, but as he stepped toward that ancient tower he knew, suddenly, that there were few places he would rather be.

This day is for you Helena.

The four guards at the entrance looked puzzled when an unfamiliar officer with the insignia of their regiment marched past, but they did not object until Selkirk gave a crisp order and the Reivers fell on them. Rourke and Crosier disposed of their men quietly and without fuss, but Wells was slow, and the Turk managed to let out a single shout of warning. Only one, and then Wells knocked him cold. Sinclair was on top of his target; hand clamped over his mouth when Selkirk landed a blow with the butt of his revolver to the back of the man's head.

'Prop them against the wall,' Selkirk ordered, 'and let's hope that nobody comes in here in the next few moments.' He glanced in the direction of the city, where the sky reflected the fires the mob was burning. 'Our Jewish friends are doing a good job in distracting the garrison,' he said.

'It is not hard to rouse the people of Jerusalem' Rachel did not smile. 'We spread the word that the Turks were going to flatten a mosque to make way for a soldier's brothel.' She shrugged. 'It may be true.'

'Who should the Jews care about a mosque?' Selkirk saw the slow innocent smile on Rachel's face as she spread her hands.

'It is not the Jews who are rioting,' she said.

'That's smart.' Selkirk admired her duplicity. She would have fitted in well in the old Border.

'Obviously,' Rachel said without the hint of a smile.

They pushed on, with Rachel and Selkirk in the lead and Crosier as rearguard. There was a flight of stairs climbing upward, well lit for the occasion, with rugs decorating the limestone blocks of the wall and an occasional array of crossed swords and shields to give a martial effect.

When the guard on the first floor stiffened to attention, Crosier cracked him over the head. He slid downward without a sound.

'Prop him up,' Selkirk ordered, and they moved on, step by step. Now he was committed, his mind focussed, so everything outside this operation dimmed into irrelevance. All that mattered was a successful outcome here; nothing else counted, not casualties and not his death.

They reached the first floor without incident. A sentry stood on either side of the great wooden door, an *onbasi* and a private, both with the square patches on their sleeves and both looking extremely efficient. The *onbasi* barked a challenge, to which Abraham responded. It was apparent that the *onbasi* had orders to let nobody in, whatever their rank.

For a second the *onbasi* faced the group of Reivers. Selkirk could see that he was trying to recognise faces. The *onbasi* frowned as Abraham issued an order, shouted something to the private and began to unshoulder his rifle.

Damn; that's put the kybosh on it!

Without saying a word, Selkirk grabbed the onbasi by the throat as Rourke and Sinclair moved to the private. The onbasi was determined to do his duty, but Selkirk tightened his grip, preventing the man from shouting a warning, and then Crosier smashed his sandbag over the man's head. The *onbasi* stiffened and fell. Rourke and Sinclair had dealt with the private.

'Well done lads,' Selkirk whispered. 'Now comes the important part. You know what to do.' He looked at Rachel, 'are you ready?'

She nodded. For the first time since Selkirk had met her, Rachel looked nervous, with sweat dampening her forehead.

'In we go.' Without waiting further, Selkirk turned the brass handle and stepped inside the room.

Selkirk's first impression was of an array of splendid uniforms and self-indulgent faces, with eyes staring with indignation at being disturbed. There were seven men seated at a highly polished table, with two more guards behind them. They all looked up as Selkirk barged in, followed by Abraham, Rachel and the Reivers, with Crosier bringing up the rear. One man in a very ornate white uniform complete with gold braid and a plethora of medal ribbons barked out something in German as Selkirk entered the room.

Crosier closed the door and put his back to it.

Selkirk nodded to the nearest guard: 'Rourke– that man; Wells, Sinclair, take care of the other.'

The Reivers stepped toward the guards, rifles jabbing as the delegates rose in protest. The man in the splendid white uniform shouted until Abraham spread his hands and spoke above them all. A man in a slightly less ornate white uniform peered at Selkirk and opened his mouth to speak until Rourke jabbed the muzzle of his rifle at him.

'Keep quiet, you!' The broad Glaswegian accent seemed homely amongst the dazzling array of uniforms and Eastern splendour.

Abraham waited until there was silence and continued to speak. Abraham no longer looked small and insignificant but dominated the room with his surprisingly powerful voice.

'He is telling them not to be alarmed,' Rachel reported. 'He is saying that we will not harm anybody if they co-operate, but if they resist there might be trouble.'

The two guards had been disarmed and forced to sit in a corner with their hands on their heads. Selkirk stepped to the top of the table.

'Right lads, uniforms.' He pulled off the Turkish tunic, so the British uniform he wore beneath could be seen. He tapped the butt of his revolver but did not draw it. 'Translate for me please Rachel.'

Rachel nodded.

'I am Major Andrew Selkirk of the Royal Borderers and Selkirk's Reivers, both units of the British Army,' Selkirk began. 'And most of you are in no danger.' He ran his eyes over the delegates who sat at the table. Please identify yourselves.'

The man in the white uniform was first. He gave a German name with pride and confidence. Selkirk did not catch the name but noted it started with a Von, so he presumed this man to be the German delegate. His neighbour in the less ornate uniform glared at Selkirk with genuine malevolence, declared he was Colonel Hefferman of the Imperial German Army and sat down again, holding Selkirk's eye the whole time. The third man did not rise; he was immensely dignified, neatly bearded and wore a splendid Eastern dress complete with a bejewelled dagger. He announced he was the representative of Persia and as such was a neutral and had immunity.

'Your neutrality will be respected, sir,' Selkirk told him.

The fourth man was darker and more nervous, with a plain uniform that was more European in cut. He smiled ingratiatingly and said he was also from Persia and claimed neutrality.

Something in the man's tone alerted Selkirk. He glanced over to Crosier, 'you've been in that part of the world, sergeant,' he said. 'Is this fellow a Persian?'

'No more than I am, sir,' Crosier said. 'He's a Bengali Hindu, or I'm a Dutchman.' He raised his voice. 'Hey you, Abdul! You know the Ganges better than the Chalus River don't you?'

The man shook his head and repeated that he was a representative of the Persian nation and an undoubted neutral.

'I'll come back to you, sir,' Selkirk told him.

Selkirk spoke to the next of the delegates. 'And you, sir? From where are you?'

The man sported a neat white beard and a scarlet uniform. There was a glittering diamond in the centre of his ornate turban.

'I am Kamran Khan' he said, 'from Afghanistan.' He did not smile and spoke as if he expected Selkirk to recognise the name.

'Christ,' Crosier said, 'sorry sir, but this man is genuine enough. He was one of the big guns behind the Pathan Revolt back in 1897.'

Khan looked at Crosier and gave a small smile. 'That is correct, sergeant,' he agreed.

'So that leaves you in the cold, Abdul,' Crosier addressed the darker skinned man.

'Try him with Jitendra,' Selkirk said and saw the suspected Bengali start. 'That's your name, isn't it? Jitendra Gupta?'

The man shook his head violently and proclaimed again that he was a neutral Persian until Crosier fired a direct statement at him in a language that Selkirk presumed to be Pashto. The man tried to stutter an answer, but Crosier did not wait for him to finish.

'He's no Persian or Afghan sir, that's for sure,' he said, 'I called him a pig-dealer, and he just mumbled some rubbish. The Persians are Muslim sir; that would be a terrible insult. A real Persian would have at least insulted me back and probably tried to kill me.'

'Jitendra Gupta,' Selkirk said, 'that's our traitor.'

The last man spoke in Turkish. His uniform, accent and words confirmed his identity. He faced Selkirk without flinching.

'We should kill the Turk and the Germans,' Rachel said at once.

Selkirk held her back. 'No; we are soldiers, not murderers,' he repeated his previous words.

There was a shout from the courtyard outside, and the Turkish delegate replied with a full-throated roar until Sinclair clamped a large hand over his mouth. 'You shut your teeth, Jackie.'

'They've found the sentries,' Rachel reported and ducked as the Turkish delegate thrust Sinclair aside, pulled a pistol from his holster and fired a wild shot that ploughed into the wall behind Selkirk. The sound of the shot was deafening in the confined space.

'That's put the kybosh on it,' Crosier echoed Selkirk's earlier thought.

'Grab Jitendra Gupta and the Von fellow!' Selkirk ordered and aimed his rifle at the Turkish diplomat. Rourke was quicker that Selkirk. He fired a single shot that crashed into the table at the Turk's side and sprayed wooden splinters around the room. The Turk shouted something and aimed his revolver again, but Sinclair jabbed the muzzle of his rifle into his chest and fired a single round. The force of the bullet knocked the Turk against the wall, where he remained for a second before slowly sliding down, leaving a thick trail of blood.

'It looks as if we must leave you, gentlemen,' Selkirk threw a quick salute to the Persian and Afghani delegates, 'but be assured that whichever side you back, the British Empire and our allies will win this war.' He spoke rapidly as Crosier cracked Jitendra Gupta over the head to quieten him down and Sinclair pushed the German towards the door. 'We hope that you will remain neutral, or even join us in our just endeavours,' he heard footsteps thundering up the stairs and loud orders in Turkish, 'and you now have an example of just how far our arm reaches, even into the heart of the Ottoman domains.'

'Ready sir,' Crosier said. The remaining delegates remained seated, some shocked at the death of their Turkish colleague, but Heffernan's eyes never strayed from Selkirk's face.

Gupta held his head and struggled as Crosier grabbed him by the hair and dragged him from his seat. 'Come on, you!' He pushed Gupta to Wells. 'You take care of this traitor.'

'Come on, Fritzy,' Sinclair prodded his prisoner. 'Out you go!'

'Out the door lads, and upstairs,' Selkirk allowed Crosier to lead, with Rachel and Abraham next and then Sinclair and Wells, forcing the struggling Bengali and the silent German between them. Rourke was just in front of Selkirk, keeping his Mauser pointed at the remaining delegates as Selkirk shut the door.

Somebody shouted from below, the words Turkish, the voice angry. Selkirk did not reply but dashed upstairs to the very top of the tower and the blessing of fresh air. He looked around, seeing the minaret that stabbed toward the sky, symbol of Islamic dominance of the city, but he ignored it and concentrated on the encircling walls.

'Onto the walls boys and run!' He stared ahead, 'Crosier, take the lead; Rourke, you're with me,' Selkirk stood at the head of the tower, rifle ready for the first Turk to emerge.

Jitendra Gupta was protesting loudly, trying to wriggle free from Sinclair and Wells, but they frog- marched him between them, swearing.

'Come on Abdul,' Sinclair grated, 'time to go home you bastard.'

'Keep that bloody traitor secure,' Crosier shouted. 'And watch the Hun!'

There was shouting from the tower behind them. Somebody fired, with the crack of the rifle sharp even against the noise from the riot. Selkirk walked backwards, rifle at the ready. He flinched as a bullet hit the parapet at his side and sprayed slivers of stone around him.

'Down there, sir,' Rourke pointed. There were Turks in the court-yards of the Citadel and others beneath the minaret. All were looking up at the British soldiers on the wall, and some raised their rifles. Selkirk took deliberate aim at the men under the minaret and fired.

'Did you get one, sir?' Rourke asked hopefully.

'I don't think so,' Selkirk replied. He watched as Rourke dropped to one knee, took aim and fired, once, twice, three times. One of the Turks in the courtyard crumpled but the others hardly glanced at him. A bullet splintered the wall a foot from Selkirk's head; another flicked overhead.

'Move, Rourke; we are just targets for them here.' Selkirk ordered.

Turkish soldiers exploded from the tower behind them, shouting, gesticulating and firing the occasional shot.

Selkirk fired back, dropped the leading man, worked the bolt of the Mauser, wished he had his Lee-Enfield and fired again. The Turks bunched then scattered, some returning inside the tower but others kneeling or lying prone to return fire. Selkirk withdrew step by step with Rourke, alternately shooting and moving, so their pursuers were always under fire.

'Careful, Fritzy!' Sinclair yelled as his prisoner suddenly dropped to the ground. 'Get up, you bastard!'

There was a sudden fusillade from behind them, and Sinclair ducked. The German grabbed his opportunity and leapt for freedom, running toward the pursuing Turks.

'Sir!' Rourke shouted and ducked as a bullet crashed into the war at head height. He turned and fired. 'Fritzy's down, sir!'

Selkirk glanced over his shoulder. The German delegate lay in a crumpled heap on the ground with Hefferman standing at his side, pointing a pistol. Selkirk was not sure if a Turkish or British bullet had hit the German. *Damn! We wanted him alive.*

'Come on, Rourke,' Selkirk pushed him onwards as Hefferman fired again.

'Here we are sir,' Rourke shouted. Crosier had halted the Reivers at an angle of the wall and was organising them into two groups. Behind them, the Turks moved cautiously along behind the parapet, but the density of the buildings had halted any pursuit at ground level.

'Down there,' Selkirk pointed. They were a hundred yards from the Jaffa Gate, and the ladders in position as he ordered. Two of them balanced against the inner wall, with Black and the remainder of the Reivers at the foot. The ladders looked long and precarious in the dark, but they were the only lifeline.

'You first, Sergeant,' Selkirk ordered, 'and then Abraham and Rachel.' He watched them climb slowly down, just as the pursuing Turks began a more accurate fire.

'The Turks are close,' Sinclair kept hold of Jitendra Gupta.

'They reacted faster than I expected,' Selkirk admitted. 'Wells, you get on the ladder first; Sinclair, you put the prisoner on and follow. Rourke and I will hold back the Turks.'

He watched as Wells shouldered his rifle and clambered onto the ladder. 'This is nothing like Herefordshire,' he said as he skimmed down.

Jitendra Gupta struggled as Sinclair wrestled him onto the top rung. He looked at the drop with the Reivers waiting below, shook his head, shrieked loudly and tried to get back onto the parapet.

Wells reached up and grabbed Gupta's foot, while Sinclair grasped his hands and thrust them onto the rungs. 'Get down you treasonous bastard,' Sinclair snarled and lifted his boot as if to smash it onto the man's head.

'None of that,' Selkirk said, 'we need this man alive to see how extensive their network is in India. Be gentle; he could save thousands of lives.'

'Be gentle ...?' Sinclair glared at Gupta with loathing, then nodded, 'yes, sir. I'll be gentle with the traitor.' He grabbed Gupta by the hair and shoved him downward, 'get down there, but gently, you bastard!'

As Sinclair bent to persuade Jitendra Gupta to descend, the bullet caught him under the jaw, travelled through his head and came out behind his left ear. He was dead before he began to fall. His blood and brains sprayed out in an obscene fountain that spattered both Selkirk and Jitendra Gupta.

'Sinclair!' Selkirk yelled. He recoiled instinctively as Sinclair crumpled on top of the wall.

Jitendra Gupta squealed high pitched and nearly fell down the ladder in his sudden desire to escape the musketry.

Selkirk saw the shattered mess of Sinclair's head and knew he was dead. The time to mourn would be later; the immediate priority was to get the prisoner and remainder of his men to safety.

'You next, Rourke,' Selkirk ordered, 'get down man, quickly now!'

Rourke hesitated, 'you first, sir,' but Selkirk shoved him onto the ladder a few rungs behind Jitendra Gupta as Turkish bullets struck chips from the parapet.

'Sir!' Crosier was on the ground below, supporting the sagging Abraham, 'Turks!'

He was correct. The Turkish soldiers that had been pursuing them on the ground had by-passed the buildings and now flooded into the street below. They were approaching the ladders at speed, shouting and brandishing their rifles.

Selkirk swore. He had hoped that the riot would keep the Turks occupied for some time yet. 'Get Abraham and Jitendra Gupta away' he yelled as he manoeuvred himself onto the ladder. 'Never mind me!'

For a moment he felt vulnerable, with his back to the enemy and a long wooden ladder to descend, but he balanced on top, ignored the rungs and slid down the side rail, hoping that no Turkish snipers had him in their sights. The wood was surprisingly smooth under his hands, olive wood, he thought, with the friction burning his palms, and then he was on the cobbles, and shots were spattering the wall behind him.

His men were in a rough semi-circle, sheltering in the corner of the wall with a small cart in front of them.

'Hot work, sir, the Turks have us hemmed in.' Crosier emptied the clip of his Mauser up the length of the dark street. 'They are everywhere.'

Selkirk glanced around. There were Turks in both directions, and his handful of men had limited ammunition and three civilians to protect. 'Where's Black?'

'Not here, sir,' there was no emotion in Crosier's voice. He loaded another clip. 'We should have brought more ammo sir; this is my last clip.'

Wells had one hand firmly on Jitendra Gupta's arm and was trying to fire his rifle with the other. He flinched as a bullet ripped the hat from his head. Rourke was lying prone, shooting and swearing with equal ferocity, while Rachel was firing her revolver to protect Abraham.

The Turks were advancing from both sides, encouraging each other with loud cries as they moved from doorway to doorway with ruthless professionalism.

Selkirk looked left and right, judging which direction posed fewer dangers. 'We'll break left, lads,' he said, 'it's only a hundred yards to the stables.'

Jitendra Gupta opened his mouth and called out to the Turks until Wells rammed the butt of his rifle into the man's ribs. 'Shut your mouth, Abdul.'

The Turks were closing, two groups of ten, maybe fifteen men, shifting from side to side in the streets, keeping to the shadows and covering each other with supporting fire.

'These Ottoman lads are good soldiers,' Crosier approved. He fired two quick shots, 'that's one who won't get back to Constantinople.'

The Turkish fire was increasing as they built up for an attack. Selkirk ducked, fired and flinched as two bullets smashed into the cart right in front of him. Splinters of wood flicked past his face, with one nicking his cheekbone. He felt the blood trickle onto his lips; it was warm and salty.

'Here they come,' Rourke yelled. He rose to his knees and began rapid fire as the Turks rushed forward from both sides at once.

There was another sound, deeper than the incessant crackle of musketry, and more shouting, the words deep throated and familiar.

'Reivers! Selkirk's Reivers!'

The words echoed from the high walls, a slogan that called up a hundred emotions. Selkirk glanced to his right to see Black at the head of the Reivers, nearly galloping down at the advancing Turks. They scattered before the unexpected threat to their rear, and Black fired as he passed, hitting one man.

'Reivers! Come on Major!' Black reined up at the cart, with the front hooves of his horse pawing at the air.

'Come on Major! Time to go!' Black indicated Kimberley, who was running a few yards in the rear.

Selkirk threw himself on the saddle, 'about time you got here, Black.' He patted Kimberley. It felt good to be on horseback again, even if it was inside the confining walls of the city. 'Wait for the others to mount,' he yelled.

'I thought you might want more help than just me,' Black said.

The Reivers surrounded them, still firing at the Turks. The muzzle flashes were brilliant in the dark of the streets and the sound a constant cacophony that hurt the ears in that confined space. Some of the horses were near panic, bucking and kicking; he heard the terrible scream of a wounded horse and the strangled yell of a man.

Selkirk waited until Jitendra Gupta was thrust over the saddle of a loose horse and tied in place, kicking, struggling and shouting in some language that Selkirk did not recognise.

'Come on lads; out of here!'

Crosier and Rachel bundled Abraham into the saddle, as Black remained at the front, firing furiously. 'Come on Major!'

'Spur lads! Spur to the gate!' Black led the way, loading as he rode, swearing mightily as the body of horse crashed into the Turks, knocking men down in their passage, firing and taking fire in return.

There was a terrible exhilaration about riding like this, knowing that death or injury was a constant possibility but not caring in the mad gallop through Jerusalem. It was stimulating to fire at the enemy, to have friends and colleagues all around, to have Black at his side laughing like a careless youth although he was a mature, hard bitten man in his late thirties.

'Reivers!' Somebody shouted.

Others took up the call: 'Reivers! Selkirk's Reivers,' but then they were approaching the gate and Selkirk had no time to shout. Black had been busy; there were dead Turks crumpled on the ground, and two mounted Reivers with Australian slouch hats and barking Lee-Enfields guarding the Jaffa Gate.

Selkirk took the lead, charging under the ancient arch with his men behind him and the spatter of shots from the Turks on the wall only a distraction. The whole of Palestine lay before them, and then the road home to Egypt. They were the Reivers, irregular horsemen of the British Crown in their natural element once more, free of the constraints of city streets.

'Come on Kimberley!' he urged, glorying in the feel of a horse under him, in movement and freedom again after weeks tied up behind confining walls. He wanted onto to ride on, to stretch Kimberley into a full gallop and feel the wind against his face and see the miles roll past, but he had his men to care for and his mission to complete.

Already the night was passing: what had happened to the time? Dawn was growling on the Eastern horizon, and behind them, Jerusalem was alive with Turks.

'Straight east!' Selkirk shouted across to Rachel. 'No holding back now!'

'Eastward to Masada,' she yelled, and for the first time, he saw she was grinning with pleasure. The sulky, intense woman had vanished. Riding with the Reivers must agree with her. Black was laughing, whooping like some Australian Dervish let loose on the countryside.

'Eastward it is, but first I will check the men.'

They had lost Edwards, victim to a Turkish bullet as they clattered through the streets, and Matthew was nursing a wound that seeped blood down his left leg, while two horses were dead and another three were limping badly.

'Leave them,' Selkirk decided. He saw the anguish on the face of the men at the prospect of losing their horses. 'The locals will pick them up and care for them,' he explained, 'but if we keep them, they will slow us down, and we could all get killed.'

He wanted desperately to push on, to put as much distance between his men and Jerusalem as possible, but he knew the men had to say farewell to their horses. It was a matter of balancing morale and safety, and in this instance, morale won. He allowed the men a few moments and then spurred on, eastward toward Masada; eastward toward the wilderness.

He could smell it. Selkirk could sense the presence of the wasteland that stretched with hardly a break for a thousand miles, and the idea was exhilarating, enticing and familiar. Although he did not know this part of the world at all, living on the edge of the Kalahari made any desert part of him, and he welcomed the freedom and space.

But this was not like the Kalahari that he knew so well. This Middle East desert lacked the freshness and sense of re-birth that entered the Kalahari each spring. There was the same heat that advanced in wave after wave; there was the space that sucked him in and impressed upon him his insignificance when compared to the vastness of Creation. There was the stark aridity that compared so unfavourably to Selkirk's early years farming in Scotland, but here in the Biblical wilderness, there was also a deadness and the pressure of human history.

As they rode eastward through the rounded hills of Judaea, Selkirk also became aware that this was a populated wilderness. Every mile or so there were signs of the hand of man, either in a Bedouin encampment or in some ruined dwelling so old that its function and history had been lost long before the dawn of recorded history. In the Kalahari each man made his imprint; here he merely followed the footprints of his predecessor. Selkirk was aware of his place in the eternal hierarchy of existence, and his place was not great.

'Dust, Major,' it had to be Black who noticed the slight suggestion of a cloud rising in their wake. 'It could be Turkish cavalry.'

Selkirk looked over his shoulder. The dust rose from the direction of Jerusalem, a single column that spread out above ground and drifted slowly in the nearly still air. 'It might be a caravan of camels' he said.

'It could be, Major.' Black sounded doubtful. 'But they must be racing camels, judging by the speed of that dust cloud.'

'Go and check,' Selkirk ordered. He watched as Black trotted away, keeping his pace under control, so he made no tell-tale rising of dust. Black knew what he was doing.

Selkirk had checked and re-checked the route until he thought he knew every twist and turn of the country, but as always the reality on the ground was different to the theory of the map. It was about seventy miles by road, but as the Turks learned of the attack, they would rush troops to block the roads.

We will use the roads as long as possible, then cross country

They rode east and south, with the Reivers pushing hard and the column of dust creeping closer as the terrain became rougher and wilder by the mile. 'Major!' Black galloped up beside him, 'they are Turks. Half a company of cavalry I would say, riding fast on fresh horses.'

'Thanks, Black.' Selkirk checked his men. They were coping well enough, even after their weeks of inactivity but Abraham was flagging, with Rachel and Wells taking it in turns to support him on his horse. Jitendra Gupta looked in a bad way; he was moaning as he lay over the saddle, and his position and the constant movement had made him vomit.

'Time to leave the road,' Selkirk decided. 'Form a single column, lads.'

They had practised this manoeuvre a hundred times in Egypt, with each man lining up exactly behind the other, so it was impossible for anybody following to work out exactly how many horsemen there were. After a few moments, they hit a patch of rock without a covering of sand and Black led the rearmost men off the road and into the desert. They would ride parallel to the column on the left-hand side but out of sight until Selkirk decided otherwise.

Selkirk rode on with the remainder of the column in single file. They moved at the speed of the slowest, with Abraham flagging in the saddle and Gupta openly moaning as he jostled across the saddle.

'Can we not allow him to ride astride, sir?' Wells asked.

Selkirk glanced at the prisoner. 'He'll live,' he said, 'we can't jeopardise all our lives for one traitor.' He raised his voice, 'how is Abraham, Rachel?' His thigh wound was throbbing, and the scrape on his face was stinging.

'He can't go on much further,' Rachel said quietly. 'His wound has re-opened, and he is losing blood.'

Selkirk nodded. In all the training he had given the Reivers there had been no provision for carrying a wounded civilian. His emphasis had always been on hard riding with hardened soldiers. 'We'll try and lose the Turks, and then we can rest,' he said.

Rachel looked over her shoulder, where the Turkish dust cloud was now evident in the harsh sunlight. 'They are getting closer.'

Selkirk did not answer. Rachel was correct, and if they continued to ride at the speed of a wounded civilian, the Turks would catch them within the hour.

'How long until dark?' He asked.

'It's barely noon,' Rachel said, 'six or seven hours yet.'

No escape that way, then.

A mile further on the road plunged into a small ravine between two high round hills. Crosier spurred toward Selkirk: 'this is a perfect place for an ambush sir. If I were the Turkish commander, I would have men waiting here.'

'I agree, but he has not had time, and this is not the Khyber.' The hills wavered in the heat, hard and without mercy: the wilderness indeed. Selkirk made his decision: the only one he could make. 'Take the next group and leave the column!'

'Sir,' Crosier hesitated for only a second. 'And you, sir?'

'Follow orders, Sergeant!' Selkirk said.

'Yes, sir.' Crosier waited until there was a shelf of hard rock and led another five men away, trotting to the right where the flanks of the hills would shield them from any Turkish scouts.

Selkirk waited until Crosier was out of sight. He now had the weakest part of the column, two civilians, one suffering prisoner and Wells.

'The Turks,' Rachel sounded anxious. 'We can't let them capture us. They will torture us until they extract all our knowledge.' She glanced at Abraham who was now slumped sideways in his saddle, blank faced and open mouthed. 'I must kill him before the Turks get to him.'

Rachel's essential practicality nearly shocked Selkirk, but when he considered, he saw her logic. Better a quick death than prolonged torture at the hands of the Turks, but that was not why he had come to the Holy Land.

'No!' Selkirk grabbed her hand even as she reached for her pistol. 'I am not going all this way just to shoot the man we came to rescue! We lost too many men to do that.'

'Then do something, Major Selkirk,' Rachel pleaded.

The dust from the Turkish column was creeping closer every time Selkirk looked. They had already entered the valley, and he could hear the drumbeat of horses on the hard ground. Selkirk made the decision he knew had been inevitable from the moment the Turkish column first got on their trail.

'Ride on, Rachel,' he said. 'Get Abraham and the prisoner to Masada.' He scribbled out a message and handed it to her. 'Follow the instructions on this and everything should be well. Brigadier Smith has something arranged to get us home.' He forced what he hoped was a reassuring smile, 'I'll hold back the Turks.'

'Major Selkirk...' Rachel began to argue, but Selkirk pulled Kimberley back and slapped the rump of her horse, 'go!' The animal started and lunged forward. 'Stay with her, Wells,' Selkirk shouted, 'send off a message to Brigadier Smith and make sure the prisoner gets to the British lines!'

'Yes, sir' Wells tried to salute on horseback, nearly unbalanced and followed in the wake of Rachel. 'Come on you,' he said to Jitendra Gupta. 'We have a nice dungeon waiting just for you.'

Selkirk just had time to see Rachel's face as she peered back over her shoulder at him and then he turned to face the Turks. He saw the dust of Rachel's passage settle and knew he was alone.

I am alone now. There are no Reivers and no spies here, just me and my thoughts of Helena; I am alone in the Judean wilderness with fifty Turks on my trail.

Selkirk allowed Kimberley to stand for a long moment. He had made his commitment, and now he was alone. No Helena, no Reivers; just himself, a horse and his rifle against half a company of Turkish cavalry.

Behind him, split into three small columns were his Reivers with the man they had come to rescue and the prisoner they had come to capture. Both held information he could only guess at, but returning both to the British lines was vital. His life was secondary.

Selkirk remembered Wilson's vision of a coffin over Masada. Perhaps it had been his death that Wilson had predicted. He shrugged. So be it. Without Helena and the children, did it matter? He looked around; he was deep in the Holy Land; was there ever a better place to die?

The road wound between hills here, curving and rising without a single straight stretch, so no real killing ground to choose. Selkirk could hear the drumbeat of Turkish hooves now and fancied he heard a hoarse shout of command. He guided Kimberley off the road and up the flank of the hill on his right. It was bare and hot, with minimal cover. He pushed on until he found a section where there had been a fall of rock, with a hundred yards of broken, splintered boulders that afforded cover. He pulled Kimberley into the rear.

'And here we stay, Kimberley.' He had two bottles of water, one pack of iron rations and two hundred and fifty rounds of ammunition. And he had his Lee-Enfield rifle which he understood better than the German Mauser.

'And after that, Kimberley, it is finished.' Selkirk looked upwards; about half past twelve. The sun was relentless in the hard blue bowl of its sky; there was no solace there, no pity, nothing to be expected but never-ending heat hammering down on them from above.

'Here we stand, Kimberley, and here we fall.' He checked the rifle, worked the bolt and balanced the very familiar weight in his hand. He patted the horse's muzzle, 'sorry to bring you to this old man.'

Flies buzzed around, seeking food, and a small bird hovered with its mouth gaping open in the heat.

The first Turkish soldier came at the gallop. He was obviously a scout riding in advance of the main body, and his uniform was so dusty and close to that of the Reivers that for a second Selkirk thought it was one of his men, a forgotten straggler. The man even wore a hat similar to the Australian bush hat, but he rode differently, and as Selkirk peered through the dust that surrounded the rider he saw that it was a Turk.

The scout rode urgently, possibly having been ordered to find the Reivers and report back, but with a clear sight of vision, Selkirk took him in his sights, took a deep breath and squeezed the trigger.

The report of the rifle echoed around the valley between the hills, while the scout jerked back his head and slumped in the saddle. His stirrups kept him in place, so his body hung loose, falling backwards. The horse sped up in panic and galloped forward in the wake of Rachel. The echoes drifted away, and only the dust remained, to gradually fall back to the ground; there was silence.

Even the drumbeat of the Turkish cavalry hooves stopped. The absence of sound was so intense that it hurt.

Selkirk imagined the Turkish commander's actions. He would halt his men and wonder what that single shot indicated. After consulting with his officers, he would send another patrol forward; perhaps three men with orders to keep wide apart and cover each other.

Selkirk moved slightly and placed his rifle in a cleft in the rock, with the barrel pointing directly at a point where a spur of the hill opposite forced the road to curve to his left. Any oncoming horseman would have to move wide to avoid the spur and would be an easy target. He eased back the bolt as quietly as he could, well aware how far travelled in the desert, and waited. Every minute gained gave Rachel and his Reivers more time to get away. The longer he held the Turks, the more he increased his men's chances of survival; and Rachel's.

I will see you soon, Helena

There were five Turks, not three, and they moved at the trot, more bunched than he would have permitted and making a lot of noise. His intention was to hold the Turks back as long as possible to allow his men to get Abraham to safety, so the more damage he caused, the more likely the Turks were to be cautious. He dropped the last man first, then worked the bolt of his rifle and aimed at the white cross belt of the second last. The initial victim was still falling when Selkirk's bullet hit the next, and without waiting to see the result Selkirk fired twice more in quick succession, aiming at the horses. Much as he disliked causing animals to suffer, the horses here were more valuable than the men, and a cavalry man without his mount was merely a burden.

Two of the Turks were down, one dead, one injured and two horses were screaming. The remainder of the Turks turned and fled, with Selkirk's parting shot going nowhere.

Selkirk knew that the sound of horses in pain would unsettle his men, but he was unsure if it would have the same effect on the Turks. He aimed carefully and fired twice, putting each animal out of its misery. The next Turkish advance would have to pass the bodies of one of their men and two horses. The wounded man had extricated himself from his stirrups and was crawling painfully back down the track, leaving a thin trail of blood. Selkirk sighted on him but did not fire.

I should kill him; he is the enemy, but I am no murderer.

What would the Turkish commander do next? He had three choices: he could give up and retreat, he could move forward en masse and try and force the pass against an unknown number of assailants, or he could try and outflank his ambushers.

Selkirk considered: the Turks were redoubtable soldiers and would not give up after a single setback, so they would not retreat. He may try and force the pass, but it was human nature for the survivors of the last attempt to magnify the number of men they fought, so they would swear blind they had seen a score of British soldiers, and they would earnestly believe their own words. The Turkish commander may or may not believe them, but he would not want to take chances with his men, so that left option three.

Selkirk patted Kimberley's muzzle again. 'Come on boy, time to move again.' He poured some of his water into a depression in the rocks and allowed the horse to drink and then headed up the steep slope with the sun baking him and a score of flies a torment he tried to ignore. There was no movement from the Turks; they were playing it very cautiously, which suited Selkirk. The longer he could hold them, the better for his men.

He checked the time. The sun was well past its zenith and headed for the horizon. He calculated it was about three o'clock now; he had at least three hours to keep back the Turkish cavalry, and then he could run toward Masada.

I might even survive this day.

He heard the whine of the ricochet before the report of the rifle, dismounted quickly and dived to the ground. A second bullet slammed into the rock a yard from his head, and he swore.

The Turks must have seen me crossing the slope; I should have remained where I was.

'Go, boy! Run!' He slapped Kimberley on the rump, 'go on!' The horse hesitated until Selkirk pushed him away and he moved reluctantly over the harsh ground. Selkirk watched for only a second and then turned his attention to defending himself.

There was a sudden spatter of shots that cracked and screamed off the rocks around him. Selkirk gasped as a splinter ripped through his sleeve and cut open his forearm. The blood was warm and bright red as it soaked into his tunic. There was a dip ahead, a piece of dead ground into which he slid, just as a bullet smacked onto the rock where he had lain.

Jesus; these Turks are good!

Selkirk felt the wind of another bullet pass him, and then looked backwards. The road was empty, but there was movement in the hills on either side. The Turks were advancing toward him, keeping low and covering each other. Selkirk grunted and pushed forward his rifle; he was lucky he only faced Turkish cavalry, brave as any soldier in the world on horseback but not as good when acting as infantry on barren ground. He remembered the deadly snipers at Gallipoli.

There were five men on either side of the road, spread out in a long line. Selkirk aimed at the leg of the nearest on the opposite side of the road, waited until he moved out of cover, altered his aim slightly and squeezed the trigger. The rifle recoiled, and the man stiffened, grabbed his stomach and yelled shrilly.

Selkirk nodded; he had aimed to wound, not out of any thoughts of mercy, but because a wounded man would make a noise, distract and perhaps unnerve the enemy and might remove another of his attackers if they decided to help their colleague back to the Turkish positions.

A second of the Turks rose to help the wounded man. Selkirk killed him with a head shot, but then the Turks on his side of the road were advancing quickly toward him, yelling. Selkirk took a snap shot that missed completely, took a deep breath, aimed again and fired. The leading man staggered and fell. Selkirk worked the bolt, aimed at the second and squeezed the trigger. The man flinched and threw himself to the ground, with his remaining three companions quickly joining him. Selkirk swore as a bullet smashed right in front of him, and a shower of splinters sprayed his face. That had come from the hills on the opposite side of the road.

The three remaining men had moved closer, so they were only a hundred yards away, and while one dashed forward, the other two opened a rapid fire that kept Selkirk under cover. The muzzle flashes were apparent; that meant it was growing darker.

I must have miscalculated the time, or I have been here longer than I thought.

'They're learning,' Selkirk said grudgingly. He thrust his rifle over the lip of his rock and fired blindly, more in hope than in any expectation of hitting anybody. The reply was a fusillade of fire that cracked and whined around his position. He lifted his head slightly to check his side of the road. Three men were crawling toward him, dim in the sudden gloom.

Selkirk slid forward his rifle, ducked as a bullet ruffled his hair and fired a single shot. The leading Turk flinched back, and Selkirk raised his voice. 'Reivers!' he yelled. 'Selkirk's Reivers!'

The reply was a chorus of Turkish yells as the men on both sides of the road moved forward.

There was a new threat approaching, the thunder of hooves as a body of horsemen clattered from the west. The sun was setting in a glorious show of brilliant red and orange fire above the desert, but there was sufficient light for Selkirk to see the Turkish banners flying above the cavalry.

Selkirk nodded. He had held them for over five hours. He was wounded and tired. His Reivers were in safe hands, for between them

Black and Crosier had enough guile and experience to take them to Masada where Brigadier Smith had promised to rescue Abraham. He could do no more.

He reached forward, fingers extended in the hope of touching Helena, but she retreated behind that veil.

'Helena!' Selkirk stood up. 'I'm coming, Helena! Wait for me.'

She shook her head, her eyes unreadable, but he needed her now. He was ready for death.

Selkirk reloaded his rifle and slotted the bayonet in place. Even against the background of Turkish hooves and the bark of Mausers, the distinctive click was sinister, and the twelve-inch long blade flashed in the rays of the dying sun.

He stood up with his rifle at the high port and stepped over the lip of his rock just as the sun disappeared behind the western hills.

'Reivers!' he shouted 'come and get me, lads!'

There were three shots, but he did not see their result, so he walked forward, lowered his rifle and fired in the general direction of the road. He saw the dim figures that lurched out of the dark toward him and lunged with the bayonet, but he did not understand the order that a Turkish officer shouted. Then something hit him hard on the head.

Chapter Eight

December 1915

'Your name?' The speaker accompanied his words with a kick in his ribs and what seemed like a bucket of warm water emptied in his face.

Selkirk opened his eyes. He was aware only of the thumping pain in his head and the flickering fire nearby.

There was another kick, hard, on the wound on his thigh. 'Your name?' The voice was hard and heavily accented, but not Turkish. 'What is your name?' A face peered into his, chilling blue eyes above a Roman nose disfigured by a broad scar, with cropped blonde hair turning grey. 'Are you Major Selkirk of the Royal Borderers?'

I know that face. This man was at the meeting in Jerusalem. Heffer-man.

Selkirk turned over on his side and spewed on the ground. The man kicked him again, grunting.

'Are you Major Selkirk?'

Selkirk tried to struggle up to a sitting position, but the man put a boot on his chest and forced him back down.

'I am Major Selkirk.' Each word felt like powdered glass in his throat. 'Who wants to know?'

The man squatted at Selkirk's side. 'Major Klaus Hefferman,' he said, 'a name that evidently means nothing to you.'

'You were at the conference in Jerusalem,' Selkirk said, 'but you are obviously a German officer and as such a representative of a nation that signed the Hague Convention that gave rights to prisoners of war.'

Hefferman kicked him again. 'You are a murderer, Selkirk!'

'I am a soldier, Major Hefferman.' Selkirk battled against the hellish pain in his head and his leg. 'We were in and out of the tower in five minutes and murdered nobody. The only men we shot were men who fired on us.'

Hefferman kicked him again, 'before that, Major.'

I do know your face. 'I don't understand, Major. You are mistaken.'

'On Fir Tree Spur in Gallipoli, Selkirk, in June; do you remember what happened there?' Hefferman spoke in a low hiss.

'I remember,' Selkirk said, 'the Turks cut our attack to pieces.'

Hefferman stood up. 'There was a counter attack.'

'There was,' Selkirk agreed cautiously.

'A young Hauptmann led it,' the anger made Hefferman's eyes nearly transparent as if Selkirk was seeing deep into his soul.

'He was a brave man,' Selkirk remembered the laughing German officer.

'You murdered him!' Hefferman spat out the words and leaned closer; 'he was my son.'

Selkirk realised that Hefferman had the same eyes and nose as the young officer he had fought on Fir Tree Spur. 'You should be proud of him,' he tried to calm the man down. 'He fought well.'

'You murdered him,' Hefferman repeated. He looked up as a Turkish cavalry officer joined him. Both men stood over Selkirk, and the Turk spoke in heavily accented English.

'Where is the Hebrew spy?'

'Which Hebrew spy?' Selkirk wished they would go away and leave him in peace. His head felt as if it was splitting, his leg was aching, and now his ribs were also on fire. 'Prisoner of war; Hague convention.' He touched his insignia of rank, 'I am a British officer and a Prisoner of War. The Turks are chivalrous people; you fought as gentlemen in Gallipoli...'

'But you used Turkish uniforms in Jerusalem,' Hefferman said, 'even when the British shot their enemies for doing the same thing.' He spoke to the Turkish officer, who looked at Selkirk with sad brown eyes.

'Major Selkirk,' the Turk said. 'You have information that we need. I am afraid that we must insist that you give it to us.'

'I don't know what you are talking about,' Selkirk said.

The Turkish officer sighed and crouched down at Selkirk's side. 'I am talking about the Zionist spy you call Abraham,' he said. 'And I am talking about the Indian gentleman named Gupta who you abducted as well.' He patted Selkirk's face with a hard hand. 'We know you were with them, and we want to know where they are now.'

Selkirk shook his head. 'I honestly do not know where they are now.'

The Turkish officer sighed again. 'I think you do know, Major Selkirk, and you are going to tell me.'

Selkirk closed his eyes and turned away. His head felt as if it would split in half.

Hefferman barked an order that saw three Turkish soldiers run toward him. One had recently been wounded and glowered at Selkirk.

Without hesitation, the cavalrymen grabbed hold of Selkirk and began to tear off his clothes. He struggled, but with two holding him down and the third ripping at the material and buttons, he had little chance.

Within seconds he was stripped naked and spread-eagled on his face. He shouted and swore, but a man stuffed a piece of crumpled cloth into his mouth.

The Turks used horse whips, began at his shoulders and worked their way down to his feet, then started all over again on the return journey. Selkirk writhed and tried to fight back, but at least two muscular Turkish soldiers held him down. When the torturers reached his shoulders, they flipped him over again, and Hefferman was standing over him, his face lit by the reflection of a fire.

'Have you remembered yet?' The Turkish officer asked. 'I don't enjoy this any more than you do, you know.'

Selkirk nodded. 'Then stop doing it.' He tasted blood in his mouth where he had bitten through his teeth in an effort not to scream. 'I won't object.'

'Here,' Hefferman took a whip from one of the Turkish cavalrymen. 'I will show you how we do this in Germany.' He flexed the whip, 'and if this does not work, then we will try fire.' He straddled Selkirk, 'You will tell me what I wish to know, Lieutenant Selkirk.'

* * *

Selkirk lay on his back, fighting the pain. He tasted the blood in his mouth and tried the cords that held him at wrist and ankle. They cut into the flesh, adding to his agony, but the Turks had tied them securely, and he could not move an inch.

'Tomorrow, in daylight, we try again,' Hefferman told him. 'We will start where we left off.' He leaned closer to Selkirk. 'Perhaps we will take out one of your eyes.'

Selkirk tried to speak, but the words only came out as a croak. 'I won't have to endure your ugly face then,' he said.

'Better to tell us and save yourself more pain,' the Turkish officer said. 'Hefferman will not stop until you tell everything.'

Selkirk closed his eyes. Perhaps he would die overnight. Maybe the war would end, and he would be released.

Hefferman shouted an order and two soldiers mounted reluctant guard. As soon as the officers disappeared, they lit foul smelling cigarettes and began to talk. One flicked ash over Selkirk and laughed, while the other gave him a casual kick and walked away, cupping his cigarette against the night breeze.

The smoking sentry looked around and then settled down on top of Selkirk. He seemed quite content there, rising every so often to walk around the encampment and return to his comfortable seat. Twice he stubbed out his cigarette on Selkirk's chest, and then somebody took hold of him by the neck and cut his throat. The surge of warm blood spurted over Selkirk.

'Silly bugger,' Black's voice had never been more welcome, 'letting Jacko capture you like that.' He sliced through Selkirk's bonds. 'Can you stand, mate?'

Selkirk staggered as he tried to put his weight on his feet, but Black grabbed his right arm, and another figure ghosted through the night and held his left.

'Right, sir, we've got you.' Rourke did not bother to lower his voice, so the Glasgow accent was quite clear through the night.

'Quieten down!' Black hissed, and together they half dragged, half carried Selkirk away from the camp.

'Don't you worry sir,' Rourke said, 'the boys are waiting for you. And that Jewish woman was a bit concerned.' He swore as he stumbled over a loose stone. 'We've been watching them torture you half the night, sir. Bastards.'

Selkirk said nothing. He felt relief wash over him.

They passed a Turkish sentry lying dead, and there were more shapes in the dark as the Reivers rose around him.

'We've got him,' Rourke reported cheerfully, 'naked as a baby and chopped to bits but still alive.'

'Glad you're safe, sir,' Selkirk could sense Crosier standing to attention and saluting even in the dark.

Somebody threw a coat over him, the cloth rough on his abrasions, but Selkirk welcomed the humanity and pulled it close against the bite of the desert night. It smelled of British cigarette tobacco and honest sweat. The trousers were even rougher on his legs, but he hid his wince and pulled them on, thankful for the covering. Even among his close companions, a man preferred to cover his modesty.

'Did you get to Masada? Is Abraham away safely?' Selkirk tried to focus through his pain.

'All in hand, sir but Abraham is still with us,' Crosier said.

'Right,' Selkirk decided he could deal with that problem in the morning. 'How many men do we have here?'

'Six, sir, I thought that would be sufficient.' Black said. 'Two are looking after the horses.' Selkirk thought of Kimberley, abandoned to the desert, and hoped the horse had survived.

His night vision was returning as his head cleared. He tried to control his pain. 'You'll find the Turkish horses on the other side of their camp, Black. Take one man and let them loose; scatter them so these Turks can't follow us.'

The flash of Black's grin was visible. 'Rourke, you're with me.' He hesitated for a moment, 'You'd better get away sir.'

'We'll wait here for you,' Selkirk said. He knew he was not fit enough to pick his way in the dark and despite his training, he doubted that Crosier had the skill to move confidently in this environment.

He heard a small slither of sound as Black slipped away. Then he waited. One of the horses whinnied softly, and there was the call of some animal deep in the desert. Crosier checked the bolt of his rifle, the sound distinct in the dark.

'Are you fit to ride, sir?' Crosier's voice was soft.

'I am, sergeant.' Selkirk knew he had no choice.

The long yell penetrated the night, the 'Coo-ee' call of an Australian bushman followed by a loud voice swearing in broad Glasgow and then the thunder of hundreds of hooves. Somebody fired a rifle, the sound lost in the drumbeat but the muzzle flare distinct. There were more shouts, more shots and a strangled scream, long drawn out.

'That's the Turkish horses loose then,' Crosier sounded as calm as if he was back home in peaceful Liddesdale.

'Aye,' Selkirk agreed. 'Get the men mounted up, sergeant.'

'Here's your horse, sir.' Crosier handed him a set of reins and Selkirk felt a familiar face nuzzling him.

'Kimberley!' He tried to conceal his pleasure.

'We found him following our trail,' Crosier said. 'So Sergeant Black followed his until we found you.' Those straightforward statements revealed a great deal. Selkirk could only imagine the hours of patient searching that had led to his discovery.

'Thank you,' Selkirk said. He did not ask for help but was grateful when Crosier supported him into the saddle. The hard leather bit into him painfully.

'Here they come now,' Crosier said, as Black and Rourke emerged out of the dark.

'Permission to ruffle a few Turkish feathers, Major?' Black pulled up at his side. 'We could shoot up the Turkish camp and get them even more annoyed.'

'How long was I a prisoner, Peter?'

'About three hours, Major.'

Is that all? It felt like three days.

'Give them hell, Black, but don't lose any men.'

'Rourke, you and Walker come with me. The rest remain with the major.'

There was not long to wait. Only a few moments after they left, the noise started with a spatter of shots, followed by a chorus of cries and yells. There was a long scream, then a regular volley and Black's distinctive Australian accent shouting, with the words clear through the night.

'Selkirk's Reivers!' and then: 'Australian Light Horse!'

'That will confuse Jackie Turk,' Selkirk approved, 'well done Black.' He looked up as a thought came to him. 'Have you sent the news to Brigadier Smith yet?'

'Yes sir,' Black said. 'You rest easy there; we released the pigeon before we came back for you.'

Another volley of shots sounded, and Black came trotting back, re-placing his rifle in its holster. 'That will shake them up,' he said happily. He caught Selkirk before he fell out of the saddle.

* * *

A million stars broke the darkness, illuminating the scene, so it was a surreal landscape of stark shadows and ghost-white rock. Selkirk swayed in the saddle, recovered and wrapped the reins around his wrists to retain his balance. For a moment he thought he was back in the Berwickshire Merse, riding home after a ploughing competition, and then he was in Africa with Helena and the children. He smiled at old memories before the reality of pain and responsibility returned, and he tried to focus on his most immediate problem of retaining his seat and not letting his men down.

The shooting started behind them. First, there was a single shot and then a whole fusillade with the sharp crack of the Mauser joined by the rapid clatter of a pistol. 'That's Johnny Turk shooting at nothing then,' Crosier said. 'That should keep him occupied then.' The firing intensified until it sounded like a full-scale battle had broken out behind them.

'The Turks are shooting at shadows, or each other,' Black said, and gave a grim little laugh. 'With luck, they'll wipe themselves out.'

Selkirk said nothing, but at that moment he felt nothing but hatred for the enemy. He wished that Helena was here. He wished that she was alive.

I wish I were with her. I wish the Turks had finished me off.

Chapter Nine

December 1915

'Lie still!' Rachel commanded. She knelt over his naked body, busy with a damp cloth but little apparent sympathy. 'Now you know what the Turks are like.'

Selkirk lay on his face and winced as she dabbed the cloth on his injuries. He felt dazed as the trauma of the past day washed over him. 'What is the date? Have you heard from Brigadier Smith yet?'

'It's the twentieth of December. No, we have not. Lie still I said.'

As Selkirk struggled to turn over, she pushed him back down. 'You need to rest,' she said sternly. 'Your men need you fit.'

'I'm fit enough, damn it,' Selkirk told her and swore as he found his wounds had stiffened while he slept. He looked sideways and saw the fabric sides of a tent. 'Where am I?'

'You're not fit, damn it back,' Rachel pushed him back down, less than gently. She probed at one of the deeper cuts. 'You were lucky,' she said, 'the Turks usually do worse things to their prisoners than this.'

'The German, Hefferman, had worse planned,' Selkirk told her but did not go into details.

'Did you tell them about us?' Rachel's ministrations paused.

'No,' Selkirk said shortly. He looked around. 'How did I get here?'

'Your men carried you in,' Rachel said shortly. 'You passed out on the journey here.'

'Where is here,' Selkirk again struggled to rise, but she pushed him down once more. 'Are we up Masada?'

'Not yet,' Rachel said sternly, and then relented. She smiled. 'I will help you up.' She gave an arm in support as Selkirk rose to a crouch and crawled out of the tent.

They were in the heart of the wilderness with red rocks a tangle all around them and the sun a flail of heat. Directly in front of them a massive rock formation up thrust from the desert floor to rise hundreds of feet into the air, with a steep sloping base that appeared to be of shingle leading to walls that were sheer cliffs, seemingly unscaleable.

Selkirk scanned the cliff, looking up and up toward the relentless bright bowl of the sky. They were like Edinburgh Castle Rock but much taller, much steeper and covering fifty times the area. Waves of heat rebounded from the cliffs so that Selkirk gasped for breath.

'Masada' Rachel told him and said no more.

How in God's name do I get my boys up there?

The cliffs looked unassailable, high and vertical, with no trace of a path that he could see. Selkirk estimated the great rock to be well over a thousand feet high and perhaps a third of a mile long, a massive lump separated from the plateau of the Judean plateau by an un-bridged ravine.

Why the hell did Brigadier Smith want us to take Abraham up there? He could not have picked a more inaccessible place.

'This is where the Jewish Zealots made their last stand against the Romans,' Rachel stood at his side. Her hand sought his, held it for an instant and abruptly tore itself free. 'And when the Romans eventually built a ramp all the way up, the Zealots committed mass suicide rather than be sold into slavery.'

'That's a cheering story,' Selkirk said, 'I won't tell the boys that.' He nodded, 'I have only respect for them, but we have to get up there somehow so that the RFC can collect Abraham and Gupta.'

'There is a path to the summit,' Rachel told him. Her hand returned, holding his arm; she squeezed slightly and remained, stroking his bicep. 'But there is a tribe of Arabs camped at the foot, and they are not allowing us passage. Your Sergeant Black suggested that your men just blast their way up, but the other sergeant did not permit that. He said to wait for you.'

Well done, Crosier.

Selkirk looked around, 'where are my men?' he asked.

The Reivers were encamped hard against the cliff face, enclosed by a low wall of loose rock on which Crosier had built two Lewis Gun positions. The horses were in the centre, heads drooping in the heat.

'How are you, sir?' Crosier asked when Selkirk limped painfully up to him. 'The Turks gave you quite a beating.' He jerked his head backwards, 'I think there may be some trouble with the locals though; the Arabs are trying to stop us getting up there,' he motioned his thumb backward at Masada.

There is always something.

'Where are these Arabs?' Selkirk asked.

'All around us sir,' Crosier said. His voice was flat. 'Look.'

Selkirk looked. At first, he saw nothing but the golden-white ridges and long sloping plateau that surrounded him, but then he saw a small group of Bedouin sitting immobile on their camels about a mile away, just below the skyline. He shifted his gaze around and saw another group, and then another, all sitting on camels and all static, watching the small group of British soldiers at the base of Masada.

'How many are there?' Selkirk wondered. As his eyes grew accustomed to the glare and the terrain he saw more and more, Arabs in groups of eight or nine, surrounding the Reivers. Nearly all carried rifles in their right hands, with the muzzles pointing skyward.

'Quite a few, sir,' Crosier reported. 'We're not sure exactly how many because they move from time to time, and sometimes men from one lot ride to another, but I would estimate there are a good three hundred Arabs there.'

'And we have sixteen men, with four of them wounded, one prisoner and two civilians.' Selkirk said. 'The odds are not in our favour if they decide to attack.' He ran his gaze across the desert. 'What do you think Sergeant: will these Arabs be hostile?'

'In my opinion sir, the natives are always hostile if they believe we are weak.' Crosier said, 'If we appear strong, then they will be all smiles and good fellowship, but the minute they suspect they have the advantage, the smiles will drop, and the knives come out. That was always the case on the Frontier, sir, and everywhere else I've heard of.'

'This is not the Frontier, Sergeant,' Rachel's voice was cold, 'but unfortunately, you may have a point. Arabs are nomads; they wander from water to water, and if they see somebody weaker than them, they may well attack.'

'Thank you,' Selkirk said. 'They might just be wondering who we are.'

'Yes, sir,' Crosier sounded doubtful. 'Do we want to chance it, sir?'

Despite their precarious position, Selkirk had to kill his smile. The old, regimental Crosier would never have dreamed of questioning an officer's word. A few weeks in the less constricted atmosphere of the irregular horse had opened up a whole new world to the Borderer's sergeant.

'Perhaps not; best get the men organised into defensive positions, Sergeant.'

'Already done, sir,' Crosier said.

Of course, it is.

'If the Arabs move too close, then give them a burst with the Lewis gun,' Selkirk decided, 'but fire over their heads. They will know all about rifles, but the Lewis might be new to them.'

'Yes, sir,' Crosier sounded happy with Selkirk's decision.

'They are moving closer,' Selkirk said. 'Can somebody find my binoculars?' Black thrust them in his hand, and he scanned the desert. With the aid of the binoculars he could pick out many more Arabs, some waiting in the dead ground between ridges, others moving slowly and seemingly pointlessly at an angle, but always drifting closer to the small band of Reivers.

'They will be here in a minute, sir,' Crosier said, 'shall I give them a burst now to make them keep their distance?'

'Not yet, sergeant' Selkirk decided. 'We don't want to make enemies of them until we are sure they are hostile. I'll go and talk to them.'

'Yes, sir,' Crosier said. He looked at Rachel, and there was a long pause before she spoke.

'You will make quite an impression on the Bedouin like that, Major Selkirk. Perhaps it would be better if you wore a uniform?'

Only then did Selkirk realise that he had been standing stark naked for the past ten minutes, but Crosier and the Reivers had been too tactful to remind him.

'That would be better,' he agreed.

His uniform was still in the hands of Hefferman and the Turks, but Crosier managed to gather up bits and pieces from the Reivers to make him at least decent if hardly as smart as a British officer should always look, even on campaign.

The Arabs were closer now, with the small groups coalescing into larger and all riding tall camels as they slowly approached.

'Stand ready on the Lewis guns,' Crosier shouted.

Selkirk heard the metallic clicks as the Reivers prepared both guns. The snick of Lee-Enfield bolts being pulled back reinforced the Reivers determination to resist any attack by the Bedouin.

As the Bedouin came closer, their bands combined, so a loose ring of camel riders approached the Reivers, each man carrying a rifle but with no shots fired and no weapon aimed toward the British positions.

'That's close enough,' Selkirk decided. 'I'm going forward, Crosier. If I get shot, you're in charge, but Black, you take over in any mounted operation. Get Abraham and Gupta away, and get my Reivers home safe.'

'Yes, sir,' Crosier said.

Selkirk stood upright, took hold of the Lee-Enfield of the nearest man and stepped over the small rock parapet.

As he walked steadily forward, he lifted the rifle high above his head with both hands so the Bedouin could see it, and then deliberately bent forward and slowly placed it on the ground so there could be no mistake as to his intentions. He was very aware of the still approaching Arabs in their long robes with their rifles still pointing to the sky.

When he was about thirty yards from the Arabs, Selkirk stopped.

'I am Major Andrew Selkirk of Selkirk's Reivers and the British Army,' he heard his voice echo from the cliff wall of Masada but the Arabs seemed to give no need at all. They continued to walk their camels forward, step by slow, methodical step. Selkirk heard Crosier's voice:

'You have ten more steps, Arabs, and then I give the order to fire.'

Rachel's voice followed; the languages unintelligible to Selkirk but he knew she was repeating Crosier's words.

The camels continued; eight steps, nine, and then ten.

'Hold your fire!' Selkirk ordered. 'I want no firing!'

The camels walked on; they formed a solid semi circle now as they closed on him. Selkirk stood still, waiting. He had faced African tribesmen, Boer fighters, Turkish infantry and German soldiers but these Arabs were different from anybody he had ever seen before. They surrounded him, circling him but keeping ten feet away. They halted.

The dust settled. Selkirk stood still. The Arabs stood still. One voice roared high:

'Shout out when you want us, Major!' and then the supporting call: 'Reivers! Selkirk's Reivers!'

One Arab dismounted from his camel and stepped toward Selkirk. He stopped when he was within ten paces.

'I know you,' Selkirk said, 'you were at the ambush! You are the father of the boy.' He patted an imaginary child on the head, and the man nodded rapidly and smiled.

He stepped toward Selkirk and took him in a brief embrace. He tugged at Selkirk's sleeve and pulled him into the mass of Arabs. For a moment Selkirk wondered if he was to be killed or carried off on the back of the camel, but one by one the Arabs pulled their camels back to form an avenue for him to walk along. The Arab tapped his chest 'Asad' he said, 'Asad.' He jabbed his finger in Selkirk's chest and nodded again.

'Selkirk; I am Andrew Selkirk,'

When Asad looked puzzled Selkirk realised that he had given too many names. 'Selkirk,' he said and tapped himself on the chest, 'Selkirk' he pointed to Asad, 'Asad.'

'Selkirk,' Asad said the word and repeated it loudly, 'Selkirk' and the surrounding Arabs laughed. Some repeated the name; others merely smiled, most nodded gravely and said nothing, but all made way as Selkirk and Asad walked through their ranks.

Both Lewis guns were pointing to the mass of Arabs, with the Reivers on high alert. Selkirk could see the muzzles of the rifles through the gaps in the rock parapet and could sense the tension.

'It's all right, lads,' he shouted, 'this is Asad. He and I are old friends.'

The rifles did not waver, but Crosier stood up from behind the barricade of rocks. 'Are you all right, sir?'

'Perfectly; send Rachel out, please.'

'He is a Bedouin,' Rachel said when she emerged from the Reiver's position. 'I would not trust him.'

'I think he already saved my life,' Selkirk said. 'If the Arabs had wanted to kill me, they could have done so, and if they had wished to over-run the Reivers, they would probably have done that as well.' He smiled, 'anyway, we have little choice. He has local knowledge that we certainly lack. Could you translate what he says, please?'

Rachel shrugged. 'Obviously' she said, but she kept a full six feet distance from Asad, and Selkirk noticed that she placed one hand within her long jacket as she spoke. He knew she was holding the butt of her revolver.

With Rachel translating it took only a few moments to ask the Arabs the best route to the summit of Masada, and within twenty minutes the Reivers were mounted and walking around the massive rock, with a curious escort of some two hundred Bedouin on camels all around.

'There's nothing like this in Herefordshire,' Wells said as he looked at the colourful throng of wild desert warriors.

'Wait till I tell the wife what I was doing in the war,' an anonymous voice said, 'yes, dear; I was walking across the desert with a thousand Arabs when you were working in the factory.'

Asad took Selkirk to the bottom of a small path that stretched like a piece of string to the summit of the rock.

'He says this is the Snake Path,' Rachel translated, 'but he asks why you want to go up there. He says there is nothing but the sun and old ruins.'

Selkirk followed the undulations of the path with his eye, 'I can see why it is known as the Snake Path' he said, 'it is a series of coils and loops.' He looked at his men. 'Can we get the horses up there?'

Asad said a few words to Rachel. 'Why would you want to? He asked,' Rachel translated.

'My men won't part from their horses, and my chief wants me to go up there.' Selkirk tried to explain, but Asad looked doubtful. He spoke to Rachel again.

'He says that he does not know of anybody who has ever taken horses or camels up that hill, but the British are strange.'

'Tell Abdul that we're the Reivers,' Black said, 'we will do what no Arab, Turk or Briton could ever do.'

'Is there any water on top?' Selkirk asked.

'The Zealots had cisterns up there,' Rachel answered. 'And Herod had a royal palace so he must have had water.' She did not ask Asad the question.

'That was thousands of years ago,' Selkirk said, 'how do we know it is still there now?'

'This is Israel,' Rachel said with a shrug, 'where a thousand years is like yesterday and a day can be a thousand years. Time is different here.'

Selkirk did not argue. Rachel had not let them down yet; she had always provided them with a place to stay and with help and support when needed. 'All right, Rachel; I will take your word that there is water on Masada.'

Asad had tried to follow the conversation and now disappeared for a few moments. The other Bedouin watched and said nothing, inscrutable as the Egyptian sphinx. Asad returned with a spare camel laden with goatskin bags, each full of water, which he distributed to the Reivers before leading the camel away. Selkirk's shouted 'thank you' seemed a very inadequate expression of gratitude. He watched as the Arabs rode sedately to the south and suddenly the felt a very lonely place without them.

'Best to be up and doing,' he said at last.

'Aye, sir,' Crosier said. 'You heard the Major; dismount and get ready to walk up that path.'

'Bloody hell,' Batsford said, 'I'll never get up there.'

'We all will,' Crosier snarled.

The lower section of the Snake Path did not look too severe as it meandered around the less steep slopes that led to the escarpment, but as Selkirk looked up, the top section appeared virtually impassable. He took out his binoculars and followed the path as it seemed to cut into the solid rock of the cliff.

I am not sure that we can get the horses up there, but if we leave them here either they will stray, or the Turks will pick them up. Either way, we lose them, and without the horses, we can't get back home. We certainly can't march out of Palestine on foot. We take them.'

The Reivers listened as Selkirk told them they were going to the top of Masada. Some looked up at the great cliffs, or at the tortuous route of the narrow path, but nobody openly voiced their objections. They were British soldiers already in an alien land; this was just one more ordeal to survive, one more trial to endure in the passage of the war.

'Anyway lads,' Kelly said, 'it's a bloody sight better than fighting at Gallipoli or digging a hole in the mud in bloody Flanders.'

'How would you know, Scouse,' Rourke jeered, 'you've never been nearer to Flanders than bloody London.'

For once Kelly did not retaliate with hot words. Instead, he rolled up his trouser leg and showed a white scar across his calf. 'That was Fritz at Mons' he said and turned away.

'I'll take the lead,' Selkirk decided. 'Crosier, I want you in the centre to keep the men together, and Black, you're the strongest horseman; you act as rearguard and make sure that nobody falls behind.'

The path was narrow, steep and littered with loose stones that slid under the hooves of the horses, while waves of heat seemed to recoil from the rocks and assault them as they climbed. Selkirk rode on Kimberley for only the first hundred yards or so, and then he dismounted and led the horse by the reins. The other Reivers followed suit as they dragged themselves up step by laboured step.

Selkirk heard the complaining voice of Gupta and shouted to Wells to: 'make sure the traitor reaches the top and does not try and run for it.'

'The bastard may have a nasty accident if he doesn't stop complaining,' Moffat grumbled. 'I've had about enough of his moans.'

'And I've had enough of yours, Moffat! You help Wells get that lovely Bengali gentleman safely to the top, or it is you who will be having a nasty accident,' Crosier promised.

In the desert air, sounds travelled far so Selkirk was aware of the click of every hoof on the ground and the rattle of every stone that careless boots kicked over the edge. He heard the snicker of unhappy horses and the grumbling of his men as they toiled up this near perpendicular 1300 feet cliff.

'The Major's gone a bit crazy, hasn't he? What for are we going up here?'

'To see what we can see, of course. What other reason is there? Major Selks is an officer; they're all crazy. Keep that bloody mule of yours away from my horse; Daisy is particular who she associates with, so she bloody is.'

With every step, the view increased. The desert opened up around the Reivers, with the immense panorama of golden-white rock blistering under the sun and only a short distance away to the east, the long blue streak that was the Dead Sea.

'Christ man, just looking at that makes me thirsty,' Rourke said. 'I wish we had taken a dip in there before we climbed this bloody hill.'

'It would not do you much good,' Rachel broke her habit of not talking to the men. 'That is the Dead Sea; it is as much salt as water. If you drank that you would go mad and die.'

Rourke grunted. 'What's the use of it then? It's like the rest of this bloody country, it all looks pretty on the map, but once you get here, it's all rock and sand and bloody flies. Christ, even the bloody lochs are just bloody salt.' He moved on, still grumbling, with his hat tipped forward to give maximum protection from the sun and his boots scuffing the small stones. 'Why don't we let the bloody Turks keep the bloody place?'

'Because it's not theirs,' Rachel sounded angry. 'It's ours.'

Our land; here we are again. It is always our land.

Upward toward the sun, with the path undulating and coiling back on itself, winding a terrible route up that cliff as a million flies sought their human prey and a score of drab-bodied birds fluttered in the still air, mouths open as they strove to reduce the impact of the heat.

'No! I refuse to go further!'

That was Gupta's voice. Selkirk looked behind him at the column of Reivers strung out on that naked path. He had put Gupta in the leading section with Crosier close behind to encourage him if he lagged, but now the Bengali had stopped completely with the result that the column was no longer a unified entity but split into two parts. The second and larger part had telescoped as tired men and horses walked into each other or halted with that dizzying drop to the desert floor at their side.

'What's the trouble?' Selkirk shouted. His voice seemed very loud in the crisp desert air. It carried far down the rock, so Black at the foot of the column looked up and waved. 'It's that bloody traitor' he shouted.

Selkirk handed the reins of Kimberley to Rachel and worked his way back down the path, squeezing past the Reivers to reach Gupta.

'What's the trouble, Gupta?'

'I'm not going any further,' Gupta said. 'I have rights as a prisoner of war, and you must treat me humanely. Forcing me to climb a mountain in this heat is contrary to the Hague Convention.' He edged into the centre of the path, looked Selkirk squarely in the eye and folded his arms. 'Prisoners of war shall at all times be humanely treated and protected, particularly against acts of violence, from insults and from public curiosity.'

'Shoot the bastard, Major,' Black suggested and was supported by a chorus of assent from the Reivers.

'Push him over the bloody edge, sir!'

'That would not be humane treatment,' Gupta said. 'As a British officer, you are constrained to obey the Hague Convention to which your nation is a signatory.' He gave a tight little smile. 'I know my rights, you see.'

'You are a traitor to the Crown, not a prisoner of war,' Selkirk told him bluntly, 'and as such, I don't know if you have any rights. Now get up that path, or I'll have you tied back over the horse and dragged up.'

'I am a citizen of Free India' Gupta said.

'You are a subject of the king,' Selkirk denied him the chance of an audience, 'and as such are a traitor. Either get up that path or be carried up.'

Gupta tried to hold Selkirk's eye but failed. He muttered and began to walk again, but so slowly that the entire rear section of the column was shuffling rather than walking and the gap between the two sections grew with every minute.

'Sergeant Crosier: get Gupta moving. I don't care how you do it.'

Selkirk struggled to the front of the column and looked down at his Reivers; strung out on the Snake Path with no cover as they were they would be a perfect target for any half decent body of Turkish infantry. Having experienced the skill of Turkish snipers at Gallipoli, Selkirk knew exactly how dangerous they could be.

'Get up the path, lads! I want us all at the top as soon as possible!' Selkirk saw Crosier grab Gupta by the neck and drive him in front of him up the narrow path. The Reivers at his back gave a short cheer, and the gap between the two sections at once began to reduce.

'Keep them coming, Sergeant!' Selkirk called.

'Dust, sir,' Black's voice carried from the very foot of the column. 'Could be the Arabs again or Turkish cavalry.'

Just what we need.

'Thank you, Sergeant; push up, lads. Get to the top before Jackie sees us.'

When the path reached the foot of the cliff, Selkirk saw that the track was even narrower and the drop even steeper, but rather than hesitate he pushed on, leading a very nervous Kimberley.

'This is Masada,' Rachel said quietly. 'This is our sacred mountain.' She looked at the vertical cliff across which the path stretched. 'It would be fitting if a Jew were first up, and Abraham is getting tired now.'

Between the heat and the exertion of the climb, Abraham was visibly flagging, leaning on his horse for support as he carefully placed one foot in front of the other. To their right, the drop sucked at them: a hypnotic invitation to fall into oblivion.

'Do you wish to go first?' Selkirk asked.

'Obviously,' Rachel told him. Her eyes were pleading.

'Then do so,' Selkirk invited. 'Your horse will follow mine; he has more sense than most humans.' Before he had finished speaking, Rachel had passed him and pushed herself up the final steep few hundred yards. He watched her nearly run up the path, slip on a loose stone and totter on the edge of the cliff for a heart stopping moment, and then she vanished over the lip onto the summit plateau.

'Masada.' The single word sounded like a prayer.

Selkirk glanced behind him; his men were pressing forward hard now they could see the result, with even Gupta moving forward without Crosier pushing him. The thought of possible Turkish cavalry spurred Selkirk onward, 'come on Kimberley; nearly there.'

'Masada!' Rachel repeated. 'Welcome to Masada.'

'On you come, Kimberley.' Selkirk encouraged. The path was steeper, the thought of the fall dizzying, but he pushed on until Rachel reached out a hand and took hold of his sleeve.

'Well Major Selkirk, you are the first British soldier to ascend Masada.'

Kimberley scrambled up, to stand in a lather of sweat at the top. 'Best find that water, Rachel, or we'll lose all the horses.' Selkirk said. 'I'll get the lads up.' He fought the weakness of his own body as the pain of the torture hit him in waves.

Come on, Drew; you are the officer, you have to set an example. Control the pain and move on.

One by one the Reivers staggered to the top of the Snake Path and onto the scorched plateau of Masada. Abraham fell onto his hands and knees the second that he arrived, but Selkirk could not help him as he ensured his men were all safe on the surface. Matthew was gasping with pain, using his horse as a prop as he limped up with the blood from his wound crusting his trousers and attracting a host of flies.

'Up you get Matthew; that's the worst over now.'

Matthew nodded. 'Thank you, sir.' Watson thrust a shoulder under his arm and eased him to a sitting down position.

'He'll be all right sir, after a bit of a break.'

Selkirk looked around the surface of Masada. It was an arid plain of red-gold rock and dust, with a grouping of ruined buildings at the north eastern side. Sundry boulders were scattered around, and a few pieces of ruined walls.

'Not much here, sir,' Crosier reported. He held Gupta by the arm, 'what shall I do with the traitor, sir?'

'Not sure, Sergeant.' Selkirk said, 'I doubt he can do much harm up here, though, so just set a man to guard him.'

'Yes, sir.' Crosier sounded doubtful. 'Shall I have him tied up, sir? He will try and run.'

'Run to where sergeant? We are a thousand feet high with only one way down. Give the poor fellow some space while we find water for the horses.' Despite Rachel's assurances, Selkirk could see no trace of water.

If we don't find some very soon, the horses will begin to die, and then so will we. I hope to God that Rachel was correct.

'As you wish sir.' Crosier raised his voice. 'Kelly; I have a job for you. I want you to make sure Mr Gupta does not get up to any mischief.' He gave Selkirk a meaningful look. 'He is not to be restricted, but only watched: carefully.'

'Right sergeant,' Kelly said. 'Come on, Gungha Din, you can help me look after my horse.'

'I am a prisoner of war. I am not obliged to work for a common British soldier.' Gupta tried to stand on his dignity until Kelly landed a heavy boot on his backside.

'You're a traitorous black bastard, and you'll obey orders, or I'll kick your arse up through your throat.' Kelly kicked again until Selkirk ordered him to treat Gupta gently.

'He's a valuable man, Kelly; he might save thousands of lives.' He raised his voice, 'Rachel: any sign of that water yet?' The horses were suffering even more than the men, heads down in exhaustion and shivering in the heat.

'Not yet Major Selkirk.'

'Major: over here.' Black sounded urgent, so Selkirk left Kimberley in the care of Wells and hurried to the head of the Snake Path. 'Down there, major. Can you see?' Black sounded as calm as if the 1300 foot climb in punishing heat had been a casual stroll around the block. 'There is the dust cloud.'

Selkirk nodded. 'What do you think, Black?'

'It's the Turks, major.' Black said. 'They have been moving at a steady pace all the while we've been climbing up here. Arabs would maybe stop for something, or move slowly; whatever makes that cloud is travelling fast and steady.'

'Following us perhaps?' Selkirk asked.

'I would say so, sir,' Black said. The fact that he said 'sir' was an indication of how serious he considered the situation. 'And we are stuck on this rock with only one way off.'

Selkirk saw the dust drifting on the west; the direction from which they had so recently come. Even as he watched, he fancied that it had moved a fraction closer. 'How many men would it take to make that size of dust cloud?'

Black was silent for a few moments. 'Hard to tell, major. It depends on the speed they ride at and the weight of the horses. I am guessing, but I would say about four to five hundred men.'

'Too many for us to fight, then,' Selkirk said. 'The Turks must be keen to get Abraham.' He watched the dust cloud. 'Keep the boys back from the edge, sergeant, in case the Turks have eyes scanning the heights. If they see movement they will know somebody is here; if they don't see anything, they will keep moving and leave us in peace.' He remembered how far sound travelled in the desert and added: 'best keep the men quiet too. I know we are quite a bit away from them, but we don't want anything to alert Jackie.'

As Black withdrew to attend to the men, Selkirk watched the dust column creep ever closer. After a few moments, he heard the slight noise of hooves on the hard ground and then, as he listened, the sound increased.

A scout trotted ahead, hard riding on a white horse with his bush hat folded back and his rifle carried at the side of his saddle. Without looking to the right or left, he skirted the outermost flanks of Masada. His dust had settled before a small troop of men followed, riding much more slowly and staring around at the surrounding desert.

Selkirk slid back from the skyline and lay prone as he focused his binoculars on this group of horsemen. There was a dozen of them, very professional in appearance as they checked the route. Selkirk hoped the Turks did not have any trackers of Black's skill or they might find the trail of his Reivers, but hopefully, the much more extensive signs left by the Bedouin had obscured most of their tracks.

'You useless bloody Orangeman,' that was Kelly's voice, upraised as usual, and it got the habitual response from Rourke,

'You Scouse bastard!'

Selkirk dragged himself back from the lip of the plateau in time to see Rourke with his hands at Kelly's throat and the Liverpool man responding with a swinging punch. For a moment the two grappled together, and then Crosier pulled them apart, cursing in a harsh growl that was intended to be a whisper but which was louder than many men's shouts.

'Watch out, fucking Gunga's escaped.'

Torn between watching the Turkish cavalry in the desert below and his Reivers on the plateau of Masada, Selkirk had temporarily forgotten about the prisoner. Now he saw Gupta run free of Kelly and make a dive for the head of the Snake Path. If he reached that, he might be able to catch the attention of the Turkish cavalry, so Selkirk ran to head him off.

Gupta took half a dozen steps, saw Selkirk and abruptly altered direction, so he ran at an angle for the lip of the plateau a hundred yards to the north of the path. Selkirk opened his mouth to shout but closed it again before he alerted the Turks. Gupta did not have such inhibitions as he shouted, yelled and screamed.

'Catch that bastard,' Black shouted, and half a dozen Reivers formed a long line in Gupta's wake.

The Bengali glanced over his shoulder, screamed again and plunged back toward the plateau but at an angle that could see him evade the end of the Reivers' line.

'Head him off!' Black yelled, oblivious to the noise he made.

Gupta must have seen the Reivers alter direction for he ran for the edge of the cliff. He poised on the very lip, faced outward, waved both hands and yelled in a desperate effort to catch the attention of the Turks.

The poor bugger must know he is in for a bad time if we get him back to Egypt.

'I'll get him, sir,' Kelly launched himself in an impressive rugby tackle that brought the Bengali to the ground in a bone-jarring crunch, but which also loosened a clutch of stones that bounced down the face of the cliff and then slid their way down the lower slopes. One large stone rolled to the side of the Snake Path, teetered for a few seconds and settled there. Selkirk breathed out slowly.

'Hold him tight!' Selkirk said as Kelly put a headlock on Gupta, 'but don't strangle him! We need him alive!' He looked anxiously over the edge.

The Turkish cavalry seemed not to have heard the commotion as they rode past, rank after rank of them enveloped in their curtain of dust.

'The buggers are deaf as well as blind,' Crosier said. 'Hard luck Gunga; your little plan failed.'

Gupta said nothing but Selkirk could sense his dismay.

'Come on, Gunga; time to get away from your Jacko friends,' Kelly released his hold on Gupta, gripped his collar and hauled him backwards away from the edge. As Gupta struggled, his flailing feet dislodged a small pebble that rolled to the edge and toppled over. The stone was only the size of a sparrow's egg but gathered others on the way down until it created a minor landslide that connected with the larger boulder on the Snake Path. The entire collection crumbled over the path and rattled down to the ground beneath like a volley of artillery, and this time the passing Turkish cavalry heard the noise. The officer at the head raised his hand, and the whole company halted and looked up.

Hundreds of curious faces scanned the edge of the plateau. First one and then another man pointed upward until the officer gave a sharp order that carried to the Reivers and the leading section walked their horses toward the edge of the path. An NCO dismounted and studied the ground, then shouted something to the officer.

'They've found our spoor,' Black said quietly.

'That's put the kybosh on it,' Crosier said.

Selkirk watched as the Turkish officer rode slowly over and looked at the ground. He raised his voice and shouted something, so the entire Turkish force moved closer to Masada.

'That's a bit of a bugger,' Selkirk said, 'the Turks know that we are here.'

'Hello,' Rachel's voice sounded through the tense silence. 'You all are looking very grave, but I have good news. I have found water,' she looked around at the circle of Reivers. 'So we can stay on Masada for as long as we like.'

'We may be here for a very long time,' Selkirk indicated the Turkish cavalry who were exploring the lower levels of the Snake Path, 'for we can't get down as long as the Turks are there, and I am damned sure that we won't let them up.'

'What happened to these Jewish fellaes that held this place?' Rourke asked.

'They all died,' Rachel said quietly.

Rourke was silent for a moment. 'Bugger that,' he gave his opinion.

Chapter Ten

December 1915

The summit plateau stretched all around, a baking wasteland of stone, with ancient ruins adorning roughly a quarter of the space and rocks of various sizes scattered all around. Selkirk took off his hat to use as a fan, but the sun seemed to redouble in force, and he replaced it, swearing.

'This is some place,' he said.

'This is Masada,' Rachel told him, 'where my people defied the Roman Empire.' She sounded very proud; her eyes were bright as she looked around her.

'So you told us,' Selkirk said. 'I would be a bit happier if you said that they all escaped and lived happily ever after.'

'Their sacrifice was one of the foundation stones of our nation,' Rachel said.

Selkirk thought of the Turks milling around the foot of the Snake Road. *I want no more sacrifices here.*

'Show me your water supply,' Selkirk ordered.

He had hoped for a miracle, a bubbling spring perhaps, or a limpid pond in the centre of the plateau, but instead Rachel brought him down a flight of steps to a sheltered chamber that held a shallow basin perhaps thirty feet long and ten wide. The water inside was warm but relatively clean, certainly drinkable by horses, although Selkirk would not have allowed the men to touch it until they had thoroughly boiled it.

'How did this get here?' Selkirk looked around, 'there is no source, no spring to bring it.'

'When it rains in the desert, it rains hard,' Rachel explained. 'We get quick flooding, and then the water drains away. When the Zealots held the rock, they had water brought from the wadis over there…' She pointed to the neighbouring massif of the desert, 'by an aqueduct, but they must also have had this built.' Selkirk realised that the water was in an artificial tank carved out of the rock and lined with plaster to make it waterproof. 'Any rain that lands on Masada must drain into this place, and because it has the roof above, it does not evaporate.'

'Clever people, these Zealots,' Selkirk approved.

'It was not them, but King Herod, perhaps,' Rachel began, but Selkirk interrupted.

'Sorry Rachel, but we have no time for the history lesson just now. We have a mission here, and half the Turkish army is prowling around at the foot of Masada. I have to let my men water the horses; then you can give me the Cook's tour of this desert stronghold of yours.'

'You are not yet fit,' Rachel said.

'I got this far; show me,' he insisted. Rachel was correct; he was not yet fit, but he had to carry on even though each step was agony and his entire body was screaming for relief.

The surface of Masada was relatively level, with scatterings of boulders among the ancient ruins, and tremendous views of the surrounding desert, stark and bare and red.

'The Dead Sea,' Rachel pointed to the long streak of the inland water that ran north and south for miles. 'And beyond that, there is nothing but desert for hundreds of miles, all the way to Baghdad and Babylon.'

The names rang with the exotic Orient and a suggestion of magic carpets and djinns but looking east Selkirk could only see bad territory to ride over and wondered how many men the Turks could raise from such wild lands, and what sort of enemies they would make. The men he had faced in Gallipoli had been formidable; these harsh lands would undoubtedly produce tough warriors.

They walked around the rim of the plateau to the extreme south.

'How far is Suez?' The ground looked unprepossessing, comprising harsh desert with a few scatterings of green that might be oases or merely plantations of palm trees.

'About three hundred miles,' Rachel said. 'And the Turks have an army in Sinai.'

'It is one thing to have an army in position,' Selkirk said, 'and quite another to patrol it effectively.'

But that is the future. We have to get Abraham and Gupta away from here, and then avoid that Turkish force camped at the base of this hill.

Selkirk remembered that last crucial line of the message he had received from Brigadier Smith. He turned his attention to his more immediate problem. 'We have to make an airstrip here,' he said. 'An area of level ground without obstructions so an aircraft can land, pick up Jitendra Gupta and Abraham and take off.'

Rachel put an involuntary hand on his arm. 'The British are going to take Abraham away on an aircraft?' Her mouth gaped open. 'I have only ever seen two in the air and never one close. Will he be safe?'

I've never seen one close either.

'Of course, he will be safe! He will be flown to Egypt and maybe after that taken to Great Britain,' Selkirk said. 'He will be as safe as any man in the world.'

And then I can get my Reivers home as well; somehow.

Selkirk looked southward to the endless panorama of arid territory that separated him from Egypt. It would be a daunting task to take his men across that and past the Asakr –I Shahaneh, but there was no alternative unless Brigadier Smith arranged a rendezvous with a ship on the coast.

'How long an airstrip will we need?' Rachel asked.

Only God or Brigadier Smith knows: how long is an airstrip?

'As long as we can make it,' Selkirk decided.

That first night on Masada was tense. With the horses watered and strictly rationed, Selkirk organised his men. He set sentries at the head of the Snake Path and returned Wells to his original task of guarding Gupta. The Herefordshire man had developed a strange relationship with the Bengali, who obeyed his orders without much argument.

'Don't let him get away again,' Selkirk warned.

'Yes, sir,' Wells tapped his rifle.

Selkirk checked his sentries, fought the pain of his injuries and walked around the perimeter of Masada.

'Get some sleep, Major Selkirk,' Rachel advised.

'Yes,' Selkirk agreed. He looked out at the fires that marked the Turkish camp. They spread around the base of Masada, close to the foot of the Snake Path to ensure the Reivers could not escape in the dark.

Brigadier Smith has effectively got us trapped.

The shouting started at midnight when the Reivers were fighting the chill.

'Andrew Selkirk' the name floated from the ground beneath. 'Andrew Selkirk. I am going to kill you, Andrew Selkirk.'

Selkirk struggled awake and listened to the voice.

'You're going to die Andrew Selkirk. You and your men are trapped up there, and you are going to die.'

'It's only to frighten you, Major.' He had not realised that Rachel was at his side, pressed close to share body heat.

'That's the German, Hefferman,' Selkirk said. 'We have a bad history.'

'Obviously,' Rachel pushed him back down, 'but he is down there, and you are up here, and he cannot kill at this distance. Leave tomorrow's troubles for tomorrow.'

'Andrew Selkirk' the voice came again, edged with menace, 'if you surrender and bring the Zionist and Gupta I will guarantee correct treatment for your men.' There was a pause, broken only by subdued mutterings from some of the Reivers, and then Hefferman continued. 'If you do not surrender, your men will all die.'

'Come and get us you bastard!' That was Rourke, but many of the other Reivers joined in, greeting Heffernan's offer with a chorus of jeers, catcalls and obscene insults that made Rachel smile.

'Your men are not intimidated, Major Selkirk' she said.

'It's hard to intimidate British soldiers,' Selkirk heard the pride in his voice, 'and impossible to intimidate the Reivers.'

'The Turks have turned intimidation into a profession,' Rachel said. 'Look what they have done to the Armenians.' She put a hand on his arm. 'We need you to free this Palestine from them, Major Selkirk, so we can have peace and security in our land. We must have our country back, so we belong again.'

Selkirk nodded. 'Everybody needs somewhere they feel they belong.' he agreed.

No idea of country is worth losing a wife. Is the idea of a country worth losing a husband? Or a son?

Selkirk stood up, intending to walk to the head of the Snake Path but Gupta was in his way. The Bengali looked at him through liquid brown eyes but said nothing and stepped aside as Selkirk pushed past.

'I ordered you to watch this man, Wells,' Selkirk ordered. 'He may try and break through to the Turks in the dark.'

'Yes, sir,' Wells held up his hand; he had attached a rope from his wrist to that of Gupta. 'I have him, sir. He won't escape again.'

'Good man.' Selkirk nodded and stepped away. The stars were brilliant above him, uncountable white lights in the incredible clarity of a sky with which he never tired. After growing up in the shaded greyness of the north, the brilliance of the desert night always captivated him. He looked up, momentarily lost in the wonder of nature.

Why do men fight when we have all this splendour free for all? Can we not share it?

Greed: that was the reason: greed and selfishness and fear. Selkirk sighed; *the love of money was perhaps the root of all evil, but the lust for power and fear of one's neighbours also contributed.*

Crosier and Black concurred that the most level area to build an airstrip was in the south west of the plateau, near a structure that Rachel told them was a great pool.

'This will do,' Selkirk said. I want it as level as possible, with all the rocks and boulders removed, with the holes and undulations filled in as far as possible and as much flat ground as possible for the air craft.'

'How long do aircraft need to land and take off, Major?' Black asked.

'I have no idea,' Selkirk told him, 'but if Brigadier Smith ordered us to build an airstrip here, then he must believe that the surface of Masada is long enough and flat enough for the purpose.'

'And symbolic enough,' Black added. 'This whole operation has been about symbolism, Major; the use of sea power to land us, the freeing of the Zionist Abraham, the Indian fellow we grabbed to symbolise the reach of the British Empire and now using the buckle's holy hill as a place to send Abraham back to Britain. It's all symbolism pure and simple.'

'Why?' Selkirk asked. 'What is the point?'

Black shrugged. 'Smith is showing Jackie Turk that we understand their Empire and can use its symbols against it.' He jerked a thumb at Gupta, who was an interested observer, 'take the traitor there. He is nothing really, a fat babu from Bengal; if he dies there will be a hundred to take his place, but the Prussians are using him as a symbol of supposed British oppression over the Indians.' He looked away; 'anyway the whole war is about symbols; our king is meant to symbolise the British Empire, but he is related to the Kaiser, who symbolises the Germans – same blood, same family but different countries. What are we fighting for? To free Belgium?' Black looked around him at the desert, 'I am an Australian, and you are Scottish, fighting the Turks in Palestine to free Belgium from the Germans. I can't see any sense in that.'

'This war is greater than just symbols,' Gupta interrupted the conversation until Wells jabbed him in the ribs: 'keep your bloody mouth shut, Gunga, see?'

'No, let him speak,' Selkirk said. 'Go on Gupta; have your say.'

Gupta pressed his hands together and gave a little bow. 'Thank you Sahib' he said without a trace of sarcasm in his voice. 'Don't you Europeans yet know what this war is all about?' His smile more than compensated for his previous show of respect. 'It is Europe tearing itself apart. All the Great Powers that have dominated the world for the past two centuries are fighting each other at the same time, with hundreds of thousands of casualties. 'Gupta gave another smug smile. 'Do you imagine that there will be a victor? All sides will claim victory, but all will emerge weaker than they were. Already the world has seen that Germany, the great European power, could not defeat a small British Army at Mons, while the maritime power of Great Britain needed its colonies of Australia and New Zealand to attack the Asian Ottoman Empire but still were defeated in Gallipoli and lost the Sinai peninsula.'

'The war is not over yet,' Black reminded.

'It has hardly started,' Gupta said solemnly, 'yet already there are a million deaths and the British and French Empires are calling on their colonial soldiers to fight for them.' Gupta's laugh caused the hairs on the back of Selkirk's neck to prickle. 'The European hegemony is dying, and their empires are proving only paper tigers.'

'So you hope to destroy the British Empire?' Selkirk asked quietly.

Gupta spread his arms. 'I have no interest in the British Empire. I am only interested in the future of the peoples of India; my people, our land.'

Our Land

'Your land?' Black's laugh mocked Gupta and the entire concept of Indian Nationalism, 'how is it your land? When you mob had it, India was a hundred different states all squabbling with each other.' He turned aside and spat on the ground. 'Your land, my arse.'

Gupta did not seem upset by the criticism. 'It was stolen by the Honourable East India Company and passed to the rule of the British government, without any thought of asking the people of the land.'

'Ask the bloody wogs? May as well ask the Abos!' Black shook his head. 'I hope they bloody shoot you!'

'Oh, the British won't shoot me. They will ask me all sorts of questions first, and when they have extracted all the information that they think I have, they will send me for a fair trial in front of a British judge and twelve British men in a splendid British court of law. Then they will hang me, fairly and without prejudice to serve the ends of British justice.'

Gupta turned around on his heel and pointed directly to Abraham. 'Indeed, my fine and honest British soldiers, you are sending me to the same fate and for the same reasons as you are saving that man from.' He paused and smiled, 'for wanting our land for our people.'

And Helena fought because the Boers wanted the same thing.

'You're a bloody traitor,' Black gave his opinion, 'and a rabble rouser and a trouble maker. It's your sort that causes wars you idealistic bastard.'

'Your ideas were tried back in 1857,' Selkirk reminded, 'and they caused tens of thousands of deaths.' He shook his head. 'If we were ever to leave India, the country would revert to little principalities and rival nations all jostling and fighting each other; Moslem would fight Hindu, and all the old barbaric ways would come back.'

'Yet you would help the Jews come to a Palestine homeland, although the Arabs already live in this land.' Gupta said. 'The needs of the British Empire at the moment are more important to you than the thousand years of trouble you are creating for the future.'

'Or the hundred thousand deaths that you will cause in India,' Selkirk said. His men had gathered round to listen to the conversation. 'Come on lads; we have an airstrip to build to get Abraham to safety and this traitor to his desserts.' He raised his voice, 'put him to work Wells; he may as well do something to help the Empire he hoped to destroy.' Some of the Reivers laughed at that, but others looked more thoughtful as they returned to the pressing problem of creating an airstrip before the Royal Flying Corps brought an aircraft to take Abraham to safety.

Clearing the scattered rocks in the punishing heat drained the strength of the Reivers, but that was the easier part. Filling in the cavities and trying to level the bumps was harder.

'We don't even have a spirit level,' Crosier said as he checked the line of the ground by eye.

'I know; keep working.' Selkirk toiled with the men. They had no tools but their hands, no power except their strength and only their determination and motivation to push them through the muscle-tearing ordeal of each hour. Within a few moments, the sweat had rendered their tunics sodden, but the sun dried them in seconds.

'Permission for the men to take their tunics off, sir?' Crosier asked.

Selkirk looked at Rachel, who was in the process of carrying an upturned saddle full of small pebbles to help even a declivity. 'Would that offend you, Rachel?'

Rachel shook her head, so her dark hair flopped around her head. 'Of course not, Major Selkirk.' She lowered her voice so only he could hear. 'After all, I have seen you naked, and one man is made much like another.' Her wink was unexpected and wholly delightful.

'Rachel can do the same if she likes,' Kelly suggested until Crosier blasted him to make an apology.

'Rachel won't get sunburned if she does,' Rachel was capable of answering for herself, 'but you British soldiers from your northern towns will peel if you are not careful.'

Gupta was holding out well, but not working as hard as his captors, while Abraham and the wounded Moffat were carrying goatskins of water from the pool to the men. However reluctant Selkirk had been to allow his men to drink that water only the previous day, now he was glad of it. He had hoped to boil the water before use, but there was a lack of fuel, so it was drunk just as it was, with no apparent after effects.

'Sir,' that was Batsford, panting for breath as he had run from the head of the Snake Path. 'Something is happening down below.'

Wilson was the second man on duty watching the Turks. 'They had reinforcements, sir; another company of cavalry or mounted infantry.' He pointed down the slope. 'They have set up a camp now.'

Turkish tents spread around the desert slope for about quarter of a mile. They were in neat rows, with horse lines in between. Selkirk used his binoculars to see the scurrying figures of men dashing here and there as a new unit merged with the old.

The Turks have a quandary; they need to get up here to grab Abraham back, but there is only one path, and we hold that. They have no water down there except what they carried with them, and no infantry to make an assault.

'Thank you, Wilson.' There must have been about six hundred Turks now, as unable to hurt the Reivers as he was incapable of getting away.

'The Zealots must have felt like this as they watched the Romans besiege them,' Rachel had joined them. 'Imagine; we are in the same position as these mighty men of old.'

'And they all died you said,' Wilson said. 'They killed themselves.'

'And became martyrs whose deeds we still recall,' Rachel said. 'We might join them in the memories of future generations; the founders of a new Israel.'

'I saw a coffin in the sky above Masada,' Wilson said quietly.

'I don't want to be a martyr,' Batsford said. 'I just want to get home to Bermondsey.' He moved to the edge of the plateau and looked down on the Turkish positions below. 'But they won't let us, will they? We can't get past all of them.'

'Major Selkirk will think of something,' Rachel said. She raised her arm and for a second Selkirk thought she was about to hug Batsford, but she changed her mind and patted his shoulder instead. 'I am sure you will see London again.'

'Yes; the major will get us home.' Batsford agreed, 'I won't end up in a coffin in Masada as Wilson says.'

'Of course, you won't.' Rachel's glare should have turned Wilson into a pillar of salt.

'You two keep watching the Turks,' Selkirk said.

The report of the rifle took him by surprise. Batsford stepped abruptly back from the edge. 'The Turks are shooting at me.'

'They are,' Selkirk confirmed. 'Keep back from the edge son, and you'll be safe.' He stepped to the lip, aware that there was at least one Turkish sniper down there, but equally mindful of the fact that an up-hill shot at a vertical target over a thousand feet above the marksman called for a degree of expertise that few soldiers possessed. He refused to flinch when the Turk fired again. He did not hear the passage of the bullet but fancied he saw a small puff of dust rise from a cliff a good two hundred feet below him.

'Keep low and keep watching,' Selkirk ordered. 'But move your positions, so Jackie doesn't know exactly where you are.' He scanned the slopes below but could not spot the sniper. The Turks were masters of camouflage.

'How is my airstrip coming on?'

The resulting chorus of howls and dissent told him the Reivers morale was unaffected.

* * *

There was no moon that night, only a screen of cloud that blotted the sky and spread darkness across the desert. Standing on the rim of Masada, Selkirk thought that even the ranked Turkish camp fires seemed insignificant against the immensity of space and time. He was nothing here; this entire war was only an incident in the eternal sweep of history.

'I thought I heard something, sir,' Batsford was on watch. 'It could be a goat or something.'

'Keep listening, Batsford,' Selkirk said. 'And keep your voice down.' He halted the philosophical musings that the desert seemed to draw from him and concentrated on the sounds of the night.

At first, he heard nothing save the soft breathing from his resting Reivers and the occasional movement of the horses, but then there was a faint click, as of stone on stone, and then another.

I wish I had brought some flares with me.

'Did you hear that, sir?' Batsford did not lower his voice.

'Keep your voice down!' Selkirk hissed, 'yes I heard it.' He leaned over the edge of the precipice, staring into the dark below. He could see the flicker of fires in the Turkish camp, pinpricks of watchful light, but the path itself was in darkness.

There was another sound as if somebody had stumbled in the dark. 'Go and rouse Sergeant Black,' Selkirk ordered, 'he can hear a man's thoughts at five hundred yards.'

'Bloody Jesus, major, can a man not get any bloody sleep in this country?' Black was at Selkirk's side before he had finished speaking. 'How far up the path are they?'

'You tell me,' Selkirk asked.

Black slipped over the barrier Selkirk had ordered erected at the head of the path and crawled downward. He was back within ten minutes. 'About thirty Turks are coming up the Snake,' he reported, 'lightly dressed and armed. They're about half way up.'

'We'll meet them,' Selkirk decided. 'Rouse the men quietly. You and I, with Rourke and Kelly, will go down the path. Bring the Lewis Gun. Crosier will take charge here,' Selkirk touched Batsford on the shoulder. 'You did well to hear them Batsford; good man.' He could feel Batsford grow taller under the brief praise.

Stepping onto the Snake Path in the dark felt like leaving security behind. The drop sucked at Selkirk as he thought of the predatory Turks creeping silently up to kill him, but the presence of Black was always reassuring while Kelly and Rourke were natural warriors, men he would want at his side in any dangerous situation.

They did not speak, and moved slowly, testing the ground before every step. Selkirk knew that Black was a past master at night movement, but he was the officer so he must take the position of most danger. The path sloped down, barely visible in the night; he knew that the Turks were coming up as cautiously as he was moving down, remembered their skill and courage in Gallipoli and tightened his grip on his rifle.

The Turks could be around any bend; he could meet them any second. Selkirk wished he had fixed his bayonet first but too late now. He wanted a spot where he could set up the Lewis gun on a straight stretch.

Jesus!

Even although he expected it, the shock of contact took Selkirk by surprise as he walked right into the advancing Turks.

More prepared, Selkirk reacted faster, lowering his rifle and firing a single shot that broke the silence of the night and took the man in the stomach. The Turk grunted; his eyes gleamed in the dark, and let out an agonised moan as Selkirk closed on him.

'Sir!' that was Kelly, always willing to talk. 'Are you all right?'

The Turk slumped to the ground, still clutching his rifle, and Kelly callously pushed him over the edge of the precipice. 'A scout,' Black said, 'but he did his job. Jackie will know we're here.'

'Set the Lewis up, Rourke,' Selkirk ordered.

'There's not a decent field of fire,' Rourke complained, but sat on the path and readied the machine gun, 'here, Kelly you Papish bastard, make yourself useful for a change and hold the magazines.'

There was a barked order ahead and a burst of deep-voiced cheering.

'Here they come,' Black said, 'hurry with the Lewis lads!'

The path was only wide enough for two men abreast and then only with care, so Selkirk fired straight ahead and kept loading and firing as long as he sensed movement ahead. After Selkirk's first three shots, Rourke had the Lewis ready. He opened up, sending short burst of fire down the path.

There were more shouts, a few screams and then a long moan. A few shots came back, but the Turks had not expected resistance and withdrawn to safety.

'Cease fire,' Selkirk ordered, 'and pull back from the path before the snipers start. Keep down!'

'These Turks are persistent,' Black said. He withdrew facing down the path and fired an occasional round to dissuade any Turk who may have decided to try again.

Rachel was waiting at the head of the path. As the Reivers passed, she reached out her hand and touched Selkirk on the arm. She did not say a word, but Selkirk felt the imprint of her fingers for a long time.

'They'll be back,' Black said.

Selkirk nodded; 'before they are, we have an airstrip to build.'

That was a minor incident; a few moments in a war that has lasted over a year, yet it will cause widows and mothers to grieve across the Ottoman Empire.

* * *

'Sir; over there!' Batsford pointed to the sky in the south. 'I can see something.'

The sound came an instant later, a high hum similar to the buzzing from a distant bee-hive. The Reivers left their work on the airstrip to peer into the sky, hopeful of seeing the aircraft that would signal an end to at least this part of their ordeal.

'There, major,' Black nudged him with a sharp elbow, 'but there is more than just one.'

Selkirk had not been sure how many aircraft would come. His knowledge of flying machines was limited, but he knew there were single- seater and twin seater machines, so he expected two at least, with a pilot and a seat for Abraham and Gupta, and perhaps a third air-craft to act as escort. Now he looked and saw a whole array of specks in the sky.

'There must be about twenty aircraft,' Black said.

Crosier shaded his eyes as he peered into the sky. 'Where have they come from? I didn't think they had the range to come this far into Jackie's territory.'

'Here, sir,' Batsford sounded excited. 'Maybe they are going to take us all away by air. The horses as well! Like Noah's Ark.'

Selkirk shuddered at his immediate vision of trying to load Kimber-ley into the seat of a fragile wood-and-canvas flying machine. 'I can't see that happening Batsford.'

As the aircraft came closer to Masada, Selkirk saw that Black was correct: there were many more aircraft than he had expected. He saw three flying low and two further groups above them, just specks in the sky, but definitely aircraft.

'Three squadrons, I think.' Crosier knew more about the Royal Flying Corps that Selkirk did. 'I think the top two are escorting the lower ones; I would guess the top two are fighters and the lower ones maybe two seater machines; spotters or the like.'

'I will take your word for it,' Selkirk said.

There was a small group of aircraft flying below two larger groups.

'I've never seen so many flying machines at one time,' Batsford sounded amazed. 'I never knew there were so many.' He grinned, 'maybe I was right, and they are going to take the horses as well. Imagine my Daisy flying in the sky.'

'Let's hope they're ours,' Wilson said, 'and Jackie has not called in some Fritzy aircraft to get us.'

'You're always the optimist eh, Wilson? Keep your stupid mouth shut!' Crosier blasted him into silence, but Selkirk remembered Wilson's earlier comment about seeing a coffin above Masada.

He nodded to Moffat, 'grab Rourke and get a Lewis gun ready, just in case.'

The aircraft passed high overhead before circling a mile or so to the south and returning, gradually decreasing in altitude until they were only a few hundred feet above the surface of Masada.

'They're ours,' Crosier said. 'See the roundels on the wings? Fritz has got bloody great black crosses on his, and I don't know if Jackie has any aircraft, anyway I doubt he knows how to fly them.'

The Turkish soldiers had woken to the fact that there were British aircraft overhead and opened up a torrent of ineffective fire. The aircraft took no notice as they continued with their seemingly leisurely manoeuvres until the smaller squadron was only a hundred feet above the surface of Masada.

'That one is coming in,' Crosier said, as one of the lower aircraft headed directly for the landing strip.

Selkirk gestured for his men to stand back 'Clear a space, boys; keep out of the way!' Very few of the Reivers had ever seen an aircraft before so nobody knew what to expect when it came roaring toward them. The noise was deafening as it swooped overhead with its double spread of wings much larger than Selkirk had expected and its wheels not quite touching the hard ground, then it passed by and rose up again, soaring upward with a blast of power and a whiff of aero-fuel that had Batsford coughing. The passage of the machine raised great clouds of dust.

'That's marvellous,' Selkirk said. 'I would love to fly in one of these.'

'It's bloody un-natural that's what it is,' Kelly muttered. 'Man wasn't made to fly. If we were, we would have bloody great wings.'

'Here, Wells, bring Gupta forward,' Selkirk raised his voice above the constant buzz of the aircraft that were slowly circling overhead. 'Abraham; you'd better get ready to jump on board as well.'

'Maybe it can't land,' Wilson said. 'Maybe there's not enough room.'

'It can land, and there is room,' Selkirk spoke with more conviction than he felt. He watched the aircraft circle and return, its wings dipping as it approached the strip they had created. Some of the Reivers ducked as the aircraft came lower, with the downdraught from its propeller lifting a cloud of dust from the ground and sending more of the Reivers into paroxysms of coughing.

The rifle fire was sudden and urgent and came from the direction of the Snake Path.

Chapter Eleven

December 1915

'The bloody Turks are trying again,' Kelly said, 'don't they know when they're beaten?'

Not with Hefferman there to encourage them.

Selkirk looked around; one sentry at the head of the Snake Path was aiming and firing while his companion was running toward the airstrip, waving his rifle and shouting. The noise of the aircraft engine drowned out his words.

'Crosier: go and see what's happening,' Selkirk decided that his place was with Gupta and Abraham, that was the prime reason for the Reivers' mission. He spent only a moment watching Crosier hurrying to meet the returning sentry before he turned to face the oncoming aircraft.

The machine levelled at the far side of the airstrip with its long wings swaying from side to side and its wheels a few feet above the ground. It seemed to hover there as the pilot cut his speed, then the wheels touched the stone surface with a long rumble and a spurt of dust. It bounced once, twice, thrice, each time raising clouds of dust, and then it rolled to a noisy halt with the great double wings flapping slightly. A curtain of dust slithered all around as the propeller slowed to a stop.

The rifle fire from the head of the Snake Path grew in intensity 'Pembroke; Rourke, go and help Crosier: move!' Selkirk watched the two men have a last glance at the aircraft and then sprint toward the firing.

The biplane was nothing like Selkirk had expected. It looked terribly frail, with its fabric-covered wings held up by light wooden struts and pieces of wire, a small body with two cockpits and an open framework that stretched from the winds back to the tail. The engine sat behind the body of the machine, ticking slowly. The pilot emerged from his cockpit, removed his goggles and smiled. His very young face was streaked with oil. The second cockpit was situated in front of the pilot right in the nose of the aircraft, and like the pilot's, it was open to all the elements.

'Lieutenant James Dale,' the pilot pulled off thick fleece mittens and held out a slender hand. 'Royal Flying Corps.' His wide grin made him look even younger than he probably was. Selkirk did not grip his hand tightly in case he broke the delicate fingers. 'Do you like the machine? It's an FE2b; brand new.' Dale's grin would have looked more in place in the front row of a school rugby club rather than in a war aircraft in the middle of Palestine.

'It's a beautiful machine,' Selkirk agreed. He looked forward as the firing from the Snake Path increased in volume. 'I have two passengers for you.'

'Only one for me, old boy,' Dale's grin did not falter as he indicated the single vacant cockpit. 'No room for any more in my crate you see.' He reached inside his leather flying jacket and produced a sealed letter. 'These orders are for a Major Andrew Selkirk or his successor if he's gone west.'

'No, I'm still here,' Selkirk confirmed.

'Jolly good,' Dale listened to the musketry, 'Bosche? Or Turks?'

'Turks,' Selkirk tried to block the rifle fire out of his mind. 'But don't mind them; they can't get to us up here.' He tore open the letter.

Selkirk
Send Gupta first, then Von Stahl and Abraham
Smith

'That's direct enough,' Selkirk said. *We don't have Von Stahl.* He raised his voice 'Bring Gupta over; he's first up.'

Wells and Wilson frog marched the Bengali over to the aircraft. Gupta pushed back against them, protesting that they could not fly him to torture and death in England.

'Haig Convention! I am a prisoner-of-war!'

'Oh I say; he's a most reluctant passenger. I thought it would be a grateful spy; it normally is,' Dale shook his head at the shouting Bengali. 'It's quite all right old chap. I'll tie you in so you don't fall out and hurt yourself.' He watched as Wells and Wilson lifted Gupta bodily and thumped him into the open front cockpit.

'I think Mr Gupta is more concerned about what happens after he arrives in British hands,' Selkirk explained, 'he intended to start another Indian Mutiny.'

'Oh my eye,' Dale eyed Gupta, 'we can't have that.' He stepped forward and bent over Gupta as Wells and Wilson held him still. 'Soon have you all snug and secure my troublesome little fellow.'

Selkirk watched as Dale fastened a series of webbing and leather straps around the protesting Indian. 'If you are allowed to move,' the pilot said, 'you might fall out, and what's worse, you might unsettle the machine, and I may fall out, and I won't like that.' He pulled one of the straps tighter and smiled as Gupta gasped. 'Sorry old man, but it's for your own good, you know.'

The firing intensified, and Selkirk heard the mechanical stutter of the Lewis Gun.

'Sounds as if you're busy,' Dale gave Gupta's bonds one last tug, patted him on the head and climbed into the pilot's cockpit. 'Must go; lot's of flying to do.' He gunned the engine and raised his voice above the sound. 'Hold on tight Gupta old chap, and let's hope the Turks don't have any Archie; it's a long way back to Egypt!' He thrust his helmet and gloves back on, waved a cheerful hand and began to taxi his aircraft along the runway.

The Reivers stood back to allow him space as he reached the end of the air strip, slowly turned and then raced along again, picking up speed by the minute. Dust rose in choking clouds as he passed them, then the wheels lifted from the ground; the aircraft dipped, bounced and took off, dipped again when they reached the very edge of Masada and roared upward in an impressive array of aerial power that left the Reivers staring.

'That's one gone,' Selkirk said, 'only two to go.'

'Two?' Black asked.

'Abraham and Rachel,' Selkirk explained. 'They wanted the German diplomat, but he's dead.'

Black gave him a sideways look. 'I rather thought you were thinking of keeping Rachel here, Major.'

'No; here comes the next machine.'

The second aircraft approached faster than Dale's had. It flew so low overhead that the Reivers ducked as the fixed undercarriage passed only a few feet above them, and then it circled and returned with the pilot leaning slightly out of the cockpit to study the ground below. He circled again and then roared in.

'He's confident,' Black said as the aircraft dropped right above them, approaching from the west so it would land facing the drop. The pilot cut his engine and came in at a glide; his wheels touched the ground and rolled, but then there was a loud bang from the engine, the machine veered to one side, scraped along the ground in a screaming array of sparks and came to rest right at the edge of the cliff.

'Jesus,' Selkirk began to run forward to rescue the pilot when the machine exploded in a pyrotechnic display of smoke and orange fire. The heat and blast of the explosion drove Selkirk back, and he could only watch in horror as the aircraft rapidly became a funeral pyre on the plateau of Masada.

The firing from the head of the Snake Path increased, with the staccato barks of rifles augmenting the clatter of the Lewis. Selkirk glanced across; his men were firing hard.

'Sir,' Black pointed upward. The third of the low flying aircraft was circling still, but rather than fly away after witnessing the death of his companion; the pilot zoomed over for a closer look. He soared upward again, with his propeller pushing the body of the machine over the heads of the Reivers.

'Black;' Selkirk took hold of his arm, 'if that aircraft lands, get Abraham on board safely. I am off to ensure the Snake Path is secure.'

Crosier had the defence of the Snake Path well in hand. He had placed the Lewis Gun behind a barricade of loose rocks, with an arc of fire that caught the head of the path and two areas further down, while his three riflemen could pick off any Turkish advance at four separate points.

'There is only the one way up,' Crosier was quite calm, 'and we have it covered. Jackie can't get up here no matter how he tries.' He jerked a thumb downward. 'He's losing men every time he comes.'

Selkirk glanced downward; the path and surrounding slope were littered with crumpled Turkish soldiers and the writhing, groaning wounded.

'If they keep coming up,' Crosier said quietly, 'we can keep knocking them down.' He nodded to a point half way down the slope, 'they are gathering again, sir.'

Selkirk watched as dozens of Turkish cavalrymen dashed from cover to cover up the lower slopes of Masada. They gathered at a dog leg bend a hundred feet below the beginning of the cliff, where an overhang sheltered them from fire from above.

'Ready, Rourke?' Crosier asked quietly.

'Ready, sir,' Rourke lay prone with the Lewis gun pointed at a section of the path just a few yards above the dog leg. Pembroke held two spare magazines ready.

'Here they come again,' Crosier pulled back the bolt of his rifle and pointed it at the edge of the path.

The Turks surged forward in a yelling mob, with a group in the rear firing at the summit of the cliff so far above. Bullets cracked and pinged around the defenders, sending splinters of rock around and raising spurts of dust.

'Wait,' Crosier said, 'wait...'

The Turks charged forward until they arrived at the steepest and straightest part of the path, where it cut into the cliff itself. There was a direct line of fire for the Lewis Gun.

'Right, Rourke,' Crosier said quietly, and Rourke opened up, with the rifles adding their barking to the metallic machine-gun rattle. The fusillade knocked over the Turks as if they were toy soldiers at a fairground.

'Cease fire,' Crosier yelled. The musketry stopped. Most of the Turks were lying in untidy bloody bundles on the path, with some having fallen off to roll down the slope. One man stood among the wreckage of his comrades, miraculously unhurt but paralysed by fear or shock and even at this distance, Selkirk could see he was sobbing.

'Will I shoot him, sir?' Rourke asked.

'No; he's broken,' Selkirk decided. 'Let him go.'

The sound of the engine came as a shock. Selkirk had nearly forgotten about the aircraft as he concentrated on the Turkish attack, but now he looked upward. The aircraft was approaching the airstrip, its wings level with the plateau.

'These pilots are brave men,' Crosier glanced up and then returned his attention to the Turks. 'You wouldn't get me up in one of these things.'

The aircraft came lower and cut its engine, so it was gliding down toward Masada. The firing ended as both sides watched the show, with only the lone Turk standing still among his dead comrades unaware of the movement above. A few Turks opened desultory fire on the aircraft.

'Here he comes,' Crosier said quietly.

'You have things well in hand here,' Selkirk said. 'I'll go and get Abraham away safely.'

There was a short burst of sound as the pilot blipped his engine once, twice and then his nose dipped, and he made his final approach. Selkirk saw the Reivers step back from the airstrip as the aircraft brushed through the tall column of smoke from the burning wreckage, and then it was on the strip with both wheels bouncing on the hard rock.

'Well done,' Selkirk shouted as he ran forward, 'well done.' But then the aircraft shuddered, rose up again and turned over on its nose. It somersaulted and turned end over end on the strip, spraying bits of itself in a display of broken struts and ripped fabric as it shattered to pieces on the rock. The wings collapsed, and the body rose high, floated through the air and crashed down in a cloud of dust, sending a group of Reivers running for safety.

There was no fire, but by the time Selkirk arrived, it was evident there was nothing he could do. The pilot lay face down fifteen yards from the wreckage of his aircraft, virtually decapitated and with his legs splayed at acute angles from his body. A group of Reivers clustered around the shambles.

'It's Wilson,' Wells shouted. 'He's dead.'

Leaving the unfortunate pilot, Selkirk ran across. The body of the aircraft had landed squarely on top of Wilson, with one wooden strut piercing him as neatly as a thrust from a rapier. He had died immediately, and the remainder of the aircraft had landed around him like a box.

'He got his coffin then,' Wells said quietly. 'He knew it would happen.'

Two more good men gone; two more martyrs on Masada.

Selkirk saw Abraham holding on to Rachel for support as he watched the remaining two squadrons of aircraft. He turned scared eyes to Selkirk and spoke.

'Abraham wants to know if the other machines will try to pick him up.' Rachel asked.

'I don't know,' Selkirk said. The other aircraft were still circling, lower than before but still far too high to land.

One broke away from the rest and swooped lower, so Selkirk could see the red ribbons streaming from its struts and the British roundels on the underside of the wings. It came lower and dropped something, before flattening out and soaring high again. The object it had whistled as it dropped, while a long red ribbon marked its passage down. It bounced three times and lay still.

Wells brought it to Selkirk. 'It's a message tied around a steel dart, sir.'

Selkirk tore the strip of paper from the dart. He read it out loud to the Reivers as they gathered around him.

'Head for Egypt' he read: 'good luck.'

'Is that it?' Rachel snatched the message from him and scanned it. 'There's nothing else. They are abandoning us here!' She looked upward. Both squadrons of aircraft had turned around and were heading south. Already they were little more than specks in the sky. The Reivers watched them go, wordless at first and then they responded in the time-honoured way of British soldiers, with catcalls, jeers and insults.

'Aye, run away you bastards,' somebody shouted. 'We don't need you anyway.'

'Dirty flying cowards,' another yelled.

'How about us, Major Selkirk,' Rachel sounded near panic, 'How about Abraham and me? We are trapped up here and if the Turks capture us…' She put her arms around her body and hugged tight. 'We will die first,' she decided. 'This is a good place to die.'

'Bugger that,' Kelly said bluntly. 'Top yourself in case something bad happens?' He spat on the ground and repeated, 'aye, right, bugger that! I hope you don't want us to cut our bloody wrists in case Jackie gets us. They're not that bloody frightening.'

As Rachel raised her voice to a shout, Selkirk put a hand on her shoulder.

'There will be no suicides in my unit and no defeatist talk. We got Gupta away; now we no longer have to worry about doing as Smith tells us. From now on we make our own decisions.'

'And the first one,' Black interrupted, 'is to decide how to get off this bloody rock.'

Nobody argued with that.

There are fifteen of us left, plus me and two civilians. We have thirty horses and water, plus a limited supply of ammunition. We are stuck on top of Masada with only one way up or down, deep in Ottoman territory, with some hundreds of the enemy blocking our escape route. The enemy knows we are here and they desperately want the civilians; surrender is not an option. The British have not offered to send a ship so we have to ride for Egypt so we must break through the Turks at the foot of Masada and head south.

'Any ideas Major?' Black asked.

'I'll let you know,' Selkirk said. 'Let's take care of Wilson and the pilots first.'

The Reivers scraped shallow graves and piled rocks on top. They used struts from the wreckage to form three crosses that looked sad and forlorn in the Palestinian sun, but British soldiers expected some form of commemoration of their dead. The Reivers stood in a solemn clump as Selkirk repeated as many of the correct funeral words as he could. He had heard them said often enough to remember the gist of the meaning, but each brief funeral got harder as the sheer futility of the war sunk home.

'Black; ensure the horses are well watered and fill the goatskins and water bottles. We might have to leave in a hurry. Crosier, check the men's equipment and weapons.' Selkirk raised his voice. 'Conserve your ammunition lads; I intend to start for home soon, and we might have to fight Jackie to get there.'

'When are we leaving, sir?' Walker asked.

'You just want to get back to your bint in Cairo,' Kelly jeered, and the other men gave a small laugh; anything helped ease the memory of the recent ceremony.

'As soon as we can, Walker,' Selkirk promised. 'There is no point in staying up here any longer, and we don't know if the Turks expect infantry or even artillery reinforcements.' He glanced at his men.

Sun bronzed, hard eyed and ragged, they looked like the veterans they were. They also looked lean and tired; they needed rest and decent food. 'We've come a long way from that day we first mustered in Egypt,' he told them, 'and now it's time to get back home. I want you all ready to ride at ten minute's notice so keep your water bottles full and your rifles to hand.'

The Turks had retreated to their tented encampment at the base of the Snake Path, and except for a few desultory shots, they seemed content to sit there and keep the Reivers trapped on Masada.

'They just have to wait for us to die,' Rachel stood beside Selkirk on the edge of the plateau. 'They don't know we have water up here, but they must know we have limited food and sooner or later we will have to surrender.'

'There will be no surrender,' Selkirk told her.

But what other option do we have? Do we emulate those Zealots from so many centuries ago and kill ourselves? No: we are British soldiers, we are the Reivers: we fight our way out.

The sun was disappearing in another of these blazing desert sunsets that still astonished Selkirk. Out here there was no dreaming sadness as the light faded away, as there had always been in the long slow dusks of the Merse. Here the day rushed to a close in a bright explosion of colour, and then the stars burst out across the desert sky; the northern melancholy was lacking.

'I love sunsets,' Rachel said suddenly. 'My husband and I used to watch the sun go, just like this.' Her voice was soft and far away as if she was reliving old memories rather than watching over the camp of hundreds of enemy who would torture and kill her without compulsion.

'So did Helena and I.' Selkirk merged with her mood.

'Do you miss her?' Rachel asked the expected question.

'Yes. Do you miss your man?'

'Obviously' she stepped closer. 'But my husband is gone, and your Helena is gone, and soon we may be gone too. Life is short in wartime.'

'Life is short in wartime,' Selkirk echoed.

The sun had already vanished below the horizon, leaving a yellow-orange sky where clouds were only a memory, and the moon was already a silver sliver. Tiny lights appeared in and around the Turkish camp; despite their function, the tents seemed ethereal in the deepening gloom, something from the land of romance rather than a place of men at war.

'We should make the most of what we have,' Rachel's voice was softer than the hand she slid into his, 'while we have it.'

Selkirk closed his eyes.

Helena? Why are you not here? I need you now.

Rachel's hand pressed his. 'Major Selkirk? Andrew? Are you with me? Or are you with Helena?'

'Both,' Selkirk said truthfully. He could not help but squeeze the small hand that was on his own.

'It is cold,' Rachel said, and he pulled her close out of instinct, but held her there for the company of her body.

'Come, Andrew,' Rachel guided him away from the edge of the cliff and the lights of the Turkish camp.

Wells and Moffat were guarding the head of the path, and the remainder of the Reivers were settling down around the water, with some talking to the horses and others playing cards or trying to sleep. Pragmatic as always, the British soldiers had salvaged material from the wrecked aircraft, so their camp fire burned bright, giving much-needed warmth as well as cooking the eternal bully beef of the iron rations.

'Unless we get out of here we will be eating the horses soon,' Selkirk said, 'and the lads won't like that at all.'

'No, Major Selkirk,' Ruth pressed two fingers to his lips. 'That is not a concern for tonight. That is a concern for another time.'

I am their officer; they are my concern at all times. But he allowed Rachel's fingers to linger on his mouth and said no more.

'Oh,' Rachel gasped as she tripped over a loose stone, so Selkirk had to put his arm back around her to offer support. She leaned against him as they walked across the uneven ground.

Selkirk had thought they were just wandering, but when he felt her lean harder, he knew she was leading him somewhere. 'Where are you taking me?'

'Somewhere a little bit sheltered,' Rachel told him and guided him to a small building.

'This was part of Herod's palace,' she said. 'It is not as luxurious as it once was, but at times like this, luxury is not something we can expect.'

Moon and stars contributed to Selkirk's night vision, so he could see they were in a small chamber that had once had mosaic walls and flooring, now sadly decayed by time and neglect.

'Come, Andrew,' her hands were insistent on his tunic.

'Rachel...'

Helena; please forgive me.

'No talking, Major Selkirk.' Rachel's fingers were on his lips again, and then they slipped away, and her mouth was there. Selkirk pulled back as he thought of Helena.

But you are dead, Helena.

And Rachel was not dead. Rachel was alive and vibrant and here. Rachel needed him for comfort and reassurance, and he needed her for comfort and release. He did not rationalise his thoughts; instinct pushed him toward him, and they met in an embrace that embodied need as much as desire.

'Rachel...' Selkirk began, but she stopped him with her mouth, and after that, he did not speak at all as nature took control.

The noise woke him from sleep.

At first, Selkirk could not remember where he was. It was cold and dark, and Helena was next to him.

Helena is dead. Dead? Then who is...?

'Rachel?'

'Major Selkirk?' Rachel covered herself with urgent hands before the memories of the previous night reminded her that there was no longer any need. 'Andrew?'

The noise increased; Selkirk made out some words in the babble of sound: 'Murder', 'Turks' and 'Major Selkirk.'

Chapter Twelve

December 1915

'Jesus; something's happened.' Selkirk scrambled for his clothes.

'Andrew?'

'Get dressed, Rachel and quick!' Selkirk hauled on his trousers and grabbed for his tunic. His belt was next, with the revolver a reassuringly heavy weight at his waist.

He waited a moment and grabbed her by the arm. 'Dress as we move,' he said. 'Come on.'

Dawn was still beneath the eastern horizon; a faint band of silver-red that promised another day of insufferable heat.

Dragging Rachel behind him, Selkirk ran to the Reivers' camp. 'Sergeant Crosier! What's happened?'

'Turks sir!' Mathew stumbled over, nursing an eye that was beginning to swell. 'I have no idea how they got here; they can't have gone past the guard on the path.'

'Where are they now?' Selkirk peered through the pre-dawn dark. He saw shadowy figures flitting about but could not tell if they were Turkish soldiers or Reivers. He pulled his revolver from its holster.

'Dunno, sir. One just ran into the cave and started yelling in Turkish. Rourke put the head on him, but he got up, shouted something and made a dive at Abraham with a bayonet. It took two of us to pull him off but he was all covered in slime, and we couldn't hold him, and he ran for it.' Mathew looked shaken. 'He was nearly naked sir. I've never seen anything like it.'

'Abraham?' Rachel grabbed hold of Mathew's shoulders. 'How is Abraham?' She burst into a torrent of Hebrew before she calmed down. 'Is he much hurt?'

'Dunno, miss. I don't think so. Me and Kelly pulled the Turko fellow off the old man. Old Abe was bleeding though...'

'Abraham!' Rachel was running as soon as she heard Mathew's last words, 'Abraham!'

Abraham's voice sounded in reply, the Hebrew words soft.

Rachel took a deep breath, 'this, Major Selkirk,' she said sternly, 'is what comes of our dallying at night.' She straightened her back and stalked away toward Abraham.

'And that's you told, Major,' Black sounded amused. 'No harm done here except a mad Turk climbed up the cliff and got chased away. There may be more than one.'

'He climbed the cliff? That was some feat!' Selkirk peered into the gloom. 'Where is he now?'

The dawn was above the horizon now, and pearly white rays were streaking the sky. In another ten minutes, it would be light enough to distinguish faces and features.

'I don't know sir; he ran away. Kelly was chasing him last I heard.'

Selkirk raised his voice. 'Kelly! Make yourself known!'

There was an immediate hail from Selkirk's left. He moved toward the sound, shouting Kelly's name.

'Here, sir,' Kelly said. He loomed out of the lessening gloom, bleeding from mouth and nose.

'Where's the naked Turkish fellow?' Selkirk asked.

'Over that way somewhere, sir,' Kelly pointed in the vague direction of the head of the Snake Path. 'I saw him run after we pulled him off the old buckle.'

'Here! You!' the words were loud and followed immediately by, 'halt' and the high crack of a rifle.

Selkirk ran to the guards at the head of the Snake Path. He saw a sentry with a distinctive Australian bush hat struggling with a bare headed, stocky man and jumped to help.

The Turk was muscular and covered in grease, so he slithered through Selkirk's grip and flicked a long bayonet from the leather belt that was his only clothing until Rourke reversed his rifle and cracked the butt against his head above the ear.

'That'll quieten you down, Jackie,' he said. The Turk fell, rolled and lunged at Rourke, who sidestepped and knocked him down a second time. 'You can't beat me Jackie; it's not worth your while trying.' Rourke glanced at Selkirk, 'shall I shoot him, sir?'

The Turk rolled once and rose again, but rather than attack Rourke he ducked low and ran toward the cave.

'Hey! Jackie: come back here!' Rourke yelled.

He's going after Abraham again.

Selkirk leapt over one of the many boulders that littered the surface of Masada and followed the Turk.

The Turk did not hesitate but ran straight toward the Reivers' cave, yelling and wielding the bayonet, but a row of Reivers emerged, each with his rifle levelled. Selkirk heard a sinister click as of half a dozen Reivers pulled back the bolts of their Lee-Enfields.

'Don't fire,' Crosier roared, 'you might hit the major.'

'Fire away!' Selkirk threw himself onto the ground, but the sight of the levelled rifles had forced the Turk away. He tried to sidestep the Reivers, but Crosier growled an order and the last two men altered the angle of their rifles.

'Shoot the bastard!' Selkirk shouted.

'Hold your fire, Batsford!' Crosier countermanded. 'You'll shoot the major!'

The Turk glanced back over his shoulder, his eyes wide. He shouted something, but Selkirk did not understand the words, turned away from the Reivers and plunged toward the Snake Path.

'Now you can shoot him,' Crosier said, and the Reivers let loose a volley that spattered against the rocks all around the Turk, but did not hit him.

'Shoot him then,' Crosier roared 'before he gets back to his mates.'

The Turk jumped the barricade at the head of the Snake Path and ran down without hesitation.

'Leave him,' Selkirk ordered, 'he's no harm to us now.'

We're soldiers, not murderers.

Selkirk watched the Turk run down the first part of the path. 'You're a brave man,' he said. 'What a pity you are on the other side.'

The bullet took the running man under the chin and blew the top of his head off. Pieces of bone and brain were in the fountain of blood that sprayed against the cliff wall and pattered against Selkirk, ten yards away. The second bullet caught the Turk under the breast bone, lifted him bodily and smacked him against the cliff. He bounced back and rolled off the path.

'Who fired?' Selkirk asked.

'Not us, sir,' that was Crosier's voice. 'That came from below.'

'Jacko shot their own man.' Rourke shouted. 'Stupid buggers!'

The Turk fell down the face of the cliff and onto the slope below, bringing a tumble of stones and pebbles as he rolled over and over toward the ground hundreds of feet below. It was too dark to make out anything down below, but Selkirk could hear Turkish voices as the mini-avalanche ceased and he imagined the Turkish soldiers backing away from the rolling body and its attendant torrent of stones.

As the Turk was falling, a third bullet smashed into the cliff beside Selkirk, so he ducked, swore and headed back for the surface of the plateau.

Crosier shrugged. 'That's him gone, then,' Crosier was unemotional. 'I wonder how he got up here. He did not come up the path, so he must have come up the cliff.'

'He was a brave man,' Selkirk repeated, 'maybe he came part way up the path and climbed the rest? I can't see him clambering up any-where else.'

'Why did he come? One man with a knife against sixteen with rifles; he must have known he could not win.' Crosier shrugged, 'Was it just desperation? Or was he a fanatic, like the Ghazis of the Frontier.'

'He was here to assassinate Abraham,' Rachel joined in. 'The Turks don't want him to reach the British.'

Selkirk nodded. 'All the more reason to make sure we do get Abraham back then. These Turks are brave men; they are going to keep trying until they find a flaw in our defence.'

It is not the Turks; it is Hefferman, and he wants his revenge on me.

Selkirk raised his voice, 'Sergeant Crosier, take a roll call; make sure nobody else is hurt. We'll have to institute constant patrols and guards along the summit of this Masada now in case Jackie has any more like that one. See to it.'

'Sir,' Black said. 'Look at this!'

The rope had a grapnel hook on the end and hung down the side of the cliff.

'That's how he got up,' Selkirk said. 'He must have thrown it from the path.' He pulled on the rope and then peered downwards. A rifle cracked from below, with the bullet going nowhere. 'Jacko has a sniper down there,' Selkirk said. 'Tell the boys to keep back from the edge today.'

'Major!' Black reported. 'Walker is missing.'

'He was on guard,' Selkirk said. 'Check to see if he's lying injured. The Turk may have caught him by surprise.'

'I have a patrol out searching, Major.' Black said. 'And I've posted Rourke and Wells with Abraham.'

'Sir!' Crosier said. 'Here's Walker's kit, and it's empty. He always cuddled that bag sir; he used it as a pillow.'

Selkirk nodded. 'I remember Matthews laughing at him.'

The crack of a rifle made them all duck. 'Where the devil did that come from?' Selkirk had his revolver in his hand.

'Up here somewhere, sir,' Crosier was crouching, rifle ready to fire as the echoes of the shot died away.

'That was a Lee-Enfield.' Selkirk looked around. 'What the hell is happening this morning? Who is firing at whom?'

'I don't know sir,' Crosier said.

'Sir!' Well's Herefordshire accent was distinct. 'Somebody took a shot at Mr Abraham, sir!'

'Christ! There's another Turk on the loose,' Black said.

'A Turk with a Lee-Enfield?' Selkirk tried to make sense of the situation as a horrible possibility entered his mind. 'Sergeant Crosier, go and take care of things with Abraham. Make sure he is secure, and the boys are ready for an attack. Sergeant Black, call back the patrol that's searching for Walker and send them to Crosier. You and I are going to hunt this sniper.' He took a couple of quick steps backwards and grabbed the rifle from a surprised Matthews. 'I'll bring this back,' he promised.

'The shots must have come from somewhere on Masada,' Black lay prone with his eyes busily scanning the surface plateau of the great rock. 'They were not from the ground below. Another Turk must have come up that rope.'

'Maybe so,' Selkirk said. 'Cover me, Black.' Keeping his head down, Selkirk ran to the nearest prominent rock, which gave him a better view across the southern half of Masada. The sun was already casting shadows across the landing strip, highlighting the folds in the ground and the ruins of the Western Palace, one of the many relics of ancient times that decorated Masada.

Clambering on top of the rock, Selkirk felt the heat rising. He scanned the surface of Masada, quartering the ground as he had done so often in South Africa when he hunted the Boer commandos. Aware that the heat would distort distance and movement, he eased forward his rifle and waited. The art of the irregular fighter was a mixture of patience and the sudden strike. As long as he was there, his quarry could not move without being observed.

'Right, Black!'

Black was moving before Selkirk finished speaking. He zig-zagged across the ground to spoil the aim of any possible sniper, and threw himself in the shelter of the walls of the Western Palace. I'm going in, Major!'

'I've got you covered!' Selkirk adjusted his sights as Black vaulted the sandstone walls. A single bird flew up, wings beating and beak open. He saw brief glimpses of Black's hat as he moved from room to room in the palace, but nobody else emerged.

'Palace's clear,' Black announced. 'I've got you covered, Major.'

Selkirk took a deep breath of the hot, dry air and slid from his rock. There was another group of ruins about fifty yards away, across frighteningly open ground. Holding his rifle in both hands, he ran forward, swore when a Lee-Enfield barked out, altered direction and slammed himself down behind the rubble walls of the ruin. The echoes of the rifle bounced around Masada.

'It's all right, Major. He wasn't shooting at you!' Black said reassuringly. 'He's holed up behind the wreck of the aircraft that crashed.'

Selkirk looked up. The wreckage was about a hundred and fifty yards away, a pile of tangled wood and fabric, with the engine in the middle. 'I'll move toward it, Sergeant. You cover me and pot him if he shows himself.'

'Right, Major.'

Aiming for the wreck, Selkirk fired a single shot, worked the bolt and fired another, and then ran forward. He heard the crack of a rifle and saw a figure emerge from behind the aircraft. The man stood, Lee-Enfield levelled, and then Black fired. The man staggered and Selkirk jumped on him with a rugby tackle that he had learned on the playing fields of Kelso.

'Walker!' Selkirk stared in astonishment at the sniper.

Walker lay on his back, bleeding from his mouth and with a bullet hole in his chest. 'Sorry, sir,' he said. 'I was not after you.'

'What's it all about, son?' Selkirk knelt at his side. 'You're no traitor.' He raised his voice. 'Bring bandages and a water bottle!'

Black arrived in a haze of dust. 'Walker? What's your bloody game?'

'Did I get him?' Walker asked. 'Is he dead?'

'Is who dead? And more importantly,' Selkirk asked. 'Are there any more assassins up here?'

'Abraham! Is he dead? No; there are no more.' Walker coughed, spitting up blood.

As the other Reivers arrived, Selkirk glanced at Crosier, who nodded.

'Abraham is well, sir.'

Walker closed his eyes and spoke in a language that Selkirk did not recognise, yet alone understand.

'Who are you?' Rachel bent over Walker and spoke in Hebrew. When Walker did not answer, she shook him roughly and slapped him across the face.

'None of that,' Selkirk said.

Walker coughed up more blood as Selkirk ripped open his tunic and pressed a bandage over the wound.

'It's no good, he's dying,' Rachel said.

Selkirk nodded. He had seen sufficient gunshot wounds to know that Rachel was correct. 'Ask him why he did it.' He watched as Rachel and Walker held a private conversation in Hebrew, with Walker growing progressively weaker and the words coming with more effort.

'He's going,' Black said without emotion as Walker heaved forward and opened his eyes wide. Blood gushed out of his mouth, and he died.

'God rest him,' Selkirk said.

'God will not,' Rachel said. 'His name was Yeffet Samiri, and he was a Samaritan.'

'A Samaritan?' Selkirk stared at Walker. 'I thought they were just in the Bible. Anyway, Walker was a Londoner. He had a London accent.'

Rachel shrugged, removed her Australian bush-hat, pushed back her hair and replaced the hat. 'He must have lived there,' she said. 'He was a Samaritan from Nablus, beside Mount Gerizim and he despised us, the Jews. He says he tried to shoot Abraham during the ambush.'

Selkirk remembered the rifle shots that had narrowly missed Abraham during the rescue and the fact that Walker had been one of the two volunteers for the Reivers. *I brought an assassin with me.*

Crosier shook his head. 'Does everybody hate each other in this country?'

'Not always,' Rachel stood up.

'Bury him,' Selkirk said. 'Whatever his beliefs, he was a brave man. Thank you for translating, Rachel. Now get back to work, everybody.'

Now I have to try and get Abraham back to safety, somehow. How? I do not know, but I do know that Smith has put us in an impossible position and now it is up to me to get us out. At least we are alone now and thank God for that.

Selkirk did not realise how he looked until he caught Rachel's eye. 'Walker's death upset you, Major Selkirk?'

Selkirk shook his head. 'Yes, Rachel. He was one of my men.'

'He was an enemy of my people and of your Empire.' Rachel said.

'So it seems.' Selkirk was more shaken than he liked to admit. 'We can't let it bother us. We are left to our own devices now.'

'No more help from Brigadier Smith?'

Selkirk forced a smile. 'No; we are entirely alone.'

'And that makes you happy?' A deep groove formed between Rachel's eyes.

'We are better on our own,' Selkirk said. 'No ties, no orders from on-high; we make our own decisions from this moment on.'

We don't have the manpower to stay here and guard this place. We have to leave soon.

'Hey, Wellsie, you're next to go,' Rourke gave Wells a wave.

'Why me, you Scotch bastard?'

'Because your name begins with W. Wilson and Walker were last. See?'Rourke lifted his rifle. 'Both their names begin with W, like yours. Best keep the old bundook handy.'

'We'd all better keep our rifles handy,' Selkirk said. 'We're getting away from here.'

'When do we up-saddle and ride, Major?' Black raised his eyebrows in hope.

'Tomorrow morning at dawn,' the idea took shape even as Selkirk spoke. 'But we have a lot of work to do first.'

'Ride? Ride where?' Rachel tugged Selkirk's sleeve. 'There is nowhere we can go.'

'We are going to the En Gedi oasis,' Selkirk said, 'and from there we go south to the Suez Canal.'

Rachel looked over her shoulder, grasped Selkirk's sleeve, turned and pointed to the Turkish tents that were spread out at the base of Masada. 'How do we get past them, Major Selkirk?'

Selkirk felt the grin spread right across his face. 'Oh they will move for us,' he said, 'we'll make sure of that.'

The Turks have made a fundamental mistake. They are camped far too close to the foot of the path. They are so intent on trapping us here that they have forgotten about the law of gravity.

With his decision made, Selkirk issued a string of orders that had his Reivers running around Masada. He had Black, Wells and Moffat caring for the horses, muffling their hooves and equipment and ensuring the Reivers filled their water bottles and goat skins. The remainder of the men were collecting rocks and boulders from the surface and piling them high at the head of the path and for fifteen yards on either side.

'Jackie won't get this far, sir,' Crosier was puzzled at the function of the enhanced wall. 'They've tried twice already, and we've kicked them back.'

'He won't get this far with you on guard Sergeant,' Selkirk confirmed, 'keep the men working but don't tire them out. We have a busy day tomorrow.'

'Major Selkirk; what shall I do?' Rachel asked.

Selkirk tried to kill his pangs of guilt at having allowed a potential assassin to come so close to his charge. 'You look after Abraham, Rachel. Keep him rested, and tend to his hurts. He has had plenty of them recently, and he is not a young man.'

'We are used to hurts,' Rachel said, but she gave a half smile and left to look after Abraham.

'What's your plan, Major?' Black asked when he had the horses groomed and fed, with all the water bottles and goatskins topped up.

Selkirk called Crosier to join them. 'We only have one way down,' he said, 'so we must leave by the Snake Path. We can ride in daylight and have the Turkish snipers play cat and banjo with us and then their entire force will be waiting for us at the bottom, or we can leave by night and have the boys fall over the edge in the dark.'

'Best try by night,' Black said at once. 'We'll lose fewer men that way.'

'I plan to leave an hour before dawn, so we are well down the path before it is light enough to be seen.'

'They'll hear us, sir, and we'll be under rifle fire and picking our way in the dark,' Crosier pointed out. 'That might be the worst of two evils.'

Selkirk indicated the growing collection of rocks and stones. 'I hope to give them something else to think about.'

Black looked confused. 'I don't follow, Major.'

'Hopefully, neither will the Turks,' Selkirk said. He explained his idea.

In the late afternoon, Selkirk had the horses exercised, as he did every day, and ordered everybody to try and rest except for the men on watch. The Turks were quiet, with only a few speculative shots by a sniper to remind the Reivers that they were still there, waiting at the base of the hill.

'Major Selkirk,' the German voice carried up from the camp, distorted by whatever mechanical device Hefferman had used. 'Give yourself and the Hebrews up, and your men will be well treated. Otherwise, they will all die!'

'Come and get us you Jacko bastard!' Rourke jeered, as the other Reivers whistled and jeered.

'That was a Fritz, not a Jacko!' Kelly sneered, 'you can't get anything right you Orange bugger!'

Selkirk allowed Crosier to restore discipline among the men.

'Will we get away?' Rachel asked, as night fell and Selkirk stood behind their makeshift wall of loose rocks, looking down on the regular lines of camp fires from the Turkish positions.

'We'll try our very best.' It somehow seemed natural when Rachel pressed her hip against him. 'We know there is no possibility of a relief column coming to rescue us, and I'll be damned before I surrender, so a breakout is our only option.'

Rachel's hand reached for his. 'Thank you, Andrew.'

'You've nothing to thank me for,' Selkirk said. 'I am obeying orders; it is my duty. Anyway, I nearly allowed the Turks to murder Abraham and I harboured a viper.'

'You could not have known about the Samaritan and your men saved Abraham's life,' Rachel said. 'These two flying men died to try and save Abraham, to help the cause of Zion,' she spoke quietly and pressed harder against him. 'We will not forget their sacrifice.'

'They were also following orders; they were doing their duty.' Selkirk shook his head. 'I don't think they will have heard of the cause of Zion, Rachel. We have a mutual enemy in the Ottoman Empire, and we are only fighting them because they are the allies of Germany.'

There were a few moments of silence before Rachel spoke again. 'No, Andrew. I think you are also fighting for Zion,' her pause was significant, 'and for me.'

Is Rachel correct? Am I attracted to her? I like her, certainly, but why? Is it because she is so like Helena with her strength and her dedication to a cause? Am I fated to fall for women who fight for their land rather than those with more feminine attributes, whatever that may mean?

Selkirk found it easy to put his arm around her and pull her close. She did not resist. 'Perhaps I am,' he said.

'After the war...' Rachel said, and stopped.

'After the war?'

Without Helena and my children, there is no 'after the war'. I have no reason to survive. The war gives me purpose.

'After the war, will you remain in the British Army or go back to Africa?' She twisted in his arms to look up to him.

'I have nothing except memories and graves in Africa,' Selkirk said.

'The Turks killed my husband and my children,' Rachel said. 'But there are ways of making more.'

Was that an invitation? Be careful now Drew.

'I am sure there are.'

'And children need a mother as well as a father.' Rachel allowed the words to linger in the air, 'and women need children as much as they need a husband.'

That was a clear invitation.

Selkirk breathed in deeply. Despite the hardship of their lifestyle, Rachel still smelled sweet and floral. He did not reply.

'Perhaps some men also need a woman,' Rachel added. 'But perhaps British soldiers are different to other men.'

'We are no different,' Selkirk said. He did not release his hold of her. She was firm and strong beneath his hand, with no surplus flesh. The night hid any expression on her face as she spoke again.

'Nor are we,' Rachel said.

There is so much unsaid here. But I cannot make any commitment; my loss of Helena is still too recent and too raw. I cannot jump from one woman to another as easily as I could swap horses.

'We must talk of this later,' Selkirk said. 'We have to rest before tomorrow.'

'Yes; we have a war to win first.'

'We have a war to win first.'

Mention of the war broke the mood. Rachel slipped clear of his grip and walked back to the Reiver's camp. Selkirk watched her hips sway in the dim star light. That image remained with him until he eventually slumped into a fitful sleep.

* * *

'Up, lads; time to get moving,' Selkirk walked around his men, 'keep the noise down; grab some breakfast.'

One by one the Reivers stirred, yawned, rubbed their eyes or swore, depending on their natures, then looked to see what they could eat.

'Not much food left, sir,' Crosier said. 'We brought enough for a fortnight, and that is long past now. We've been on half rations for days.'

'I'm well aware of that, Sergeant and I hope to find something on the way back,' Selkirk said.

I can't think of that now. I have to get these men safely down this hill. And Rachel.

'Do you want the men to mount up, Major?' Black stroked the nose of his horse.

'Not yet. We'll lead the horses down; it's quieter than riding.' Selkirk looked upward. 'Was that a drop of rain just now?'

'Could be a shower; it is winter.' Black grunted, 'in fact, it's 25th December, Christmas Day.'

'So it is, Merry Christmas Thomas.'

'Thank you major; Merry Christmas.' Black managed a wan smile, pulled his pipe from his pocket and thrust the stem in his mouth.

'I wonder if the shepherds are watching their flocks tonight...' Selkirk realised that he was rambling. 'Get the men ready to move down the path, sergeant.' He saw Rachel and Abraham standing in the corner of the chamber. 'Are you two ready? We are moving out.'

Only fourteen Reivers left now, and I am taking a huge gamble on their lives.

'Right lads; we're on our way home. Keep as quiet as possible. Sergeant Black; you lead. Sergeant Crosier, you are in the middle, and I am in the rear.'

'That's the most dangerous place,' Rachel pointed out, 'but you know that.'

'One thing to do first,' Selkirk took a deep breath. Either this would be a success, or it would cost the lives of many or all of his men. 'Roll these rocks down the hill, boys. All of them.'

'That will wake the Turks...' Rachel warned.

Black stared at him, his eyes bright in the starlight. 'You're an evil bastard, major! Come on boys! Do as the officer says!'

'Roll them, men, roll them all!' Selkirk set an example by levering a four-foot-wide boulder over the edge. 'We've no artillery, so we'll do this the old-fashioned way. Get these rocks rolling!'

The Reivers responded with a will, pushing every rock down the slope, from small fist sized stones to giant boulders the size of a horse until the rumble of rolling stones multiplied into a constant roar that nearly deafened the Reivers on the summit.

'The Turkish camp is around the bottom of the path and the base of Masada,' Selkirk explained. 'When that Turkish assassin rolled down he created a small avalanche; imagine what devastation this lot will do.' He forced a grin he hoped would be visible in the dark, 'this is our artillery barrage, boys, make Jackie keep his head down.'

'Roll them, you bastards!' Black roared. 'Squash Jackie flat!'

The Reivers shouted and yelled as they worked, sometimes with two or three men combining to uproot an unusually large boulder and send it bouncing down the Snake Path. 'Die, you Turko bastards!' Rourke laughed, as he and Kelly worked together.

The second that the last rock was sent crashing over the cliff, Selkirk ordered Black to lead the Reivers down. 'Move as quickly as you can but keep quiet as long as possible; the avalanche should keep the Turks occupied for quite some time.'

The noise increased as the rocks rolled down the hill, gathering speed and volume with every yard.

'Wait, sir,' Crosier looked upward. 'It's raining!'

The first drop was warm; the next came a few seconds later and then followed a torrent that formed rivulets on the path and soaked the Reivers even as they attempted to negotiate their way back to the ground.

'I thought it should be snowing at Christmas,' Batsford complained.

'Only in Britain you stupid bugger,' an anonymous voice told him.

When the last man led his horse onto the path, Selkirk followed. He raised his head and opened his mouth, welcoming the rain after so many hot, dry days. In front of him, the line of Reivers and horses slithered on the now slippery path with the horses' hooves, padded with pieces of spare uniforms, nearly silent in the pre-dawn gloom.

There were new sounds from the ground below, the high screams of the injured, sharp voices shouting orders, the clatter of hooves and neighing of horses.

Poor buggers, it must be hell down there.

''Push on,' Selkirk urged, and the Reivers moved as quickly as they could, with the horses sliding on loose stones and the men leading them, cursing as they leaned backwards in their attempts to balance as they hauled on reins and held on to manes, feeling their way step by careful step.

'Come on Daisy, behave,'

'Get down that path, Zulu,'

The words were hissed or whispered as the Reivers negotiated the twists and turns and slopes in the dark. The rain kept dimmed the dawn, so the Reivers were half way down the path before it was light enough to see.

'The rain's a mixed blessing,' Selkirk murmured to Rourke, the man in front of him, 'for if we move slower because we can't see the path, neither can the Turks see us.'

'Well, they'll see us in a minute, sir' Rourke predicted. 'The rain's lifting.'

'Keep moving then,' Selkirk said. 'Pass that on; try to get down the path before Jackie finds out.'

'Right, sir,' Rourke said. He raised his voice to a shout, 'the major says to bloody hurry up!'

'Quietly!' Selkirk snarled, but too late.

That was my fault. I did not emphasise the need for silence.

Others of the Reivers passed the message on in full voiced chorus but even so it was a good five minutes and a few hundred yards later before the first Turkish bullet came whistling overhead.

'Keep moving,' Selkirk shouted. 'I don't think they can see us properly yet so don't fire back. The muzzle flashes will give us away.'

The initial shots were un-aimed, hitting all around the cliff and the Snake Path, but within a few moments, the light had strengthened sufficiently for the Turks to see the Reivers and the shooting improved.

'How far is it to the bottom, Black?'

'About fifteen minutes at this speed, major!' Black sounded unusually nervous, 'by the time we get there, Jackie will be ready and waiting.'

'Mount up, Black; mount and ride down the hill!'

'He wants us to ride on this? Old Selks has finally gone doolaly!'

I have no idea who said that, but he is correct.

'Mount and ride boys- up-saddle!' Selkirk found he was grinning as he roared the order. 'Come on men; we are the Reivers!'

'About bloody time, major! Black let out a long yell: 'come on Reivers! Get down the hill!'

There were other shouts as the Reivers mounted and pushed down the path. As the sun vanquished the final curtain of cloud, Selkirk saw his men sliding and riding downwards in a row of bobbing bush hats and shouldered rifles. Batsford had an expression of sheer terror on his face, but he was holding on bravely while Black was laughing and Wells holding Abraham in the saddle.

But the Turks could also see them. The rifle fire began to take effect. A led horse screamed and kicked wildly then plunged off the path in a terrible flurry of flailing legs and flying mane.

'Spur it, lads,' Selkirk shouted, 'get down the path.'

Matthew was the first casualty as a bullet plunged into his thigh. He yelled and stiffened, but a Turkish sniper targeted him and fired again. The shot took him through the head, and he slipped sideways in the saddle, killed instantly. Matthew's horse sensed his rider was dead, panicked and bolted, barging his weight against the led horse in front, so both pushed against Mackay, the next in line.

'Rein in, Mackay!' Selkirk shouted, but the pressure of two horses was too much for the strength of the wounded man, and he lost control. The reins slipped from his hand and, deprived of guidance, his horse reared up, with the fore-hooved barging into Mackay's back. Mackay swore and fell sideways, over the edge of the path and onto the loose rocks deposited by the avalanche. He yelled once, then again as he realised what was happening. He continued to scream as he rolled head over heels until he was half way down when a Turkish bullet mercifully ended his ordeal.

Two of my men killed; how many more?

'Fire back,' Selkirk ordered, 'unsettle the bastards!' He showed the way by pulling his Lee-Enfield from its holster and firing an entire magazine in the direction of the Turkish camp. The most competent of the Reivers did the same, so the long thread of horsemen was punctuated by a succession of rifle fire. Selkirk saw Batsford try to obey the order and fire as he fought to control his horse.

'Good effort, Batsford!' Selkirk encouraged.

'Rocks ahead!' Black shouted, 'rein up boys!'

Selkirk's avalanche had worked a little too well and deposited a formidable litter of rocks on the lower reaches of the path. Black held up a hand to halt the Reivers, dismounted and began to remove the obstacles from their road. Others of the Reivers joined him, bunching up and inadvertently providing a better target for the Turks who were now only a few hundred feet away and slowly recovering from the shock of the avalanche.

Selkirk dismounted and helped Abraham from his horse. 'Keep your head down, man; you're too valuable to sit up tall as a target for every Jacko in Palestine.' He glanced over his men. 'Rourke; you and Kelly get on a Lewis gun and make these Turks keep their heads down. The rest of us will make a path through this mess. Rachel; you keep under whatever cover you can find.' He patted Abraham on the shoulder. 'You are our priority, Abraham. You must stay safe, or this whole mission was a waste of time.'

With the stutter of the Lewis a reassuring backdrop, the Reivers toiled in the growing heat. Most rocks were small and could be kicked or pushed away, but some of the larger required considerable effort.

The Turk's fire was still desultory but increased by the minute, so the Lewis was hard pressed to keep them quiet; Kelly fired in short bursts.

'Keep that gun working, Kelly!' Selkirk roared.

'We're nearly out of ammunition sir,' Rourke answered for him.

'Where's the second Lewis?' Selkirk called.

'It went over the side with one of the horses sir,' Rourke said, 'and half the Lewis ammo as well.'

Christ!

'Clear these bloody rocks, Black! Get us out of here!'

The Reivers redoubled their efforts, tearing at the obstructions with bloody fingers and aching muscles until they eventually came to the foot of the path and a scene of utter devastation.

The avalanche had flattened around half of the Turkish camp. Tents, equipment, horses and men sprawled in a hundred different positions. Rocks and rubble spread over the area nearest to the path, burying tents and men alike, while some of the larger boulders had trundled further on; one had smashed the makeshift fence that contained the Turkish horses, and they had run free.

'That's why they took so long to see us,' Crosier said. 'It's like a major artillery bombardment.'

'I wondered that there were so few men firing at us,' Selkirk looked at the devastation, 'but now I am surprised that anybody could recover so quickly.'

As the British reached the foot of Masada, more Turkish soldiers had managed to find their rifles, but their resistance had been spasmodic, and the Lewis had sent most scurrying for cover. There were only a couple of shots aimed at the Reivers as they picked their way across the stone-strewn shambles of the camp. Selkirk glanced around, hoping to see Hefferman among the dead, but without success.

'Spur!' Selkirk noticed that some of his men hesitated, perhaps wishing to help the Turkish casualties. 'Ride on boys! Rachel – lead the way to the oasis!'

Without another backward glance at the Turkish camp, Selkirk kicked in his heels and headed south and east. It felt good to be in the saddle again with Kimberley beneath him and the wilderness all around. It felt good to have the wind in his face and to see the blue smear of the Dead Sea to his left and the high escarpment of the Judea Hills to his right. It felt good to be leading his men with the sound of hooves drumming on the hard ground and Rachel smiling at him from his right as her black hair blew over her shoulder.

'We're free,' he said to Black, 'free of that bloody hill.'

'Free?' Black shook his head. 'We're hardly that, Major; we're manipulated by bloody faceless men in suits to fight a bloody stupid war in somebody else's bloody arse hole of a country. Free? We're just warrior slaves of the British politicians.'

Before Selkirk could think of a response, Rachel spoke.

'It is not far,' Rachel promised. She was laughing, with her teeth white against her tanned face and her dark eyes wide. With Rachel beside him and his Reivers at his back, it was nearly possible for Selkirk to forget the hardships and losses of the past days, but he knew that in the dark of the night or in any moment when he was alone and without a pressing problem, the images would return. He would remember the death of Sinclair, the way Matthew fell down the cliff, the terrible final scream of the horses and the loss of so many of his men in this expedition. Despite those memories, at the minute he was free, and he was moving, riding and in good company; if he kept busy he could chase the spectres away, at least for the time being.

Warrior slaves of the British politicians? What the hell did that mean?

En Gedi Oasis was much larger than Selkirk had imagined; an area rather than a single pool of water. The name was applied to a region some three miles long, a place of palm trees and cool water and a delightful pool with an idyllic waterfall. The contrast between the surrounding desert and the fertility of the oasis could hardly have been greater.

There was a small group of Bedouin camped with their tents and camels beside one of the pools.

'They are nomadic people,' Rachel said. 'They belong in this environment, and their home is the wilderness that stretches from nearly the very walls of Jerusalem east as far as God made, and south and ever south.'

'All over the Ottoman Empire, then,' Selkirk said. 'I wonder how they view the Turks.'

Rachel shrugged and looked away without interest. Arabs and British watched each other with wary respect, but Selkirk had his men in hand, and the Bedouin would not break the sanctity of water in the midst of the desert.

There were six springs and two streams where the horses luxuriated in fresh water, a multitude of birds, lizards that darted among the rocks and small herds of ibex with the ubiquitous wild goat that hopped casually among the rocks.

'Water the horses,' Selkirk ordered, 'knee tether them and let them graze.' At that time of year, the fodder was not of the best quality, but it was better than nothing and the horses needed any nourishment they could get.

'This is heaven,' Rachel said. She glanced at Selkirk, 'How far behind are the Turks?'

'A long way,' Selkirk promised. 'They are in such disarray that they will not be on horseback today and maybe not tomorrow.'

Rachel looked at the inviting pools of water. 'We have time to bathe, yes?'

The idea was so appealing that Selkirk had to agree.

The men have been on that hot rock for days; they were locked up underground for weeks before that; they have fought across Palestine and lost a good many of their friends. A few hours relaxation will boost their spirits. That boulder assault will have demoralised the Turkish cavalry; even such excellent soldiers as they are will need to recover.

'Bathing parade, men.' Selkirk ordered, and then grinned at Rachel, 'you'd best find somewhere a little more secluded' he said, 'or you'll have a dozen lusty British soldiers ogling after your body.'

Her eyes twinkled at him. 'And perhaps I will be able to ogle twelve British soldiers as well?' Her smile took him by surprise. 'Or maybe only a single British officer?'

Maybe you are correct.

Rachel was looking quizzically at him; 'are you all right, Andrew?'

'Obviously,' Selkirk said and winked at her.

'I've posted Wells on guard, sir,' Crosier reported. 'We can spell him, so he gets his chance at bathing.'

'Well done, Sergeant.'

Rachel widened her eyes and raised her voice, 'I think I had better leave now, Major Selkirk. There are some things a well brought up Jewish girl should never see,' the lift at the corner of her mouth gave the lie to her statement, and she looked deliberately past Selkirk and Crosier at the already bathing men before turning slowly away.

Selkirk glanced behind him, where the Reivers were splashing in a pool, laughing as if they were at Brighton or Rothesay beach rather than hundreds of miles within enemy territory. Selkirk glanced back at Rachel, saw she was smiling at him, but he left her to find her space, and he joined his men. He desperately needed a wash and guessed that he must stink. He rasped a hand over his face and wondered when he last shaved; two days, maybe three days ago?

The water was refreshing, with a dozen frogs and a crab or two swimming around the reeds that edged the pool. Selkirk allowed himself to relax. He had got his men down from Masada, and now they had water. There were even some old dates hanging from the trees; he would have them plucked later, and maybe shoot one of the goats for meat. He could not remember last time he had tasted fresh meat. Selkirk stripped and washed his clothes as best he could in the limpid water, knowing he could not achieve perfection, but any semblance of cleanliness was better than none.

The men were laughing, some just lying in the water, others splashing each other; one or two were searching for the remains of last season's dates. Most were washing their clothes or washing their bodies. It was a scene of relaxation and fun, entirely opposed to the tension and murder of the early morning. Selkirk allowed himself to relax for a moment.

'Permission to go hunting sir?' Black asked, and indicated a goat that grazed within two hundred yards of them.

'Yes, off you go,' the prospect of fresh meat was too tempting to turn down.

Black hardly shifted from his position. He hefted his rifle, aimed and shot the goat all in a single movement. Selkirk remembered that Moffat had been a butcher in civilian life before there was a discrepancy in the till and he thought it expedient to do his duty for the country and sign up. 'Show us your skills, Moffat,' Selkirk invited. For the first time in weeks, he lay back and enjoyed the healthy buzz of soldiers relaxing without fear of Turkish attack.

Smoke from the campfires drifted pleasantly across the oasis as men, naked or nearly naked, emerged from the water to eat, joke and laze together. All had desert sores, some still bore wounds from Turkish action, and all were bronzed so presented a strange picture of dark brown faces, necks and arms, with white torsos where their uniforms protected them from the sun.

Selkirk allowed them their time to rest. He lay back in the shade of a clump of palms and let the pleasant sound of men relaxing ease away his cares. He turned his head and saw Rachel. She was emerging from the water, dripping wet and nearly fully clothed. Selkirk smiled; she was either too modest or too send sensible to take off her clothes in the presence of a dozen soldiers. How would Helena have acted? Helena would have placed her rifle on the bank and dared anybody to look.

Rachel looked up suddenly, caught the direction of Selkirk's gaze and waved. Turning her back, she began to undress.

Well done, Rachel. That takes courage. You are safe with my Reivers though.

Selkirk closed his eyes as fatigue overcame him.

'Sir!' That was Well's voice, waking him from unexpected sleep. Selkirk looked up. Wells was at his side, holding his rifle at the trail. 'Turks, sir, coming from the West.'

Oh God, here we go again.

'Thank you, Wells,' Selkirk stood and grabbed the clothes he had left to dry beside the pool. 'Cavalry or infantry?'

'A mixture of both, sir.'

'Were they moving fast?'

Wells screwed up his face. 'Not very fast, sir. They were not force-marching anyway.'

If they are not moving fast, they are on a routine patrol and not out hunting for us.

'Get back on watch and shout out if they get close.' Selkirk watched as Wells returned to his post. 'Right lads; Jackie has come to spoil the fun; we have to up-saddle again.'

Rachel was in the adjoining pool, luxuriating in the water. She looked startled when Selkirk called to her but stood without any display of modesty.

Jesus, woman; this is not the time and place to display yourself like that!

'Turks are coming from the west; we have to leave,' Selkirk tried to ignore the nakedness that shortly before he had applauded. 'I don't think they know we are here, but we are moving out before they come. Out you get and dress.' He did not spare even a moment to admire her charms as he returned to his men. 'Abraham! We're moving again!'

However brief the halt, it had refreshed the men, so they were nearly jovial as they hoisted themselves back into the saddle and waited for the next order. They were soldiers; their lives were dictated by others until the unbelievable happened and the war ended.

'Fill the water bottles,' Crosier was not going to be rushed by any number of Turks, 'grab what food you can find; we don't know how long it will be before we find food and water again.' He raised his voice. 'Let the horses drink their fill and ensure all the water bottles are full! Jildi, Reivers!'

The Reivers pulled out of the oasis within fifteen minutes of Wells giving the alert. Some were still dressing, others chewing on hard out-of-season dates or hunks of roasted goat, but all carried their rifles, and nothing was left behind except memories.

'Black, scout ahead and see what is happening; Kelly, you have a look at the Turks and tell me what they are doing.' Selkirk checked his compass and map and headed south and west.

'Where are we going Major Selkirk?' Rachel asked.

'Gaza,' Selkirk told her. 'I think we have more chance of meeting the British if we are on the coast than inland.' He looked back at his men. 'I am more hopeful of seeing a British ship than a cavalry patrol in Sinai. Last I heard we were still tied up in Gallipoli and Mesopotamia with few men spared for this theatre.'

Rachel smiled. 'You will help us free Zion,' she said, 'the British Empire will get us our land back after so many centuries.'

He looked at her. 'I hope you are right, Rachel; you deserve it.'

'Right, Reivers, here we go again. Egypt here we come!'

The further south they rode, the more the desert closed on them, great gaunt hills of rock, shimmering red in the heat, with dry wadis on either side and an occasional ibex or jackal watching their progress. The sun battered them with relentless heat, torturing them, evaporating sweat even before the beads formed. Selkirk looked at his tiny force of men and felt a stirring of pride. He had led them from the coast of Palestine right across to the Dead Sea and south into this terrible wilderness, and they had not been found wanting. His collection of unwanted and misfits had welded together into an expert fighting force.

Dust enveloped them, sticking to sweaty faces, covering uniforms and horses, grating in throats and clogging nostrils, making it hard to breathe. Veterans of the conditions, the Reivers rode on regardless, with the miles slowly passing and with the desert unforgiving on either side.

'Sir,' Kelly cantered up to him. 'The Turkish force split up. The infantry remained at the oasis, but the cavalry spotted our trail and are following us.'

We are still hundreds of miles behind Turkish lines, with limited ammunition and no clear route back to British territory. We have fourteen privates, two civilians, one an elderly man, and some wounded. But we are rested and fed and experienced. It will take more than a few Turkish cavalrymen to stop us now.

'Thank you, Kelly. We'll keep riding as we are. Join the ranks and send Wells to watch the Turks.'

With Black scouting ahead and Selkirk hoping his map was accurate, he led the Reivers for the rest of that day, riding through a landscape of bare red rocks with jagged mountains all around. The heat was incredible, battering them, pressing down on them, as dangerous an enemy as the Ottomans.

'Is this all your Zion?' Selkirk indicated the surrounding wilderness.

'This is our land,' there was pride in Rachel's voice.

'If this is the Holy Land you can keep it,' Wells was riding immediately behind Selkirk, 'it's nothing compared to Herefordshire. There's not a patch of green anywhere.'

Rachel looked at Selkirk and smiled. 'Our land is not England,' she said.

Nor Scotland, but it has the same atmosphere of stubborn defiance.

'Sir,' Crosier trotted over. 'If I remember from the maps we looked at, there should be a wadi near here with a well in it.'

Selkirk nodded. 'Good thinking, Sergeant.'

It was late afternoon when they halted at a pool the size of a bathtub with water they would normally not consider fit for washing in, yet alone drinking.

'Black,' Selkirk said. 'Post sentries to watch for the Turks.'

'Yes, Major,' Black was staring at the ground. 'I wouldn't recommend staying here for long,' he said. 'Somebody else is using this place.'

'Probably the Bedouin,' Selkirk said. 'This is their part of the world.'

'Over there, sir.' Black pointed to the ground. 'Look at the tracks. There are marks of horse shoes and something with wheels.'

'Rachel!' Selkirk called. 'Do you have merchants with carts here?'

'Not in Sinai,' Rachel said at once. 'Not in the desert.'

'Military,' Selkirk decided. 'Water tha horses and up saddle!' He shouted. 'We're moving out!'

The Reivers responded without question, climbing back into the saddles and following Selkirk as he rode away south.

'Trace them, Sergeant,' Selkirk said. 'See which direction they took.'

They camped in a dry wadi, with the stars bright overhead and the night air crisp and cold. Selkirk ensured that Rachel and Abraham were safe, turned down the Reivers request for a fire in case the Turks smelled the smoke and circled the camp to check the sentries. Black rode in an hour after dark.

'Well, Sergeant?'

'It was a Turkish column, right enough, Major,' Black said.

'Are they following us?' Selkirk asked.

'No.' Black shook his head. 'They were here a few days ago, maybe as long as a week.'

'It could be a routine patrol then,' Selkirk said. 'We'll have to watch out for them.'

Selkirk had his Reivers moving before the sun rose, hoping to cover as much ground as possible before the heat grew intolerable.

'How are you holding up?' He asked Rachel.

'I am well, thank you.' The Australian bush hat suited her, but her smile was weak. 'Abraham is not good.'

Selkirk handed over his water bottle. 'Make sure he drinks enough,' he said.

Twice that morning he stopped to consult his map, laying it on the ground with the compass on top while he calculated distances and times. 'This will be a longer trip than I had hoped,' he said.

'Abraham...' Rachel said.

'We'll look after him as best we can.' Selkirk promised.

By the middle of the afternoon, even the staunchest of the Reivers was flagging, and Selkirk called a halt. Luckily the area was seamed with wadis, and the map led them to another small well which provided water for the horses.

'Sir!' Black again approached Selkirk. 'The Turks have been here as well.'

'Show me,' Selkirk said and viewed the distinct trail of horses and wheel-marks. 'There were four wagons,' he said, 'and more than a hundred horsemen.'

'That's right, Major.' Black agreed. 'They're heading south and west, the same direction as us.'

Selkirk nodded. 'When were they here, Sergeant?'

Black screwed up his face. 'About three days, at a guess. They are a bit fresher than the tracks we saw yesterday.' He grinned. 'At this rate, Major, we'll catch them up.'

'Do you think it is the same column as we saw yesterday?'

'I would think so, Major.' Black said.

'It's gone then,' Selkirk decided. 'We'll stay here and rest.' It was a calculated risk, but he had little choice. His Reivers could not ride in the heat indefinitely, the horses were drooping, and Abraham was nearly falling out of the saddle.

The Reivers watered the horses first and then sought whatever shade they could find. Selkirk posted sentries, checked on Abraham and fretted as the sun beat down upon them.

'How far is it to Egypt?' Rachel was at his side.

'It's about a hundred and eighty miles,' he spread out the map. 'By my reckoning, we are here,' he stabbed downwards with his forefinger.

Rachel studied the map. 'And the Turks could be anywhere.'

'Anywhere at all,' Selkirk said. 'But we are fast and mobile, and they have to find us first.'

She took off her hat and tossed back her hair. 'And if they do, Major Selkirk?'

'Then we fight them,' Selkirk said. 'Or we run.'

'One-hundred and eighty miles is a long way to run.' Rachel said.

'Let's hope that they don't find us then.' Selkirk was hot, tired and anxious about his men. He was in no mood for polite conversation. 'Try and get some sleep. We will be on our way long before the sun comes out.'

'And you, Andrew?' Rachel asked. 'Will you sleep as well? You spent last night watching over your men, and us. You need sleep as much as we do.'

'I'm all right,' Selkirk snapped. 'Just do as I tell you for once, damn it!' *Honestly, this one woman gives me more trouble than all the Reivers combined.*

Rachel looked up with her mouth open. 'Yes, Andrew,' she said with surprising meekness and then she flicked back her hair. 'If you do as I tell you for once, damn it back!'

For a moment Selkirk was astonished. He was not used to having his orders questions. He could not help his smile. *That is what Helena would have said.* 'Good for you,' Rachel,' he said. 'Let's both get some sleep.'

They all heard the sound that night, the steady drumming of horses' hooves and a rumble that could have been wheels over rock, or something completely different. Selkirk was up in seconds, grabbing for his revolver.

'It's all right, sir,' Crosier was already awake. 'It's miles away. Sound travels far at night in the desert.'

'Turks.' Selkirk said quietly.

'I reckon so, sir.'

'And if we can hear them, they can hear us.' Selkirk glanced around the wadi. 'Before we move, I want all the men's equipment muffled and cloth tied around the horse's hooves.'

'Yes, sir.' Crosier said. 'And if I might make a suggestion, sir?'

'Yes, Sergeant. Anything that might help.'

'We should dull the metal work sir; bayonets, rifle barrels or anything that could reflect the sun. Flashes can be seen miles away, like heliographs.' Crosier stepped back as if he had said too much.

'Good thinking, Sergeant. We'll do that.'

They set off again in the early hours of the morning, with hooves and equipment muffled and every man alert for sign or sound of Ottoman soldiers. Moonlight gave a ghostly glow to the desert, casting intense shadows, so the Reivers rode through a nearly surreal landscape of white rocks and dark shade.

'I like the desert,' Selkirk said. 'It is clean somehow.'

Rachel gave a small smile. 'I will like it better when it is behind us, and better still when it is cleansed of Turks.'

'We'll do our best.' Selkirk said.

'They haven't gone yet,' Crosier said. 'Listen.'

Selkirk held up a hand, and the Reivers halted. The dust settled slowly. The sound came to them, the grinding of wheels on rock, combined with the rhythmic tramp of many boots.

'It sounds as if Jacko had the same idea as us,' Black hefted his rifle. 'Go and see, Sergeant.'

Black lifted his rifle in salute, turned his horse and trotted away.

'Right, Reivers,' Selkirk moved onward, knowing that Black would find them without difficulty.

Moving slowly to minimise the dust they created, the Reivers followed Selkirk south by south-west. He called over Crosier. 'Ride to the flank, Sergeant; watch out for Turkish scouts.'

Selkirk checked over his shoulder. Rachel was on one side of Abraham, with Rourke on the other. His Reivers were riding well, relaxed in the saddle and watching for danger.

'Major Selkirk! Be careful!' Rachel hissed. 'Horned viper!'

Selkirk hauled on his reins, swearing as the snake curled away, its brown striped back distinctive under the moonlight. 'Thank you, Rachel.' There were other predators other than the Turks out in Sinai that night.

The sound of the Ottoman convoy faded and died within half an hour. A leopard coughed in the distance, disturbing the horses, and the Reivers rode on.

'Major,' Sergeant Black appeared in front of the column. 'The Turks are in front.'

Chapter Thirteen

'How many? And where?' Selkirk held up a hand to stop the Reivers.

'Thousands, Major and they're in a wadi.'

'Show me,' Selkirk ordered. He looked up as Crosier rode up. 'Look after the men, Sergeant. There are Turks ahead.'

The moon threw long shadows as Black led Selkirk across a plateau of cracked rock. The sound of horses carried to Selkirk, with the drift of smoke and an occasional murmur of laughter. Without talking, Black dismounted and tied his horse to a slender outcrop of rock. Selkirk followed, and they dropped to all fours and crawled up a ridge that overlooked one of the many wadis that seared the area. Black indicated that Jack should look over.

Even with the aid of binoculars, moon-shadows prevented Selkirk from seeing more than a fraction of the wadi, but what he saw was sufficient. Water gleamed along the wadi floor in a series of pools, with an irregular line of palm trees hinting at more water underground. On either side of the palms, lines of tents stretched into the shadows, with an enclosure for horses and camels and open space that held ranks of wagons.

'Dear God,' Selkirk said. 'There are thousands of them. This must be the main Turkish army in Sinai. You've found Frederich von Kressenstein's camp, Sergeant.'

'Yes, sir.' Black agreed.

Part of the Reiver's original mission was to find this place. Now we have another reason to get safely to Egypt.

They withdrew to the Reivers, with Selkirk even more thoughtful than he had before. *We have to alter our route now to avoid Von Kressenstein's army and his patrols.*

They moved on, quietly, with scouts out all around and the desert seemingly watchful as they passed through.

'How is Abraham holding up?'

'He's all right, sir.' Wells had taken over the job of supporting the spy.

'Increase the pace a little,' Selkirk decided. 'We are too close to Von Kressenstein for my liking.' They accelerated to a fast walk, which raised dust but covered more ground. Every mile away from the main Turkish army was a bonus in these conditions. Riding with his compass in his hand, Selkirk tried to head south by south west, winding through the tortured rocks of Sinai, keeping away from the larger areas of sand desert where the enemy might more easily see them.

Dawn was spectacular, an incredible sky of banded orange, silver and yellow light that made Selkirk wonder anew why humanity fought wars in the midst of so much beauty. Taking a deep breath, he moved on with his Reivers behind him and the heat already beginning to mount.

'Dust, sir,' Crosier reported half an hour later. 'Behind us and to the east.'

'Thank you, sergeant.' Selkirk hid his agitation. 'Rourke; have a decko and don't be seen for God's sake.' He watched Rourke check the magazine of his rifle and ride off.

'When are we stopping to rest?' Rachel asked. 'Abraham is getting tired.'

'Not yet,' Selkirk said. 'I want as much distance as possible between the Turks and us.'

'But, Abraham...' Rachel put an arm around the spy.

'He'll have to hold out as best he can,' Selkirk hardened his heart. 'Better for him to be tired riding than for the Turks or Germans to capture him.'

'Sir,' Rourke galloped beside them with his hat hanging loose and the sweat drying on his face, 'more Turks. The Turkish cavalry is coming fast, and some others have joined them; they are riding hard and look a bit ragged.'

'Ragged?' Selkirk glanced at Rourke, 'ragged in what way?'

'They look as if they have been in action sir;' Rourke said.

'I'll have a decko,' Selkirk decided. 'Take over here Sergeant Crosier.'

Ragged had been a good description of the Turks. There were around eighty of them, in a loose formation but pushing their horses as they followed the Reivers' trail. Some were wounded, and others had extra horses on long reins. The man who led them wore a dirty white uniform and rode some ten yards in front of his men, spurring and whipping his horse without mercy.

'Hefferman,' Selkirk said.

Now we have to run. I have gone too slowly and allowed Hefferman to catch up.

'We'll try and lose them,' Selkirk told the Reivers what was happening. 'Up the pace lads; Jackie is on our trail. Sorry, Abraham but we have no choice.' He sent a rider to warn Black, who was scouting ahead and pushed Kimberley on, with the desert now a trap rather than a place of freedom.

'There's no sign of Turks in front,' Black reported. 'Nothing but desert.'

'Ride around and see what is happening,' Selkirk ordered. 'Find out the condition of Hefferman's boys. He has scraped together his survivors, and he wants to kill me; not you.'

Black nodded; he was tired and dried sweat had stiffened his uniform to his body, but he was a South Australian bushman, and he would ride and work until he died.

'I'll change horses,' he said, 'this one is all-in.'

Black was back within fifteen minutes. 'There are two distinct units with the German, the lot that we fought at Masada and another force of Ottomans. 'He reported calmly. 'Hefferman's mob is badly beaten up, with about half the men carrying injuries, but the German is pushing them hard.'

'He's determined to get me,' Selkirk said.

'He's determined to get Abraham and me,' Rachel said.

'He's determined to get all of us,' Black corrected.

'I killed his son,' Selkirk told him. 'He wants revenge for his boy.'

Selkirk pulled Kimberley around and returned to the head of his men. They rode on, south west by west with the landscape dictating their route and the sun scorching them. Unable to ride fast in case a high plume of dust gave away their position, Selkirk kept them moving steadily, rotating the scouts to ensure they remained watchful. Keeping to the same general direction, he jinked them around wadis and mountains, obscured their trail by dragging palm fronds and encouraged Abraham with kind words. By midafternoon the horses were flagging, and Selkirk ordered a ten-minute break to water them.

'They can't go on much longer,' Crosier reported, 'and nor can the men. The old buckle is suffering.'

'How is Abraham, Rachel?' Selkirk asked.

'He'll survive,' Rachel said, 'but I don't know how long he can keep riding at this pace.'

'It's either that or Jackie Turk will catch us.' Selkirk played the uncaring commander, but he saw the strain on Abraham's face and knew he was not capable of much more.

I'll have to do something here. I'll have to divert the Turks somehow.

'Come on lads! Keep it moving!' Selkirk rested Kimberley and transferred to Frigga, one of the spare horses, a dun mare with a hard mouth and a wild mane. He circled his Reivers, encouraging, haranguing, exchanging lewd jokes and swearing at the two men who complained.

'Major!' Black spurred up. He spoke urgently. 'There is another body of Turks about ten miles ahead of us. A different unit I have never seen before.'

Selkirk grunted. 'How many are there, Sergeant?'

'A couple of hundred at least, Major; they are big fellows riding in column of twos.'

'They must be from Kressenstein's army,' Selkirk gave a wry smile. 'It seems they are hunting us, rather than us hunting them. Can you find us a safer route?'

'Follow my lead, major.'

With Black riding three miles for every one the Reivers travelled, they pushed through the heat of the day and into the stark cool of the night.

'Abraham's about done in sir,' Crosier reported, 'and Moffat and Pembroke are flagging as well.'

The wounded men. 'We have Germans and Turks behind us, and Turks in front and on our flank,' Selkirk said, 'they'll have to cope as best we can and hope Jacko gives up for the night.'

The Turks did not give up. Hefferman pushed them hard, decreasing the distance to the fleeing Reivers. Selkirk knew his men were tiring. Abraham looked grey, with a Reiver constantly propping him in the saddle and Pembroke was nearly delirious, passing from consciousness to unconsciousness from minute to minute. *Unless I do something soon, the Turks will catch us and all our efforts will have been wasted.*

'Right lads; follow my lead,' Selkirk gave a quiet order and abruptly altered direction to the East.

'We're heading away from the coast.' Rachel's weariness slurred the words.

'I hope to circle Hefferman's cavalry,' Selkirk said, 'if our horses have any strength left in them.'

Sound travelled even further in the desert night, so the Reivers slowed down and walked their horses step by cautious step. Selkirk led, checking the route under a night sky where clouds obscured the moon.

'Dismount,' Selkirk passed the whispered order, 'except the civilians and the wounded. Give the horses a bit of a respite.'

Rachel was first to slide off her horse; her eyes defiantly fixed on Selkirk. She took off her hat, wiped her face with her neckerchief and covered her head again.

'You'd better stay on horseback, Rachel,' Selkirk told her. 'Conserve your strength.'

'I'll get back on the horse when you do,' Rachel told him sweetly, 'You are injured as well, major Selkirk.'

You are a stubborn creature.

They walked for an hour, hoping to save the horse's strength while simultaneously draining their own on the harsh terrain. Twice Selkirk stopped to listen, and each time heard the distant clop of horses and the murmur of Turkish voices drifting through the night.

'I'll have a decko, Major,' Black eased away. He returned within ten minutes.

'They are still coming Major.' Black refused to give way to the weariness that forced his shoulders to droop and made his eyes appear like deep dark pits in his face. 'They have spread out into a long line, yards apart and are walking toward us. You can see their lanterns now.'

Black was correct. The line of glinting lights stretched from horizon to horizon as far as Selkirk could see, moving slowly toward the Reivers, combined with a constant murmur of sound as the Turks shouted to their neighbours.

'They are too close together for us to slip between and there are too many of them to ride around,' Selkirk said. 'Hefferman and the Turks must have been reinforced.' Even the shrouding of night could not conceal how tired his men were. 'Right lads, Jackie is still following us; we have to keep moving.' He patted his horse. 'Sorry, Frigga old girl. Needs must when the devil drives, and he is certainly driving now.'

There were no complaints; the Reivers mounted up and headed away from these sinister lights. Pembroke was trying to stifle his moans of pain while Wells and Rachel supported Abraham in the saddle.

Step by step, the Reivers moved on with the sound of their horse's hooves loud in the echoing dark and the lights a constant in the night.

From time to time the contours of the land, or a wadi or intrusive outcrop of rock, forced the Reivers to alter their line of march, but always the Turkish lights were there, and always they drove the Reivers to the south and east through the long hours of the night.

'Keep moving,' Selkirk said as he put a supportive hand on Pembroke's shoulder.

'Keep moving' he said as Moffat swayed and nearly fell. 'Keep moving,' he intoned as tears of exhaustion streamed down Batsford's slum-thin face.

They kept moving, pushing the horses beyond the limit of their strength, changing mounts every two hours, gasping with fatigue, no longer concerned that their colleagues heard them sob or knew they were suffering.

'Keep moving lads; help your mates.'

A hot wind came from the east, blowing sand in their faces, so they wound scarves around their mouths and noses and tried to shield the horses. With the stronger supporting the weaker; the Reivers rode on through a curtain of dust. Wells hand a hand on Abraham's shoulder as Rachel reeled in the saddle.

When the wind dropped, the lights were still there, slightly closer, paler as the night eased before the onset of yet another flaming desert dawn.

Pembroke was the first to fall, slumping sideways in the saddle and then sliding softly to the unforgiving rock.

'Pemby!' Batsford nearly jumped off his horse in his rush to help. He crouched over the fallen man. 'Up you get Pemby, the Turks are coming.'

Crosier helped hoist Pembroke back into the saddle. 'You hold on Pembroke, and we'll get you home safe.'

The Reivers rode on as dawn burst the eastern sky, and the heat began again in wave after pitiless wave that beat down on them, drawing sweat from bodies that were at the limit of their endurance.

'The boys can't carry on, sir,' Crosier warned. 'We'll have to stand and fight while there is still some strength left in us.'

'We keep moving,' Selkirk grated. 'If we stop, the *Asakr –I Shahaneh* will surround us, and there is no way out. We keep moving.'

'Yes, sir.'

'Major!' Black was still riding twice as far as anybody else. 'Some of the Turks are pushing ahead of the rest. That German officer is leading a party of a dozen men from the cavalry.'

They are going to try and run us into the ground, they hope to break us, so we are an easy target for the larger body.

'Thank you, Sergeant,' Selkirk tried to appear calm, so Rachel and Abraham were not alarmed. 'I'll come and have a look.' He handed his map to Crosier. 'Take over here, Sergeant; keep the boys moving.'

The Turks were only quarter of a mile behind; twelve men on powerful horses following the trail of the Reivers.

'We could turn around and ambush them,' Black suggested. 'That would warn the Turks not to get too close.'

'It would also delay us and tire our horses, so the main Turkish force will catch us easier.' Selkirk said. 'It is exactly what they wish.' He focussed his binoculars on the Turks. 'You are right; that's Hefferman, but he's not after the Reivers. He just wants me.'

At that moment Selkirk would have gladly just laid down to sleep exactly where he was.

'What are you thinking, Major?' Black studied the Turks, 'You are not going after him alone.'

'If I kill Hefferman, or he kills me, the driving force of the search will be gone. The rest of you will have a better chance of escape.'

'It's suicide, sir.'

'It's logical, Sergeant.' Selkirk said.

The Turks were moving at a fast canter, with Hefferman not sparing his horse or his men. *They will have a host of additional mounts to replace their losses.*

'You are more capable than I am of getting the men and Abraham away. Hefferman will follow me until one of us is dead.' Selkirk tapped Black on the shoulder. 'Look after the Reivers; get them safely home.'

'Major: you can't,' Black put a hand on Selkirk's arm, 'sir...'

'Get the lads home, Sergeant.' Mounting Frigga, Selkirk rode forward alone to meet Hefferman and the Turks.

This ride is my last; I cannot kill Hefferman and all the Turks, so why am I doing this?

Why not? Wait for me Helena: I will be with you soon.

Hefferman rode a few yards in front of the Turks, spurring his horse so fiercely that blood dribbled from its flanks and it frothed at the mouth. Selkirk watched him for a few moments and then rode onto the ridge of the nearest hill, so Hefferman could see him highlighted against the skyline. He withdrew his rifle from its scabbard, held it muzzle upward and stood there in plain view.

'Hefferman!' He shouted the name. 'Here I am!'

He saw Hefferman look up. For a second their eyes met across the wasteland and then Selkirk turned his horse and spurred away, trying to buy time for his men as he led Hefferman away from the Reivers. He heard the snap of an order and hooves drumming behind him. There was the sound of a single shot and then a fusillade, but nothing came close. A man on a moving horse had little chance of hitting anything at which he aimed, yet alone hitting a single rider moving at speed.

Selkirk felt Frigga tremble under him and fondled her ears. 'Sorry old girl,' he said. 'I promise you it won't be long now.' Glancing over his shoulder; he saw the Turkish cavalry following Hefferman in a long, broken line with the stronger riders outpacing the weaker.

'On you come, lads,' Selkirk said and kicked in his spurs. He had no route to follow and no idea in his head except to divert the Turks away from his men. Nothing else mattered; he accepted that his death was inevitable, even welcome. Crosier and Black would get the Reivers back.

Frigga staggered as they entered a wadi, whose sides seemed to waver with the unbelievable heat. There were more rifle shots behind them, and Selkirk heard the vicious whine of a ricochet and the echo of hooves from the rocks. He tugged at the reins, jinking from side to side, ducking and weaving as his dust rose behind them like an improvised smoke screen.

'Sorry, old girl. Sorry.' Leaning forward, he fondled her ears again.

There was a gap ahead, a narrow, rough-bottomed pass out of this place up which he forced Frigga. 'Come on, girl, you can do it.'

Something splintered the rock to his right, and for a fraction of a second, he saw the bluish smear of lead on the sandstone. He looked behind him. Some of the Turks had dismounted to fire while Hefferman led the rest in his wake. The gunshots echoed in the wadi; a double report coupled with the whoosh of passing bullets. The Turks were making better practice now, with rock splinters spraying around Selkirk.

The pass opened into a viable opening in the wadi wall. Selkirk forced Frigga through, ducking as a bullet whizzed past his head. Ahead was a plateau of level ground, sun-tortured rock that led to a nightmare landscape of sharp ravines and savage hills. It was a picture of Hell and a fitting place to die.

'Come on Frigga!' Selkirk pushed forward, feeling his wounds open and blood soak through his shirt and trousers. Flagging with the heat, he knew he had to stop soon and face the enemy. He had run as far as he could. It was time to join Helena.

There was a raised rock in the centre of the plateau, a natural defensive site with a level surface and all-round visibility. 'Here we are, Frigga,' Selkirk pushed her to the rock. 'This is as good a place as any to die.' Dismounting, he lifted off his ammunition pouches and water-bottle.

'Here.' He raised the bottle to Frigga's muzzle. 'Drink all you can and then run free. There is nothing for you here.' He watched Hefferman lead the Turks through the gap. They spread out across the plateau and trotted on, unhurried and professional. 'They've seen us.' Allowing the horse a last swallow of the water, Selkirk unfastened the saddle and let it fall to lie forlornly on the ground. 'Off you go, girl. Find water.' He slapped Frigga's rump. 'On you go.'

Turning, he ascended to the top of the rock, feeling the heat burning through the soles of his boots. He checked the magazine of his rifle and worked the bolt to ensure that sand had not entered the mechanism.

Hefferman's Turks advanced in a broad line. They moved slowly, confident of victory against this lone and dismounted British soldier. Selkirk looked around. There was rising dust in the south which meant more cavalrymen. He would never have got through them; the Turks had him boxed in whatever he did.

Gasping at the touch of baking rock through his ragged uniform, Selkirk lay down, worked the bolt of his Lee-Enfield and aimed at the nearest man. The heat distorted his target, making the soldier appear elongated, with his legs and feet detached from the ground. Selkirk's plan had not altered; delay them as long as possible to give his Reivers time to escape. There was nothing else in his mind as he aimed and fired, with the shot impossibly loud in that hushed desert. Hefferman's Turks did not falter. He did not see anybody fall. He worked the bolt again, sliding a bullet into the breach with the brass cartridge glinting in the sun.

'Come on then, Jackie; come for me!'

Time to join Helena. The longer I detain the Turks the better my Reivers chance of escape.

The thin blare of a trumpet made Selkirk look around. What was the point of that? The Turks knew where he was; why waste breath and effort in announcing themselves?

Selkirk swore. The dust cloud to the south was much closer than before, and there was a long line of men trotting toward him, chasing a smaller, scattered group that he instinctively knew was his Reivers. After all their travails, his Reivers must have run straight into this other Turkish force. Now the Turks were herding the Reivers toward Hefferman's cavalry. He had failed. He had not saved his men; they were as doomed as he was; their mission had failed. Abraham and Rachel, Black and Crosier and all the rest would be captured or killed.

Unable to help, Selkirk could only watch as the Reivers cantered across the plateau with the fresh force of cavalry three hundred yards behind. The bugle sounded again, ear-piercing, insistent and surprisingly similar to British calls. The pursuing cavalry changed from a trot to a canter and opened their formation.

'What's happening?' Selkirk asked himself. He heard the crack of a rifle from Hefferman's force, and then another. A bullet pinged from the rock a yard from where he stood with a splinter slicing through his trousers. Selkirk gasped at the sting of a wound and felt the warm blood flow.

'Oh dear God,' Selkirk said as the Reivers galloped past, shooting from the saddle and hitting nobody. 'The Reivers aren't running away; they're leading an attack!' He tried to shout but his throat was dry with dust, and only a harsh croak came out. The cavalry he had thought were chasing his men swept past his rock, teeth gleaming in dark faces and khaki turbans light and reassuring under the Sinai sun.

The men closest to him suddenly shouted: *'Jo Bole So Nihal!'*
They're on our side! Dear God; they're Sikhs!

The turbaned warriors shouted again *'Sat Sri Akal!'* After shouting their war cry, the Sikhs drew their swords, the bugle sounded the charge, and they galloped toward the Turkish line.

Selkirk watched, ignoring the occasional bullet that still buzzed toward him. Hefferman continued forward as if the Sikhs did not exist; he thrust toward Selkirk, single-minded in his quest to avenge his son.

Come on then, Hefferman. This fight is between you and me. Come on.

The Turks were undoubtedly brave men. Some dismounted to fire at the advancing Sikhs, others fired from the saddle, and one or two spurred forward, but the Sikhs were unstoppable. With the bugler sounding the charge again and again and the Reivers taking their place in the centre, they crashed into the Turkish ranks, bowled over men and horses, rode on for a hundred yards, turned and charged again.

Selkirk watched, unable to say anything. He saw Hefferman moving forward, still shouting orders.

'Sikhs!' Selkirk shouted. 'Don't kill the German. He's mine!' His voice vanished in the increasing roar of battle, the shrill call of the bugle, the deep-throated Sikh battle cry, the clatter of Sikh swords on the metal parts of the Turks' equipment, the scream of horses and the rattle of musketry.

'Hefferman!' Selkirk tried again. 'Hefferman! Here I am!'

Perhaps the German heard Selkirk's shout. He turned toward him and for a second their gazes locked through the turmoil of the Sikh charge. Selkirk saw the hate in Hefferman's eyes, and then a Sikh officer slashed downward with his sabre. The blade took Hefferman at the top of his head and sliced his skull in two. The German died without a sound as the Sikh recovered his sword and rode on. Hefferman lay where he had fallen, a crumpled, insignificant heap on the desert rock.

'God rest you,' Selkirk said. 'You were a brave man.'

More riders appeared around Selkirk. His Reivers, battered, bloody, with tattered uniforms and blood-stained bandages, dirty, unshaven, sunken-eyed and yet every man held his rifle and every rifle was ready to use.

'Sir!' Sergeant Crosier dismounted at his side. 'I'm glad you are all right sir. We met these Sikh lads on the way and thought you might need a hand.'

'I was just getting on top of Jacko,' Selkirk said. 'Where is Abraham?'

'He's safe, Major,' Black said.

The Reivers surrounded him, laughing and joking, a tattered, rag-tag unit drawn from the unwanted and disregarded, yet they had done the impossible. He looked at them, fighting the emotions that welled within him.

Helen had gone; his children had gone, but these men made life worthwhile. What did we achieve? We failed to capture Von Stahl and lost nearly half our number, but we rescued Abraham and captured a very dangerous traitor. We showed that we can hit the Turks in this part of the world and we got back. My Reivers are all right now.

'We're all safe, sir,' Crosier shouted up. 'This is a long range patrol looking for Von Kressenstein. We told them the Reivers found his lair and now they'll take us back to Egypt.'

Safe? Selkirk tried to speak, but the words would not come. He could not think of the concept of *safe*, even while these superb fighting Sikhs chased the Turks back across the desert. 'Safe?' He nodded. 'Good job, Sergeant,' and saw Rachel looking up at him.

She was smiling.

Dear reader,

We hope you enjoyed reading *Our Land of Palestine*. Please take a moment to leave a review, even if it's a short one. Your opinion is important to us.

Discover more books by Malcolm Archibald at
https://www.nextchapter.pub/authors/malcolm-archibald

Want to know when one of our books is free or discounted? Join the newsletter at http://eepurl.com/bqqB3H

Best regards,
Malcolm Archibald and the Next Chapter Team

Historical Notes

Selkirk's Reivers are a fictional unit; they did not exist yet the idea of a small irregular unit follows a pattern that has occurred in British military history for centuries and continues with the Royal Marine Commandoes and the SAS in the present day.

There is a great deal of fact in the background of this story. In 1914, the Ottoman Turks did attack the Suez Canal. The British repelled them, but the Ottomans captured and retained the peninsula of Sinai. The campaign in Gallipoli did include the attack on Fir Tree Spur, the first action of 52 Lowland Division which took terrible losses in a daylight attack.

The district of Wazza in Cairo was indeed the scene of a major riot involving British and Anzac soldiers where some of the Military Police, the redcaps, were roughly handled.

There was also a Jewish intelligence service active in Palestine during the First World War; the information it provided was vital in helping the British, Indian and Australians conquer the area from the Turks.

The Germans and Ottomans also intended persuading Persia and Afghanistan to join the war against the Allies, coupled with a rising in India. That gave the idea for this story.

After the war the League of Nations handed Palestine, Transjordan and Iraq to Great Britain as mandated territory. There is still trouble in Palestine.

About the Author

Born and raised in Edinburgh, the sternly-romantic capital of Scotland, I grew up with a father and other male relatives imbued with the military, a Jacobite grandmother who collected books and ran her own business and a grandfather from the legend-crammed island of Arran. With such varied geographical and emotional influences, it was natural that I should write.

Edinburgh's Old Town is packed with stories and legends, ghosts and murders. I spent a great deal of my childhood walking the dark streets and exploring the hidden closes and wynds. In Arran, I wandered the shrouded hills where druids, heroes, smugglers and the spirits of ancient warriors abound, mixed with great herds of deer and the rising call of eagles through the mist.

Work followed with many jobs that took me to an intimate knowledge of the Border hill farms to Edinburgh's financial sector and other occupations that are best forgotten. In between, I met my wife. Engaged within five weeks we married the following year, and that was the best decision of my life, bar none.

At 40 the University of Dundee took me under their friendly wing for four of the best years I have ever experienced. I emerged with a degree in history, and I wrote. Always I wrote.

Malcolm Archibald

Our Land of Palestine
ISBN: 978-4-86752-917-1

Published by
Next Chapter
1-60-20 Minami-Otsuka
170-0005 Toshima-Ku, Tokyo
+818035793528
12th August 2021

Lightning Source UK Ltd.
Milton Keynes UK
UKHW010653070922
408471UK00002B/508